MARA

a novel

by Lilly Barnes

Dec. '09

For my long term/
forever friends
Beth and Berhanu,
with
love
Lilly

stb
STORIES THAT BIND

OTHER TITLES BY LILLY BARNES:

A Hero Travels Light
5 books for children, including 'Toe Tapper'

Published in 2009 by
Variety Crossing Press
PO Box 45035
5854 Yonge St.
Willowdale, on, m2 m 4 k3 , Canada
Phone and Fax: 416-222-7935
E-mail: dt_huh@yahoo.ca and
varietycrossing@gmail.com
Web site: www.varietycrossing.org

Library and Archives of Canada Cataloguing in Publication Data

Barnes, Lilly
Mara : a novel / by Lilly Barnes.
ISBN 978-0-9782020-9-5
I. Title.
PS8553.A7628M37 2009
C813'.54 C2009-904423-4
Publisher: Dae-Tong Huh
Copy Editor: Martha Uniacke Breen
Design and Layout: Sandra Huh
Cover Design: Sandra Huh

Variety Crossing Press acknowledges support from the Ontario Arts Council.

ONTARIO ARTS COUNCIL
CONSEIL DES ARTS DE L'ONTARIO

Printed and bound in Canada.

For all the Musicians in my life,

including my Mother,

and, of course,

my Sons, Daniel and Micah

MARA

a novel

by Lilly Barnes

stb
STORIES THAT BIND

TED

The whole thing started up way back in June, before I even met Mara. I was home playing that Sunday night. My pad was steaming. I remember I was wearing a towel around my neck for wiping sweat off the keys. Around midnight, somebody starts knocking on my door. I had no intention of opening it. No way. I was going on the road the next morning, three weeks with only the electric keyboard and all that time not even touching my old beauty and her ivories. No, man. Let them knock all night long, I was not yanking my ass off the piano bench or my fingers off the keys.

First I figured it was the landlord knocking. Spring of '64 was slow, so by June I probably owed him a couple of months' rent. Except the landlord I had on Broadview was chickenshit. The kind shoves notes under your door when he knows you're out.

Then whoever's out there knocking decides to add a vocal line:

"Come on, Ted. Take your knuckles off the keys. Open up."

It was Bear. The one dude who knew I was going out on the road, not getting to play any of my own music for three weeks till it starts buzzing around in your head like flies trapped in a bottle. And Bear knows exactly what that feels like, too, so if he heard me playing and he's still out there, it has to be something big, right?

I get up, wipe the sweat off my face and neck, and open the door.

Bear leans into the doorway, six feet long, with a three-inch Afro on top. Not stepping inside.

"Get a shirt on, Ted. And grab some beer. We're going to Henry's. Somebody there you've got to hear."

I'm still hungry to play so I'm in no rush to jump.

"Who's got beer? You think I'm going on the road to get cash for caviar? I don't even have enough bread for a tuning. Listen to this!"

I send Bear a couple of out-of-tune blues chords that should have made him yowl, but his ears aren't here.

"Move it, Ted," he says. "You don't want to miss this one."

We get to Henry's place, head for the basement, and halfway down the stairs I stop moving. Practically stop breathing, listening to a voice I never heard before. A lived-in kind of voice, sliding into full round notes, reaching right down, dark and sad, and then slowly climbing, getting brighter, and soaring up to a high clear finish.

After that I jumped the rest of the way down and nodded at the guys set up around the piano: Roscoe Wildman at the potluck set of drums, thin long arms with lumpy muscles like strings of sausages. Rex on bass, eyes half closed, suspenders so long, his crotch hangs around his knees. Elliot taking off the guitar, looking like a wrinkled baby with freak hands, his fingers so thin and long. And Henry the host, clutching his ever-shiny Selmer sax to his chest, ever-ready to become a living legend. The singer is just moving away from the piano.

"Hey, singer lady! This is no time to be taking a break. I just got here. How about one more tune?"

Everybody's for it except the singer. She's still moving away. About 26 or so, short dark hair, slim body. Bear steps around me, grinning at her.

"Michelle," he says. "Meet Teddy Tantrum. Any kind of waiting causes him to hurricane."

The singer turns to look at me. Eyes dark and shy. Bear is not letting go.

"Listen, Michelle, I dragged the man away from his own true love all the way over here, so he'd get to hear you sing."

"'Own true love,'" I tell her, "is Bear's quaint way of referring to my piano. And just so there's no scratch getting on my record, I might let off a blast here and there, but I do not throw tantrums. Now what do you say—

one more tune? I'll play for you."

She is going to do it. She comes and stands beside the piano and says to me: "How about 'Stormy Weather'?"

"Brave lady."

I was willing to give her the benefit of the doubt. Maybe she actually could come up with something worth listening to without copying Billie Holiday or Ella. Maybe.

Well, she did. She sure did. And she made me play the hell out of the piece, and Bear grabbed the bass, and he was nodding and bopping and swinging like a motherfucker! Man, it was one helluva night! That Michelle had her own way with every old jazz standard we played—no pyrotechnics for the hell of it, no facile sentiment, no cliché endings. On "Lover Man" she just blew everybody away. We kept her singing till her voice was a croak. A swinging kind of croak, mind you, but by then we really did have to let her quit. She had to get to a day gig in a couple of hours. Rex said he'd give her a ride home. So we all stood around for a minute and nodded a lot, and Henry said he'd get another jam happening soon, and then we all climbed out of the basement into humid dawn air.

Bear said to drop him at his place. No, he couldn't hang out, have a beer, talk about this new voice: out of the blues and into jazz, a full-blooming musician and we've never even heard her before.

"Where the hell did she come from?"

"She lives right here in Toronto," says Bear, climbing into the van. "She just doesn't come out to sing. She's had no training except for listening, man. She's unique. And she's a real Susan."

"A real Susan" is rare, in Bear's book. John Coltrane is a "real Susan." And Alicia, Bear's wife, is a real Susan. I'm driving west on Dupont. Slowly, so I can get to hear more about the singer. Bear tells me to step on it. "I've got to be getting home."

"What kind of shit is this, man? Tell Alicia what we just found here tonight. She'll dig it."

Bear looks like all his toes are curling the wrong way.

"I've known Michelle for a couple of weeks," he says. "And you can stop staring at me. Just keep your eyes on the road," says Bear. "How many times do I have to tell you: you can't drive the way you live." Bear thinks I careen around in my life like a dragonfly and instinct alone keeps me from crashing. I didn't say anything. Not one word. Nothing to take him off course.

"Okay, okay," he says. "The first time I heard Michelle was two weeks ago, at Pat's after-hours. Late, after everybody split except for a couple of musicians. We were playing and she came over and joined in. Man, ever since then I can't get enough of playing behind her. Three times so far. I like talking to her, too. But now it's all getting fucked up. I guess I mentioned her name too much around Alicia, I don't know. The woman is giving me cold looks and a voice I don't even recognize."

"Bear. Listen to yourself. Alicia?!"

"I'm telling you, Alicia. Meantime I never even touched Michelle. I mean fucking is not what's on my mind, with her."

"Not too far away, I bet."

"What are you? The Keeper of Measures? Purveyor of Purity?"

"Listen, Bear," I told him. "I'm gone in the morning. Three weeks. When I get back, I want to hear Michelle sing again, and I want to hear that everything is cool with you and Alicia."

"Yes, Ted Terrific. And now we go to commercial."

Which pissed me off because it's Bear's way of telling me I was going on this tour strictly for the cash. He thinks I can afford to stay away from out-of-town gigs. Bear doesn't have to support a van. He can put his bass on his back, if he has to, and get around by bus. I have to drag an electric keyboard around, sometimes the B52 organ, sometimes both. You try hoisting those onto a streetcar.

Bear doesn't do tours. He says it's because in small Canadian towns, it's hard to tell who it is, staring at him: somebody just curious, never seen a real live Negro before? Or is it somebody who's looking to tar and feather him for showing up in the white world?

Actually, Bear does not get confused. He's got the sharpest eye for people I've ever run into. I'm no slouch myself, but Bear can spot bullshit coming from a longer way off.

I pull over in front of Bear and Alicia's place. Bear says, "See you later," jumps out of the van and heads for their front door. I can't fucking believe it. I'll be three weeks on the road and all that time wondering what the hell bit into Bear, keeping a singer like that secret for two weeks. Too late to jump out after him or even phone him when I get home, because Alicia hates hearing the telephone at 5 a.m. Better call tomorrow, from the road. If I can wait that long without busting a vein.

Or maybe I can just sit right here and figure it out? "Sink, Ted, sink," says grandma's voice in my head. (Grandma doesn't do "th.") Figuring it out is not actually that hard, once I remembered this peculiar notion Bear has: that every female who gets a whiff of Ted Terrific instantly turns into a cleaving vine. As though he wasn't around to watch when Dona took off on me. As though he doesn't know the only one clinging on me is a creature from redneck lagoon we call the Tic.

Anyway, there it was: Bear wanted Michelle undistracted. Singing jazz, not moon/joon/cottage for two. Right then and there I decided to shift my dick sideways. There's a bit of squawking from below but hell, I can still hear Michelle sing, and I can play piano behind her, and I can even talk to her. The rest just isn't worth it, if it could get between Bear and me.

I drove back to my pad. About three hours left before I had to pack up the electric keyboard and wrestle it into the van. I parked and dragged myself up the stairs, my eyes half closed, my breathing already starting to reach down for some dreams. All of a sudden some horrible screeching starts up.

"Don't you ever answer the phone? Don't you ever stay home like normal people? It's five in the fucking morning! And your phone's been off the hook again. All night."

It's the Tic, of course, getting up off the top stair, spewing down at me.

The Tic's red hair makes her head look like a strawberry with an unripe side where her face is. She's actually what's called a dish to look at, but once you find out what's inside that head, who wants to look?

"I can't deal with you now, Tic. Just go home."

"This is my home now," she spits at me. She didn't mean Toronto, you dig. She meant my pad.

"Never was and never will be. Go home to North Bay."

"Maybe I will," says the Tic, which was a new one and got my attention, for about a second, but then we're back to the same old tune we've both played too damned often and which ends like this:

"Let me just stay the one night, Ted. I don't have anywheres I can go…"

So I have to part with my last ten-spot—and how the guys are going to love me in the morning, borrowing gas money for the van before we're even out of town.

"If you spend this on booze or dope instead of a bed, I hope you poison yourself. Now move it."

I make it through the door and lock it behind me and in about five minutes I hear her starting down the stairs. So I stop cursing myself for being a sucker, handing over cash every time she sounds really down and out, and finally get to fall into my bed to catch a couple of hours before I have to crawl out again and hit the road.

All right. It's three weeks later now, early July. Late afternoon on another Sunday and so hot even keeping the windows open in the van doesn't help. I'm wasted after ten hours driving, and I'm pissed off at the pickled bass player sitting beside me because he keeps trying to haul his upright acoustic bass into the front, to show me some chord progressions he thinks are new. Never mind. I've dropped him off and now I'm home.

I pull myself up the stairs and open the door to my pad and the cockroaches aren't done running yet when the phone starts ringing. I figure it's the Tic, so I lift the receiver and let it drop to the floor. I fall on the bed and right into sleep.

I don't know how long I slept, only that it wasn't long enough. Maybe if I'd had enough sleep that night we'd all be singing a different tune here, but I don't really believe that. I remember I woke up all of a sudden, as if I'd been shaken, and there was Bear sitting on the chair beside my bed, hanging his head. Now he sees I'm half awake, lifts his head and stares at me, and then he opens his mouth and drops what he's been carrying:

"Michelle is dead."

I don't get it.

"What are you saying, man? Michelle isn't singing any more? Or maybe she's singing you that old Bessie Smith tune: 'I ain't gonna play no second fiddle'? What do you mean, 'Michelle is dead'?"

"Dead, man. Life over, body buried. About a week ago."

By now I'm sitting up in bed. I can just reach the bottle of Scotch I brought in with a couple of fingers left in it, so I pick it up and hand it to Bear. Bear pours it down neat. Makes a terrible face, because Bear never drinks anything but Bourbon. Then he just lets the empty bottle drop on the floor and stares at it.

Thinking about it, trying to remember, I'm not sure how much sank in, at that point, about Michelle being dead. See, I'm not the kind of dude lets a lot of people get to him. In my kind of life, people are here one day, the next day they're gone. You spend three weeks on the road with a guy, eating and sleeping and farting in the same room, borrowing each other's razors and socks, playing on the same bandstand with the guy every night, and then, after three weeks, you come off the road and you don't see the guy again maybe for three months. Then, when you do see each other, it's: "Hey! How you doin'?" That's it. Or maybe you never see him again at all, because he went and OD'ed on some bad shit the day after you all got back with some cash.

I know I didn't ask Bear "How did Michelle die?" I must have figured, yet another overdose, accidental or otherwise, because I remember being pissed off at Michelle. For being yet another one dead and lost to jazz much too soon.

Bear is still staring at the bottle on the floor but now I'm awake enough to see his eyeballs are red with purple half-moons underneath, and his skin is grey, like he's been crawling through ashes. I never saw him so low.

First I was going to say, "Let's play, man," thinking that might get him past the worst of it. "Let's play a sendoff for Michelle." But then I caught a look at Bear's hands, dangling between his knees like dead fish, like they never knew how to pluck music out of catgut.

And then Bear shook his head and laid something else on me.

"Listen," Bear said. "I wasn't going to drop this one on you today but here it is anyway, so listen hard because I'm doing no repeats on this one. Right after Michelle died, body not even cold, her own mother cut off both her earlobes! Michelle's earlobes. Her own mother cut them both off! Can you even get that past your eardrums?"

Then there was a pause. Total silence. And then I was doubled over, like I'd been stabbed in the belly with a red-hot knife but there was no blood, no screaming.

"How can a mother do that to her own child?"

That was the last thing I heard: "...how can a mother do that to her own child." Right after that, my stomach hauled me up on my feet and over to the toilet bowl and I hung there, heaving and puking, heaving and puking.

Let me tell you something about heaving and puking: it gives you time out. Like a hook is reaching down into your guts, trying to turn your stomach inside out, and that's all you know. No matter what-all else is going on, heaving and puking is all you know.

By the time I was empty down to my toes, my whole head was soaking wet because Bear kept throwing cold water in my face. It helped. Puking and cold water in the face will cool you out. Enough so the roaring waterfall in your ears fades into the distance. Enough so you can brush your teeth and towel your head dry and pretend to be okay, more or less, and set out for the Pilot tavern. Which is where Bear and I went. To toast the memory of Michelle and of her singing: her way of sliding into the second chorus on "Stormy Weather," her scatting on "Don't Get Around Much Any More."

Then Bear remembered something else: how he wanted to go to the courthouse to check out Michelle's mother, that fucking earlobe freak, but Alicia said, "'No. Put it behind you. I mean it.'"

And then I heard it again:

"How can a mother do that to her own child?"

I know it was my own voice said that, though it sure didn't sound like it. Not to me, and not to Bear, either. He stared me in the face and started shaking his head.

"Jesus, Ted. You look more freaked by that mother cutting off Michelle's earlobes than by Michelle checking out altogether. Michelle is dead!"

We were staring at each other.

Then Bear remembered. "Oh, shit!" he said. "Oh, shit, Ted! I forgot. I completely forgot what you told me..."

Then I passed out. Passed right out and still can't remember what happened after that.

LENA

There's not much I can tell you about those early weeks after Michelle's death; I was barely attached to the world ongoing. Her mother was living downstairs in Michelle's apartment but we rarely met face to face. I would see her coming and going when I was curled up on my window seat—which was a lot of the time—but I couldn't see her face from up there.

The house was quiet all the time, even when she was home. No voices, no lamentations, and thank goodness, no music. I couldn't even turn on the radio back then, lest I hear a song Michelle used to sing. If her mother had played any of Michelle's records, if I'd heard Ella Fitzgerald or, heaven forbid, Billie Holiday floating up from downstairs, I'd have cried till I was a puddle on the floor. Actually, any music at all made my heart too heavy to carry.

I remember thinking: Now I understand why people talk to the dead. Why my mother was always talking to her dead sister. We can't bear to stop. If I stopped talking to Michelle, I'd lose a whole part of me. Amputation of a way of talking, of exploring ideas together. "Improvising," Michelle used to call it. On any subject, any idea that popped into our heads, following it where it took us, like making footprints in fresh snow.

I remember our last long talk, before Michelle got too sick. We started with the social organization of bees, don't ask me why, and the life of a queen bee, and Michelle said, "I'll stick to being a human female. More choices than a queen bee, and we can fight for ever more of them." But then she didn't fight hard enough to stay alive!

You hear me, Michelle? You didn't fight hard enough to stay alive!

Oh, hell. Do we have a choice about when our heart stops beating?

All our talking, for hours at a time, about the afterlife, if any, and about god, if any—all open-ended, because it was always "to be continued." If I thought about an afterlife now, I would only slide into wishful thinking. I so desperately want you to be ongoing, somehow, somewhere.

If you've got some answers now, Michelle, you better find a way of getting them to me!

Since I pulled the sheet over your face, covering those mutilated ears and the blood, I have not been able to see your face in my memory. But I hear your voice.

Can you hear me?

(Yes, even now I sometimes still slip back into talking to Michelle.)

What I should tell you, what you need to know, is that I fully intended to do what I could for her mother, if occasion arose. For Michelle's sake and for my own, as penance.

TED

Okay. It's the next day, Monday, and I'm sitting in a courtroom. At ten o'clock in the morning! After three weeks on the road, then a night of libations, maybe a couple of hours sleep, tops, some demon from hell grabbed me by the scruff, dunked my head into cold water, and hauled me over here.

Every little move like stepping on tacks. Barefoot. But I did promise Bear I'd go, so here I sit, shaved, buttoned, third row from the front. Fighting to keep my eyelids up.

The courtroom has a high ceiling and wood panelling all around, the kind of room makes you want to clap and tap, to check out the acoustics. All the polished wooden benches are filled with very quiet people, waiting.

My eyes keep skipping over to the right, to the three big cops standing in a row beside the exit door. The youngest one is parading his uniform. The fat one is trying to keep his snores down to *sotto voce*. And the biggest one, the one with a furnace for a chest, he's doing a slow burn. He's expecting some falutin' lawyer language to go swooping over his head where he won't catch the half of it. But he's the one: if he looks my way for two seconds, he'll have my number: hung-over jazz musician, trying to clean up his act for the day.

Yeah, well. I may have sold my ass to the Devil's music but I'm not chained to it, and I proved it, too. Quit my last jazz gig two and a half months ago. My thirty-third birthday. Walked off the stage, and told the snotty little club manager to go fuck a goat. Then I went home and ripped the phone right out of the wall. I was up-to-the-eyeballs sick of playing in dark holes and caverns full of smoke, seeing only the shadows of people. Except for those few at the front tables, reserved by Mr. Suburbia and his anniversary wife, out slumming in memory of hot pursuit. Man, I was even sick of playing for the jazz aficionados, up there in their cerebral nooks, with everybody sitting in rows like goddamn effigies, and every note you play echoes like a hollow tooth. And I sure as hell didn't want to be waking up one day 20 years from now, a 53-year-old sideman still doing shit gigs to pay the rent. No, let's face it, man, it don't add up to a great life in music!

So I quit. And I was damned serious about finding some other way. But what do you do, if you're hooked? You swear you're gonna leave town and run your uncle's motel out on Highway 117, or you swear you'll play pop till you've got some bread together, and then go off and...man, what you do in the end is always the same: go back to playing jazz, scuffle, swear, and play some more. You can tell it wasn't the first time I chewed over that one.

I see the three cops and everybody else turn towards the back of the courtroom. A woman comes in through the big open door. The woman is tall and beautiful. She moves down the aisle and every step she takes says: I am Dignity and Grace, submitting to an Ordeal Imposed. I promise Drama Larger than Life.

I knew from the first second I saw her that my life just took a hairpin turn.

The woman walks all the way to the front row and sits down. And now the whole courtroom sounds like a field of dry grass, whispering: *pshpsthp-shtpsht.*

I'm three rows up, to the right of her, so I see the woman in three-quarter profile. She is sitting very still. She has a hat on, with a wide curving brim over dark hair. She keeps her eyes pointing down. She's waiting. Once, she tilted her head and said something to the guy on her right. He nods a lot and shifts his ass around on the chair. Has to be the lawyer.

Everybody in the courtroom seems to know who this woman is. I've been taking that break, remember, two months without LBJ's double talk about Vietnam, without the Beatles on Ed Sullivan, without Lester Pearson's one-per-flag-two-per-flag magic maple leaves. So the only thing I know about the woman sitting there in the front row is this: I cannot take my eyes off her. Not for one second.

She is sitting very still, not moving at all or making a sound, but I'll swear it to this day: I heard her. A sustained note, full of harmonics, humming in her veins.

I have to meet this woman.

She's unbuttoning her right glove at the wrist, one button at a time, pulling it off, one finger at a time. Every single eye in the courtroom is watching her. But it's not theatre. I can't tell what it is. She's like some instrument you've never heard, or maybe a very ancient one—you can't even guess what kind of sound it would make.

In the meantime the court proceedings are passing me by like distant traffic. All I heard was her name: Mara deJong. Then it's over.

The woman stands up and the whole courtroom gets up on its feet, to watch Mara deJong walk back up the aisle. I jump up and have to step on a few toes so I can slip into the aisle just behind her. I follow her out the door, down the hall, click-clack on the marble floor, out the heavy front doors into the heat and the blowing dirt and glaring sunlight, and down the concrete steps to the sidewalk. There she stops. Now I'm right beside her.

In front of us, there's a guy backing into the street. His belly is tangled up in leather straps and cameras and he's getting ready to snap. Mara deJong turns sideways, one hand up to her hat. Her elbow is completely blocking the camera shot. And her eyes are looking at me, Ted O'Sullivan. The great improviser.

"Would you like a ride?"

Just like that, out of my own mouth.

Then I get a flash of my beat-up old van full of assorted travelling gear, like foam rubber covered with a ratty old Mexican blanket, a dolly with straps for moving the B52 organ, a few empty beer bottles rolling around, and that damned wobbly passenger seat. Mara deJong is still looking at me. Not smiling.

"Yes, please," she says. "In my taxi."

And then a cab pulls over to the curb and she climbs in the back and I follow. Never occurred to me to do anything else.

"Right on time," says the cabby, big grin in the rear view mirror. Mara deJong is one fare he doesn't want to miss. He's driving off and he already knows where to go.

At that point, I finally remember that I was supposed to be sitting back in the courtroom, waiting for Michelle's mother, the earlobe freak, so I could check her out for Bear, as promised. I'd better just ask this Mara deJong for her phone number and then get my ass back to the courtroom.

I turn to the woman who is sitting upright, looking straight ahead like she is totally alone in this cab. Thinking. Not even a quick glance in my direction. So I had to ask myself: what the hell does this woman have me here for?

I knew it wasn't as a stud. I've heard that old tune often enough to recognize it from the first chord and I was willing to bet all my Fats Waller records that wasn't it. But say this Mara deJong just likes having men tag along here and there, and say she doesn't mind picking a stranger, nobody else being handy—even then I was not a likely candidate. I mean I don't usually inspire confidence at first sight in people à la mode. My hair's too long, for one thing. And my face? Well, I never was the ugliest kid on the block but my face would not sell breakfast cereal. And my eyes make some people real nervous. As I've been told more than once: "You know something, Ted? When I first met you, you scared me a little bit." So then you know: this woman likes taming bad boys. Or maybe she likes getting treated bad so she can cry. Either way you'd better play it smart, Tedboy, and beat it.

I shift my ass sideways and look the woman over some more, this time at close quarters. Mara deJong is older than I thought, maybe around forty. Eyes hiding in the shadow of the hat. High cheekbones, lips delicately sculpted. A face that makes you think about—no, not photos of Garbo, but portraits with titles: "Beautiful Lady suspected of harbouring strong Character." And, let me tell you, a first-rate poker face. Even today I have no idea what she was thinking about on that drive. What she handed me later as her reason for picking me up sounded nuts.

Mara deJong is facing forward and she still hasn't said one word. Hands in her lap, holding each other, still wearing those long buttoned gloves. Perfect legs—long, slim, European legs. I'd already guessed she was a foreigner and I even thought, maybe that's what it is, but let's face it, Mara deJong was not the first foreigner I ever met. No, man, what pulled me in like a magnet the first time I saw her was this: I couldn't read the woman. Not at all. And that sure as hell was a new one on me.

I should tell you this: jazz musicians meet a lot of women. Maybe too many. The last time I got tired of floaters, I ended up living with a very nice college graduate. An anchor with doilies. When we split up, Dona forgot to pack the tapes I made for her: all my own pieces, and some of them damned good ones.

Meantime, the cab is turning left, from St. George onto Bloor, and suddenly I really want to hear the woman's voice. So I say: "I'm Ted," sounding cool and easy because I can do that no matter what, except when I'm seriously pissed off.

"Ted O'Sullivan."

Mara deJong holds out one gloved hand and turns her head in my direction.

"Mara deJong," she says. "Pleased to meet you." Polite. Nothing but polite.

The taxi stops and the cabby hops around to open the door for Mara deJong. With a smile. By the time I'm out of the cab, Mara deJong has the house key in her hand and she is taking for granted that I'll come in.

The hallway is a lot of dark polished wood. No sounds. One of those antique wall mirrors with ornate hooks. A smell in the air of something gone sour, like a note in the wrong place.

I follow Mara into the ground floor living room, which is casual and comfortable and confusing as hell, because Mara deJong is neither.

"Please sit down," she says, taking off her jacket. Her blouse shimmers like dove feathers after the rain. (One of my favorite Coltrane tunes, "After the Rain.") She takes off her hat. Very dark hair, with waves. She doesn't fuss with it. Doesn't even reach up and pat.

"May I get you something to drink? Wine? Scotch?"

English is not her mother tongue. She speaks it well, no hesitations or obvious errors, but her delivery is a bit stiff and there's a faint accent, hard to place.

I ask for Scotch, of course, on the rocks if any.

Mara deJong nods and leaves the room. Still wearing those long gloves. The whole house is quiet, just a few low rumbles coming in from the city. Nothing like the traffic noises attacking my own pad all day and most of the night.

The couch I'm sitting on is deep and soft, dark blue. There's a fireplace in the right hand wall, not recently used. There's an antique rolltop desk in the corner. All the walls are bare. Nothing anywhere talks about Mara deJong.

Next to the fireplace, there's an old cabinet with a record player in it. The albums are on a shelf above. A fair-sized collection. I want to go see what music Mara deJong listens to. I know that's like checking out a horse's teeth before you've even seen it walk, but I have to find out all I can fast. I have to get myself out of here and back to the courtroom.

I'm halfway off the couch to go look at her albums when Mara deJong comes back with two glasses. Hers looks like mineral water. I raise mine high, then pour half of it in. She sits down across from me. She takes a sip and puts the glass on the low table between us. And speaks.

"Do you have a family, Mr. O'Sullivan? A wife? Children?"

"No, I don't. Call me Ted."

Mara nods and now she is looking me over. Like I'm a chimp and she's the buyer for the zoo. I guess it's fair enough: the curiosity is mutual. Only my question is, "Who-and-what-the-hell are you?" and Mara's question about me is this: "Let me see now, is he going to be useful to me?" Which does finally tell me something, of course. Just enough to make me want to drop my glass on the rug and take off.

I swallow the rest of the Scotch.

Mara's inspection tour has reached my eyes, and right away hers bounce off. She takes a while looking at my hands. Finally she's done with her all-over tour, tilts her head and says:

"What is your line of work, Ted?"

"I'm a jazz musician."

"Ah..."

She sounds faintly pleased, so I ask her outright about the record collection.

"Yes. Nearly all of it is jazz," she says. "But these record albums do not belong to me." Dismissing the owner's taste in music.

"So this is not your apartment."

"No, no," she says. "It was my daughter's."

Mara deJong gets up and walks to the rolltop desk in the corner. Dark old wood. Makes exactly the sound a rolltop desk should make. She takes out a pile of newspaper clippings, and pulls out one short square column with a loud headline. She hands me the clipping.

I read the headline and look up and Mara deJong is walking out of the room. My eyes start doing a kind of jumpy samba over the printed lines:

"...unnatural....heinous....evidence clear-cut..."

And the headline again: MOTHER ACCUSED OF MUTILATING BODY OF DEAD DAUGHTER

ALICIA

That Monday I came back from work early and found Bear pacing back and forth, back and forth, turning our home into a cage. I knew it had to do with Michelle, dead though she was, or with her monstrous mother Mara deJong, so I turned around and went out again. Went to the library until it closed. By the time I returned home, Bear was gone. Yes, I know there's no point in it, but just the same, I keep wishing I had stayed home with Bear, to talk and clear out those dark-looming clouds, maybe avert the storm.

TED

That headline, "Mother mutilates," jumped out at me and then everything went dark and I was falling, in complete silence, into a bottomless pit. That's what it felt like: falling down a pit, in complete black darkness, complete silence.

It used to happen to me in nightmares, till a few years back. When I woke up I was always gasping for air. This time it's just more falling, and then I hear something and it pulls me up and out of there and then it's over.

I take a long deep breath. I raise my head and see Mara deJong, just coming out of the kitchen, followed by a dark shadow. I see the dark shadow bending way over with grief, and then it dissolves and is gone and there's a glass of Scotch right in front of me. I take it and gulp down most of it, and feel the Scotch land in the pit of my stomach. Okay, not a bottomless pit after all.

Mara deJong is just sitting down across from me, putting her glass on the table between us. She is calm and poised, crossing her legs at the ankle, taking a sip from her glass of mineral water, waiting for something. I drink down the rest of the Scotch, which jogs my brain: Mara is way back at the point where she left me reading the Monstrous Mother clipping and she's waiting to see what I'm going to do. I check in with my gut, expecting to hear "Run! Run like hell and don't come back!" But what's coming through loud and clear is this: "Stick to the woman like a burr. Stick to her, find out everything about her, till you know what makes her tick."

Mara deJong is still waiting for my reaction. She's looking down at her own hands. They're in her lap and they're holding each other. The hands say: "I need help. Should I trust myself to a stranger?" But it's a pose. I know it and I'm not about to let her get away with it, but now—I can feel it in my bones—the woman is getting ready to leap a hurdle. She flashes me a quick look, then she leans ever so slightly forward and proceeds to interview me.

"Tell me, please, Ted: do you by any chance speak German?"

"Well enough to do a loose translation of something, I suppose. Something simple..."

"I knew it! I could tell that you have some German in you," she says.

"One grandmother, all told."

Mara deJong isn't listening. And she doesn't look one bit in need of help. More like triumphant.

"Please tell me, Ted," she says. "How soon could you be ready to travel?"

"Travel?"

"Yes. By any good fortune, could you be ready tomorrow?"

"To travel where?"

"To Paris, then Bergheim in Germany, then Vienna."

"Quite a tour," I say, and then I remember she's never even heard me play, so it had to be something else.

"Okay, say I went to Europe. What would I be doing there, in Paris and Germany and Vienna?"

"You would help me make preparations for my court case. I have a list."

Mara deJong's arm moves, her hand descends on a knob, pulls out the drawer of a small table. Lifts out a shiny black notebook. Starts leafing through it.

"Did your lawyer tell you...?"

"My lawyer has nothing to do with this," says Mara deJong. "In fact, I shall be changing lawyers. Did you see him today? He must recently have gained weight: his jacket was so tight it stuck right out over his posterior. And that tie..."

"Wait a minute. You are firing your lawyer because his jacket doesn't fit?"

Mara deJong does not smile.

"Surely you can see, Ted. His appearance is an important tool. If he doesn't know that..."

Mara's voice is completely serious. She deposits the black notebook on the table. Maybe she's decided that I'm all wrong, too. Not my weight—I never carry around more than I need—but one of my shoelaces is definitely shorter than the other. Mara has gone back to her I-need-help pose: hands in lap, eyes on hands. No medley ever had a smoother transition.

"Tell me something, Mara, are you an actress?"

Surprised. "No. Why do you ask?"

I don't want to call her on the "I need help" pose, so I go back to my first sight of her. "Your entrance at court today. I mean in the courtroom. You almost had me yelling 'encore.'"

Mara nods. "It was good, wasn't it? I do believe I made exactly the impression I intended. Yes, I think it deserves a toast. To the first fruit of my labours."

Duly raised glasses. I drink, Mara sips mineral water. But she's excited. Her eyes flicker across mine. She wants to talk.

"Go ahead," I tell her. "What labours?"

"Well," she says. "Since you witnessed the success of my appearance at court, I'll describe to you how it was achieved. I'll start at the top, shall I? You'll remember the effect."

Now Mara deJong starts a hymn, delivered in operatic *Sprechgesang*.

"First, the light grey felt hat," Mara recites, "wide-brimmed, imperceptibly tilted: playing on tall slim elegance with a rather discreet worldliness, yes?

"The suit: so well-cut as to draw no attention to itself. A grey-blue surface upon which reflections are cast as on water: by each observer according to his or her inclination.

"The shoes: sturdy. Providing a note of trustworthiness, of conservative reasonableness.

"The long buttoned gloves: saucy or staid, depending on the perceiver's age and experience. A keyhole on mystery, a stimulant to the imagination, which I intend to mould and to shape.

"No handbag, of course. My progress down the aisle had to show me unprotected, concealing nothing."

Mara stops talking, eyes still bright. All of a sudden I get a picture of Dona's brother, the painter. Jumping around like a grasshopper on bennies because he'd just found a way to paint the texture of winter bark. Eyes shining and excited like Mara's.

"Please tell me, Ted," says Mara deJong, leaning forward a tiny bit, "did you happen to overhear anything? Among the public?" Then, without pausing for an answer:

"Let me tell you what they were saying, in one way or another, or thinking. 'This lady I see could not have committed the crime of which she stands accused—though I can see that some people might think her capable of it.' " She smiles a genuine smile. "You see, Ted, that is precisely what I intend people to think."

"So you intend to plead 'not guilty'?"

"No, no, Ted. Today it was not a question of guilt or innocence. The impression I created today was merely a first tactic in my strategy."

Mara gets up and heads for the window. Not sure she can trust me with her strategy. Well, why should she? I am a stranger, for Christ's sake. Though it sure does seem by now that we've jumped into the middle of something.

I turn to talk to Mara at the window, her back to me, and there it is again. A sound you can't quite hear. You know it's in there, you think it's a kind of hum, but that's just a word. Real sounds are a lot more specific. Time to get the woman turned around and talking.

"Tell me something, Mara: how come only one single photographer at the courthouse? Your case must be making waves all over."

Mara turns, walks back to her chair and sits down.

"I arranged that all the—how do you say it: newshounds? I made sure that they all had precisely wrong information. They believe I shall be in the courtroom tomorrow to receive my trial date."

Not even a hint of a smile, her voice sounding like a shrug. Like it should be obvious: a woman who designed every detail of her appearance can certainly take care of business all around. Okay, I'll try a different route.

"Where were you born, Mara?"

"Russia. In Leningrad."

"When did you leave Russia?"

"Just before the war. World War II."

"Really! How did you get out through the Iron Curtain?"

"I was married to a German. But, Ted, none of this is really pertinent right now. All the information you will need is in here."

Mara is picking up that black notebook again. It's looking fatter and shinier.

"All right, Mara, tell me what is pertinent right now."

"Whether you can go to Europe for me," she says and goes on with what has to be a prepared little speech. "I need friendly character witnesses at my trial. I cannot afford to fly everybody I know to Canada. The selection of character witnesses has to be made there, in Europe. I myself cannot leave Toronto at this time. I can assure you that you will be well paid for the work."

I'm still back with the first part of all this and tell her:

"By the look of that notebook, you want to stuff the whole courtroom full of friendly witnesses."

"Oh, no," she tells me, "this contains not only a list of names and addresses. There is information, as well, about each person. And, most important, a list of questions to ask them."

"But how the hell do you know that I'd do a good job? That I wouldn't just take your money and fuck off?"

"Ted! Please!"

"Ted Please what? Offensive language? Or how can I doubt your infallible intuition about people?"

"Intuition has nothing to do with it. I am very scientific in my assessment of people."

"Like lawyers by the fit of their jackets."

"Never underestimate appearance, Ted."

She still sounds serious. So I stand up and show her the appearance of my entire wonderful self. Bottom to top.

Black leather shoes, the ones I wear to "refeened" gigs and to court. I.e., no holes and showing bits of shine.

Jeans, clean.

Leather jacket, and a damned good one, too. Soft leather, dark brown, fine stitching, well cut like a suit jacket. Bought it off Sam. Sam is a pimp and a badass but he does have good taste in clothes. He wears only the best and he tires fast.

Under the jacket, my clean white shirt and the tie. I really wanted to get into that courtroom without a hitch.

Under that, though Mara can't see it, a T-shirt that says: "Life's a bitch and then you die." (The whiner's T-shirt, said Alicia when she saw me wearing it. Since then it's been strictly an undershirt.)

Mara is looking at my hair, which is creeping down to my collar but is clean, light brown, and wavy. The way it gets when I remember to buy shampoo.

No beard these days, but my mustache, of course. A bit darker than my hair and a bit rough, but thanks to the Great Joker Up Above, not the kind of mustache that gets tangled in your shoelaces if you don't trim it every day.

That's it: Ted O'Sullivan. Not the ugliest kid on the block. I take a bow and sit down.

"Well, Mara, let's hear your scientific assessment."

Mara says: "Attractive, easy-going, impulsive, decisive..."

"'Easy-going?' That's a hoot and a riot, that one. Impulsive? Okay. What was the last one? Decisive. Where did you get the 'decisive'?"

"Few men act as promptly as you did, when they want to meet someone."

"You were pretty decisive yourself, inviting me to come home with you." Wait a minute, is this going anywhere I want to go? Before I can think about that, Mara gets back on track. Her track.

"Ted, do you have commitments which you cannot postpone?"

"No commitments. Now tell me how you know I'd do a good job for you, if I went."

"You responded most perfectly to every aspect of my design."

I don't know if she's pulling my leg or what. Not something I generally get confused about. And does the woman really believe she's got me pegged?

"Okay," I tell her. "You are right this far: I saw, I boggled, I followed."

Mara is getting up. Has she even heard me? She goes to the window again. In a world of her own. And inside there, I get the feeling she's right on course. No meandering, looping or wavering. Like breath going into an oboe: that direct and precise. Amazing! Bloody amazing. I mean, I'm all of one piece behind the piano, sometimes, but in the rest of my life? More like a pendulum gone berserk.

But I do know what's next on my own agenda: another drink, and then some serious poking and prodding, to find out what that world-of-her-own is, inside of her.

Mara turns to me and says: "Would you excuse me for a few moments? And please, help yourself."

She steps out into the hall, walks up the stairs. If she's going up there to change into something tactical, I'll get pissed off. I hate it when women take that route.

What I really needed right now was a joint. Grass gives me new perspectives and I sure did need one of those. I didn't have any grass on me, of course. You do not go to court carrying. So I went for the Scotch.

The kitchen is disgusting. Dirty dishes everywhere, overflowing garbage can, empty cartons and containers on the counter, a dishtowel on the floor where she mopped up something brown. If this kitchen was in my neighbourhood, the roaches would load it up and carry it away. The liquor is in an upper cupboard next to the spices. A nice selection. I take a sample direct from the bottle of Johnny Walker and pour a healthy one into my glass. No point in looking for the good herb anywhere in this place; I'm willing to bet my piano on that. Well, maybe not my piano, but the stepchild, my electric organ. Actually, I've been thinking about hawking the B-52, if cash runs out altogether. Old Hopper on Church Street would give it decent storage. He pays less than some pawnbrokers, but he doesn't turn your ax into a pile of dusty junk.

I get back to the couch and Mara is back on her chair, waiting again. Ah yes, she wants me to go to Europe for her. On a gig. Why me?

"Tell me something, Mara. Why don't you hire a private investigator for the job?"

"The people I want you to see would not be at ease with a professional."

That actually makes sense.

"But what the hell made you think I'd even consider hopping off to Europe for you?"

"I lose nothing by asking."

"What if I said yes and then messed up? Turned out to be the wrong man for the job?"

"In such a case I would terminate the arrangement." Stated like it's so obvious I should have deduced it from her shoes. From their note of "conservative reasonableness."

"You certainly cover all the bases," I tell her. "I really have to hand it to you." Mara looks confused again.

"I mean you think of everything. The photographers at court, your lawyer's appearance, your own..."

"I never," she says, "permit myself negligence in serious matters. I remember exactly what I wore on every important occasion in my life."

(Oh, sweet Jesus, here comes a recital of proms and graduations and weddings.)

"I remember," says Mara, "what I wore each time I was interrogated by the SS, I remember what I wore at the murder trial in Indonesia, I remember...."

"SS? Murder?"

"Yes, Ted. Are you hungry?"

Mara is heading for the kitchen to warm up some food. I feel like I've been spun and dropped off too fast, no idea where.

Suddenly, there's a crash from the kitchen: the sound of broken glass. Then a lament starts up. Mara, sounding like she's lost at least a favourite relative. I jump up and rush to the kitchen doorway. Mara has her back to me. She is holding her head in her hands and she is weaving like a mourner at the graveside. The dirge is in Russian, an ancient lament, going on and on.

"Mara," I really want to bring her out of this. "Was it very old? Sentimental value?"

Mara doesn't answer but she gradually stops weaving; the lament is fading out. Now she looks down at the shards of glass and says "One year bad luck." In a voice of eternal doom. Then she turns away, leaving the mess on the floor, and goes to the stove to stir something. She's frowning into the pot.

"You see?" she says. "Something has already gone wrong. I hope you like vinegar." She dumps a spoonful of sugar into the pot and then stirs some more.

"This is borscht. With meat and potatoes. Russian cabbage soup."

We carry large bowls of soup, bread, butter, utensils, and napkins to the back part of the living room, sit at a round table, and eat. The thick soup is heavy on the vinegar all right, the potatoes aren't warm all the way through, and the bread is stale. Mara deJong is eating very fast, getting it over with. And then she sits, looking down at her hands, waiting for me to finish. I'm not all that turned off by the vinegar, so I keep eating and try slinging in a question.

"You don't look much at people's eyes, do you?"

She flickers her eyes across my face and says:

"Please tell me why you wanted to meet me."

Her tone of voice makes it clear she's not looking for compliments. She wants just the facts, ma'am, and well, she had me there. If I said "curiosity," she'd think it was only about the crime. I didn't know the word that would tell it all. But by then I knew this much: I was sticking because I couldn't pry myself off.

"If you had a piano, I could play it for you," I tell Mara. "A jazz tune. 'Bewitched, Bothered, and Bewildered.'"

"Do play it for me some day," she says. Polite phrase, polite voice. But she is actually looking at me.

Now there's a knock on the door, interrupting. Mara says: "Come in." The door opens; a woman stands in the doorway. Long shiny brown hair, bare feet in leather sandals, maybe 35, standing in the doorway because Mara hasn't asked her in.

"I wondered how it went today," says the woman, voice low and sad.

Mara says: "It was a complete success."

The woman nods. I am confused. "Mara, what exactly happened in court today?"

Mara looks at me and sighs. "I'll continue my report in a moment, Ted." Spoken as if we've been interrupted in an important board meeting. The woman takes the hint and splits, and Mara immediately uses her as a way to dodge my question.

"That was Lena," she says. "Her apartment is upstairs. She was my daughter's friend. Lena spends most of her time sitting on her windowsill or under the big maple tree in the garden—I think you call it backyard? Sometimes she makes notes in her lap."

"Is she a writer?"

"I doubt it. She has no temperament. I don't understand her at all—she could be quite attractive."

"She *is* attractive."

That surprised Mara, I could tell. I ask her again what exactly went on in the courtroom today, but now she is looking down at a pile of newspapers beside the doorway.

"Oh, dear," she says. "I forgot to give those to Lena to dispose of. I have never read daily newspapers before. They are ghastly, aren't they? As soon as the court case is over, I shall never touch another one. Right now, I have to clip out all the pertinent reports and editorials and letters. This letter, for example."

Mara reaches into an invisible pocket in her skirt and hands me a clipping. A letter to the editor.

> *"I have been endlessly reading about Mara deJong and her 'heinous crime.' Most of it is sentimental tripe. Let the people who concern themselves so passionately with 'Unnatural Acts' and 'Punishment' look at the world around them: hundreds of thousands of people are killed, tortured or starved to death every day! And the Master Criminals continue to pile up the Instruments of Death to the entire human race.*
>
> *Why the great outcry over a pair of already dead earlobes?"*
>
> *Val Johnson,*
> *Lindsay, Ont.*

Mara is watching me. I have barely skimmed the letter because I have just realized something: this is a moment Mara has definitely and carefully planned.

"Mara, tell me, did you write this letter to the editor yourself?"

"Certainly not," says Mara. She did have the clipping mighty handy, though, ready to draw.

"What else?" I ask her. "In your pocket, Mara. What other guns in your arsenal?"

"There is nothing else in my pocket," she says. Then she reaches for her handbag, which is dangling from the back of the dirty gold chair. She opens a zippered inside pocket and pulls out a piece of cardboard the size of a postcard. A photograph. She's looking at it, wondering whether or not to show it to me. Tempted, but hesitating.

Finally she hands it to me. It's a posed picture: a little girl with round cheeks and big solemn eyes, wearing a traditional dress of some kind, with lots of red embroidery. The little girl is standing on a chair, looking regal. Portrait of the princess as baby.

"Very pretty, Mara. You?"

"Yes, when I was three years old. I remember that day very clearly. I insisted that I must stand on that chair. I knew that if I was photographed standing on the floor, I would be dwarfed and distorted by the angle."

"As in 'nobody looks down on me, buster'?"

By the way Mara takes back the photograph, I've missed her point by a block.

"Why are you carrying the picture around with you?"

"It is," she says solemnly, "a talisman."

She is depositing the photo back in her bag, shutting it away. No further explanations unless of her own choosing. I have a sudden hard urge to shake the woman off her agenda. To crack her composure.

My mouth opens, intending to ask more questions, but the one that comes bursting out surprises the hell out of me. "Mara, *why*?"

Holy shit! Now both of us know it. I believe that Mara deJong is guilty. I believe that she did actually cut off those earlobes. Not only that: I'd been assuming her guilt all along. Ever since I found out she was the mother. And now it's completely clear to me why I have to stick to the woman like a burr, like a splinter: I have to find out how a mother could do such a thing. To her own child.

MARA

Dear Theodore,

A day of elation and of despair. A day such as only artists and scientists encounter, survive, and transform into triumph.

At court, the proceedings went as expected. The date for my trial is set, for Sept. 6th. That much was merely a matter of diligent research and of detailed instruction to my lawyer.

Not long thereafter: elation. My meticulous preparations for today conjured the very person who should prove most useful to me in the coming months. His name is Ted O'Sullivan. He is like a Pushkin character: gallant, impulsive, loyal, obsessed, unpredictable. There is no caution in him.

And then, while still in the midst of interviewing this young man, I broke a glass. And was immediately thrown into the vat of roiling superstitions, emanating fumes so pungent as to rob me of rational thought. Suddenly all my confidence was shaken, making me question even my victory in that other trial, in Indonesia. Could it be that it was won not as a result of my research and deductions but rather by way of a bribe to the judge (from Albert, of course)? Or even as a result of sheer blind luck? You know how I detest the notion of luck. It rides in tandem with superstition: both are anathema to the scientist in me. In the end I must believe that the years of dwelling in Indonesia made possible that sure-footed progress towards victory, and that, in my present trial, I can and will be successful as before.

How our father used to rail against our mother's superstitions. Do you remember my "lucky dress"? The one I wore for all recitals until I could no longer fit into it? How I cried and stormed, how father paced and pontificated, and how mother quietly removed the dress to the sewing room where she cut it into squares the size of a handkerchief, and came back to assure me that each piece of the dress would be as lucky for me as the entire dress. Neither father nor mother understood that the dress was not a "lucky" dress, nor did it hold magic of any kind. Neither listened to me to find out why I was so desperately crying. I daresay I was too young to give a coherent explanation of the power lost and wherein it lay.

And do you recall that recording I made the same day, when I was 12, while I was still furious, absolutely volcanic about the loss forever of the dress, and how that very performance was afterwards praised as yet more proof of my great talent?

Our father would turn in his grave to see me now, toiling in the fields of science. Just as he would turn and turn again to see me succumb, albeit rarely and always briefly, to superstition. I console myself with the knowledge that this struggle against superstition is surely an epic battle. Think of the millennia of accumulated proverbs, folk sayings, superstitions in Russia alone!

And superstitions do not depart because reason has discovered their lair. No, they retreat for a while, stay hidden as you laugh at them, laugh at the hold they once had over you; they might even feign death, but let your guard down for even a moment and they are back, dancing their demon dance, pulling you into their dark circle until, swamped with fear, you succumb and offer whatever appeasement they demand. Thinking yourself lucky indeed if it is only a pinch of salt thrown over your shoulder. Not admitting for a moment that even this is surrender.

And when you are weakened, or perhaps when you are hopeful, then the demons circle and whisper: could it be that superstitions are but the boiled-down wisdom of myths? Just as clichés so often turn out to be nuggets of truth, and proverbs splinters of stories which broke off and, floating free, yet retain some of the story's essence. And just so, could superstitions not be the vestiges of ancient knowledge which are exiled from their origins but are nevertheless powerful and true?

You see how devious, how insidious are those whispering voices, awaiting moments of weakness or of hope.

And what are rituals if not another form of superstition? Appeasement of the jealousy of gods?

Today, amidst the gathering evidence of success, there were two moments of doubt about my own perceptions. The first, that the lawyer I chose after interviewing several has an incomplete understanding of his role. The second, that Lena, my neighbor, whose casualness about her appearance amounts to neglect, is yet perceived as attractive.

"Small potatoes," as Michelle used to be fond of saying at the most inappropriate times, but nevertheless a warning: Canada and Canadians are bound to present me, recently arrived as I am, with unsettling surprises.

How glad I am for the rigorous training I received as a child in discipline and in permitting neither my feelings nor my thoughts to show themselves. When my role was so tightly proscribed and deviation meant father's thunderous eyebrows and mother's sighs of exhaustion, I honed the skills which stand me in good stead to this day.

(You must remember endlessly fiddling with lights and focus while I stood, though only three years old, not moving even one muscle until my legs cramped and I grew dizzy and fainted dead away. I believe that if you had had the courage to pursue your love of photography as a profession, I, too, might have defied father. It was too late, of course, by the time I fled Russia only to fall prey to yet another dictator.)

The discipline I acquired during my lost childhood and which saved my life during the Nazi years, that same discipline seems to be akin to something I see all around me here, among the "Anglos" (Canadians of British descent). They, I understand, have had generations of such training in hiding their emotions. Sometimes I do ask myself whether what I see is lack of demonstration of feelings, or an actual lack of the feelings themselves? Or perhaps they feel a mere tremor where we Russians experience cataclysmic eruptions?

The question is, of course, whether such differences are cultural, or in fact, deeply seated in the psyche. My travels tell me these differences do exist; it remains only to find their roots. That search, however, is beyond my field of endeavour. My focus must be the preparations for the trial.

This young man, Ted O'Sullivan, believes himself to appear nonchalant, perhaps even inscrutable, but he is neither. His eyes betray him. I do not know the source or nature of his quest, but I suspect that I have become a part of it—whether I am a dragon to be slain or a damsel to be rescued is not, as yet, clear to me.

I know there will be no answer to this letter. I confide in you as I always have, knowing you to be the one who understood me from the beginning.

As always, your beloved sister,

Mara

TED

About an hour ago, Mara deJong ushered me to the door of her apartment like a gracious hostess, and then told me straight: unless I went to Europe for her, this was goodbye. That was the gist of it and no discussion: go to Europe for her or I'd never see her again.

Well, fuck you, Mara deJong, and fuck the donkey you rode in on.

I'm sitting in the Pilot Tavern, facing the back wall and yet another glass of Scotch. What I want is to get drunk, so drunk I'll forget my own name, let alone Mara deJong's. Forget her, forget the earlobes, forget mothers can do such things. Work up to another clearing-house puke and spew it all out of my guts. And tomorrow, join up again with my own life, such as it is. But the Scotch isn't working.

I pay the tab and go sit in my van, motor running, thinking: this being about midnight on a Monday, where is Bear likely to be hanging out? And remember, only about two hours late, that this is the night we were going to jam at Henry's again. I signal and pull away from the curb, a model driver, and head for Henry's. I promise myself to skip over the last time I was there and played behind Michelle. I park the van smack in front of the door and then, halfway down the stairs, I get stopped anyway by an echo of Michelle's voice, singing "Stormy Weather."

When my ears finally clear so I can tune in, the guys are doing an up-tempo "Salt Peanuts" and they are sounding good. Roscoe on drums, Biddle on the trumpet, and Reggie, the finest tenor player around, when he's not too busy whittling the perfect reed. Bear on the upright bass.

Bear catches sight of me and he's waving me over to the piano. My legs take me over there and my ass puts itself on the stool—one of those old round ones with claw feet that ain't too steady, so you'd better not leave the ground with both legs at the same time. So there I sit, and I must look like I'm all ready to play, but something's happened to my fingers. I can't feel them. I look down at them and they're there, all right, but they're hanging on my hands like limp dicks. Like nothing is ever going to pump them into life again. I close my eyes and try to figure out what's going on, but how can I? This has never happened to me before. Never. No matter what shape I'm in—drunk, hungover, so tired I can't sit up straight, so fucked up I can't remember my name, so down and out I want to howl like a dog—no matter what, I have always been able to let my fingers tell it to the keys. Right now, with all the yammering and bleating and blasting going on inside of me, none of it—not one note—is getting out.

I turn my head away from those dead fingers and see Bear is looking at me.

"I'll be out in the van," I tell him, and get myself up off the stool, out of the basement and back into my van. And sit there, staring at my hands.

I used to think I was pretty good at figuring people out. After a couple of hours with somebody, I'd know at least the main themes: what makes them purr, what bothers their ass, how much do they see, looking at life? That stuff. About Mara deJong, after four hours in the same room, with my eyes and ears and antennae on full alert, I know nothing. Except that she did the deed. Other than that, abso-fucking-lutely nothing.

I've hit the steering wheel so hard my hands are hurting. It feels good, proof my hands aren't dead. And it's jogged my brain into coming up with a plan: I'll take Bear over to Mara deJong's place and get him to check the woman out. Yes! With his eye and mine along for another try, Mara deJong is as good as x-rayed, tagged, and filed away under "deranged, temporarily."

Leaving me to get on with reassembling all the pieces of my life, including reconnecting my fingers with piano keys.

Right on cue, Bear comes out of Henry's basement and climbs into the van. I concentrate on driving us over to Miguel's, the small after-hours place where we go when we want to talk. The owner, Michael, is from the Caribbean and he thinks all black Americans like Bear should go back to Africa. "A fantasy," says Bear. But it's one he likes arguing about.

Bear hasn't asked me what happened back at Henry's; he knows it'll spill when it's ready. We sit down at our usual table. Bear orders two Ex and waits. Oh, shit. All of a sudden I've remembered my promise to Bear: that I'd be in the courtroom today to check out Michelle's mother, the earlobe freak, and then give him some kind of report.

"Forget it," I tell Bear. "Do not ask me what makes mothers tick, okay? Just don't ask me. Because I don't know what makes mothers tick."

Bear says: "What's all this tick tick tick? And what the hell you jumping on me for? Be cool, okay? I wasn't even going to ask about the earlobe freak. Do what Alicia keeps on telling me to do: Put it behind you!"

Bear has a way of cooling me down faster than a fire hose. Or at least jumping me off the track.

"What the hell is going on with you and Alicia? You still hassling about Michelle? Who died over a week ago? Make some sense!"

"As a matter of fact," says Bear, "hang on a minute. Let me just give Alicia a call and say I'll be late getting home."

Bear heads for the phone and it's a damned strange sight to see, let me tell you, Bear beetling off to check in with the wife. But then, what isn't strange? I have never in my life been so fucked up I couldn't play!

Bear comes back, shaking his head.

"Alicia knows what you and I are talking about, and she sends you the same message: 'Put it behind you, Ted. I don't want to see either of you till you do!'"

Bear throws me a look like I'm the one giving him a hard time.

"Listen to me, Ted. Here's what I am going to do: I am going to give you a few more minutes yammering, and then I am going home and I am not mentioning Michelle or her mother the earlobe freak ever again. Because Alicia is turning cold on me and I can't take it. You listening to me? Ice picks for words, ice picks for looks. I can't take that from Alicia. So is that all clear now?"

"Okay, okay, Bear. But first you've got to help me out. You really have got to come with me and check out this Mara deJong."

So now I tell Bear all about it. Going to court, the woman I saw and had to follow, and how I found out, *after* all that, she's Michelle's mother.

"Listen," I told him. "There she was, sitting on the other side of the coffee table, and I know she's Michelle's mother who cut off her daughter's earlobes, but I can't put them together. The woman right in front of me and that mother. And it's driving me nuts. I tell you, man, the whole thing is playing pizzicato with my nerve strings so nothing is making any sense. I have got to figure out what would make a mother do such a thing or I'll go nuts."

Bear's been listening but I can see he hasn't stepped all the way in.

"You'll find out at the trial," he says. "You'll go and listen to the court case and figure it out from between the lines. Take it easy, will you?" Shaking his head as if he has no idea that waiting is something I cannot do. Like he hasn't had to bail me out of bars and hospitals and jail, too, because there'd been some waiting and waiting makes me go berserk.

One last squawk is all I have left in me.

"Bear, if you don't come with me to check her out, I'll have to take off and go to Europe for her. She wants me to go there, do something for her for the trial. So maybe I have to go and find out what I can over there."

"Oh, Christ," says Bear. He stretches his legs so he's practically lying on his chair, and starts up a grin. "Don't tell me," says Bear, "that this whole thing is one of your 'Ted to the Rescue' trips! Mara deJong pitifully sighs and Ted flings himself on his white horse, rides all the way to Europe, and starts hunting for the magic ring? Man, when are you going to come out of story-ville into the real world? Remember the time you took it on to help move that poor little mother and her kid with your van? The landlord threw them out, so Ted Terrific rides to the rescue. Loads every damned pot, blanket and crib into the van, says 'hop in' to the poor little woman and her kid, and then, all bloated with goodwill, he finds out the little mother and her kid have no place to go. So our man Ted Terrific takes them home and he sleeps on the floor. For two months. At which time the little woman's husband shows up and throws a fit and Tedboy gets kicked out of his own pad. Want to hear another one?"

"No, thanks," I told Bear. "You are totally off-base. I took those two in because of the kid. His mother was going to leave him at Children's Aid."

"By the way," says Bear, *sotto voce*. "The Tic just sat down at the bar."

"Oh, shit. Did she see us?"

"Oh, she knows you're here, all right. Alicia must have told her."

"Alicia wouldn't do that."

"These days, I don't know what she'll do. Anyway, here is something you have got to take care of: get that Tic out of our hair. She called every damned day to find out where you were and then she wouldn't believe you were on the road. We have to keep the phone off the hook, nights, so we can get some sleep."

Right then Jack the bartender calls over: "Hey, Ted." He's nodding his chin at the Tic, who is sitting at the bar with her back to us. "This lady a friend of yours? She says you're paying."

"Okay, okay," I told him, probably snarling by then. "I'll pay for what she's got here. Then she has to be going."

"Me, too," says Bear. "I have to be going."

So then I had to come right out with the worst of it. "Listen to me, Bear! I can't play, man! You hear me? My ears are getting nothing but buzz and my fingers won't move! That has never happened to me before, not once, and it scares the shit out of me. Do you hear what I'm saying? I can't play!"

Bear is sitting there, one hand on his beer, and he looks like he's listening to me, but he's not hearing me.

"Cool it," says Bear. "Take it easy! You're frothing like a bee-kicking mule! I mean it! You're likely to do yourself harm. Shit, man, I don't know what's happening with you. I mean, you're never as rational as you think you are, but this is nuts. It's morbid. Here is something to put up for a good hard look: You've already got more ways than a snake to slither out of being one-hundred-percent serious about your music. Your own music, I mean. And here you go, chasing into one more fucking detour off what you're supposed to be doing. And you want me to say it's okay? It's not okay. I do not think it's okay. So if you have to go on back there for a while to find out about your lady monster, you go ahead and do that, but I'm out of it. You get that?"

"That's fucking lousy," I told him. "I can't go back there. Mara says she'll be busy doing one thing and nothing else and that's prepare for her court case. So if I'm not going to Europe for her, that's it. Goodbye. Sitting on my ass and waiting for the court case, and you bloody well know that'll drive me nuts."

"Oh, shit," says Bear, sounding really pissed off like he's the one with reasons. "You're turning into a fucking ghoul! I want you to get this loud and clear: don't you ever mention any of this whole mess to me, ever. Or to Alicia. I mean it! Nobody and nothing is going to fuck up Alicia and me, and this here shit is coming damned close to doing that, so if you can't get yourself off that shit pile, and you can't clear it out of your head, then you just make damned sure you don't come around until you do!"

Then Bear split. Got up and split and left me sitting there feeling like I've been kicked in the head. Feeling like I've been kicked, and like I might never play music again, and now here's the Tic standing in front of me. The proverbial straw.

"You sure look awful," she says.

"I can't deal with you right now, Tic. You've got to leave me alone."

For once she doesn't start screeching. She keeps looking down at me and then she opens her hand in front of my nose and says:

"Here. You can have this one."

She's got a ball of foil paper in the palm of her hand, the size of a marble. She unfolds it like it's made of fragile gold leaf and holds out her palm again: a tiny white pill.

"What the hell is this?"

"It's my last one. Take it, it'll make you feel okay."

I swallowed it and it worked. Thanks to the Tic and her tiny Tac, I forgot about everything. When I woke up the next morning, I was in my own bed, and the Tic was lying on my shoulder, sleeping, with her eyes showing a slit of white.

I couldn't remember how I got home to my pad or to my bed. I left her a note and split.

LENA

Want to or not, I have to talk about my oath. I wouldn't have been around for any of this if not for my oath. I would have been ensconced in my studio, being the artist, instead of meeting Alicia and Ted and Bear, instead of getting embroiled in Mara's court case, instead of partaking in life.

It's actually what led to the oath that was so terrifying. I was sitting at the bedside of Michelle, my dearest friend. She was breathing with difficulty, only opening her eyes to smile now and then, and that's when I heard myself think: 'You should be in your studio, working!'

I heard that voice and right then and there I took the oath. I swore that I would not go near my work, would not even enter my studio, for one hundred days. One hundred days, I thought, would be long enough to break myself of obsession.

Nobody ever discourages artists from their obsession, have you noticed that? (Except of course, the spouse. Mozart's wife with paper twists of hubby's compositions in her hair.) In fact, they even tell you that unless an artist is obsessed, she will never do her best work.

But sooner or later—sooner, if you are a woman—you come to a fork in the road and there you have to decide: art or comforting, art or listening, art or holding the hand of your dying friend.

I know what Michelle would say: "You're making too much of it, Lena. It's just your monkey-on-the-shoulder berating you wherever you are, whatever you're doing, *whenever* you're not working."

Maybe so. Maybe so. But how horrifying to think that nothing is sacred to that voice. While others wrestle with the Angel of Death, I was defeated by Monkey Voice.

One hundred days without the escape hatch of work also meant that the pain in my heart remained unsiphoned and undiluted. My only solace in those days was the beleaguered Maple tree in the backyard. I could practically feel how her roots had to strain under that hard-packed city soil.

I always thought of the roots of trees as tentacles but now I think that they are the arteries and heart of the tree. Sometimes, when I am sitting under the Maple, I think I can hear her pulse. Well, I daresay it's my own pulse I'm hearing. I daresay I could become obsessed with Trees.

In the meantime, yes, Alicia, I had met Ted, but it was no more than an introduction. He was a young man downstairs, talking with Mara. Wishing me to blazes for interrupting. Ask him.

TED

Okay. I'm skipping right over a lot of heavy fog here, a lot of dozing with buzzing ears, all the way to Paris, France, where I'm sitting in the back of a cab. My brain is pea soup, my eyes are bloodshot and sore as hell and I figure hey, this is no way to have my first look at Paris, so I close my eyes. And think back to meeting Mara deJong, just last Monday, about Bear fucking off on me that same night. The next day lost in chemical limbo. So now, I figured, it had to be Wednesday. Early July, anyway, but not humid like it is back home and...two seconds later I'm asleep. The Parisian driver takes this as a grave personal insult and has his revenge: he hits the brakes so hard, I slide right off the seat, my eyes jarred open, looking at a black rubber mat and two little empty cognac bottles rolling back and forth. Where the hell am I? I pull myself up and nearly collide with the cabby's suspicious face, demanding his francs.

Then, at the hotel desk, I have to part with my passport, like it or not, and right after

that I have to come up with an enormous dollop of faith in a contraption out of ye olde antique shoppe. I mean, Bear and I could have a great tap-and-bang percussion session on all the iron curlicues, with no doubt great sounds coming off it everywhere, but I am supposed to trust my life and limb to this medieval cage! Forget Bear and get in there.

The contraption does get me up to the fifth floor all right, and I find my room and flop down on the bed, intending to sleep off the rest of the Tic's potent little white Tac. But all of a sudden I'm wide awake. Fog and sleep both gone, eyes finally open all the way, and now I can't believe I'm sitting on a bed in Paris. What am I doing here? What in this crazy fucked-up world am I doing in Paris, having agreed to run errands for a total stranger?

I sat there, staring at my gig bag, the only familiar thing around, and gave myself hell. The gist of it being: if it was important to Bear and Alicia that I walk away from some stranger I just met, then I should have gone ahead and done that! Good luck, Mara deJong, and goodbye!

I have three friends in all: my grandmother, Bear and Alicia. The rest are people I play with. Musicians. And as far as family goes, I'm all for it as long as I get to pick it. I do not play son to a pickled puff of hot air which calls itself my father, and I do not play brother to Pinocchio, a puppet who keeps yapping about how he wants to be real but when you give him a chance to be real, like can I crash here for a couple of nights till I find a new pad, then he has to ask his wife. That one helped me a lot with not letting people get to me and give me nasty surprises. And it helps me say no every time grandma takes it into her head to try for a family reunion.

Anyway, that was my life: Bear most days, Alicia often, and my grandma on Sundays when I'm not on the road. And every minute in between, Music. So once more from the top: what was I doing in Europe, running errands for a stranger?

That morning when I went to her house, Mara deJong wasn't even home. "Keeping an appointment," said Lena the neighbour, who opened the house door. She handed me a thick brown envelope from Mara, and said:

"I'm glad you are going. Mara will need friendly witnesses at her trial. She could so easily be misunderstood here in Canada." A friendly woman, this neighbour, but before I could get even one question out about Mara deJong, she'd wished me a good trip and was gone.

The envelope contained a notebook and a folder with hotel reservations, cash in francs, Marks and Schillinge, and all kinds of information. I was surprised there wasn't a tag in there with my name on it to hang around my neck. I stuck the folder into my luggage, an old saxophone gig bag somebody left in my van ages ago.

In my hotel room, still wide awake, I decide I'm going to do two things in Paris: one, go see the first person on Mara deJong's list of potential witnesses, and get the woman to tell me every single damned thing she knows about Mara. Two, go check out some of that famous Paris jazz. And right after that, I'm heading back to Toronto. Back to my own life. That was the plan.

I grab Mara's folder and look up the telephone number of the woman I am going to see in Paris, a Tanya Volnikoff.

"Hello? You don't know me. I'm Ted O'Sullivan from Canada, with greetings."

Mrs. Volnikoff says to come, come, right away. She'll send a cab to my hotel and I'm to be downstairs in five minutes.

Language was not going to be a problem. Mrs. Whatsnikoff speaks Russian, French, German, and English. How did I know that? From Mara. Who also told me: "Anything else about her that is relevant is in the notebook." But where in hell is the notebook? That fat black notebook of Mara's I was supposed to study and never, ever leave unattended?

I find it inside Mara's folder in the gig bag, a bit bent but all there. I grab it and jump down four flights of stairs, glad to be in motion. I was going to spend the next hours listening to Mrs. Whatsnikoff explaining Mara deJong. Life from birth to today, character, and tendencies with earlobes and cutting tools. Then I could hang that picture of Mara away in the closet and close the door on it. Maybe bring it out once a year for a reminder: You're not shockproof, Tedmeboy. You can be yanked and spun around, so watch out.

The cabdriver Mrs. Whatsnikoff sent over is Russian and he knows where she lives. We are whizzing along so fast it's damned hard to read much of anything in Mara's notebook, but I try.

> ***Tanya Volnikoff.***
> *...petite and slim but do not mistakenly think that she is frail.*
> *...my first husband Karl and I helped her to leave the USSR and come to Germany.*
> *...she has been married twice. Her first husband left her. The second spends much time in a convalescent home. He is an invalid.*
> *...she has a son from her first marriage. The son is a member of the French Communist party. He and his mother are not on speaking terms.*
> *...she is an intensely jealous woman, inclined to make scenes like a fishwife.*

And then there is a question I am supposed to ask the woman: What happened to the shawl?

By now the taxi is driving through a suburb of Paris: tiny houses with tiny gardens. Thousands of them.

"All Russians," says the cabby, proudly.

He pulls up to one of the tiny houses and refuses to accept a single franc. I have no rubles and consider kissing him on both cheeks, and then I see Mrs. Whatsnikoff. A tiny woman standing on the doorstep of her house. Old enough to be Mara's mother.

Tiny Mrs. Whatsnikoff has black and grey hair pulled tightly back into a bun, black button eyes, and skin like weathered barn wood. She pulls me into the house and then leaves me standing and zips off somewhere. The little room I'm in is stuffed with bulbous furniture, and cluttered. And drenched in the smell of cooking oil, like the whole place is a plateful of nobbly fritters. And Mrs. Whatsnikoff, a housefly all over everything.

She comes zipping back, points me to a chair and asks about Michelle, in Canada. She has assumed I am bringing greetings from Michelle, Mara's daughter. Michelle who is dead but Mrs. Whatsnikoff obviously doesn't know that. Her eyes are excited black dots in her pointy face. I dodge.

"Actually," I tell her, "I'm here doing some research into Mara's past."

"Mara is dead?"

"No, no."

By the look on her face, Mrs. Whatsnikoff is not happy to hear that Mara is still alive. No doubt about it. She looks—forget the housefly, she looks like a scrawny old hen, the brown, skinny kind, more wild than domesticated, and right now she's ruffled as hell and grating on something nasty stuck in her throat. A good thing I didn't tell her at the door that I'm here on Mara's behalf, because I swear she would have slammed the door in my face. Her mouth is puckered tight, her small black eyes are burning and shooting sparks. She decides that she needs a drink, picks up an unmarked bottle full of something clear that has to be Vodka, and pours out two glasses of it.

She's got me sitting in a fat old armchair between two end tables beset by porcelain ballerinas. She hands me my drink, frowns, and swallows her entire glassful in one go. Then she sits down across from me. We're both holding onto our glasses, because there's nowhere to put them down without bothering the ballerinas.

Mrs. Whatsnikoff points her eyes at me and says:

"I have not heard from Mara in a very long time and I hope I never will."

That stopped me, I have to tell you. I mean: What was this woman doing on Mara's list of friendly character witnesses? She knows nothing about the heinous act—she doesn't even know Michelle is dead—but she looks ready to fly off in any direction, including my face.

We're looking each other over from our battle stations among the ballerinas and it's clear she's a tough old bird and no TV-watching zombie, out here in the suburbs. Her voice is hoarse, her English has a heavy accent—Russian, not French. All her languages are locked shut over the subject of Mara. Where the hell is her gratitude?

"I understand," says I, "that Mara helped you to leave the USSR and come to the West. Could you tell me how?"

"As her maid," says Mrs. Whatsnikoff.

Maid? In the Soviet Union? Did they hand Mrs. Whatsnikoff a visa so that a good Soviet citizen like Mara, in the process of defecting, would not miss the comforts of home?

"Karl arranged it," says Mrs. Whatsnikoff. (Karl being Mara's husband number one.)

"We rehearsed our story very well. We said that I wanted to come to Germany with Mara and Karl so that I could become a student of hotel management. We told them that I would earn my tuition by being Karl and Mara's maid for two years. That was our story and we tried it on the bureaucrats and it worked. They chose to believe it. Of course, Karl as an important foreigner had always a special treatment. And then, two months after we all arrived in Germany, I married my first husband, a friend of Karl's, and we moved far away to a different town. Since the day we moved I have seen Mara only twice, and I hope never to see her again this side of the grave."

And that's it. Mrs. Whatsnikoff gets off her perch with a little hop and I expect to be shown to the door and sent on my way, all wound up and strung so tight I could pop anytime. But no. Mrs. Whatsnikoff is moving one skinny arm with a lovely, grand and gracious sweep towards the doorway to another room, and then tippy-toes ahead in there. It's a tiny dining room with a table filling up most of it. The table is loaded with enough shiny silverware to light up the house. I squirt myself into the chair she wants me on, between wall and table, and Mrs. Whatsnikoff pops off into the tiny backroom kitchen. Outside the small square window three fat pigeons are guarding the pigeon coop, which takes up most of the yard. The pigeons look ferocious in this suburb of miniatures. How come Mrs. Whatsnikoff hasn't turfed me out of here?

Mrs. Whatsnikoff comes back carrying a plate stacked with skinny little pancakes she calls blini and a platter with stuffed cabbages, ringed with slices of spicy sausage. Delicious, all of it. Mrs. Whatsnikoff enjoys scurrying off to the kitchen for other tidbits like pickles and sour cream and this and that, and she enjoys watching me dig in. Her husband is away, her son is in French Paree, not talking to Mama who loves Mother Russia and hates the Communists, and here is Mrs. Whatsnikoff, alone in this tiny box of a house, buzzing and pecking, and maybe the reason she's not throwing me out is that she's hungry to feed somebody.

Now the food I'm chewing becomes strategy: as long as I keep eating, I'll be allowed to stay. As long as I'm allowed to stay, I can keep trying to get the old bird to feed me what I really want: information about Mara.

My job for Mara is done, I know that much. It's damned clear that Mrs. Whatsnikoff isn't going to make it as a friendly character witness. Unless there is some marvelous deed of Mara's only Mrs. Whatsnikoff knows about.

Over my fifth blini I casually ask Mrs. Whatsnikoff whether she and Mara were friends in long-ago Russia.

"No," she says, perched on the edge of her chair. "We came," she says, "from very different social backgrounds. Mara's family was 'intelligentsia.' I was the daughter of a postal clerk."

So we talk a bit about the classless society and then Mrs. Whatsnikoff sits back and I am pretty sure she is finally warming up.

"How did you two meet?"

"We were assigned to the same Cultural Group," she tells me. "Yes, after we graduated it was our turn to bring Culture to the North. They put together a group of artists: ballet dancers, musicians, one poet, one terrible old bore who played different kinds of folk music on old instruments, two singers—both of them basso profundi, can you imagine!—Anyway, they sent us to a new industrial town in the Ural mountains. A mining project. Ten thousand people in the mud, without roads, without meat, without indoor bathrooms, and only two hours for women in the public bathhouse. Can you imagine!

"I had by then eight years of ballet school in Leningrad. The best teachers. Twelve hours a day minimum, for eight years. And then they sent me North to the provinces, into the mud. And not just for one year, in my case, you understand. No, no, I had not, you see, been chosen for the Kirov. No influence!"

She pecks at the air a couple of times and then shakes her head. "Ah, who knows...maybe I didn't have the talent? How could I know, at that age? But Karl thought that if I came out, in the West I would be accepted by a very good ballet company. Of course, Karl, well, he thought everything was possible. He was the one who brewed up the hotel story."

Mrs. Whatsnikoff doesn't mind at all talking about Karl, who was a terrific and helpful guy who "knew a thing or two." I, however, want her to talk about Mara, in the same cultural group in the mud.

"Tell me, and Mara? Was she any good?"

Mrs. Whatsnikoff shrugs and says, " She would have preferred to grow long fingernails."

Meow.

But I know by now that there is a lot more to Mrs. Whatsnikoff than cattiness, and I'm not about to quit digging for the rest. I just can't take the shortest route. Mara is obviously poison to the old bird, but Karl was good stuff. He should have been a Russian, according to Mrs. Whatsnikoff. He loved Mother Russia as that perverse wife of his, Mara, never did. And he knew his way around.

"Oh yes. Karl could arrange for anything, even in that godforsaken hole in the North. A private flat so Mara could move out of the dormitory. Brand new leather boots with fur lining. A beautiful royal blue scarf with fringes and tassels. However," says Mrs. Whatsnikoff, "if he really had been Russian, Mara would never have married him."

"Ah, yes," says I. "The attraction of the exotic foreigner!"

Mrs. Whatsnikoff lets out a squawk. "Ha!" she says. "Karl was a foreigner who would return to Europe and who would take her with him."

"Are you telling me that Karl was Mara's passport out of the Soviet Union?"

Wrong again, Ted. The old hen refills my glass with Vodka and hands it to me, like: "Here, you need some of this." Then she makes a toast in Russian. To Mother Russia, I guess, lying asleep under an evil spell until the day of her awakening and rescue. By whom?

I was pretty sure right then that Mrs. Whatsnikoff was in love with Karl. Whether Karl was a tomcat isn't relevant, unless of course it explains the old bird's sharp claws. I try to get to her sideways.

"So you married a friend of Karl's. Was he anything like Karl?"

Mrs. Whatsnikoff cackles with her mouth wide open, gold fillings everywhere.

"No wonder," she says, "that your American films are such sentimental fairy tales. The man I married had three warts on his chin and a soccer knee that swelled up whenever it rained. He spent every Sunday gardening and gave away all the best vegetables, to show them off. When he left I tried to kill myself."

Mrs. Whatsnikoff downs another shot of Vodka, neat, and leaves for the kitchen, and I remember an entry about her in Mara's notebook:

...she is an intensely jealous woman, inclined to make scenes like a fishwife.

Three explanations for the hate pop up right away. One, that the two months Mrs.

Whatsnikoff spent as a maid in Mara's house in Germany were hell—but that doesn't wash, because she and Mara got together twice after that. Two, jealousy of Mara's talent and career. Not to mention envy of Mara's beauty. And three, that maybe Mara provoked jealousy and a fishwife scene over the husband who left.

Mrs. Whatsnikoff comes back in, heaves two platters on the table, and loads our plates with roast chicken, home-fried potatoes, and cold green peas. I'm chewing slowly, afraid I'll be turfed out right after dessert.

I ask her whether Karl was a Communist. Mrs. Whatsnikoff up and flaps her wings so hard, I have to rephrase the question fast. "I mean, did Karl see anything good to have come out of the revolution?"

"Oh, well, yes. I would have to say yes. Karl used to call us cynical city brats. We used to make fun of all those earnest students and their enthusiasm about the hero project they'd been sent to work on. Karl didn't even like to hear us complain about the living conditions—the mud, the isolation, the wooden barracks never warm enough. Karl would tell us about the conditions of European miners. 'One illness and they're out of a job and starving,' he used to say. 'Family and all.' Or about the miners in South Africa. "'Treated worse than slaves, like beasts of burden and toil.' Did you know," says Mrs. Whatsnikoff, "that the black people in South Africa have to carry passes, just the way we did back in Russia?"

I knew. And that they often don't see their families for years. And that 12% of the

population, all white, grows fat on everybody else's back. A subject I know something about, thanks to Bear, but a subject for another day. I decide it's time to ask Mara's question.

"Tell me what happened to Mara's shawl."

"I burned a hole in it," snaps Mrs. Whatsnikoff.

"By accident?"

"Of course it was an accident. I didn't know Mara very well back then." The old bird starts cackling again and I feel like pulling feathers.

"How about you? Did you become a great and famous ballerina, in the West?"

"I had a more important goal, once I was out," she says. "Something called 'survival.'"

The naive young whippersnapper put in his place. I am the one who used to think he could write the manual on survival. How to duck flying beer bottles onstage, brawling drunks in the alley, and anybody whose pimp was holding up the wall. How to avoid the clap. How to score dope without paying for camel shit. How to keep the landlord from discovering four buddies in your place, crashing for the night or the week. But that scrawny old bird…well, maybe she had the right.

"So you and Mara met in the Ural mountains, bringing Art and Kultur to the provinces, and Mara married Karl, and you all went off to Europe together. Plus one baby daughter, but no need to go into that. And then..."

Mrs. Whatsnikoff really smiles for the first time.

"The first baby born at the project," she says, and smiles again. "Everybody was invited to the celebration, and for a whole week nobody was sober. Karl must have spent more on the black market than he earned in a month, and he earned plenty. He bought meat and champagne. And when Mara's mother came from Leningrad, he hired a *droshka* to bring her cross-country for the last thirty kilometres.

"When we heard the bells on the horses, Karl ran out with a fur blanket and he wrapped Mara's mother up in it and just carried her inside. And she was no feather! Oh, and a jar of caviar fell out of her bag and broke and we had to throw it all out because it was full of shards of glass. Karl opened a bottle of champagne and we toasted the grandmother and the baby again and again. Of course, Mara refused to drink the champagne."

"Because she was nursing…"

"Oh, no. Mara didn't nurse the baby. She said it hurt her nipples. The woman who ran the canteen—imagine, she was still nursing her three-year-old son—anyway, she was hired to be little Lisa's wet-nurse. And little Lisa thrived on the milk. I haven't heard from Lisa in over a year now. I mean Michelle, of course. I don't know why she has a different name in Canada. You don't know her at all?"

"Not really. I don't even know Mara very well."

"You're a lucky man," says Mrs. Whatsnikoff, and prepares to clam up again. I have to prevent that, but thinking fast doesn't come easy when your belly is crying for mercy and it's louder than your thoughts.

Mrs. Whatsnikoff is slowly lifting her Vodka glass, then she suddenly tosses the whole shot into her mouth.

"Mara," she says, "calls all Russians barbarians, you know, meaning drunkards. She didn't find out about Karl's benders until after the baby was born—I told you, he celebrated for days—and when she found out, Mara wasn't going to speak to him for a month, but he never knew that. He sobered up just in time to go away to work on his next project for three months. By the time he came back it was 40 degrees below zero again and Mara needed a winter coat."

"So you are telling me that Mara is a thoroughly materialistic bitch. Is that right? An opportunist? And that's why you never want to see her again."

Mrs. Whatsnikoff slowly leans across the table and sends Vodka fumes into my face after every word.

"You...are...wrong," she says. "You...know...nothing."

It's a bloody miracle I haven't crushed the glass in my hand before it reaches my mouth. Mrs. Whatsnikoff is shoving her eyebrows up to join her hair and she is pouring herself yet another Vodka.

"To Mother Russia," she says, and drinks it down. The same Mother Russia she couldn't wait to leave. I'm sitting forward, tightening all the muscles in my ass to keep sharp.

"What was it like when you arrived in Germany, in 1936?"

"For me, it wasn't bad. I spoke enough German to get by and I was not afraid of work. But I tried to go home right away, just the same. In Russia, you know, we had no information about the politics of Germany, and in 1936 it was already very bad. Karl told us never to speak to men wearing black shirts. He was very upset. He tried to get a job in another country but it was too late for him. And for me, too, after I met my first husband.

"We had a big wedding, many miners and their families. Mara insisted that we hire a hall and dress up. She had a new long gown. In the middle of everything, came the SS men. Six men with guns, right into the hall. Mara went to them and she said to them: 'Your boots! Look at your boots! You must go and wipe them on the doormat!' And they all did. One of them went right outside and scraped muck off his heels. It was raining outside, you see. Then they came in and arrested four people from one family. Friends of my husband's. Catholics. We never saw them again.

"My husband and I moved to his family farm near another town and we stayed there until the end of the war. We were lucky." Mrs. Whatsnikoff turns her head sharply away as though she's heard a bomb go off. I can't wait to hear more about Mara at the wedding. Was she naive, about those SS men? Or was she courageous, in a foolhardy way? I risk a direct question:

"What about Mara?"

I watch Mrs. Whatsnikoff decide to answer.

"Do not think for one moment," she says, slowly, raising a warning finger, "that Mara is mad." She sticks her head in my face and says it again: "Do not think for one moment that Mara is mad."

Then she gets up and starts piling dishes and every move says this visit is now over. I get up to leave and then ask her one more:

"Tell me, what did Mara do to you?"

"Goodbye," says Mrs. Whatsnikoff.

Halfway out the door my brain kicks in with something else: would Mrs. Whatsnikoff change her tune if she knew Mara was in trouble? Would she do a turnaround and rush to the loyal support of her long-ago compatriot, colleague, and ex-wife of Karl the wonderful?

But to tell her about Mara's troubles means I also have to tell her that Michelle is dead. Oh, Christ. I've never been a Messenger of Death before.

Mrs. Whatsnikoff sees something in my face and lets go of the door and I tell her everything I know, which isn't much, but does include death and a pair of missing earlobes.

Tiny Mrs. Whatsnikoff starts shrinking. Right there in the doorway in front of my eyes, she's shrinking. I try to get back into the house, just to wait till the shock wears off. She refuses to let me in.

"I'll kill her," says Mrs. Whatsnikoff with a thin grim voice. "Tell Mara if I ever see her again, I'll kill her."

I try to make it clear that it was Mara herself who sent me to her but she's not listening.

"Now there are two of us who know about Mara," she says. "Myself, and her daughter."

"Know what? Come on, lady, know what?"

"You're a man," she says. "You will never know." And slams the door shut.

I still feel bad, all these months later, about Mrs. Whatsnikoff finding out about Michelle the way she did. Back then, I wanted to kick myself, kick the door open so I could do something for her, but what? I gave up staring at the door and waddled to the curb and sat down to wait for a cab, burping and farting and muttering, trying to wipe out the sight of Mrs. Whatsnikoff, standing in her doorway and shrinking. At that point I had no idea that her "you will never know" was going to turn into a hissing chorus in my head.

Eventually, a cab comes along, another Russian. This one takes me back to my hotel by way of every fucking gas lamp in Paris, not one of them throwing light where I need it. I make it up to my hotel room, dive for the phone, and actually get a line through to Toronto. There's a question for Mara twitching around on the tip of my tongue: "What the hell is that Mrs. Whatsnikoff doing on your list of friendly witnesses?"

Twelve rings and still no answer. Not home. Back in Toronto it was sometime in the afternoon and who knows what the hell Mara does with herself at any time, day or night?

I don't even consider calling Bear.

I grab the gig bag and head down the stairs. The groomed-greyhound lady at the front desk is all set to fight for full payment on the unused bed. My cash, so ready and willing, shocks her into offering to change my train reservation. So there I was, sitting in yet another cab, heading for the railway station. Anything's better than waiting.

Even if it's just something like getting to a gig ahead of time, I can't just hang around and wait. I step out for a beer, or a quick drive down to the lake, and next thing you know the bandleader leans on me for being late. Or the club owner kicks me off the gig. Actually, that only happened to me once and it wasn't even my fault. I had to go down to the police station and catch Bear before he lost his cool and got some organs strained through his ribs. There's always some racist fucking cop waiting for an excuse.

Sometimes I think Bear asked for it. Like yelling: "You touch me and I'll kick your balls down your throat, you fucking asshole."

When all Bear had to do was let them search his pockets, which were clean at the time. Not even a seed in the lint. We were doing a run-through rehearsal and Bear was just stepping out to a corner place that makes real coffee and he'd pulled on the bandleader's jacket. The bandleader never carries stuff in his pockets; he's a real cautious junkie. Bear's jeans don't even *have* pockets, clean or otherwise, because Bear is so vain about his ass he won't disfigure it with the lump of a wallet.

"They're going to learn not to hassle black folk in this town if I have to get busted a hundred times." Bear was still steaming that day. "Every time they take me in at least one cop gets the message."

"Man," I told him. "Don't you know you're just giving those cops a good time?"

"Fuck you," Bear said and didn't talk to me for a week, which is pretty cold when you're on the bandstand together every night. But he didn't get himself busted any more after that. Except the time he was coming to my place and when the cops stopped him and his brown paper bag and confiscated the open bottle, Bear got mad as hell and I had to bail him out again.

"Shit," said Bear. "I really wanted to make it to your place without detours."

Yesterday he couldn't even detour by Mara's for an hour.

Fuck him!

Me, I was on a train, on my way to the second person on Mara's list. And this person was going to tell me all about Mara if I had to chain myself to her big toe.

ALICIA

Bear and I hadn't heard from Ted for a couple of days—not a word—and I couldn't stand it any more so I dialled the contact number he'd left with his grandma. A woman's voice answered.

"Hello?"

"Could I please speak to Ted?"

"You must have a wrong number. There's no Ted here."

I told her the number.

"That's our number all right…oh, wait a minute. There was a young man here: tall, slim, dark blond hair, mustache, leather jacket…"

"That's Ted. But he's not there now?"

"Oh, no. He flew off to Europe two days ago."

"To Europe? Ted flew to Europe? Are you sure?"

" Yes, I handed him the tickets myself."

"I see. Well, okay. Thank you."

Damn that Ted. How could he just go off like that without calling?

Well, be fair, Alicia, If Ted had called, you'd have chewed his head off.

No, damn it! Fuck being fair!

Oh, Jesus, here she goes again, this shrew of a woman I don't even recognize. I really want to blame her on that Michelle, but she's a corpse. A corpse minus earlobes. I do know this much: she was the one standing at the fork in the road where I took the wrong turn and wrecked the best friendship Bear and Ted ever had. Maybe even my marriage. Oh, hell, hell, hell!

I can't stand it. I have to talk to Ted the minute he gets back. Where is that number? I don't care if I'm bothering the woman. I don't care if I drive her crazy. I don't care.

"Hello?"

"Excuse me, it's me again. Alicia. Can you tell me when Ted will be back from Europe?"

"I'm sorry, I don't know. I can ask Mara when she gets home. She might know. He went to Europe for her."

"For Mara? Mara deJong? The earlobe freak? Oh, sorry. That slipped out."

"Yes. Michelle's mother. Michelle was my friend. My name is Lena."

"Oh, I'm sorry, Lena. I didn't realize…"

"Mara asked me to give Ted a big envelope when he came by on his way to the airport. She also left a suitcase for him to borrow but your friend said 'no, thanks.' That he'd packed everything he was going to need into an old saxophone gig bag."

"That's Ted, for sure. How did he look? Okay?"

"Well…I'd say he looked like he had a rough night."

"Hungover, you mean."

"Definitely worse for wear. I told him he could change the ticket, delay the trip. But he said, 'Waiting is something I cannot do.'"

"That's true. He really can't."

"You're worried about him."

"Oh, yes, I'm worried all right."

"Well, I will ask Mara when Ted is likely to be back and then I'll call you, if you'll give me your number."

"I'd better call you back, if that's okay?"

"Fine. I try to be the one answering the phone in case it's for Michelle and upsets Mara."

"I see. Well, thank you, Lena. I'll call back later."

I hung up just in time or I'd have burst out with something disgustingly rude and impertinent. Like if Michelle was your friend, how can you be considerate and helpful to her horrifying mother? I picture a house full of weird and venomous women: Michelle with her fangs into Bear, now the mother snapping up Ted and flinging him all the way to Europe. But this Lena doesn't sound weird. Warm, friendly voice. Wish I could pump her about Michelle…no, Alicia! Put it behind you! Concentrate on getting yourself back to your own self and on getting Bear and Ted past this serious rift.

It's not like either of them had any other friends. There's the three of us and Ted's grandmother. That's it. And I'm supposed to be the dependable one, the rational one, and the peacemaker when they have their little dust-ups. Of course, living with Bear you get pushed into being the peacemaker. No cuddly bear, he. More like a grizzly bear. But not at home. Never at home. It's me. I've been the one poisoning the air at home.

"I suppose you're rushing out the door to go see Michelle the Marvelous again."

No wonder Bear is bewildered, eyes full of questions like what happened to my wife, the one I can talk to about everything and anything?

Well, dear husband o'mine, I don't know what's got into me. I'd say the green monster of jealousy, even though that never happened before. Maybe it's Michelle being a singer. A musician. Bear having something with her I could never share, not altogether, me being a mere teacher and aspiring writer.

Oh, shit. Listen to yourself, Alicia. When did "mere" sneak into your self-description? I just can't stand it being all my fault. I was the one who pushed Bear to stop brooding and moping and not even to mention the names or lobes in my hearing. So with me carrying on like that, Bear decided not to help Ted check out Mara deJong, and now Bear feels real bad about it, not helping out his best friend when he really needed it.

And I really can't stand not being able to talk to Bear about what's going on with me—this feeling that I'm trapped in an ongoing horrifying metamorphosis, turning from Alicia as we knew her into—what? A Kafkaesque bug-eyed shrew? Maybe this is what it feels like to go crazy, to have your feelings and your behaviour go completely out of your control?

Okay. This has to stop. I have to get a grip and make a plan. First: to get the two of them back together. Yes. I'll sit the two of them down, as soon as Ted gets back, and we'll talk and clear the air.

"Look," I'll say. "This is your first serious bust-up since the night you two met."

I've heard about that night so often, I might as well have been a fly on the wall. How neither of them intended to go to that posh Rosedale house after hours but Ted was hungry and sick of the food at Fran's, the only all-night restaurant in town, and Bear was dragged there by a percussionist he wanted to keep sweet for other low-paying gigs. Bee, the hostess, was recently divorced and had some high ambitions to get low-down in her new life: she'd invited two entire jazz bands for free food and booze after their gig, and so there they both were. (But Bear did not, he'll have you know, take his bass. He had no intention of being free entertainment at any Rosedale party.)

Now, depending on mood and whether they've got a few beer in them or some smoke, it's a tale of two forces of nature meeting up and uniting to make common front against the hypocritical rich and against racist cops, or else, in other moods, it's a story about two boy-men, mischievous, best buddies from their very first meeting, and fused together at the music bone.

I'll have to keep the Fates involved, and a vocabulary of the Mythic, for the entire Tale of the First Meeting. This was not, after all, the beginning of an ordinary friendship. Which is actually true: Ted protects Bear when he's about to erupt one more time at some racial slur, and Bear keeps Ted from sloshing Scotch all over his music, trying to fill the hole his mother left behind.

So Fate, having led them both to the party, now causes somebody to go and put some horrible music on the record player. Clichés drenched in syrup. Bear and Ted can do a ten-minute riff each on how awful the music was and in just exactly what way it was awful. Naturally, both Ted and Bear, coming from different parts of the house, start heading for the record player downstairs so they can do something about it. And neither of them was into playing "après vous, Alphonse." There they are, both of them bent over in front of the glass shelf with record albums, looking for sounds to satisfy their soul, and there they are, both of them finding the jazz section at the same time and moving over there. Ted's just pulling out Sonny Rollins' "Now's the Time" when Bear holds up Miles Davis' "Birth of the Cool," and they look at each other's choice and both of them nod and grin and Bear says:

"Sonny Rollins first and then Miles to kick ass, or the other way around?"

Then they sit down side by side on the floor near one of the speakers, and they're listening "like we had one pair of ears between the both of us," Bear told me once, and Ted swears that he knew right then and there that Bear was a musician and that they'd be playing together one day soon.

Meantime, back at the party, there's a loud crash. Everybody turns to look. The speaker near the window had fallen on somebody's head.

A big speaker, wood with sharp edges, tipped out of its corner by the window, fell off its stand and hit a woman sitting on the floor. It hit her on the shoulder and the side of her head. She passed out. Somebody called an ambulance. Bee the hostess rushed around like a demented weasel, getting ice for the head, something warm for the body, and then the woman came to and sat up and started looking just fine long before the ambulance came. But Bee the hostess talked her into going to the hospital to get checked out anyway, in case of concussion or whatever.

"And don't forget to get the doctor to write down exactly what condition you're in!"

The woman wanted no fuss and went off in the ambulance. Ted and Bear had a drink together and came up with an idea they both liked. (Whenever those two talk about an idea they both like, watch out.)

So first they went and stood around the Villainous Speaker, still on the floor, and they put on a show of studying it and shaking their heads and murmuring, carrying on like that, until Bee wasn't just watching them but was starting to make like the same hysterical weasel.

"Oh, poor Anne," said Bee. "What a terrible accident. I'll never forgive Walt if she's really hurt. That's my ex-husband. He left me the house when we divorced. It was his speaker, actually, but now, well—it's all my responsibility, I guess."

"The speaker may need repairs," said Bear.

"New woofers for sure," Ted said. "Do you still have your tools at home, Bear?"

Bear nodded and mumbled something about being very busy, these days, but Ted set about talking him into it and the two of them offered to take both speakers off her hands to check and fix them, and then they would call her to come and pick them up, or she could call them, in a couple of weeks or so.

Bee was delighted with their offer.

Bear and Ted picked up a speaker each and headed for Ted's van. Out on the sidewalk they had to stop and put the speakers down so they could have themselves a laugh without dropping them. Giving Fate time to perfect the next bit.

Ted remembered that the key to the van was in his jacket, which was still inside the house. So Ted went back inside to get them and by the time he came out again, just a couple of minutes later, there was Bear, hollering, with a cop on either side of him pushing him to a cop car.

Bear was hollering to warn Ted off. But instead of backing up out of the scene, Ted saw what the cops assumed was going on, and yelled:

"Hey! Hold it!"

But the cops didn't hold it and they didn't stop push-walking Bear towards the police car, and they wouldn't listen, absolutely not at all, so Ted hauled off and belted the cop closest to him in the belly. (Says Ted: "I have to aim for the belly so I don't wreck my hands.") And that's how Ted landed in hospital with a number of bruises and contusions and a possible fracture and Bear landed in jail. Yet again.

Bear always gets Ted to tell the next part because Ted has a ferocious memory—not only for any tune he hears, even once, but for what's been said and in what tone of voice. Here's Ted remembering the rehearsal those two cops had on the way to the hospital. Just in case there was going to be a hearing about the "incident."

"He's got a lot of damage on him just from falling down the stairs," said cop #1. The one Ted didn't hit.

"He was high on drugs at the time," said cop #2. "Maybe he had a fight he can't remember." And more like that.

But they didn't charge Ted with assault. Because Ted kept talking to Bear about his uncle, the newly appointed Judge Williams who has not been fond of cops ever since they harassed his Jamaican maid. The two cops suspected Ted made up this uncle, which he did, of course, but they couldn't be sure, these days. Anyway, they dropped Ted off at Emergency and took Bear to the police station but they didn't mess with him and released him in the morning. Bear went directly over to the hospital to find Ted and they got to talking and got real curious about each other's playing, and had this idea—both of them at the same time, of course: why not right now? And so they decided to release Ted from hospital forthwith. They picked up Bear's bass and then went over to Ted's pad and they jammed all that day and most of the night and that was it. Right from then on, they started spending most evenings together way into the night, playing music or listening to some, talking and hanging out. (Giving me precious time to do my own writing. Which I have not been able to so much as look at since I became the resident shrew.)

And if the tale of their Momentous Meeting does not have them falling into each other's arms, I can add the first time Ted came here to the house and we hung out, all three of us. That happened a few months after they first met. Bear says he told Ted, "You gotta come home with me, meet my old lady. She's getting real curious when your name comes up." (Which was true. I wanted to meet this white guy Bear trusted so completely.)

Ted said: "Then bring her along sometime. She might like to get out for a change, look around in the world."

Ted apparently had this picture of me, Bear's woman, waiting at home, not seeing her man till the early morning hours, keeping herself ready and sweet but slowly going sour, hanging there. So when Ted came in the door and saw me, he turned to Bear with a look that got me started laughing till the tears were rolling. Bear said to Ted: "Let me know when you're through thinking I'm a stupid motherfucker who doesn't deserve this beautiful intelligent sexy creature. And then take your eyes off her."

We went to an Italian restaurant and after the food and wine and a lot of laughing, Bear gave me a look: "so am I right about this guy?" and I just smiled. His buddy Ted was okay by me. Better than okay. And Ted saw me smiling and understood and after that we were family.

And now, Bear is miserable, Ted is miserable and rattling around somewhere in Europe, and me, I'm so pissed off at myself I can't sleep.

"Hello?"

"Oh, Lena, it's Alicia again. I hope I'm not calling too late?"

"No, not at all. I asked Mara and she is not sure when Ted will be back. It might be a few days, or a week, possibly as long as ten days."

"Oh, no. That long?"

There is a silence on the line. I'm sure Lena thinks I'm Ted's girlfriend, trying to hunt him down.

"Lena, it's not what you think. Ted is my husband's best buddy and I have caused a serious rift between them which I want to repair. I feel quite desperate…I'm sorry. I'm not usually like this…When Ted comes back, would you please tell him to call Alicia as soon as possible?"

"I'll do that. Good night."

TED

Outside the window, France was passing by, but it could have been Ontario for all I could see: dark night, with one thin grey line for a horizon. This was only my second time in Europe. The first time, eight years earlier, I was in Italy, hitchhiking around with a list of youth hostels in my pocket and practically nothing else except time. This trip was different in every way—including sitting in a first-class train compartment where Europeans think I'm vermin.

The plan, once I got on the train, was to spend the trip to Germany fast asleep. What happened instead was Mrs. Whatsnikoff scratching away at the roots of my teeth, hissing: "You will never know."

Listen, here's the thing: I've put in time in all kinds of Toronto neighbourhoods. I *knew* what Mrs. Whatsnikoff's red-hot Russian hatred might be made of. Like two hours of yelling on the sidewalk, making you think "war zone," and then it's all about Mr.Whosnitzky's snow bank, shovelled into a neighbour's favourite parking spot.

But whatever the hell it was about, what was that poisonous fowl Mrs. Whatsnikoff doing on Mara's list of potential witnesses? That made no sense at all. And not knowing what's going on turns me into a kid, feeling stupid. Something I had plenty of back when I *was* a kid, and my aunt kept telling my little brother and me: "We will never know." I hated it then and I hate it now. Let me tell you, it wasn't all pretzels and beer on that trip.

Outside, poles come looming up and drop away in rhythm, like a slow-swinging bass. Lots of great harmonics in the sounds of the train. And here comes the beer pusher again, smiling with his two missing teeth. Suspenders wider than his legs, a trolley stacked with the finest beers of Germany. He sells it, he smells of it, you can pay him in four different currencies and he'll throw in his life story for free. I'm wasted and more beer won't do me any good but I buy two: one for him and one for me. He grins and opens both bottles.

"Take a load off your feet."

I pat the empty seat beside me. He squints a quick look at the other passengers. They are all of a sudden playing statue. The beer pusher raises his bottle at me in salute and moves on. The statues start up breathing again.

Let it pass, Ted. Let it pass.

The train slows down and rolls into a station. Everybody in my compartment gets off. I try to picture Mara standing on the station platform out there. Hat and gloves. At least two porters rushing to her side. Mara has done a lot of travelling in her life. But was a foreigner in her compartment a parcel of germs? No idea. In a nightclub, would Mara talk through the bass solo? When we were in the cab, riding to her apartment, did she see the picture of the driver's kid stuck to the dashboard? An angel-faced little boy holding a toy machine gun. I have no idea what Mara sees.

At this point, the picture of Mara I had in my head was like one of those Polaroid snapshots—just when you think an impression is swimming up, it blurs on you and all you can make out is the tilt of the head or maybe two hands holding each other. I have a couple of old photos of my mother that are like that. Whenever I look at them, I want to scream into the blurred parts: "Come out of there, damn it! How could you do such a thing!"

I still can't believe Bear wouldn't come over to Mara's apartment to give me his reading on the woman. He could have done that much. He knows I trust his eye and ear for the sharps and flats of people, and his nose for the sour note.

Not that I'm an amateur. Being a white boy playing black music, I've picked up some keen odours myself. Some from rednecks in tight white collars, some from black players putting fences around their music, and even the scented stink from touchers—see my hand on your buddy's black shoulder, see my liberal smile.

But sometimes I still get surprises. Because in the class system of my life, the aristocracy is black. Duke and the Count, Ella the Queen, Lady Day—now there is royalty! And the Empress of the Blues, Bessie, playing second fiddle to no one. And Thelonius Monk. A dude I want to meet someday, when I'm ready.

The light in the train compartment flickers a couple of times and goes out and there is the countryside, pale grey but getting brighter, and changing so fast you want to slow down the train. Vineyards, rows and rows climbing uphill in perfect formation—in no way "drunk and disorderly." A small town crowding around church spires. Fields like checkerboards in all shades of green. A hilltop castle looking so old you think it's painted on but there's smoke coming out of a chimney; somebody's still living up there. Every inch of land is busy. Even the steep shoulder off the railroad tracks is growing hay. It's like looking at one of Jeff's piano charts that leaves no spaces at all for playing free. Not even one old pickup truck, saved in case any part of it can be used again before it rusts all to hell. I used to think the "wide open spaces" of Canada were just a cliché.

Slow clouds are moving above the quick-passing fields. Slate rooftops gleaming like old silver. I'm trying my damnedest to enjoy this trip, but I might as well give it up. It's not working. Might as well open up the notebook and look over the stuff about Mara's second witness. Helga.

I pull out the black notebook and leaf through it and while I'm doing that, I spot something I had no idea was in there: notes on Mara!

"A FEW SHORT BIOGRAPHICAL NOTES" was the heading and my eyes jumped all over that one page so fast, I had to slow myself way down and start again from the top.

I was born in Leningrad in 1912.

I remember sitting across from Mara in her apartment, thinking, maybe not 35, like I guessed when I watched her in the courtroom, slowly unbuttoning her glove. Maybe more like 40. But "born in 1912" means she's 52! Well, let me tell you: there's nothing middle-aged about Mara deJong, so 52 is just a number.

When she showed me the photo of herself at age three, she said it was taken by one of her brothers, so I asked her about her family life back then.

"Before the Revolution," she told me, "we were living in comfort." With her parents, the father a lawyer and the mother a buyer of haute couture for the finest stores of Leningrad. Big house, maid, silver samovar.

I have three older brothers, says the notebook.

Not something I'd wish on anybody. My own brother is going to get a firecracker stuck up his ass one of these days. Just to see if his legs still work without strings.

There's no description in Mara's notes of any family member or how they got along. Doesn't she know it's practically obligatory to bellyache? To hear Canadians talk, every one of us was hard done by as a child. My father the secret alcoholic. Blotto every night except after the weekly outing with the boys. All of them middle-aged colleagues of his at the university research lab, so when he was with them he had to watch his elbow. Now my father's altogether reformed and an even bigger pain in the ass.

I asked Mara at some point back in the apartment, "How can you be sure that I'm not a drunk or a junkie?" Mara said, "I know that a heroin addict would refuse to travel far from his supplier and I never fail to recognize drunkards."

Obviously, the woman didn't learn about life entirely from leatherbound books. I asked her what she remembered about the Russian Revolution and she said, "Well, I was six at the time." (Letting me know her real age right then, if I hadn't forgotten the year of the Russian Revolution.) Mara remembered that the whole family had to squeeze into two rooms in one of their own houses. The mother lost her job and learned how to cook and bake from their former maid or housekeeper. Mara remembered the sound of shooting in the streets and her father covering the windows with mattresses to stop the bullets, and about shortages of all kinds and trading clothes and jewellery for food. But she talked about all of it like it was a movie she once saw, a long time ago. I guess when you're six years old, even a revolution is just part of life, as long as your parents are there to protect you.

Mara's mother was a Coptic Christian, her father a Jew. The family had never been religious and the father had been anti-Czarist by way of Tolstoy and Dostoyevsky. It sounded to me like they had a fairly smooth ride through the turmoil of revolutionary waters. Then Mara told me that her father was hauled off to jail, twice. And both times his wife found the right strings to pull and got him out.

In the notebook it says:

My mother was a very resourceful woman. And very beautiful. My father was completely devoted to her. And to me, of course, because he discovered me.

An odd phrase. Mara's command of English is so good, you're surprised when something comes out stilted.

My three brothers became professional men. Brother #2 apparently wrote long sarcastic parables and fables about the Soviet bureaucracy. He was the doctor. The youngest of the brothers was a textile engineer called Theodore. Her closest friend.

Karl, my first husband, was a mining engineer, in Russia on a contract. He was building mines in Beresniki, a new town in the Ural mountains. We married and our daughter was born there. We moved to Germany later that year. My husband arranged false German citizenship papers for me and my daughter. He and I separated in 1939. During World WarII, my daughter and I lived in Bergheim, Germany.

That paragraph alone sounds like a whole book to me. They separated in 1939? In Nazi Germany? Could it be that Karl the husband figured being married to Mara, a half-Jewish Russian, would give him bad breath?

Mind you, Karl was also the one who arranged for the false German citizenship papers, but do false papers hide a woman's jet-black hair and—back then for sure—a Russian accent?

And why Bergheim, which was, according to Mara, a "very small town, offering nothing a young city woman could enjoy"?

Except survival.

I fished around in my soggy brain for whatever else Mara told me about her life in Germany during WWII, but all I came up with was one ridiculous bit:

"The most difficult item to procure was silk stockings. Once, I had to trade an entire month's milk coupons for one pair. The stockings had a run by the time I came home in the evening. Luckily, Helga knew how to repair silk stockings."

And later something about "a certain almost British sense of fair play among Germans."

Fair play among the people who branded and killed others like cattle? Mara waved away the Nazis as if they were an imposed aberration. She was talking about those *other* Germans.

"Fair play among their own, of course," said Mara. "And for those they could protect."

"Protect even if it meant danger to themselves?"

"You would find yourself surprised," said Mara, condescending to smile. "There are such people everywhere."

I didn't get a chance to ask whether her husband Karl had been one of those "other" Germans. Or not.

There was only one more paragraph left in her biographical notes:

In 1949, I met and married my second husband, Albert deJong, and we moved to Indonesia. We separated in 1960 and I settled in Vienna, where I still live most of the time.

Let me tell you, "verbose" is not something you can hang on this lady. Not in the notebook and not back in her apartment. Her daughter's apartment. Michelle. Who has half a sentence in Mara's autobiographical notes. Not even a "died in 1964, buried without earlobes." Or did they sew them back on for the funeral? Cover the seams with earrings? Do corpses wear earrings to their funerals? Does anybody?

Right in the middle of a hailstorm of questions, I fell asleep. So fast asleep and so far out of it, I could have ended up anywhere in Europe. But that old beer pusher handed me off his train and into the hands of a buddy on the next train, and that righteous dude eventually woke me up and pointed at the sign in the train station saying Bergheim. I am grateful to both those gentle men to this day, wherever their train might be.

So there I was, sitting on a bench in the Bergheim train station, more or less awake, looking up at the ceiling, a huge high glass dome, and listening to the echoes. Important, booming echoes.

Then I got up and moseyed around to find the john. Right inside the door, there's a vigilant gnome sitting on a low stool. She was obviously guarding the WC from the likes of me. The only toilet paper around was in her domain, and I had to point and nod and smile to get her to dole out two bits of sandpaper.

Definitely awake now and back on my bench, I started ferreting around in my brain for the bits of German left in there. My grandmother always speaks German to me at home so I can understand it all right, but speaking it, that's a different tune.

Never mind. Time to move out of this air that's at least a century old, out through the huge station doors to the sidewalk and into a fresh mountain breeze. Just a few breaths of that stuff sure starts the juices flowing. And just one look at the sturdy middle-aged couple walking along, and some German comes plopping out:

"*Bitte,*" I say, "how do I get to 21 Bündheimer Strasse? Is it walking distance?" Something like that.

"*Ja, ja, natürlich,*" they tell me. "You can easily reach it on foot."

I have no reason to believe they are kidding around, so off I go. Following their directions.

Man, let me tell you something: the good burghers of Bergheim must have legs like tree trunks! I walked till all my tendons turned into vocal chords. Lots of vibrato and tremolo, like Venetian songs. I should have bought myself one of those heavy-duty walking sticks before I set out on that trek. Maybe a little green hat with a feather on the side. I *definitely* should have bought underwear.

I hiked! And found out that hiking gets you lots of time to look around you. And time to think.

So here's Bergheim ("Mountain Home"). A small town, plinked down over the foothills of the Harz Mountains. A long time ago. The Harz Mountains are nothing like our Rockies. Nothing wild. These mountains are tamed, rounded, and covered in pine forests, all reforested in rows but long ago, so they're very tall pines, and regal. Nothing like our bush back home, with messy underbrush and a dead tree across the creek. The town is a ski resort in winter; in the brochure, they'd call it "picturesque." Red gabled roofs, white and green striped awnings, ancient cobblestones worn smooth. Lace curtains and flower boxes in all the windows, filled with red and white flowers. Ornate wooden doors. Nothing raw. Nothing temporary.

Not a town built for cars, obviously. The few cars I saw were erratic, snarky-sounding little beasts. I would have bet no bus could ever make it around those narrow curves, but I watched one do it.

I tried picturing this little town in 1939. Nazi times. Tried picturing Mara deJong arriving here, with her little girl. Heaps of elegant, big-city woman luggage. And then she's stranded here for the entire duration of WWII.

At a crossroads I stopped walking and looked down the streets in all four directions. Tried to put marching SS on these streets, or the Hitler Jugend in full uniform, flags with swastikas hanging out the windows—it was hard to picture it like that. War movies never show you a town like Bergheim, with Germans walking around, holding their children by the hand, licking ice-cream cones. Not American war movies, anyway.

I tried seeing Mara deJong walking down these streets and I couldn't picture that, either, but she did. For ten years!

I started hiking again and tried to remember what else I knew. This was the town where Mrs. Whatsnikoff played Mara's maid for two months. Or was it two years? It was around here somewhere that they had the wedding and Mara told six SS men to stop and wipe their feet before arresting people. It was for sure in this town that, wherever Mara went, every man, woman and child could tell by the look of her and by the sound of her that she was no German. So she had to be wondering all the time who was a Nazi and might inform on her. Not all Nazis wore uniforms, you know. And she must have spent all those years waiting for the war to end.

And there were bombing raids! And living on rations and food coupons. I remembered Mara telling me: "We had no shortage of money, but there was nothing in the stores to buy with the money." So Mara traded clothes for food. And then she told me that story about trading milk coupons for silk stockings. Which sounded damned weird to me, at the time: giving up milk for silk stockings?

Now here I was, walking down the streets of Bergheim, and those silk stockings told me a different story altogether. Now they were telling me that Mara went right on with her eye-catching city-woman elegance when the safe thing would have been to hide. Right? Loden green coat and sturdy brown walking shoes and definitely no silk stockings. And that started a whole avalanche of questions. For instance: was Mara being brave and defiantly herself when she ordered the SS men around and wore silk stockings? Or was she arrogant? Or was she a young woman, first time out of Russia, still naive?

A whole list of questions to put to this Helga in Bergheim, the second friendly witness on Mara's list. If I ever did reach 21 Bündheimer Strasse, that is, which was not something I was still counting on.

But after I made another left turn, there I was, standing right in front of the house where Mara used to live. Plain old house, solid, lace curtains in the windows but no window boxes. High stone steps up to the heavy carved wooden front door.

The door wasn't locked, so I walked into the front hall. Big hall, a spotless tile floor, stone hard. Not a hall you can cross unheard. On the left, a wide wooden stairwell, shiny wood banister. I remember thinking about my grandmother and how she probably grew up in a house like this. But there was something odd about this one: there were no sounds. No voices, not even sounds of movement anywhere in the house. Nothing but closed doors and silence. Like the house was taking a break from life. Like it was waiting for Mara to come back. Ridiculous, I know. I must have been train-lagged.

I climbed to the second floor landing, then up a steeper narrow staircase to the third floor. To Helga Müller 's apartment. I pushed the button and I could hear the doorbell ringing inside, but nothing and nobody was moving. Shit! Mara told me that Helga would definitely be waiting for me, but I was way ahead of schedule because of that damned old hen, Mrs. Whatsnikoff. And Jesus, just the thought of waiting around, who knows for how long, made me want to run down the stairs and take off again. Maybe go find the local pub I passed on my way. Have a beer. Only my legs wouldn't play. They kept yelling at me to sit down, damn it, and right then, my legs were boss. So I sat down. On the doorstep of Helga Müller 's apartment, in Bergheim, Germany.

I opened the gig bag, intending to get out my clean shirt, and there was that damned notebook, reminding me I had yet to read the notes on Helga Müller. Well, as Sonny Rollins says, "Now's the time."

Helga Müller is 62 years old. She was once pretty in a nondescript way and is now plump (Canadians would consider her fat). She has no wrinkles at all. She wears printed flower dresses and aprons and sturdy walking shoes. Her hair is grey blonde, worn in a bun with perpetually unruly fringes except on special occasions, when she gets a tight-wave permanent, parted on one side.

On my trek from the railway station I'd seen at least ten women who fit that description. Every one of them carried a brown leather shopping bag. And I bet every one of them was real sure that looking sexy was bad enough in the young, and quite unthinkable in "women our age." Mara walking down the streets of Bergheim? Like a peacock among the pigeons. Ruffling a lot of feathers. Oh, yeah.

Helga has lived in the same house all her life, as did her parents and grandparents before her. Hardworking burgher stock with a nearly complete disregard for the aesthetic side of life; the entire family has a tenacious grasp on the practical realities.

Helga cooks, cleans, gardens and looks after a dozen relatives and neighbours when need arises. She is a widow with three children, none of them living in Bergheim.

I wonder if my grandmother would have turned out like Helga if my grandfather hadn't carried her off to Canada. "Your grandfather," grandma likes to say, "was a wild Irishman." Shaking her head, with a smile on her face. In Canada, my grandmother took evening courses in plumbing and home repairs, she fought daily battles with the butcher, and eventually she brought up her grandson Ted. I remember hoping that Helga would have my grandmother's sense of humour. Back to Mara's notes.

During the years when I lived in the Müller house (second floor apartment, front), Helga was doing war relief work with the wounded. Most of the men are still keeping in touch with her so that she has to spend many evenings writing letters.

Helga loved looking after my daughter and frequently did so. Nevertheless, I think that she will be a friendly character witness, for the following reasons:

1. Helga knew me during the most difficult years of the war (WWII) and has often said that my courage and my ability to carry on were admirable. She believed that I was bravely risking arrest when I listened to the strictly forbidden Allied Radio reports late at night. She lied valiantly on my behalf when the SS was investigating my background.

2. Both in 1940 and in 1941, when I returned to my daughter after prolonged absence, everyone was quick to condemn me underneath their odious politeness. Helga never asked for explanations—she understood.

3. Though not a churchgoing woman, Helga acts on the Christian dictum about throwing stones. She knows why I kept company with a German officer.

4. Helga pacified the maid who was unreasonably angry and threatened to go to the police because I accused her of stealing my best silk nightgown. Before I left Bergheim, I gave Helga many articles of clothing and she greatly enjoyed distributing them among friends and relatives.

And that was it for Helga Müller . And all I really got out of the notes was that Helga was a saint. The rest was questions. Like how do you fit together the Mara with a Nazi boyfriend and the Mara who listened to Allied Radio in the middle of wartime Germany? Mara's life was a goddamned B-movie, except she didn't sound or look one bit like a martyred heroine. I remembered Mara walking down that courtroom aisle: a woman who would get a first-row seat anywhere.

And then I was back to waiting, and where the hell was Saint Helga? She sure better have some Scotch behind that door. No sense in hoping for the impossible, like a joint. Maybe better that way. If I was high and if that Helga was sanctimonious, I might just blow the whole thing.

I should have been thinking in German, to prepare for Helga. If she talked dialect, I was sunk. I pushed the notebook into the outside pocket of the gig bag and pulled out my clean shirt. Better wrinkled than stinking. I was still tucking in when I heard footsteps—steady, heavy footsteps accompanied by the clink clink clink of thick glass bottles.

LENA

I was still cocooned in my sadness but Alicia's second phone call touched me: here was a woman who was passionate about the loss of friendship, and life did go on. For the first time in ages, I could feel the house around me taking a breath.

I started noticing things again.

All my windows were open and I sat in the front window to catch the summer breezes, so I saw Mara go out and come back, sometimes several times a day. Always looking elegant, always composed. I started waiting for her to erupt with tears and howling, or to collapse. Hoping she would, so I could stop being furious about her composure.

Mara received no phone calls or mail, had no guests. She never went shopping for groceries; all her food was delivered already cooked, from the Chinese take-out on Harbord Street.

When we accidentally ran into each other in the downstairs hall, Mara and I exchanged polite phrases and that's all. Except once, after I asked her Alicia's question: when was Ted O'Sullivan coming back from Europe? Suddenly, Mara gave me a penetrating look. Nothing friendly in there, nothing warm. It startled me so much I had to go back upstairs to think. And the first thought I had was this: could it be that Michelle was scared of her mother?

Michelle and I had agreed, quite early in our friendship, that neither of us wanted a life anything like our mothers'. I had assumed the rest: suburban Hausfrau, hairdresser once a week, girdle at all times except to sleep, never seen without make-up, housework done in time for watching the soaps on television. My mother, a fine example of the genus, waged war all my life against the person I was becoming: no hairdresser, no girdle, no make-up ("Look at you! No wonder your marriage didn't last!"), leaving university in mid-course and taking off for a place nobody ever visited, and now working in an art form nobody ever heard of. To protect myself, I eventually applied my university education and became "an anthropologist in the field, studying my mother the Hottentot."

Mara deJong, I now realized, was obviously no suburban Hausfrau, but an entirely different sort of Hottentot.

Mara's penetrating look shocked me. And it became a warning: in my sad and weakened state, I had imperceptibly been drawn into Mara's orbit and was in danger of dissolving in it. I remember being frightened by feeling so insubstantial. But I knew how to pull myself out of it. I once again became the anthropologist in the field, this time studying Mara deJong. It's a wonderful tool, that role. It makes you acutely observant, and at the same time it protects you like a shield.

Then, one day, Mara wanted my help and the house was full of activity for hours—but I don't want to get ahead of the events unfolding.

TED

Heavy footsteps come up the stairs, clink, clink, clink, across the second-floor landing, and then start climbing again. We can't see each other yet, so I "hullo" down to warn the woman, and she hullos right back.

"*Du liebe Zeit*, here he is already. Mara's friend from Canada!"

A round pink face comes smiling up at me with a fringe of grey hair, and then a big warm hand. She's as tall as I am, firmly cushioned everywhere, and she's shy. Helga's German is not only clear to me, it's so familiar it starts up a flood of grandma's favourite proverbs. Listening to Helga's inflections and rhythms, I would have bet all my Bill Evans albums on this: Braunschweig, the town my grandma's from, wasn't very far from Bergheim.

Helga grabs my bag, herds me into the apartment, and deposits me at a round table. Now she's off to fetch a beer from the kitchen. Forget the saint. She's a sweetheart.

The apartment is cluttered, but then most places are, in my book. In Helga's living room, junk and antiques live side by side and on top of each other: heavy dark brown oak furniture, little plastic souvenirs in loud jarring colours, potted flowering plants of all sizes, dainty little porcelain figurines of shepherds and milk maidens in silly poses, a rough wool Colombian blanket with a dark-orange design covering the back of an ancient wine-red velvet sofa. And three cages, suspended from the ceiling, one yellow canary in each.

Helga comes back, hands me a big blue mug full of golden-coloured beer with just the right head on it, and then she steps over to a cage to converse with one of the canaries. She's tied on a dress-sized apron and stands with one hand on an ample hip. The canary's head is cocked for listening.

"Just imagine, Hänschen," says Helga to the canary. "A guest all the way from Canada! To talk about Mara! She is well, I hope?"

The question is for me. I say, "Mara is in good health and looking fine but..."

Helga sighs. Helga knows about the dreadful deed. She sticks a finger through the cage bars and strokes the canary's head and I get one of those horrible flashes that make you swear you'll never do heroin. For half a second, I see Helga's finger stroking Michelle's head. Canary-shaped. No ears. But a very small head, so maybe it was my little sister's, the way it must have looked with all the curls cut off, right after she died. A flash of nightmare in broad daylight.

Meantime, Helga is still talking to the canary. "It's a strange world," she says. "You never know what's behind it all."

I bet even canaries hate to hear "you never know."

Helga's a bit fidgety. Not surprising: she's a small-town woman and I'm a foreigner. And not only that. Back home in Toronto, longhaired guys in faded jeans are rebels or weirdos. In Europe, they're bums. A different species. Helga's living room has never seen anybody like me. No wonder she's talking to the canaries.

"Mara knows I'll be happy to be her character witness," she says to both of us, canary and me. "I only hope I'll say the right thing."

Now Helga wants to go and cook something for me, Mara's friend, but I talk her into sitting down a while. Unfortunately, as soon as I ask my first question about Mara, up she gets. Saying we really should at least have a cup of coffee and some of her homemade cake. Off she goes to the kitchen. Leaving me to ask myself: How come, out of that long list of questions I have about Mara, how come the first one out is about the Nazi boyfriend?

Helga comes back with a large platter of something flat and glazed. Bienenstich, a specialty of the region, I really must try some. The coffee smells great and reminds me of my grandmother's brew: mixed with hot milk but still very strong. And the cake is different than any grandma ever baked, but it reminds me of her anyway. I tell Helga that I have a grandmother who must have come from somewhere around here, and Helga beams and nods and pushes the cake closer. Takes another slice herself. She considers dunking, but refrains for politeness' sake, so I dip my rectangle of flat cake into the coffee and Helga beams some more and does likewise. We're getting altogether too comfortable, so I ask her again:

"Helga, tell me about Mara's Nazi boyfriend."

Helga slices some more cake. She knows this needs some explaining: Mara, Russian and half-Jewish, probably halfway to concentration camp all through the war, snuggling up to one of the Nazis.

"Yes," says Helga, contemplating the Bienenstich, which means "bee-sting cake" and was probably served just like this to Mara and friend.

"Yes," says Helga, sliding into the past. "He was a handsome man. They looked very elegant together, both so tall, and she had the most beautiful legs. Well, I'm sure she still does." A quick look at me, wondering whether Mara's legs were gracing my life now.

"Forget her legs, Helga. I want to know how she could keep company with a Nazi. Don't you think that was a bit weird, in her position?"

Now Helga's up and finger-feeding those damned birds in their cages, a crumb of cake at a time. But she starts talking. About ration cards and getting up at five in the morning to queue up at the greengrocer's every time there were rumours he had some vegetables. "It was the child," she says, "who took the five-in-the-morning shift in the queue, and Mara would come at eight." Helga throws me the sideways look of a mischievous girl. "You see, the greengrocer, even though he was nearly deaf and had lost one eye, was still an old goat. Well, he'd been to the Russian front and he loved showing off his three words of Russian to Mara. While he slipped her a few extra carrots. Food wasn't easy to come by in those days."

Helga talks about the women with all their men in the army. They had memories of their men, or they had leftover wrecks.

"Able-bodied Mr. Schmidt from downstairs," she says, "he worked double shifts bringing logs down the mountainside and he looked after his own wife and his wife's sister, and occasionally, her niece, too. After the war, he divorced his wife and married the niece. She'd had two children of his by then. When the first wife turned bitter, everybody reminded her that she had had a husband around when nobody else did so what was she complaining about?"

Helga's own husband came back from a French prisoner-of-war camp riddled with T.B. and gonorrhea. She nursed him back to tolerable health and made him walk with a cane until the end of the war. She had no intention of letting him get drafted again.

Helga is not digressing, you dig, talking about the women without men. Helga is treating me to context. Me, the young man from Canada where we heard occasional wartime rumours about a possible shortage of sugar. I rephrase my question.

"Listen, Helga. Was this Nazi big enough to be helpful to Mara?"

Helga goes over to the big oak buffet. Maybe it's the combination of beer and coffee and Bienenstich in my stomach, but I keep getting the feeling I'm sliding into a different world where everything keeps shifting.

Helga is bending over at the oak buffet, one hand on the counter, and for a second I really do think it's grandma, right here, and she's pausing to listen to my Irish grandfather doing a riff. Like:

"Well, Ted, my boy, here you are with your born-in-Canada passport, your bag full of British cricket and America's Hollywood, mounted on a moral horse. Wrinkling your dainty nose at Mara's Nazi boyfriend. Tell me quick now, what would you be willing to do to survive?"

That was a real jolt, let me tell you. I was kicked off that high horse before I even knew I was riding one.

Meantime Helga is hefting a huge photo album over to the table and she's smiling and nodding like she's found the answers to everything I want to know. She opens the album to page one: Helga's great-grandmother, buttoned to the chin, silver hair piled high, the beauty of the family. Followed by five generations of Müller s at family gatherings: weddings, anniversaries, birthdays, the bowls and platters of pork roast and dumplings changing to wartime hills of potatoes and herring. Christmas parties around the tree, decorated with live white candles and icing cookies. A wedding photo of Helga and hubby, Helga a perfect younger version of herself. Hubby in the uniform of a German private, thin and pale.

"We were all living on the main floor then," Helga tells me. "Three generations of Müller s and two cousins and their husbands. Their own house in Hannover burned down during a bombing. By that time, all the houses in Bergheim were overcrowded with refugees from the big cities. So then Mara stopped being embarrassed about how small her own apartment was and she started to invite her uptown friends. Dr. Weiss used to come by quite regularly and..."

Helga thinks she has been tactless and she's about to get up and feed the damned canaries some more.

"They'll die," I tell her. "They'll get hardening of the arteries and high blood pressure and you'll have to put exercise equipment into every cage. How is Dr. Weiss these days? Happily married?"

"For the third time," says Helga. "He marries his nurses and turns them into housekeepers, and then he goes hunting again."

Obviously, uptown people were fair game. Mara, however, was on the protected list, and Helga would neither speak evil of her nor even think it. I wanted to get to the photos of Mara, and finally we did.

First photo. Mara is leaning against a wrought-iron garden gate, dressed in a white suit with a narrow skirt, wearing a white hat. Yes, I'm looking at her clothes—because her face has no expression at all. Closed.

In the next photo she's smiling, sort of, but you almost wish she hadn't tried. You smart ass, I told myself. This is Mara deJong in WWII, out for a walk between SS interrogations, bombing raids, and food queues. Life goes on, enjoyment not always an option.

Finally, the Nazi boyfriend. In full uniform. Strutting at Mara's side, hat under his arm, blond hair glued to his head. GI Joe promoted to Nazi drag. In this one, Mara really was smiling.

Helga is watching me. I get the feeling this last photo was supposed to explain something to me. She sees that hasn't happened, so she sighs and turns to the next page. Mother and child, about five years old, wearing identical skiing outfits.

"Mara never learned to ski," Helga says, "but little Lisa—that was Michelle's real name, you know—Lisa took to skis like she was born with a pair strapped to her feet. A real little daredevil, too, but she never broke so much as a toe. She almost froze them all off, though, many times. She used to stay out all day until you had to soak the socks off her feet. But she certainly didn't do it to annoy Mara, she..."

I ask Helga for another beer. I'm getting altogether too much about Michelle and not enough about Mara. Helga is clattering away in the kitchen, muttering. I know she's agitated, worried about protecting Mara. Sweet Helga, who wouldn't harm a fly and who kept three birds in solitary confinement. How do I convince her that I don't intend to do Mara any harm? Pretend I'm in love with Mara? Would that work?

Helga is no fool; she's seen a lot, that woman, and kept her feet on the ground. So what does she see when she looks at me? Hardly the kind of man Mara's likely to pick.

Something smells good in the kitchen. I stand in the doorway and watch Helga stirring at the stove. Big bosom, big bum, big heart. Bounteous. There's no way I am going to lie to this woman. Now what?

"Helga, you know Mara sent me to find friendly character witnesses for her trial. Tell me what you know about the, er, crime."

"Oh, everything," says Helga. "Mara told me all about it in her letter."

"Do you know *why* she did it?"

"No. That's none of my business."

"You said you'll come to Canada to be a witness at the trial?"

"Yes, of course."

"Then you'll have to tell me the truth about Mara. Everything you know. The prosecutor is going to ask a hell of a lot of nasty questions and I have to know whether you'd be a good witness." (Not really a lie, was it?)

Helga nods and puts a lid on the pot. She comes back to the round table and sits down and sighs. Preparing herself for the hard stuff. Sitting across from her round face and fringe of grey hair, I want most of all to stop upsetting her with questions. But I really can't. (At that point, questions were hot coals burning a hole in my stomach, and not even great beer was going to douse them.)

Helga sighs and says: "I'll tell you whatever I know. Go ahead and ask me."

"Let's go back to the Nazi boyfriend."

"I told you about him," she says. "I even showed you his picture. I don't know how they met, but he was an officer sent here to recuperate from a wound. Up in the mountains there were hotels for officers like him."

"Did he help clear her during the SS investigations?"

"No, Mara met him after that was over."

"Okay, let me go way back and get the sequence straight: Mara came to Bergheim in 1939, just when the war broke out?"

"Just before Christmas. Karl had to start building new mines in the Ruhrgebiet, an industrial area, and he thought Mara and little Lisa would be safer living here. So he came and rented the apartment for them and brought them both here to live. Then he went off."

"So then they were in fact separating in 1939, is that right? And in 1940 Mara left here without the child and then came back, but did the same thing again in 1941. When were the SS investigations?"

"1942."

"And *then* the boyfriend?"

"Yes."

"Was Mara safe after the investigations were over?"

"None of us was safe until the war was over, Ted."

"What did you and your family think of Mara keeping company with a Nazi?"

"We never talked politics in our house. There was nothing we could do except wait it out. Little Lisa used to ask, sometimes: 'Will there really be no war, someday? What will it be like?' I told her about chocolate Easter bunnies, and real eggs, and shoes made of leather. Those wooden soles were hard for her little feet."

"Helga. The Nazi boyfriend."

"Yes. He had a wife, as it turned out. I'm sure Mara didn't know that at the time. He took Mara to the casino at the hotel and he arranged for her to play for the wounded officers. Everybody had to do something for the war effort, you see: roll bandages, darn socks. And the officer arranged it so that Mara could play for the wounded as her part."

Play? Play what? I'd assumed that Mara was a dancer, like Mrs. Whatsnikoff, but come to think of it, she never actually said what Mara used to do in their cultural group.

"Helga, what was it Mara played for the wounded officers?"

"Piano, of course."

"Is that right? How well did she play?"

"Oh, Mara is a wonderful pianist. At the beginning, when she first came to us, famous musicians on tour used to visit her. Sometimes they played together, right here in the house. Violinists. A cellist. Mara stopped giving concerts herself once Russia came into the war. It was too dangerous."

"Concerts? You mean classical concerts? As a soloist?"

"Beethoven was her favourite. But at home she often played Rachmaninoff." Helga stops and thinks a minute. Then: "Excuse me, Ted, how long have you known Mara, did you say?"

But I'm already on my feet. Getting out of there. Fast.

"I'll be back," I tell Helga, halfway to the door. "I need some air."

I'm so pissed off, I jump down the stairs two steps at a time and out the door. Here I am, bopping around Europe for the woman and she hadn't even thought to mention she was a piano player, too. No, pardon me, a pianist. Before I know it I'm at the corner, turning right, and there's the pub.

Everybody in the place watches me cross to the public wall phone. I call collect.

"Yes, Ted," says Mara's voice. "I am glad you called. I have a message for you, from Louise."

"Louise? I don't know any Louise."

"Well, I think you must. Let me read you the message: 'Tell Ted that

Bear called him and he is really pissed off because you missed a gig.'" Mara is reading like it's a foreign language and she's learning it phonetically. "And tell Ted from me: he's cock of the roost."

The Tic, of course. I'd forgotten her real name was Louise.

"Forget Louise," I told Mara. "If she calls again, tell her it's time to get out. That's all. Now you answer me this one: Why in the name of Hades didn't you tell me you're a pianist?"

"It was not pertinent, Ted. Please tell me why you called."

I slam that receiver down so hard it bounces off its cradle. I catch it and slam it down again.

MARA

Dear Theodore,

This old letter, its date snipped off in long-ago and dangerous times, fell into my hands as I was removing a valuable artifact from my overseas trunk (appropriately shaped like a treasure chest).

Dear Theodore,

When this war is over and mail service from Bergheim to Leningrad has resumed, dear brother, will I send you these letters I have been writing for years? At this moment I am certain only that I must write to you, to talk to the only person I can trust.

I see your pale face at the train station when I was leaving our home in Leningrad: your mustache trimmed to perfection above your not-quite-stiff upper lip. Wishing me luck and assuring me that you will always be happy to look after me, should I decide to return to Russia. You can't imagine how often I have wished that I could. Including at this very moment. But in truth, once the war is over, and the constant danger, I shall not wish to re-enter that world without choices.

Perhaps we were wrong, you and I, to divorce ourselves from those endless political discussions around the family dinner table. Perhaps if I had stayed to listen, I would have believed the warnings of our father that there was a war imminent in Europe and that it would last a long time. Perhaps I would have stayed at home in the family nest. Perhaps.

If you would enjoy it, tell mother that she has the last laugh. You know that she used to sigh and shake her head when I complained of the deadly dull state of Socialist fashions. Well, I now live in a world equally beset by shortages and getting worse. You, a textile engineer and a man of taste, can imagine what it does to a dress to have been pieced together from two or three old garments by the wrong eye and hand. Just one of the horrors which daily meets my eyes: Helga in a polka-dot dress of poison green background, with a wide olive hem from God knows where and—no, I can't go on. If I had not found my little dressmaker, I would be in utter despair.

The child is as yet oblivious of clothes, I regret to say. She clumps along in her wooden-soled shoes and asks only to be allowed to wear knee socks because the long woolen stockings are itchy.

Sometimes the child is so timid and silent for so long while in the apartment with me that I have to remind myself I have seen her from my window playing out in the street, where she is a tomboy at soccer, a daredevil on skis. Sometimes, when her silence and timidity have followed me around the apartment for hours, I scream at her: stop or I shall leave you, as your father did.

At 11:30 last night, after the alarm sounded and the bombers were droning overhead as they have for weeks, always at the precise same hour, the child jumped out of bed, fully clothed, and ran into our basement shelter to sit with all the other inhabitants of the house. I had the distinct impression that she was not scared but happy. Who can understand children? When the all-clear sounded, Helga carried the child up, fast asleep, and put her to bed. I had to hurry the woman out of here, because it was almost time for the Allied broadcast and I won't miss that for anything. The child woke up right in the middle of the report on the Eastern Front, screaming out of her endless nightmares, and I had to threaten her again.

What I cannot fathom is her recurrent whimpering, during sleep, for her father. I have done my best to make her see his perfidious character, but she clutches that damned book he sent her and, fast asleep, calls for her Papa. Since we have to share the same bed (one room per person is the allotment and with the growing number of bombed-out refugees it may shrink further), I can't escape and have to wake her up to make her stop.

I suppose I am lucky that the child is so silent and secretive. The good burghers of Bergheim have a sentimental attachment to the picture we present: mother and child, war-stranded and alone, bravely facing the vicissitudes of life. (Whenever we are out in public together, we are dressed in identical outfits, which amplifies that impression a hundredfold.)

I hope that you are writing to me as frequently and as frankly as I am speaking to you, and that, at the end of this war, we can meet and present each other with great thick packages of our correspondence.

As always, your beloved sister,
Mara

TED

Every pair of ears in that German pub heard me slam down the phone, twice, and every pair of eyes looked at me, but nobody even frowned. When I sit down at the bar and order my first Scotch, the bartender pours it right in front of me but doesn't look at my face. Smart bartender.

I swallow it down and put the glass back on the counter for another one, and right there's that damned black notebook of Mara's. I want to pour Scotch all over it and put a match to it.

I remember thinking: shit! I went and slammed that phone down so fast I didn't even tell Mara that's it, lady. I'm finished. Find another Joe-boy to go chasing all over Europe for you, because I'm through. I'll hang around Helga some more, yes, but only to get my own questions answered. And when I'm done, I'll know the one thing I've really wanted to know all along: what would make a mother cut off her own dead daughter's earlobes? And is it the same thing that can make a mother cut all the hair off her dead little girl's head? With all the windows open so the hair went flying all over the house, and for months there were little blond curls turning up everywhere—in your shoe, on the lampshade, in the box with toy animals. All the time you're waiting for your mother to come back home and put her hand on the middle of you, to stop the burning in there. Burning ever since your little sister died.

The second Scotch went down so fast, I forgot to pour it on the notebook. I order a double. That's it, I decide. After I get my questions answered by Helga, I'll head back to Paris for some of that wine, women and song. And then, home to my piano. And I may or may not report to Mara that Mrs. Whatsnikoff would make a great prosecutor at her trial, and I may or may not report that Helga Müller won't do as a friendly character witness either. Because any prosecutor not dripping behind the ears will take about three minutes to suspect the truth: that Helga can't even call a cockroach by its name, lest she hurt the little pest's feelings. As for the gig: keep it, Mara. I'm out of it!

Of course, Mara had no idea why I took on that job of hers. She didn't know I've never once taken a job just for the bread. Oh, sure, maybe it starts out a money gig, playing a wedding, say, because the rent is overdue again and you're trying to keep your organ out of the pawnshop, but then, when you get to that wedding, and the bride's mother is all worried maybe the caterer didn't bring enough butter, and the groom doesn't see his bride is still looking, and the uncle tells you he used to play clarinet in a swing band, thirty years ago, and the maid of honour is hoping to lose some of it with the piano player, well, pretty soon even the wedding gig isn't just about the rent.

The bartender is tapping a beer mug. I nod. A double Scotch needs a chaser. And Bear can go barbecue his bass, for all I care about missing that gig of his. I look up into the mirror behind the bar, the whole place reflected in it, all green and brown. Eight tables, nearly all with four or six men sitting at them. Mostly old geezers with big hands and fat fingers. One guy has an empty sleeve pinned to his shoulder. These geezers have known each other all their lives. If one of them even started wearing his dick on the other side, they'd all know about it. Not one of them was looking at me but by then, I'd bet my mustache on it, every one of them knew how many hairs were in my nostrils.

I down another half-glassful of beer, hardly tasting it.

Mara lived just up the street from this joint, but I bet she never came in here. Not her kind of place, not her kind of people. Unless there was some job she wanted done. Carpenter, plumber. Call me messenger boy.

The waitress keeps her eyes on me from every part of the room. A total stranger right in the middle of their own local pub, and a foreigner at that. One who came in like his pants were on fire and then sat down to quench the flames.

Come to think of it, even if Mara never did set foot in this place, the old geezers must have known about her!

The waitress comes to the bar, smiling at me. "*Guten Tag*," she says. "Speak you English?"

All the men turn to watch the show.

"*Deutsch auch*," I say. "German, too."

The waitress thinks that's *wunderbar,* and an invitation to chat. She's wearing a dress too tight for her and her lipstick has slipped and spread but she's a friendly, curious young woman who leans one elbow on the bar and talks to me and to everybody else in the room so we can all get some fun out of this.

"Are you one tourist?"

"No. I'm here visiting Helga Müller ."

Now the whole room is smiling and nodding. They all like Helga and any visitor of hers.

"Yes," I tell them, "I'm visiting Helga Müller and I am doing research into the life of Mara deJong." It's been a dozen years since Mara lived here but their faces tell me she hasn't been forgotten. Which doesn't surprise me a bit.

"Eine schöne Frau," says one grey-stubbled gent. "A beautiful woman." And everybody nods again. I just might get somebody spilling some beans here. The waitress wants to know if I'm writing a book about Mara.

"No," I say, and then wish I hadn't. But then something helpful comes floating up from Mara's biographical notes and I decide to try a shot in the dark.

"I just made a phone call about her. She's disappeared again and I'm trying to find her."

Murmuring. Great curiosity. Yes, I'm almost sure I can get them talking. Then the waitress flaps her mouth again.

"Oh, you're a policeman," says the waitress. "An American policeman!"

All of a sudden, not one eye looking at me. No doubt about it, these geezers are not crazy about investigators. Who knows how many of them were dragged in for questioning during WWII? Or how many of them did the dragging? Come to think of it, most of them would have been in the army.

Any of you old farts remember wounding a Canadian Air Force pilot in 1943?

No, forget that. If my father'd been born a German, he'd be right here, too, drinking beer with these old buggers.

Grandma escaped being called a Kraut, in Canada, because she had my grandfather's Irish name and because she had a son in the Canadian Air Force. Grandma never hid she was German, but she was always pointing out to people what was German and what was Nazi.

I called for my tab and paid up and my hands reached for the black notebook. Like it was attached to me by invisible strings. On the way out I got a round of waves from the men, for Helga's sake, and from the waitress a smiling *"Auf Wiedersehn."*

ALICIA

There was still no news about Ted but I had to phone Lena again.

"Hello, Lena, this is Alicia."

"Hi Alicia. Ted's not back yet, as far as I know."

"Well, I'm actually calling about something else, this time. Did a young woman show up there yesterday? Redhead, loud voice...?"

"Oh, yes. She was here last night."

"I am sorry, Lena. I'm the one who gave her the address. That damned Tic was bothering us every hour. We had to keep the phone permanently off the hook, but we can't keep on doing that. Bear gets called out on gigs by phone. Then she found out where we live and starting pounding on the door, wanting to know where Ted was, when he was getting back, accusing me of lying, of hiding him, screaming and cursing and calling me names. I finally snapped and gave her Mara deJong's address. So she could go and find out for herself that Ted's away. Was she a horrible nuisance?"

"Well, hard to say what Mara made of her. She arrived at three in the morning, banging on the door and yelling she wasn't going to leave till she saw Ted. Mara got to the front door first and let her in. Her name is Louise, right?"

"I don't know, we call her the Tic. God—three in the morning. Was she drunk?"

"Possibly. Or on some drug. Mara asked her into the apartment and Louise was so surprised, she just stared for a minute. Then she went in and I went back up to my place but about half an hour later Mara called up and asked if I would please come down to join them."

"At 3:30 in the morning? What, a tea party?"

"Not exactly. More like an interview, but don't ask me for what. She's Ted's girlfriend, is she?"

"Not in a million years."

"She claims she is."

"She's not. The woman is a pest. An infestation. What kind of questions did Mara ask her?"

"Well, I didn't hear the beginning. When I came down, Mara was asking, was that her natural hair colour? Louise laughed. She was looking pretty relaxed by then. She said no, it wasn't her natural colour. Then Mara wanted to know why Louise chose the colour red for her hair. Louise said because it wasn't mousy and she'd do anything not to look mousy. Mara asked how long she's been in Toronto and what she was doing here. Louise said waiting for Ted."

"Lena, believe me, Ted wants nothing to do with her. Really. He just can't seem to be nasty enough so she'll get the message. He probably thought he could rescue her from something or other. Unfortunately, he doesn't know this time he was trying to rescue a barracuda."

"Surely not a barracuda? After Louise left, Mara wanted to know what I thought of her. I told her Louise seemed lost to me, and desperate, trying to hang onto somebody to keep afloat. Mara looked at me as though I was speaking in riddles."

"That doesn't surprise me. Would you like to hear my assessment? Based on what came out of this poor little lost one's mouth, she's a redneck racist menace, out of control on booze or drugs or both. And so pissed off at the world she's capable of serious mayhem. I won't repeat what she called me, but I'll tell you this: I came damned close to slapping the bitch. And I'm the one always preaching "there must be a better way" when Bear or Ted threatens a fist."

"Let me assure you," said Lena, "a slap would barely register with Louise. One reason she left North Bay is her older brother who apparently beat her up regularly. He took over from the father who used to beat Louise all through her childhood."

"Oh hell, I wish you hadn't told me that. I really do."

I had to pause at that point and remind myself what this poor little Louise had called me, a "lazy dirty nigger," just to make sure I didn't go all soft and cuddly about the Tic. After that, Lena and I talked for a bit about non-violence. I thought maybe it was easier for women to be non-violent just because we're physically weaker. Lena wasn't so sure.

"This is the age of the gun," she said. "Surely that makes us equal? On the other hand, you may be right. It does take a lot more time to change long-held assumptions like 'the weaker sex' than it takes for technological change... Oh, sorry. I seem to be in anthropologist mode these days."

Lena laughed at herself.

"Never mind," I told her. "It's a relief to be talking about something besides my personal woes."

I could hear her hesitating to say something.

"Spit it out, Lena. What?"

"Well, I have a question. About Ted and waiting. Both you and Ted mentioned that 'waiting is something Ted cannot do.' You made it sound like—oh, a skill. Like 'mountain-climbing is something Ted cannot do.'"

"It's true. He just can't. Any time Ted has to do some waiting, he gets into trouble. It's like he's driven, like some demon takes over and drives him into action. Let me tell you just the last example I know about, okay? This happened a few weeks ago, when Ted had to wait for his grandma at the train station.

"Grandma was supposed to get back from Montreal by the five o'clock train. Ted's down at Union Station, standing at the gate, checking everybody coming through, and it's now 5:30 and still no grandma. Ted asked a railway official and yes, the train got in on time and yes, everybody's off it by now, but no, the man has no way of knowing whether Ted's grandmother was on it. Ted says he might as well have been talking to the uniform buttons for all the signs of life he was getting.

"'Why don't you,' said the uniform, 'just sit down and wait for the next train?'

"Ted figured that was four hours and twenty minutes of waiting and not knowing where grandma has got to and whether she's even alive or dead—Ted's words. When he has to wait, he thinks like that: 'alive or dead.'

"'Oh, no,' says Ted to the official. 'No waiting. We are going to do something about finding my grandmother right now!'

"The uniform starts to turn away from Ted. Ted grabs his arm— 'just the arm,' says Ted, and just hard enough to turn him back around, but the guy goes and whistles for the cops! Two of them were just starting to haul Ted away, when dear old grandma comes walking along. Hale and hearty, as they say. She'd taken an earlier train and was sitting on a bench all that time, just around the corner, waiting for Ted. Grandma made the cops hold on and hand her a pen and a page of their notebook so she could write down the cops' names and badge numbers. Then she told them to take good care of her grandson and told Ted she'd be bringing him soup. 'Like jail was the 'flu,' says Ted. And: 'That's my grandma.' He claims she had those cops saying 'yes, Ma'am,' to her before they hauled Ted away. Released him the same day, by the way. But see what I mean? Waiting is something Ted cannot do. I'm sure it's connected to his mother's suicide, somehow. When Ted was a little kid."

"Oh, my God, Alicia. How can a mother do that to her child?"

"There you go. Exactly the question Ted asked about Mara deJong. God, I really wish I'd remembered about his mother before I started ranting at Ted about the earlobe freak and putting it all behind him. I'm still so pissed off at myself I could howl. I really wish I could roll back time to before Michelle's death."

"Me too," said Lena. "Believe me, me too."

We both paused there and sighed. Then I made another foray into dangerous territory.

"Listen, Lena. I'm sorry if the question I'm about to ask offends you, but I'll burst if I don't ask you this one: you say you were Michelle's friend, so what are you doing helping her mother? How can you even live under the same roof with her?! Oh, shit. I'm sorry. I know it's none of my business and I should never have asked."

"Whoa, Alicia, it's all right. You think I never thought about it? Every which way? Finally I asked myself what Michelle would say and then it wasn't all that difficult. Because, let's face it, what real harm was done except to convention and customs? Michelle was already dead and beyond caring about her earlobes."

"Oh, my God, Lena! How can you be so rational? No, wait a minute. Hang on. I have to ask myself a question here: would I be more rational about this, if I was in my normal state? Not this emotional mess I am right now. I tell you, Lena, I feel berserk, half the time—weepy and then pissed off—like in a prolonged and really horrible pre-period. Oh, never mind all that. Okay. No big harm done, you say, Michelle already dead, but... no, I can't. I cannot make my mind go there. It makes me crazy to go there."

"Then don't. Go there. I'm already there because Michelle was my friend. You know what makes *me* mad? That those damned earlobes are wiping Michelle herself out of everybody's mind. My friend Michelle, who was gentle and talented and funny, with a kind of gallows humour, and who made a great cup of coffee and who really tried to do no harm to anybody..."

"Wait, Lena, I'm not forgetting Michelle for the earlobes. Forgive me if

I sound a bit bitter, but did you know this gentle funny friend of yours was hanging out with my husband?

"Michelle would never have played footsie with a married man."

"You so sure of that?"

"Absolutely. Michelle was a student of Buddhism and she really tried to live by the dictum, Do No Harm. We used to talk about how difficult that can be. Believe me, staying away from married men is easy compared to, say, not killing the cockroach in your sink."

Lena was laughing and I was starting to believe her about Michelle, which left me feeling worse than ever about the harm I had definitely done to Bear and Ted, and to Bear and me. No wonder I felt nauseated most of the time.

TED

I came out of the pub and headed back to Helga's, still steamed over Mara not even breathing one hint that she's a piano player. Pardon me, not a piano player, a *pianist*. Let me tell you about classical musicians. Some of them are so fucking snotty they need umbrellas to keep the rain out of their nostrils. Then you get a few that come hanging around the stage, wanting to know where you get it all, playing without music sheets. And not one of them has the slightest idea how much wood shedding, how many years of practicing, go into the basics of jazz— how many hours just on the chord changes alone. They hear somebody bending a note and they think it's lack of technique, for Christ's sake. They hear a virtuoso like Oscar Peterson and think he didn't have to put in his years practicing because he's black, see, and he's playing jazz, so it was just born right in him.

Cool down, Ted! Or as my grandmother would say: Temperrrr, temperrrr.

And then—man, I really hate to be telling this—I puked. Right out there on a tidy Bergheim street, I puked. Held onto a wooden fence post like a goddamned rubby and puked out everything I had in me: cake, beer, Scotch, the works. Luckily there wasn't anybody around; I don't think I could have passed it off as a coughing fit.

I picked some grass growing along the sidewalk and chewed and spat, cleaning my breath, all the way to Helga's house. No light on in the hall. Banister, good, hand-over-hand to the landing. If this is the wrong house,

I'll be busted for drunk and disorderly and certainly several suspicions of. And Mara will hear about it and say she told me to get my hair cut.

The hall light comes on.

"Are you that, Ted? Why make you not the light on?"

In English. Showing off. Helga must have been listening for me and pushed a button for the hall light. Long before I make it all the way up, the light's out again. Whatever happened to German three-quarter time? Stately waltzes, then goose-stepping marches, and now hop-skip and jump to beat the hall light.

Helga has soup on the table, and chops, and home-fried potatoes, and two kinds of dessert. Refusing would be like spitting in her sugar bowl, so now I'm actually glad I puked and made some room.

Helga is eating with gusto, asking about Canada.

"Tell me, is it truly so cold? *Ja?* And do you have mountains there?"

"Not like yours," I tell her, and she takes it as a compliment. She's obviously never seen the Canadian Rockies.

"*Natürlich*," she says. "Naturally. It's the reforestation. Every time a mountain tree is cut, another one is planted. Except one whole side of the *Spitzenberg*, where the British occupation forces took their firewood after the war. That whole mountainside is still bare."

No rancour in her voice. Just fact.

I ask Helga why the three canaries in three separate cages.

"Well, *ja*," she says, "that is kind of a long story." She's smiling and launches into a tale she's definitely told before. I know it involved her son and three successive girlfriends and jealous fights and Helga ending up with one canary after the other and if you put them into the same cage, they fight.

I realize Helga is waiting for an audience reaction so I smile and nod, and she continues:

"So then they bought themselves a hamster," says Helga.

I look around but there's no hamster.

"Oh," Helga says, "they had that hamster in the car the last time they came to visit me, Helmut and Mariette, but I told them. 'Never!' I said. 'I refuse to take an angora rat into my home and you two better stop having fights and start having babies instead.'

Helga guffaws.

My nice small-town Hausfrau, still capable of blushing at age 60 or so, lets out a guffaw the size of a lumberjack and then she looks surprised out of her tree. Not because she'd let out a raucous sound like that, mind you—that wasn't her first guffaw by a long shot—no, she's surprised because she's let it out in front of a stranger. A foreigner, all the way from Canada, whose hair is much too long.

Now we're on the last dessert, Helga and I, a chocolate-covered little cream puff that lands softly on top of the slice of cheesecake. Time to get back on course.

"Tell me, Helga, did many people know that Mara listened to Allied Radio broadcasts? It was illegal, wasn't it?"

"*Ja, ja*, certainly. It was very dangerous. Only the people in the house knew about it. You see, there was a false wall in Mara's apartment. Very thin. Even with Mara's beautiful Persian carpet hanging on it, we could hear the radio anytime she turned it on. Of course, we knew that Mara had family in Leningrad. So you see, she wanted to find out what was really going on with the war."

"Did she tell you what she heard?"

"Oh, no. We all pretended not to know that she was listening. It was much safer that way. Not everybody is as brave as Mara. Did she ever tell you how she used to meet Günter? Right out there in the old shack by the abandoned railway track? At night, in the pitch-dark of the blackout!"

"And who was this Günter?"

"Oh, Günter was the biggest black marketeer in town."

Helga is enjoying something about this memory.

"One night Mara came back after meeting Günter. She'd taken her ersatz coffee rations again, to trade for some of that black tea she loved. And that night he finally had the new blue shoes for her, the ones she'd been hoping to trade for. So when she came back, she was wearing the new blue shoes and I guess she must have heard our voices in the living room downstairs because she knocked and came in to show them. And who was sitting there on our couch but our neighbour, Mr. Rolf. Boasting away how he'd just been promoted by his Nazi cronies to deputy mayor. And here is Mara coming home at midnight, wearing new shoes and smelling of black-market tea! Well, I tell you: we all stopped breathing. Not Mara, though. Do you know what Mara did? She held out her hand to Mr. Rolf, who jumped up, of course. Standing so close and shaking her hand, he couldn't even see her shoes. Then Mara said: 'Congratulations, Mr. Rolf. You deserve your promotion, I'm sure. Now, everybody! Can you guess the aroma of the newest perfume from Berlin? Yes, yes, it's the aroma of real tea!'"

"*Menschenskind,* I tell you, it was so hard not to laugh! Mara just kept smiling at Mr. Rolf and then she waved and disappeared out the door."

Helga has a chuckle to herself, shaking her head.

"Oh, and guess who is Mr. Rolf's own brother-in-law. Günter, the black marketeer! The two of them hoist a few together at the pub every Wednesday, but Günter never told his brother-in-law about his black-market deals. We all had our secrets, I guess."

Helga, no doubt about it, is enjoying herself.

"One of our secrets was Bruno. Bruno was Karl's best friend (Karl being Mara's husband number one). Whenever Bruno came to visit he used to do the most risky things. Imitations of Goebbels: hobbling just like him and talking circles around everybody. Or he'd crack jokes about Mussolini, and even about Hitler. Oh, dear."

Helga is a bit nostalgic about those days, alone up here with her three canaries and a stranger. I lift my mug and we clink and drink a silent toast to dangerous laughter.

"In 1937," says Helga, "just when Hitler annexed Austria, we were having a party—my mother's birthday party it was, and Bruno came in, waving an Austrian flag. Goodness knows where he got that flag. And he made a long speech about cleaning up the Austrians by letting out all the Hungarian and Yugoslavian blood. Five pints per person, he said, man, woman and child. Six pints from everybody with Slavic cheekbones. And it sounded so ridiculous and we all laughed so hard. Oh, dear. We didn't know, you see. Who would have believed....Oh, dear."

Helga might have stopped there but momentum carries her along.

"Well, we found out, of course. In 1940. November 9th it was, my cousin Traude's wedding anniversary. That day the owner of the Berghotel disappeared. Herr Hoffman. They took him and his whole family in the middle of the night and those hooligans even started a fire in the hotel lobby, but it was put out. Later, in '41, the hotel burned down anyway because a bomb fell on it. Herr Hoffman came back after the war, in 1952. He only stayed three days and then he went back to New York. That's when we found out his whole family was killed in the concentration camps. He looked so old and sick and he didn't speak to anyone except Herr Bauer, the porter on the train."

"Was he Jewish, this Herr Hoffman?"

"He must have been. Or maybe Armenian. He had beautiful carpets in the hotel. He played violin and sometimes he came to play with Mara, that first year she was here. Wonderful music. Herr Bauer, the porter, told us Herr Hoffman could never play violin again, after the war, because in the camps they made him work with his hands, filling up thousands of bags with wet sand. His fingers were 'as thick as Bratwurst sausages,' Herr Bauer said."

That horror story came tripping off Helga's tongue like it's just one of thousands and maybe it is, maybe it is. I excuse myself and go to the kitchen sink and throw cold water on my face for a while and then go back into the fray. Helga has filled our beer mugs again—best beer I've ever tasted—and I lift mine as intro to the next skirmish.

"Tell me, Helga, did Mara's first husband drink?"

Helga twinkles. "*Ja, ja,* Karl certainly knew how to enjoy himself. He was a great one for parties. Singing and treating friends. Telling stories."

Another one who loves remembering Karl.

"Why did Mara and Karl separate in 1939? Why did they divorce?"

Helga can't handle that question at all. Loyalty to Mara battling with loyalty to Karl is my guess. Her eyes are darting around between the three canaries till she looks dizzy—I have to let her off the hook.

"Never mind that, Helga. It's not really relevant, let's hope. Tell me about testifying to the SS on Mara's behalf."

"Oh, they only called me down once. I volunteered and went down twice more after that, but they hardly listened. There was a different man behind the desk every time, and none of them local people or I would have told them what I thought of their manners. One of them worked on a crossword puzzle all the time I was there. Mara had coached me, of course, so I knew exactly what to wear and how to sit and what to say, but they hardly paid attention."

I have to excuse myself. Helga nods me in the right direction and I go off into a tiny cubbyhole—nothing but a toilet and a sink in it—and stay there long after I'm finished, to think. About how Mara, the arrogant pianist I've been pissed off at is the same woman who coached Helga into outsmarting the SS. And is the same woman who left her little girl alone in the middle of that war. How do you get any kind of handle on a woman like that?

Sitting at the table again, I ask Helga:

"Tell me something, did Mara ever cry?"

"Oh, yes, of course she did, Ted."

"What made her cry?"

"Well, she certainly must have cried when Russia entered the war. You see, after that there were no more letters from her family. She didn't even know whether they were alive or dead. Not for many years. And then, after the war, she found out that her parents were killed. Also her sisters-in-law, all her nephews and nieces, the whole family—they were all killed."

"By the Germans?"

"By Hitler's army. Mara's family was trying to escape Leningrad during the siege and they were all caught and shot. Only her three brothers survived. They were in the Russian army and when the war was over, they went home. But there was nobody there.

"*Ja, ja,*" says Helga, "I am quite certain that Mara must have cried when she found out about the death of so many people in her family. It was soon after the war was over. A Russian officer came in a red jeep and told her."

By now everything in my belly is turning sour, including the cream puff. Here was Mara, a young woman alone with her little daughter in a foreign country, which is at war with her own country so she's an alien and in constant danger, and most of her family gets killed, and then I come along and I get miffed at the woman because she didn't tell me she's a pianist. Why would she tell me anything at all?

Meantime, Helga has gone to the canaries. She sighs at the middle one and says: "Almost bedtime for you, *Hänschen*."

But no, she insists she herself isn't tired at all. She likes company. I'm so limp I'm practically sliding off the chair, but I'm not done in yet.

"Helga, how did Mara herself cope when she was being investigated by the SS?"

"Well, she never said anything to us but there were signs of strain, of course. Like the time her handbag broke. It was a pretty bag, a petit-point with roses, but we all knew that it couldn't be the real reason for the way Mara carried on, crying and screaming all day long, and Lisa the only one in there with her, poor little thing. The same thing happened when the heel broke off her blue pumps.

"Or sometimes Mara would be in tears of despair because a pair of silk stockings had runs. She knew perfectly well that I would repair them for her, so we all thought it must be the strain. Or one day, when little Lisa was playing outside and she climbed the old cherry tree in the back garden and ripped her stockings. Well, Lisa and Mara were supposed to be visiting uptown that afternoon, so Lisa came in crying and I tried to mend the stockings before Mara saw them but, well, Mara found us out and made Lisa change and that meant Mara had to change her clothes, too, because they were dressed in identical outfits, and by the time they were ready again, it was too late and Mara had one of her headaches and so they didn't go at all. Mara was most upset. She said it wasn't because they had to miss the visit but because she'd hoped to talk to Mrs. Kreisler up there about taking Lisa on in her ballet school. Lisa told me in secret she really didn't want to spend every afternoon in ballet school.

"I tried to explain it to her. Your mother wants you to associate with the children from nice uptown families. But Lisa said—I remember it as if it was yesterday—'I like my friends down here,' she said. 'They don't boast all the time.'"

"Mara never did go and enroll Lisa in the ballet school; I forget why. Maybe that was close to the end of the war, when everything was changing so fast. It must have been around that time."

"Tell me more about Mara, Helga. Anything you like."

Helga waggles herself into her chair so she's roundly rooted. Like I've given her a treat.

"Oh, she was wonderfully cultured, Mara. You could see that right away even though she had such foreign ways. Mara never once went bare-legged or wore wool stockings in all the years she lived here. She had regular hairdresser appointments, a manicurist, and even...for the toenails, you know. Pedicure. And a masseuse. Karl never complained of the expense. Not even if he had to send two extra cheques a month. Karl was a very generous man.

"Oh, and Mara had a seamstress, too. She made Mara dresses from the 'Berliner Mode'. Everybody said Mara was the town's own fashion magazine. Even when everything was rationed and the stores were empty, Mara looked the picture of elegance.

"She taught the child, too. Table manners, and piano and deportment, and—oh, dear—sometimes I almost went up to their apartment to ask whether little Lisa could be excused to come and help me with some chores, the poor little thing. So quiet and obedient. You'd never know it was the same child, out in the street galloping around with her friends."

"Wait a minute, Helga."

All these stories about Michelle as a little girl have started up a buzzing in my head and it's getting louder. Even Helga calling her Lisa doesn't help. I've been rooting around in my near-blotto brain for a question to steer Helga out of that memory lane and onto a different one, and finally come up with something out of Mara's notebook: I ask Helga about the maid. The one who stole Mara's silk nightgown.

"Oh, but she didn't! Goodness gracious. She couldn't have. I've known Isolde since she was a child, Ted. But Mara didn't know her, you see, and she couldn't find the nightgown anywhere. Until later—it turned up in the wrong laundry hamper. Isolde, the maid—she was so upset about losing her reputation, she wanted a police investigation to clear her name. What a scare! Well, in the end it all blew over. But it wasn't easy, finding another maid for Mara around here, with all the young girls doing well-paid factory work and so on. I finally cleaned her apartment myself now and then."

And mended Mara's silk stockings, as I remembered, and looked after the little girl a lot, especially when abandoned. And doesn't for a moment consider that she might have done otherwise. Maybe Helga and my grandmother play in the same key, after all. And what was Mara doing in the meantime? Or, for that matter, now? For example, is she still playing concerts?

I ask Helga if Mara is giving concerts these days and Helga stares at me. I guess I should know the answer to that one if I'm Mara's friend.

"Mara," I tell Helga, "is being very secretive about her piano playing."

"Oh, dear," sighs Helga, and stops herself from saying something else. Then she throws a sideways look at the canaries and comes out with a question for me.

"Excuse me for asking, please: how long have you known Mara?"

What she means is "how well."

"I am not her latest man, Helga. I'm just a friend."

Hired man, actually, but that just wouldn't come off my tongue.

There's a buzzing in my head, getting louder every minute, so I don't know which is going to bust first, my head or my belly? I manage to croak: "Hotel," and "Taxi," but Helga won't hear of it.

"Wait you right there," says Helga. "Your bed will be ready in a blink."

LENA

A few days after I asked Mara when Ted was coming back and she'd given me that penetrating glance, I noticed that Mara was actually looking at me whenever we happened to meet in the house. It occurs to me now that she might even have orchestrated some of the occasions when we bumped into each other. When we did, she always had a question for me, and always listened attentively while I answered, her eyes observant. And then one day, she dropped me out of her attention and I was invisible again.

She'd asked me, that day, what I made of Betty McDonald, a neighbour on our street, three houses over. Who did I think she was, from what background?

I couldn't tell Mara very much about Betty McDonald. I knew she and her husband owned the house, which was still a one-family home, big though it was, so they were likely well-to-do. She drove a Mercedes, actually. Two kids and a nanny and what seemed like a very straight middle-class sort of life. Why was Mara interested in Betty McDonald and family?

Mara mumbled something, shaking her head, and then asked another question: Didn't I think it odd, if they were a well-to-do family, that Betty McDonald dressed like a student, in jeans and sneakers, with a nondescript blouse hanging out?

"No," I said. "Not odd. She likes casual and comfortable clothes."

Mara threw me a sharp look and asked one last question: What was my opinion of Betty McDonald?

"You mean about her as a person?" I asked Mara, and she nodded, watching me very intensely as if my opinion of Betty McDonald would be significant.

"But how can I have formed an opinion of her?" I asked Mara. "I don't even know the woman."

And that's when Mara erased me from her view. Luckily, I was already in anthropologist mode or it might have felt a lot worse. As it was, I cautioned myself sternly not to get drawn into Mara's world. ("Easier said than done," as Michelle used to say. Most often when she was talking about living the simple life, comically sighing while easing yet another brand-new record onto the turntable.)

TED

My grandmother says I have the constitution of a horse. I know she's not thinking race horse; more likely one of those Belgian workhorses, because what she means is no matter what condition I'm in when I go to bed, by the time I wake up, I'm in pretty good shape.

It's morning in Helga's apartment; my eyes are still shut but my ears are open, getting a rousing duet: kettle and canaries. I roll over and pick up the huge feather pillow lying punched out on the floor, and then I sit up. Something Helga talked about last night is nipping in and out of my head. When I finally grab hold of it, it's Bruno, the friend. The one who cracked jokes even about Hitler. Seemed to me that this Bruno was somewhere in Mara's notebook.

I pull the black notebook into bed with me and start leafing through it, and here he is:

Bruno Hofmeister

Bruno is a miner, with some education but no ambition; he never rose above foreman. My first husband Karl was very attached to Bruno and delegated him to look after me and the child once Karl and I separated. Bruno came every two months by train all the way from the Ruhrgebiet where he and Karl worked, to see that we were all right.

Bruno was the first to come forward and swear under oath that we were Aryans and Christians. In the SS office he broke down and cried while talking about the efforts of a mother (myself) to look after her little girl during wartime.

Bruno is very loyal and good-natured, but he very often is drunk. Please try to find out whether it is still possible to have him cured. He would be a very valuable witness, but only if sober. When drunk he is sentimental and given to exaggeration to such an extent that no one in court would believe him.

Bruno is convinced that Karl and I are a Modern Tragedy, destroyed by historical events beyond our control. He is fond of remembering how beautiful a couple Karl and I were and how he himself was in love with me but would never act on it or even show it (though one had to be blind not to see it), because Karl was his best friend, after all, and I a woman cast upon hostile shores and in need of protection.

Despite the above, be assured that Bruno is no fool. He is a tall, handsome man who keeps his abundant hair well-groomed and wears shoes of the finest Italian leather.

There is no need for a list of questions. Once started, Bruno will talk ad infinitum *about anything which relates to us.*

That's it for Bruno Hofmeister, but it's plenty: finally somebody who is going to rattle on about Mara without having to be prodded at every pothole in the road. I decided right then and there that before I followed Mara's instructions to sober him up I would get this Bruno soaking it up like a pickle in a barrel, and talking about Mara every drop of the way. Yes. Bruno was going to be my personal fountain of answers and joy. Hallelujah!

I jump out of bed, pull on the man's bathrobe lying on a chair, smelling of forest-green laundry soap, and step out into the living room. Helga is feeding the canaries. Wearing an enormous frilly housecoat, hair sticking out in all directions. From the back she looks like the retired madam of a small-town cathouse, but when she turns around, her face is round and rosy-clean and relaxed as a sleepy puppy.

Helga says good morning and let me show you my new shower. Completely modern, she is proud to say. The cold white tiles and stainless steel are a jolt in that cozy apartment, but I sure am ready for a shower. I find one of Helga's hairpins in a little porcelain swan and take it with me under the shower to clean my fingernails. Which started me thinking 'piano'. Would Mara have told me she's a pianist if I'd mentioned the classical music I listened to, growing up, and all the classical albums I still lug around with me every time I move?

"You can listen to anything you like," my grandmother used to tell me. That was when I first started listening to jazz and was doing it all the time. "As long as you hear at least one great composition a night." By "great" grandma meant the dead European classical composers, what else? Not my greats. But I did listen to hers, too, and not just once over lightly. Mingus and Oscar Peterson didn't come to any harm listening to them. And some of that music *is* great, and some of those piano players, like Ashkenazy and Horowitz and Schnabel, they really blow you away.

When I get back to Toronto, I'm going to play Mara some Art Tatum and Oscar Peterson. And then Bill Evans. And when I think she's ready, Monk. That should stretch her ears. That woman has a whole world of music to discover and she doesn't even know it yet!

Ted the jazz freak. My father's nickname for me, pronounced: Ted the bum.

You're right, dad. There is no tenure in jazz and the booze is right out there on the table, not hidden behind any water tank in the basement. How did my father get into this brand-new morning?

I finish towelling myself dry and relax again because, hey, Bruno is next on the list and Bruno is going to rattle on and tell me all about Mara. First, though, I want to say hello to my grandma. Helga is in the kitchen, quietly clattering and producing great smells. I dial the operator and give her my grandmother's number, and while I'm still explaining to her I want the call charged to Mara, grandma comes on the line. Grandma in Toronto, 82 years old, eyes hunting around for her glasses.

"You don't need your glasses to talk to me on the phone, grandma. I'm calling from Germany, for Christ's sake."

"Stop your swearing, Ted," she says, preoccupied with squinting around the room.

"Maybe they're in the bathroom, with your teeth?"

"My teeth are right here in my mouth and you're not in Germany. I suppose you've been nipping again?"

"Nipping hasn't been invented yet in Germany," I tell her. "Here people drink and leave nipping to the canaries."

"So, Tedboy..." she's found her glasses. "How have you been keeping yourself?"

In English, my grandmother's mix of Irish lilt and German accent is a gas. Snatches of flute over a pizzicato bass.

"I'm all right, grandma."

"Have you called Bear? He's looking for you."

"Let him. And if he calls again, tell him to find himself another piano player."

"Now I know for sure you're fooling around again. So what's this about you being in Germany?" Grandma pauses for my punch line.

I get the telephone operator to back me up but grandma still thinks it's one of my jokes, abetted by a girlfriend. She thinks I have a girl for every day of the week, tsk tsk, but she can't help being proud of me anyway. Not that she ever lets on. Watch your language, Ted. Watch your manners. Watch where you put your feet. All reflex. One evening, on her 75th birthday, the two of us got drunk together and my grandmother said: "Ted, if I had to live life over, I'd do it as a wildcat. A tiger."

On the phone, Grandma thinks she's sneaking one in.

"Now, Ted. What about Thanksgiving, then? Wouldn't that be a fine time for a family reunion?"

"Not that again, grandma."

Grandma says there's some dough rising in the oven so she has to go now but why don't I call her back when I reach Timbuktu. A chuckle and she's hung up.

Helga is waiting with breakfast. Bratwurst, home fries, and some bread that is guaranteed to ferment in your stomach and keep you farting for days. I haven't eaten breakfast in years, but I'm not stuck on that. Helga pours herself another cup of coffee. Half of it, strong and black, comes out of a loud pink and shiny plastic coffee maker. The other half, warm milk, from a porcelain pitcher with little blue flowers all over it. Like two different centuries making coffee together.

I have my first question all ready to pop because now that Bruno the Happy Talker is on the agenda, I can just dive right in where I was wading around on tippy-toe last night.

"Helga, tell me this: why did Mara abandon her daughter? Taking off and leaving her when the kid was three years old, right? And then again when she was five."

Sure enough, Helga starts dodging. As full of evasions and euphemisms as a politician.

"Oh, we all knew Mara would come back," says Helga. "We just didn't know when."

Bit by bit I find out that they also didn't know where Mara went. She just disappeared. With two full suitcases. Think about it! Just downstairs from where Helga and I were sitting, Mara was packing two suitcases, getting ready to split but hiding it all from her own little daughter. Who woke up in the morning and found her mother gone and a note pinned to the pillow. A note the kid couldn't even read yet.

She took it to Helga, of course.

The note said: "I know you will take good care of her. Mara."

That's all. Nothing about when she was coming back. Or even *if* she was going to.

Helga remembers little Lisa asking to be taught to read, please. Right away.

"That was Michelle's real name, you know, Lisa. In this house she was never Michelle. Our little Lisa...Sometimes she worried me, she was so quiet at home. But very intelligent. She learned to read in one week!"

I do not want to hear any more about this too-quiet little girl, waiting for her mother to come back.

"And you never found out why Mara left or where she went?"

"No," says Helga, averting her eyes, clearly dying to know. Mara's notebook said "Helga understood" but I'm willing to bet those canaries still hear questions about Mara.

"Tell me, Helga, did Mara *like* the child? Did she care what happened to her?"

Helga has never heard anybody question mother love. She looks at me all sorry-eyed, and wants to know if I am an orphan.

"Only when I'm away from my piano," I snap at her.

Whoa! Take a long breath and slow down, Tedboy. But do not let up on this question.

"Come on, Helga. You've heard of mothers abandoning their children? Leaving them at the bus stop? Or killing themselves and leaving no letter or even a note?"

Helga is smiling.

"But those are women who have lost their minds," she says *(die haben doch den Verstand verloren)*. "That never happened to Mara. She might raise her voice and carry on but she never loses her wits. And whatever the problem is, she always finds a solution."

"Okay, give me an example, Helga. What kind of solution?"

Helga sits down squarely on her chair—roundly is more like it—and she folds her hands on the table. Big hands, rough-skinned, knobbly at the joints.

"One day," she starts up, in true storyteller fashion and enjoying it, "one day, we were all of us sitting in the shelter. We had our own bomb shelter in the basement, you see. We whitewashed the walls and put chairs and benches all around, and we had a miner's lamp that Karl gave us hanging from the ceiling in case the electricity went again. There aren't any windows down there so we never had to worry about blackout.

"I always liked the smell from the root cellar: carrots, potatoes, apples, and cabbages. And we had candles…"

"What about Mara, that day in the shelter?"

"Night, actually. It was night time. For about five months, the bombers flew overhead every night around 11 o'clock. You could hear them for a long time—that sound they make when they're flying high and together, deep and steady. It's the best sound. It means they're going to faraway targets and they won't be dropping their bombs on you. When they're coming back though, you sometimes get a couple of low-flying ones. That's a higher sound and sometimes kind of stuttering, and it worries you because they're likely to drop any bombs they've got left. The sound of the bombs, well..." Helga stops herself. She'd rather not remember the sounds of bombs dropping. I can hear them, too, thanks to Hollywood, but now the sound is connected to Helga and Mara in Bergheim, in the basement of this same house we're sitting in. Helga says:

"That night there weren't any bombs. Not for us.

"Anyway, Mara surprised us by coming down into the shelter that night. Usually, when the air raid alarm sounded, we all trooped down just as we were and left the house to Mara. Mara would put on her fur coat and her terrycloth robe over that, and then she'd walk all over the house, to get it ready. Opening windows so they wouldn't shatter during the bombing, turning off any lights, and so on. Mara and our grandmother always said the same thing: 'If the house is hit by a bomb, I'd rather go quickly than be buried alive under the rubble.'

"Well, that night Mara came down into the shelter with us and I could tell she was worried. Not about the bombs. About a woman called Eva. Mara had met Eva that afternoon at the shoe repair and Eva told Mara that she knew Mara's father was Jewish. Now, Eva's husband was in the SS, you see, and if Eva told her husband..."

"Helga, did you and your family know during the war that Mara is Jewish?"

"Oh, it was never spoken of. We certainly knew that Mara's papers were not her own. We had seen her real passport when she first came to us, the family did. But it was never mentioned. Then, just before Karl left, he asked me if I would look after Mara and little Lisa. I said 'yes, of course.' Then Karl said: 'You know that they might need exceptional friends, don't you?' And I said 'yes.' That was all we ever said.

"Anyway, that woman Mara met, Eva, she had a much younger husband and she was *hörig*. Do you know what *hörig* means?"

I knew the word but vaguely. Something like: "Sexually obsessed with a man and will do anything to keep him." No such word in English. I nod and Helga goes on.

"Eva's husband was in the SS and Mara was worried. She could hardly sit still that night in the shelter, but there was no room for pacing so she rocked back and forth on her chair and talked to herself in Russian.

"I asked Mara what I could do to help. Should I talk to the woman? You see, I knew Eva well. I often looked in on her after her baby died. Her husband was unemployed and getting drunk every day. Mara told me no, she'd have to approach the danger from a different angle. Then she rocked some more and I guess we all thought about Mr. Goldstein who owned the best textile store in town and who had just disappeared one day, two months earlier. His business was taken over by that ne'er-do-well son of Manfred the tailor.

"Well, Mara finally stopped muttering in Russian and asked me something: 'Doesn't Eva's husband go to the races? On Thursdays?'

"She was right. He did go to the races every Thursday and he still does, for all I know. He lost a leg in the war but he gets around just fine when he wants to.

"Then Mara asked me one more question. 'Did Eva's husband ever travel? Go to any big cities?' And we all knew he hadn't, though before the war he used to boast about how he was going to be a mechanic in the city. 'Cars are the future!' he used to say. Then, when the Nazi party came in, he stopped trying to pass the mechanic's test, pinned on a swastika and started saying 'We are the future!'

"Anyway, by now Mara looked all excited. Like she'd found a solution. She went upstairs and we could hear her prowling around up there like she usually did.

"The next Thursday, Mara went off to the races. Looking like a picture in a fashion magazine from Berlin. White linen suit with those thin stripes in red and blue, high heeled white shoes, and a white hat with one red silk poppy on the side. And then, when Mara came back, she said to me: 'All solved, Helga. Whatever Eva tells her husband about me now, he won't believe it.' And she was quite sure about it."

"Really! What did Mara do, seduce the man?"

Helga looks at me like I've just gone and farted into her favourite cooking pot. Then she laughs. Long and hearty.

"Never," she tells me.

"Not even to save her neck?"

"It would not have occurred to either of them," Helga says. "Mara is a lady, after all. And Karl was well known in our town. Generous and good-tempered but not a man to be trifled with."

"But they were separated by then, he and Mara."

"Nobody knew that, Ted. Not until much later."

"Then what do you think Mara did or said to the man?"

"I don't know," says Helga, shaking her head, dying to know. "But you can be sure it was something clever. Mara is impractical in some ways—she is artistic, you know—but she has a very clever mind, full of ideas."

Helga the storyteller senses that she hasn't delivered a good ending. She doesn't take long to find one.

"That woman Eva, by the way, she did tell her husband that Mara's father was Jewish. She even goaded her husband to go to Civilian Affairs to inform on Mara. But all he said to them was that Mara's father brought her up to be a Communist."

Helga snorts and laughs, sits back in her chair.

"Well, of course, anybody could see that Mara was no Communist," she says. "When the SS started asking Mara questions about that, she just said: 'That's utterly absurd. I even married a man so that I could escape Communism.'

"She was lying, of course. I am quite sure that she didn't marry Karl for that. But she convinced the SS that she did and when Bruno testified, he corroborated her story."

Now I'm wondering: if Mara did *not* marry Karl's passport, why did Karl and Mara separate so soon after coming to Germany? Could it be Karl took a look around, saw a flood of Nazis all over everything and decided that Mara was rocks in his pocket?

How do I ask that one of loyal-to-both Helga? I look at the lively eyes in her round rosy face and I see something: having spent a night under her roof, I'm not a stranger any more. No need to fiddle my questions. When I ask Helga why Mara and Karl separated in 1939, she leans forward and confides her own conclusion:

"Karl and Mara," she says, " should never have married. Those two were like oil and vinegar."

"Don't you mean oil and water?"

"Yes, of course." Helga throws me a quick look. Hoping I haven't guessed who the vinegar was in her pantry. Certainly not good old fun-loving Karl!

But then Helga sighs and leans even closer: "Karl," she says, "went on benders. Sometimes for days. And Mara had bad migraine headaches every time he disappeared. She'd be in bed with terrible pains all the time he was gone."

Helga was telling me that the marriage went sour not because Karl's usefulness as a passport was over for Mara, not because Karl wanted to ditch a dangerous liability like Mara, but because Mara didn't want to spend the rest of her life with his benders attacking her head. Not that Helga used those words. She didn't use Bruno's either ("Historical Events" and "Modern Tragedy"). Helga told me stories. How miners celebrate and that Karl was never one to put himself above his men. If one of his workers invited him to celebrate a birth or a wedding—funerals were quiet, in those days—well, Karl would get on his motorcycle and take off and drive around the countryside till he found a farmer—and he knew every one of them for miles around—somebody who had some extra butter or liverwurst and some real rye *Landbrot*, and then Karl would load the sidecar of his motorcycle up with food and beer and off he'd go to the celebration.

"None of them ever missed a day's work, mind you. Or overtime either. They weren't allowed to. But right after work the celebrating would start up again, till they all just had to get some sleep. Karl didn't need much sleep, I guess; he was always one of the last ones to get brought home. Well, many a night Karl just slept it off on our couch downstairs before he made it upstairs, so it would be four, five days he was away and Mara vomiting and moaning all that time. No, no, I always thought it was better that they each go their own way."

This, I have to remind myself, was back when it took guts to get out from under.

Helga looks like she could keep going, so I ask again about the Nazi boyfriend.

"Was he needed for Mara's survival or was she just..."

"Lonely?" says Helga. "Maybe she was lonely..."

"In a house full of people? With a young child of her own?"

"All females," says Helga. "We were all lonely for men. Not just for our own husbands and lovers. We were lonely for the sound of men's voices—not old ones or squeaky ones—deep loud voices, laughing and shouting. All we heard was speeches on the radio. Mara was never one to hug a woman for comfort."

Then the doorbell buzzed. Helga got up and opened the door. I heard her talking for a minute and then she came back and handed me a telegram. From Mara.

BRUNO IS DEAD ALBERT REFUSES TO CO-OPERATE. AM MAKING CHANGE IN STRATEGY. COME BACK.

MARA

Dear Theodore,

It has become apparent to me that the dragon in my path is larger and perhaps more devious than anticipated. In order to vanquish the beast, I must change my strategy and therefore my tactics.

After these weeks of attentively living in Canada, I conclude that, as character witnesses, both Helga and Tanya may prove ineffective or even damaging to my court case. In a Canadian context, they would be seen not as women of valour and experience whose portrait of Mara deJong would be deemed trustworthy. No, Helga and Tanya would here be seen as colourful characters from foreign lands, and colourful characters belong in the realm of fiction. (Why, even our dignified father, a tragic hero, would here be just another immigrant with an accent and grandiose ideas of himself.)

As for Albert, he has always been unpredictable and it behooves me to remember this. After years of marriage, I was still unable to anticipate his actions, and one day I said as much to his sister. She looked at me for a long moment and then she said: "Yes, Albert has a truly loving heart and there are even times when he is wise." Which does not help me in any way to predict what he might say on the witness stand.

Albert's sister believes in the existence of love without judgment, without conditions, without self-interest. Albert's sister is a nun.

"You are speaking of the love of God," I said. "Not something I can talk about from experience. Love between people always entails conditions and self-interest."

Albert's sister the nun dropped her head and tears rolled down her round rosy cheeks. Albert's sister is a naïf.

And Bruno, who was to be my most important, most convincing character witness; Bruno who would require no coaching in order to conjure a sympathetic and truly heroic picture of me for the jury and the judge—Bruno is dead.

"Know thine adversary," our father used to say. In the Russian courts of law where he toiled, this was no doubt a matter of life or death. In my case, victory will mean freedom to continue my Work and to bring it to its glorious conclusion. Defeat, by keeping me from my Work, will condemn me to the state of a living corpse.

My adversary: any Canadian who might appear on the jury of my trial. The Herculean task before me: learning to assess Canadians at a glance in order that I may devise precise tactics for my defence.

In the face of so daunting a task I again find myself grateful for the once-onerous law as laid down by our father so long ago: Thou shalt put no other gods, passions, concerns, needs or desires above your life's work. (It makes little difference that the nature of my work as it was then has drastically changed. The law, the Work, remain paramount and my dedication unshakable.)

And you do see, of course, that every grain of knowledge gleaned in the course of preparing for my trial will also serve as an invaluable contribution to my Life's Work.

Canadians, I find, are a far more difficult people to understand than I anticipated. I am often confused and at a loss to judge what I see. In the matter of dress there seems to be no decipherable code, nor in the manner of living. A young matron, for example, might appear dowdy as a middle-aged European housemaid. (Completely unlike Tanya Volnikoff, of course. While she was our maid in Germany, she clung to an appearance most akin to a French cabaret dancer until the day she got married, when she went directly into invisibility.)

The young Canadian matron, dressed as a student or housemaid, might drive a Mercedes, wear no make-up, go to the hairdresser twice a week to perfect a "casual" look, have a young son getting up at six in the morning, no matter what the season or the weather, to work a paper route in order, I am told, to build character. This young matron may furthermore employ an illegal immigrant from the Caribbean as maid, but do her own marketing in the cheapest stores, be a member or even president of the women's auxiliary to the Symphony Orchestra board of directors, present at all cultural functions, wearing a one-of-a-kind dress, for a single event, and according to the news photos, each gown singularly dull and drab or else festooned with giant bows in all the wrong places. And this young matron would be considered not at all odd if she belongs to the class called "old money."

Also interesting: they attempt to hide their arrogance, these old-money Canadians. Their manners betray it only in subtle ways, nuances of tone and vocabulary—difficult to apprehend for anyone whose English is not cradle-bred. A language, incidentally, which prefers understatement and ambiguity to drama and metaphor.

To recognize old money, look above all to the frosty politeness, the distant eye. (The opposite of all the above traits can be found in a young woman called Louise, or "the Tic." I shall study her in detail.)

On several occasions I joined what is called a "line-up" and deduced the following: Canadians do not speak to each other, no matter how long they stand one directly behind the other. Should someone commit the crime of intruding himself or jumping ahead in line, no one speaks up about it. Everyone becomes grim, you can almost hear them muttering, but not quite. Imagine! I compare it to the behaviour of Russians or Germans in food queues or lining up for commodities—the sarcasm, the hostility, the direct action if an intruder didn't quickly relinquish his ill-gotten advantage. Canadians, I conclude, have had no need of the hard carapace born of wars and deprivation. I try to find such innocence endearing.

Of all the countries I have come to know, Canada is the most free. One cannot help but wonder: to what purpose has this freedom been put? While the mighty democratic wind has blown away some of the outward signs of class, as yet people in places of power are overwhelmingly "Anglo." Immigrants aspiring to power imitate Anglos as best they can, while the rest form pockets of living nostalgically by the mores of "back home." I am curious about the future: in twenty years from now, or fifty—let us say in the year 2000—will the entire population be steeped in understatement, or will the now-newcomers have made significant inroads, transforming and enlivening the human landscape?

The vastness of the task before me and the constraints of time require me to seek assistance. Since I cannot as yet reveal the nature of my Work, disclosure of tactics has to be limited lest I seem to be overstepping the bounds of people's mores. Lena has indicated a willingness to help me. If I were to guess what Michelle has told Lena about me, her mother, I would say, not much. Michelle always was a rather reticent and hidden child. While in the dark about Lena's motives, I see clearly that she will be useful in several ways.

Ted O'Sullivan, the young man who should be on his way back to Toronto at this very moment, seems to be susceptible to influence. I believe some acts of kindness towards him will elicit grateful acquiescence. I have a bold plan, which should bring about the desired outcome.

As you can imagine, I am enormously busy designing experiments.

Always, your beloved sister,
Mara

TED

So now I was in Vienna, sitting on the terrace of the Schwarzenberg Café, being served by waiters in penguin suits who hate the sight of me. Tough shit.

Mara's telegram said: "Bruno's dead, come back!" But this time Joe-boy wasn't jumping. Not while there was one more person on the list who could talk about Mara. "Albert refuses to co-operate," said the same telegram, but Albert made that decision before he met Ted the Mule. I took a plane from Frankfurt to Vienna—no panoramic train trip for a man in a hurry—to see this guy, and what I wanted from him was real simple. No psychological portrait of Mara with sensitive nuances, nothing like that. What I wanted from Albert was bold stark outlines—black and white would do.

In Frankfurt I had an hour's wait for my plane to Vienna, which was about 45 minutes' too much waiting. I roamed around the airport, my pocket full of cash, and next thing I knew I bought a teddy bear. A golden-haired Steiff teddy with brown eyes, just like the one my grandma had waiting for me when she brought me home with her. I was almost seven by then, much too old for a teddy bear, but grandma said he had always lived in the room where I was going to sleep, so he'd just have to stay in there with me, like it or not. So Teddy lived with me till I left grandma's house. By then one ear was gone and one eye was dangling, and his fur was worn so thin you could see through to the mesh underneath. The teddy bear I bought in the Frankfurt airport was his exact twin. Perfect proof and evidence for grandma that I've been in Germany, just like I told her.

So far I'd had three cups of great coffee: Milch Kaffee to coat the stomach, a tall cappuccino, and then an expresso to burn the lining off again. Presumably I was now awake. But I kept right on sitting in that cafe in the morning sun, in Vienna, the city where Mara lives "most of the time." Not something I would do unless they let me make a couple of changes. Like trading in the inhabitants for something more human. The ones I'd seen were pretty good facsimiles, but they were all bent. (Maybe because they were trying so hard to jump back to their time of Imperial Glory without falling into the Nazi-infested swamp in between. Or maybe I was just piss-eyed because everybody in Vienna called me "*geehrter Herr*," which means revered mister or something like that, and all the time their eyes were calling me "bum," because of my hair. There, in the city of great musicians once known as long-hairs!)

Anyway, here I am sitting in the Schwarzenberg Café gathering my wits, checking out the monuments and the boulevards and the fountains, and the young girls. Spring flowers, they are, fresh and cool, with skin like peaches. I may get an attack of Strauss waltzes.

Pity old Albert, though, if he's looking at the middle-aged women here. They're puffed-up pastries on spindly legs, with icing on their heads. For watching older women, you have to go to Paris or New York. Except in New York you don't have the time, and in Paris a Mrs. Whatsnikoff screws up your appetite.

Any minute now, I'm off to pump Albert.

"Ah, yes. Mara," Albert will say. "Well, it's true, as Helga says, that Mara never lost her mind before, but when a daughter dies, you see, the mother is deranged by grief and in that state is entirely unlike herself. No longer a mother but a crazed being, capable of anything."

Albert said on the phone that he is looking forward to meeting me. Wanted to come to the airport, in fact, to pick me up, but I put a stop to that notion. I was so high on that trip from Frankfurt, I could have done the flying without plane or pilot. Not on booze or anything else but on watching golden rays of the sun playing on snow-capped mountain peaks, playing like the peaks were a giant vibraphone. I was high on imagining the sound!

Sometimes when you're playing music, you get a travel high like that. When it's all pouring out of your fingers direct, with a thousand variations, that's the best high of all: when everybody playing is reaching for it...

Man, after that's over you want to jump around and yell and do some high-steppin' dance with all the parts of you shakin' and movin'. But being civilized, as they say, you just grin a lot and give each other fancy handshakes. For about a minute or so after, you still know that the music really happened, and then it's all gone. Dispersed. Sound waves going out into space. You hope maybe a creature way out there, with six ears or a Martian set of antennae, is grooving on some of those basement nights. And maybe he is. And maybe he's saying: what the fuck is this? Who's gone berserk and where?

Those playing highs get you hooked. And then they drop you down deeper than any other kind. And the only way up again is a lot of playing and sweat. Don't anybody talk to me about "easy-going."

And right now, I'd give my left leg for a cup of that sweat.

Hey! Maybe Albert has a piano!

The taxi driver said that the Opera House was on the right, museums on the left, and then the University of Vienna. All massive and old, granite with flourishes, on the grand scale. And then I'm standing in front of #8 Heinzelgasse. A five-story building, Albert deJong on the nameplate, mezzanine. The buzzer lets me in and right there, about five steps up on the landing, are Albert's feet in brown leather slippers. Brown slacks with a sharp crease, brown cardigan buttoned over immaculate white shirt and brown paisley tie. Well-shaved jaw, strong bones, brown eyes. Blurred-looking eyes, with a film over them like an old dog's eyes. Oh, Jesus. The man is nearly blind!

By the time I've digested that one, I've missed Albert's opening. His voice is low and formal, but lots of timbre. This is no damaged and discarded ex-colonial here, doing a slow fade-out till death do him part. This is a handsome man about 55 and no slouching, pouching or doddering. My current landlord is about the same age, only he goes in for dyed hair and all the latest hip fashions. He looks like a clown and acts like a jerk. Albert here does not think middle age is disgusting.

He's led me into the living room and deposits me in a leather armchair. His dark grey hair is brushed back with a neat part at the side. The skin on his hands is speckled brown egg. Albert is pouring us each a Scotch with perfect precision. There is silence in the room and there is uncluttered space and there is order. A place for everything and everything in its place. Albert picks up a pair of silver tongs and puts ice cubes into our glasses from a crystal bowl.

He places our two drinks on the little carved table between us. He is sitting on the leather chair across from me. Nothing about him is slouching. And he is looking at me with those hard-to-read eyes, possibly friendly.

"Now," he says in German, "What is the language in which you would prefer to converse?"

I remember Mara's notes: *Albert speaks eight languages, four of them Indonesian.*

"How about English?"

"Of course. Yes," says Albert. "Your pronunciation is not at all French Canadian. Well, now, I am most happy to see you, Mr. Ted. Mara told me in a telephone call that you met recently and that you are being most helpful to her. I believe, however, that she is under the impression that you would not be coming to Vienna."

"Is that right? Well, maybe she figured I'd skip Vienna because you don't want to co-operate. According to a telegram Mara sent me yesterday."

"How odd," says Albert. "She is most certainly mistaken in that assumption."

Before I have time to think about that one, Albert changes gears.

"Tell me," he says. "Is Mara looking well?"

"Oh, yes," I tell him. "Mara is well."

Albert's ears are milking every inflection. He nods slowly, smiles, and wants to know:

"And is she enjoying her current tussle with the law?"

I take a slow sip and then I have to ask, just to make sure: "Did you say 'enjoying?'"

"Why, yes. I know of course that Mara has been accused of a terrible act..."

Albert turns his head away and coughs into his hand. Like he can't bring himself to name Mara's alleged act. And like he is absolutely sure that she didn't commit it! So aha! Now I figure I know why Mara wanted me to skip Albert in Vienna. She wants him to keep on believing she's innocent! Well, too bad, Mara. I'm here now and to be crude about it, I'm not leaving till I've got what I came for.

Albert seems to be looking at the wall behind me. I turn and there's a huge photo of Mara on the wall, with two dogs. Mara in a summer dress, wearing a necklace that refracts into spots of light around her neck. Her hands are holding a leash and the dogs are waiting to go for a promised walk. The whole print is grainy, enlarged from a photo that wasn't quite clear enough so now it's a bit fudged. But it was worth blowing up: the camera caught Mara before she had a chance to get self-conscious. She is looking fondly down at the dogs and she is smiling as if she's just heard something witty. She is, of course, beautiful.

Albert's been watching me look at Mara's picture; now he looks away again and tells me this:

"Mara, you must understand, is incapable of giving pain to a fly. Why, when her first dog was eaten by a crocodile, Mara wept for days. You see, the bridge over the river was swept away by the floods once again and we had to walk across the swollen waters by way of rocks and boards. The dog was swimming alongside as Mara walked—a small white dog—and a crocodile snapped it up. Mara was inconsolable. She refused to leave her room and she spoke to no one. I bought her the two new dogs; you see them in the photograph there. But it took three weeks before the dogs reached us on the plantation, and in the meantime..."

Albert looks up to face the photograph on the wall.

"I assure you," he says, "that Mara would have taken care of every mangy dog she saw, but the local dogs in Indonesia are not pets." Albert sighs and shakes his head. "Life in the tropics is difficult for European women."

Albert, I realize, is not just aimlessly rambling on about Mara. He is throwing out clues to her character, right and left, and he is doing it according to a plan. I'm listening so hard, I'm forgetting the obligatory mm-hm.

"I am sure you know," Albert is saying, "that Mara is an artist. She is temperamentally unsuited to submit to any manifestation of ugliness—whether of the spirit or of the more picayune material sort. When I started to put on some weight—a belly, in fact—Mara was genuinely concerned. And she was right, of course—every part of one's life should be aesthetically enhancing."

Again, Albert is looking up with his nearly blind eyes at the picture of Mara. Is he adoring it? Can't believe she did the deed because she's so beautiful, an artist, an angel? It's hard to read those eyes of his.

"Yes, I was telling you how difficult life is for a European woman on a rubber plantation on Java. Just think of the isolation. I am sure you know how sociable Mara is; she simply blossoms in good company, but she spoke no Indonesian languages, you see, beyond directing the servants, and so she had no one to talk to except our rare European visitors. Or when we went to the city. But going to Bandung meant five hours of driving on very rough and often dangerous roads. When we were able to get through at all.

"I wanted to teach her one of the Indonesian languages—I offered it all the time at the beginning because I had such great friends she could have enjoyed. Of course Ram, my engineer, spoke excellent English, and so did his wife who was a very fine violinist. She and Mara played together, once, but it didn't work out.

"It was very difficult also to keep the piano tuned. The nearest piano tuner was five hours away in Bandung. The fighters in the mountains were swooping down too often and we didn't have enough armed guards to bring in the piano tuner every three weeks. In the tropics, you see, especially so near the ocean, the piano goes out of tune very quickly."

Albert is talking slowly, recalling their life on Java, and as long as Mara is the main subject, I am the Great Listener.

"I tried to find solutions," Albert assures me. "One of my gardeners had a son who was very intelligent and wanted more education than our village school could offer. I sent him to Bandung to go to school and also to be apprenticed to the piano tuner. He was doing very well, we heard, but then he disappeared.

"The boy's father, well, he was very upset. We were old friends, the father and I. We played chess together and he shared my interest in geology; in fact, when we were young, we went on long trips together." For a moment, Albert indulges in a memory and smiles. Then his voice drops to a lower note.

"The son," he says, "that bright young boy, was killed in the mountains. Four of his comrades brought the body back to the village. Mara wasn't at all well just then, she had had typhoid, but she insisted on coming to the funeral."

Albert pauses to let Mara's saintly self-sacrifice sink in.

The telephone rings somewhere out in the hall. Albert excuses himself and leaves the room.

We've been interrupted but I'm not worried. I sip a little toast to talkers, especially to storytellers who haven't had an audience for a while. Albert is going to continue pouring forth, sweeping along nuggets of gold among the rocks, and all I have to do is be there with a pan.

Mara's notes said that Albert was born in Indonesia and that he spent all of his life there, except for the university years in Europe. He was visiting old university friends in Germany after the war, a 40-year-old bachelor, when he met Mara. They married and Albert took Mara back to Indonesia with him, where they lived for 11 years.

Albert is coming back into the room, apologizing. It was his sister. She calls him daily from her convent in Belgium. She has a free international line because she co-ordinates worldwide adoption of war orphans. Albert sits down and offers more Scotch, but all I want is to listen.

"Go back to you and Mara on the plantation," I tell him. Albert sighs.

"I wish I could...I was slated to retire as soon as somebody was ready to take over as manager. He wasn't even one of my own men. I had Ram, the young Indonesian engineer, all trained and ready to take over, but he was killed. By the guerrillas, swooping down from the mountains, of course, though the prosecutor insisted it was done by three of our villagers.

"You should have heard Mara on the witness stand. She was magnificent!

Her testimony saved the lives of three men!"

Albert takes a long drink, savouring the relief of that acquittal. Now I'm the one pouring us both another Scotch. All the time Albert was playing his favourite tune, "Mara in Indonesia," I've been listening very attentively, and by now I know for sure that he's picking and choosing what he says very carefully. To a precise plan. Feeding me a line, is what it's called. And he's so good at it, I can't tell what's behind the lines or in between. Mara wouldn't hurt a fly, but deserted near-blind Albert; she has an artist's bent for aesthetic perfection, but cut off her daughter's earlobes. She is brave, and loyal, and should have become a lawyer. A crusader, in fact. Justice for peasants! I can't even guess what-all Albert is leaving out.

"What about here in Vienna, Albert? Do you and Mara see each other often, here in Vienna?"

"No," says Albert, clearly uncomfortable. "Mara never sees me at all. I only see her when she goes for a walk in the *Stadtpark*. Around four o'clock."

I couldn't fucking believe it! Here I've been sitting, letting this dude ramble all over me and I know until this minute that he was never going to give me the truth. All of a sudden, Mrs. Whatsnikoff pops into my head yet again, with her: "you know nothing. You're a man. You will never know."

"Tell me something, Albert." I know I sound sharp but I can't help it. "Aren't you a bit old for June-ing, mooning and pining?"

Albert turns his head away, takes a deep breath, slowly gets to his feet. He excuses himself and goes off to the bathroom. I waste about half a second kicking myself, then I'm up on my feet. To stretch my legs, by way of a quick snooping expedition.

The kitchen is long and narrow and very clean. The bedroom door squeaks a bit, but what the hell, I'm just having a look. No clutter in here, either. On the bedside table a large magnifying glass and a small book. A framed picture of Mara on the dresser opposite: Mara sitting at a baby grand, formal portrait with smile. Only one more room in Albert's apartment and only one single thing in it: a piano. Standing on a rug right in the middle of the room, the shapeliest piano of them all, a baby grand. Gleaming and beautiful. I'm betting the piano keys are perfect ivories. I want to have a look, but when I try to lift the lid, it's locked.

Why the hell would it be locked?

Oh, shit!

This is Mara's piano. And the old fart is keeping it locked so no other hands will defile it. Now he's gone too far, has Albert. I've got to get the fuck out of here!

As soon as Albert comes out of the bathroom, I tell him "I'll be back," and split.

It didn't take long to find another café or to get the first beer to my table, but thinking turned out to be a bumpy ride. I mean, Albert was no fool. Marriage should have cured him of imagining angel wings and singing hymns to Mara, hallelujah. Shit, I hate sentimental. In music it's saccharine mush; in relationships, adoring mates are a drag in bed. Sentimentality is anti-sex. That's why jazz is so sexy: it scrapes away all the mush.

Then I thought: who the fuck are you, Ted O'Sullivan? I mean, if Albert doesn't want to touch earth, who are you to prick his heavenly balloon and then find out it was the only thing keeping him afloat? The man is already nearly blind and exiled from the Indonesia he loves. Just leave him his woman up there, larger than life.

By this time I had a surprising number of beers under my belt. (The waiter kept tabs by way of bringing a new cardboard coaster with each glass.) But the only thing I knew for sure was this: I liked old Albert. I really didn't want to chop off any part of him for curiosity of Mara. But Albert was the one supposed to be painting a clear picture of Mara for me.

Because the only picture I had of her so far was something only that guy Dali could have come up with: part lioness at bay, part opportunistic hyena, with a bird of paradise high-stepping among pigeons, a knife tucked among the feathers.

I had no choice. Albert was the only one left, so if I had to prick his balloon, well, that was too bad. The man had to be told that yes, his sainted Mara did the heinous deed. And I was the one had to do the telling.

I left the café and started roaming around in Vienna's inner city, through narrow ancient streets with houses that have their backs turned on you. Making you feel like a rolling cauldron full of beer and roiling questions, looking for a place to tilt and pour off steam.

Then I heard a sound.

Coming from somewhere down a street. Definitely the sound of live music. Man, I really needed some of that! What I would have liked, I remember thinking, is Mingus. Or Parker. Or Miles Davis.

What I got was the blues. My gospel according to St. Nick, and a great antidote to pining Albert and this sweet Vienna air. The blues, suddenly pouring out of a door, open and then closed again, leaving a hollow silence. But I knew I could find it and, sure enough, here's that door.

"Big Daddy's," it says on a tiny blue sign. Thick padded door, shallow steps down to the cellar. White-washed walls, thick stone pillars with smoke swirling around them, and onstage a big black man with a horn. Big Daddy himself.

Two things are clear right away: the music coming out of that horn is not cream puffs or pablum, and somewhere in this dark room somebody is smoking some fine-smelling hash.

I lean against one of the pillars to listen and it's good old Chicago blues, catching you right up, making you hum against the grain of life. Big Daddy sings, too, with a big deep voice that's mostly growl but swings like one of Basie's muted trumpets. He's been doing this for a long time, but he is not flying on automatic. No, he's not! Big Daddy *likes* playing and singing the blues, and he's never lost the taste for sweet jelly roll.

But there's something keeping him tied down. It's not the drummer—he's no Art Blakey but he's okay. The bass player is basic, with a nice fat sound on the funky old upright and no problem with his ears. It's that stick of a piano player! All the right chords and lots of fancy runs, but no feel at all for the blues.

I drift closer to the side of the tiny stage and by the time the tune is finished, I'm close enough to sign to Big Daddy: "Good one! How about letting me sit in?" Big Daddy looks me over some and then he gives his big head a little jerk: "Okay, come on up." Not even knowing what my ax is.

I step up on the stage and over to the piano and the piano player has no choice but to move his ass off the stool. He's not liking it, either. Maybe he's Big Daddy's brother-in–law, or maybe it's his club and he's the boss—I don't give a shit. I know Big Daddy's going to be smiling soon.

The drummer starts us up, "Ain't Nobody's Business If I Do." He's taking it too fast, but I don't want to fight him right off so I go with it, but loose and rolling. Big Daddy opens his mouth on a swinging growl, and away we go.

Big Daddy takes a nice solo on the sax, short and cocky, and then it's me and I slow her way down, rolling her over and holding back, tail draggin' and dirty, and then letting loose again, off and struttin' it, and now everybody takes off together, ridin' high. All right!

When we bring her in for a landing there's clapping and shouting, and Big Daddy is coming over to the piano and he's smiling, all right. Big Daddy says to go ahead, pick something I want to play. I hear myself say "Downhearted Blues" and my hands are rubbing on my thighs, getting ready, and then, just like that, it's all over. Nothing more getting through. Like I'm behind a steel wall. Inside of me something is clawing at my gut and hissing in my head. Yesss, I can go ahead back to Albert and bust up his perfect picture of Mara, yesss, I can march forth to search and destroy, but what's the use? When it comes to Mara, Albert will never give me anything like the truth. I wouldn't be one single beat closer to knowing what makes the woman tick.

My hands are lying on my thighs like dead fish. And there's a brand-new chorus for Downhearted Blues, growling in my ears: You will never, never know.

LENA

I was the first one to see Ted when he came back from Europe. Standing in front of the house door with a big honey blond teddy bear sitting on his arm, fuming because Mara had the temerity to be out. He deigned to come up to my place to wait for her.

When I gave him his messages he grumbled, then went into the living room and sat there like a needle stuck in a pincushion. A perfect demonstration of "waiting is something Ted cannot do."

And, of course, he went straight to the subject of Mara. Her apartment, actually. Did I have a key for it? And when I said no he looked so haunted, so at the end of his rope, I nearly handed him his teddy bear to hug.

Then, in the nick of time, I realized the danger I was in and moved away. I had much too recently emerged from my own quagmire and was not in any way equipped to rescue somebody else from the grip of obsession.

Meanwhile, Ted had asked something else: about Mara the pianist. I offered to put on Mara's recording of the Rachmaninoff Prelude and then I fled, practically panting after that narrow escape, and went to sit under my Maple tree.

TED

Mara was out.

I couldn't fucking believe it.

I crammed myself into a plane full of screaming babies, first direct flight out of Vienna, bypassed Paris, but when I got to Mara's house, she wasn't home. Shit and damnation, I have got to see the woman face to face!

Lena the neighbour opens the door. No, she doesn't know where Mara is but she, Lena, has messages for me and why don't I come and wait for Mara in her place.

I shift the teddy bear, grab my gig bag, and follow Lena up the stairs. As soon as we get inside her apartment, Lena says, "One message is from Alicia. She would like you to call her as soon as you get back."

Yeah, well.

"The other message," says Lena, "Wait. I wrote it down." She steps behind the kitchen counter and lifts a slip of paper off a pad. "It's from Henry," she says. "He wanted me to take it down verbatim. 'Where the fuck are you?'" reads Lena the neighbour in a poker voice. "Hamlyn is looking for you. *The* Hamlyn. His piano player quit and he wants you on the next record and tour. Pronto.'"

Lena hands me the scrap of paper with message and phone number and points me into the living room. I go sit down and stare at the note. I know the message is really from Bear, who knows this gig was made for me. A chance to play and record with Hamlyn, the hottest sax around, and his band the best of the younger jazz players. Next stop, New York. I should be up on my feet, jumping and yelling "Hallelujah!" But Jesus fucking Murphy, talk about lousy timing. I stick the scrap of paper into my shirt pocket and try not to grunt or bark, answering Lena the neighbour.

Lena the neighbour is in her kitchen, rummaging, trying to find something for me to drink that doesn't come in a box covered with little leaves and flowers.

Lena has told me that Mara goes out every day, perhaps to a library—Lena isn't sure. She doesn't like to pester Mara with questions. I have promised Lena the neighbour that I am made of cruder stuff.

There's no furniture in this room. Just rugs, these big colourful cushions, tapestries on the walls. A bamboo flute hanging by a beaded string.

Out of nowhere, a question pops into my head.

"Say, Lena," keeping it cool and casual. "Do you have a key to Mara's apartment?"

"No, I don't. But she should be back soon."

I pull the bamboo flute off the wall and it's a real one: the sound of wind in the rushes, when you can get it right. I'm getting mostly snake-in-the-grass, but by tonguing the breath I can at least make it chatter.

Lena shows up in front of me with two glasses of sherry. I hate the stuff, but she took a lot of trouble finding it, so I thank her and take one. Lena is looking at the flute in my other hand.

"I'm happy to hear it make music," she says. "I, unfortunately, can't get anything out of it except farts."

I take another look at the woman. She's got light brown shiny hair to her shoulders. The shape of her face must be what they call heart-shaped: broad cheekbones and a very definite little chin. Brown eyes with flecks in them. Nice eyes. Looking right at me. And something about me is bothering her! Well, isn't that just too bad.

Holding her own glass of sherry, Lena slides her butt down, smooth as water, till she's sitting back on her heels. Like she grew up squatting in some distant marketplace.

"By the way," she says. "Your girlfriend was here."

"What girlfriend? I don't have a girlfriend."

"Her name is Louise. Isn't that teddy bear for her?"

"That teddy bear has nothing to do with her. And she sure as hell is not my girlfriend. She's a piece of flotsam, sticky and real hard to shake."

Lena is looking at me like I must be protesting too much.

"Jesus, the woman is practically a stranger. She followed me from North Bay. Uninvited. And about as welcome as a tic."

"A complete stranger followed you?"

"After one night! She showed up with a couple of joints after a gig. I guess I wasn't paying attention." (Too drunk, or too tired, or too horny, or all three, but that's my own idiot business). "Anyway, she stayed the night. Next day I heard her open her foul mouth—about her kike boss at the hotel, the chink cleaner who ruined her best skirt—so I kicked her ass out of there. Then, back at my pad in Toronto, she phones me every hour on the hour, her boss catches her charging calls to the hotel and fires her, so she hops a ride and lands on my doorstep."

"Irresistible Ted."

"Last Chance Ted. An excuse for coming to the big city. 'Please, Ted, just put me up for a couple of days, till I'm on my feet.' I told her every which way I could: racist trash does not rest its bones in my pad."

"But she's been staying at your place."

"Yeah, well—that's another story. A short one. She's out of there as of today. Tell me something, Lena, you knew Mara is a pianist, right? Did Michelle think Mara was a good pianist?"

"Oh, yes. Very good. You can judge for yourself, if you want. I have her record."

I was so surprised, I yelped like a puppy.

"Yes, I want to hear Mara playing piano!"

Lena's putting a record on the turntable, about to set the needle on halfway into the side, handing me the album cover. The printing on the front is in Russian, which is Greek to me. I turn it over and there's some English in the bottom left corner telling me it's a compilation album of Russian pianists playing Russian composers. Only one Mara—a Mara Garina Petrovich, which must be her maiden name—and she's playing a Rachmaninoff prelude: Opus 23, the B Flat Major Prelude.

Lena is still holding the needle arm.

"You are welcome to stay here until Mara comes home," she says.

I nod, trying to keep cool. Put the goddamn needle on!

Lena does and leaves.

It's obvious right from the opening bars that it takes a virtuoso to play this piece and it's also obvious that Mara has all the chops she needs for it and more. And the sheer strength for it, too. For the sweeping arpeggios and the dramatic chords, all gathering momentum for one hell of a storm.

A short piece. I check the cover and see it's the only piece Mara plays on this album, so I put it on again and listen again and am bowled over again. How many years of steady practicing would it take to develop technique like that? I mean, I've listened to classical pianists enough to know that these chops were absolutely first-rate. Mara, the woman who didn't think her being a pianist was relevant enough to mention, has just turned into an even bigger mystery.

I turn off the record player. My butt refuses to sit; I've got to *do* something. I grab my gig bag and jump down the stairs to the second floor landing. Through the back window, I catch a glimpse of Lena, sitting in the backyard under a big old Maple, eyes closed, listening for something. No time to ask what she's listening to.

The lock in Mara's apartment door is no problem, thanks to Pro. That's Tim, who likes to boast he's a professional and to prove it, will teach you useful skills such as picking locks.

Mara's living room looks like it was left to grow dust since the last time I was there. If there were any changes, I don't see them. The albums on the shelf, Mara had told me, were not hers. I run a finger along the spines, just in case, but there's nothing by pianist Mara Garina Petrovich or deJong.

Looking around the room, I don't see any personal bits and pieces of Mara lying around anywhere. Except for the four candleholders on the mantel. They're definitely Mara's. Long glass stems, cool crystal petals at the top, holding tall olive green candles. Elegant and snubbing the rest of the room: the deep old couch and the fat-armed old chair, both faded brown corduroy; the smaller straight-backed chair with a dirty gold covering. There's a white rug on the floor with a border of diamond shapes in blue and red, cheerful looking, and the curtains have bright blue-green stripes. Then there's the old rolltop desk in the corner, looking a bit quaint but fitting right in beside the window. The fireplace is real; the wrought-iron tongs look like they get used. A comfortable place. Definitely not Mara's.

Shit! I should have stayed in Vienna long enough to look at Mara's own apartment there. Here, my only hope for getting some answers is the rolltop desk, but it's locked.

I head into the kitchen to get myself a Scotch and it sure doesn't smell any too good in there. Sour. Coming from the same pot of borscht we ate the day before I left, about a week ago. Congealed and almost black, with purple bubbles. Doesn't she have a nose? What's Mara been doing all week?

The kitchen cupboard on the left is still full of booze. All kinds. I know that Mara doesn't drink, so who is it for?

I stick my head out the kitchen window.

"Lena! Why all the bottles of booze in Mara's cupboard?"

"I have no idea," Lena calls back. "Michelle didn't drink anything but wine."

"What about visitors?"

"No visitors." Lena's voice sounds like it's enjoying the outing.

"You know," she calls up, "You should talk to Mara. She's been ordering her meals from that Chinese restaurant on Harbord Street, and I'm worried about all the monosodium glutamate."

The things people worry about. Mara is accused of mutilating her daughter's corpse, and Lena is worried about her monosodium glutamate. Whatever that is.

Lena waves bye-bye and goes back to whatever she's doing out there, under the tree.

By then I've got half a glass of Scotch in me and I'm finally slowing down some.

Lena, I remember, was Michelle's friend. But she sounded like she'd willingly show up in court to defend Mara. That had to mean that like me, Lena assumed Mara was deranged by grief to do what she did. Or it could mean that Lena is a good person. The other two: Helga in Bergheim, and Albert. Both willing to come to Canada to testify at the trial. I didn't know whether Helga would do any good. And Albert was afraid that Mara wouldn't let him come. When I called him to say I was unexpectedly leaving Vienna in half an hour, Albert said, "Tell Mara I would like to come to Toronto. I want to help."

Not me. I wanted to have Mara face to face till I had a clear picture of the woman and knew for sure she went off the rails, did something crazy, but wouldn't dream of abandoning her own child if she was in her right mind. And then, I wanted to get myself home to where my fingers would be re-uniting with their own old beauty and would happily play until dawn.

Meantime, I was going to ferret and snoop in Mara's rolltop desk. Maybe she kept a journal in there, explaining all? And maybe she kept her own albums in there, locked up like her piano at Albert's? And why, it occurred to me, wasn't that piano in her own apartment in Vienna?

I found a paperclip and straightened it out and seconds later the lock of the rolltop desk popped open. I remember thinking that somewhere, recently, I lost not only the old Ted O'Sullivan who could take people or leave them, but also the one who had some shreds of decency still clinging to his person. I was about to invade privacies like some cheap wino snoop paid to dig dirt and I didn't even hesitate. I just dug right in.

One pigeonhole was full of newspaper clippings, neatly stacked. I'd check those later. In another pigeonhole there were three letters in Mara's handwriting. All three letters started with "Dear Theodore," who I figured had to be Mara's brother. One of three, all of them back in Leningrad, Russia, so why was she writing in English?

"Dear Theodore,

"As you know, I have been accused of mutilating the corpse of my daughter. The trial begins early September, in Toronto, Canada. I do so wish that you could come to be by my side. There is no one at all in this land who knows me well. Am I wrong to hope that people will, for just a moment, put themselves in my place? For only if they do that, will they be able to see clearly that they too, would have acted as I did.

"Sometimes my spirit fails me but I remind myself that I have been persecuted before and have been misunderstood and reviled before and yet, even as an alien beset by fanatic enemies, I have survived with my honour and reputation intact."

The letter was unfinished. What there was of it reeked of crock to me, all carefully laid out. But who was supposed to step in it? A judge would catch the stink as fast as I did. I put the letter back into its pigeonhole and was about to start on the next one when I heard the house door opening. I popped the letters back in and pulled down the rolltop, fast. Nothing I could do about the broken lock. Two seconds later, I was sitting on the couch, legs crossed, glass in hand, listening to Mara coming into the hall.

I'm straining to hear over the racket in my chest. Then Mara's in the doorway, about to sail through into the living room. She sees me sitting on the couch and stops. Her eyes look directly at me for all of two seconds. Then she steps all the way into the room, coming closer, holding out her hand for me to shake, moving forward, and at the same time, she's also pulling back. Reeling herself in like she's a line that could get caught and snagged.

Mara is excited. Definitely excited about something, but I can tell you, it wasn't one bit about Ted O'Sullivan, last heard from in Germany and now sitting in her living room. No "hello," no "welcome"—she doesn't even ask how the hell I got into the apartment.

"Sit down, Mara. Talk to me. You look like you've had good news."

Mara smiles at me, sparkles, which is a wonderful sight to behold.

"I found something I've been looking for," she tells me. "It's absolutely perfect in every way."

Mara steps back out into the hall, giving me time to think, "If I met Mara today, I'd follow her home all over again." And then: "I sure as hell don't want to get turfed out. So any report about Europe and the character witnesses will have to be trickled out."

Mara comes back into the living room and sits down on the small dirty-gold armchair across from me. She pulls something out of a pink plastic bag. Something silvery grey—a silk scarf. She's holding it up for comment. Her hands are slim, neither large nor small, blue veins under thin white skin. Just looking at her hands, you'd never guess at the reach and power in those fingers on piano keys.

"Very pretty scarf," I say. "Why didn't you tell me you're a pianist?"

"I had no particular reason," Mara says.

She gets up and drapes the scarf over the back of the small armchair like she's preparing an altar. Placing the scarf just so, draping her jacket over it, tugging at the bits of scarf showing on either side, just so, stepping back to assess the results. Then the ritual is over and Mara turns to me.

"I hope your flight was fine. Could you please give me the notebook?"

I fetch the black notebook from my gig bag in the hall and Mara takes it from me as if it's an important state document, then leaves it lying in the dust on the end table.

"Sit down, Mara. I still want to know: why didn't you tell me you're a pianist?"

"But Ted, it just didn't come up."

"Don't bullshit me, Mara."

Mara takes hold of a corner of the scarf, slowly pulls it out from under the jacket, folds it and puts it back into the pink plastic bag. All done like one big shrug. Pissing me off.

"What do you mean, it just didn't come up? The way Mrs. Whatsnikoff's love for you just didn't come up? What the hell was that woman doing on your list of friendly witnesses?"

"Ah. She still hates me. I thought that she would be more serene by now. But she is a barbarian—she knows only friends and enemies and nothing at all of subtler shades."

Mara is not interested in Mrs. Whatsnikoff. Something has changed. She goes to the window and stands there looking out. Thinking. But I did not fly around Europe like a dizzy mosquito to come back and find Mara barely listening to my buzz.

"Mrs. Whatsnikoff laced my Vodka with cyanide," I tell Mara's back. "And when I was lying there on the floor, she held a rooster by the legs and made him peck at my eyes. And the house in Bergheim is a brothel now and Helga is the madam."

Mara turns around, comes back and sits down.

"Louise was here," she says, meaning the Tic. "She was anxious for news about you. I gather that you didn't tell her that you were flying to Europe."

"Why should I? She's not even a friend. Look, I'm sorry if she bothered you."

"She has gone back to her home town."

Mara is watching me. I must have looked surprised out of my gourd.

"Yes," she says. "Louise came again yesterday morning to pick up her bus ticket. One way."

Mara still watching me: "She may return, of course."

"Well, if she does come back, she'd better not show up at my pad. Listen, Mara, you've done a good deed and you've done me a big favour, getting her out of my hair. Now forget about the Tic and tell me what you did to Mrs. Whatsnikoff."

Mara waves one hand, dismissing Mrs. Whatsnikoff, first friendly witness on her list.

"That's a long river under the bridge, Ted."

It took me a minute to transpose that to "water under the bridge—long gone."

"Not for me, Mara. I just met the woman a few days ago and got a ton of vinegar dumped on me. Your vinegar. Did you seduce the husband who left her?"

Mara makes a sound somewhere between a sniff and a short laugh.

"I have never," she says, "seduced anyone."

It's the truth as she believes it. When it comes to telling truth or lies, Mara is actually getting easy to read, despite those hide-and-seek eyes.

"Did you allow him to seduce you?"

"I wouldn't let that man touch me with gloves on. Is this interrogation now concluded?" Mara gets up.

"Please help yourself to more Scotch, Ted. I'll be back in a moment."

She walks out and up the stairs. I wish she hadn't used the word "interrogation." Because the truth is I'll dig and chisel answers out of Mara if I have to.

I sure as hell wish I had a witness for those first minutes of seeing Mara again. Somebody to tell me, yes, that is what you did see and hear. And yes, what you saw and what you heard did not match up.

I wish I had a witness just for our handshake. Because I can't even remember touching her hand, which is damned amazing. Must have been my ears and eyes were so busy I was already on overload. You have to remember, at that point I hadn't seen the woman but that one day, in court and in the apartment. And since then I'd been finding out a whole lot about her and some of it was pretty weird stuff. So it was like checking her out for the first time all over again.

When she was standing there at the window, thinking, I swear I heard that sound again. Making me wish I knew what was humming in there, underneath all that thinking.

I hear Mara coming back down the stairs.

"Don't let me forget," I trumpet up. "Albert sends a message."

Mara stops in the doorway, surprised.

"You saw Albert? In Vienna? What did he say?"

Mara sits down, not too comfortable, waits for my answer. Let her.

"Tell me, was Albert already going blind when you left him?"

"I didn't leave Albert. He left me."

"He left you?! Albert has your piano locked away from the touch of mortal hands, he has your picture up on the wall big as life, and you tell me Albert left you?"

"Yes, Ted. He did. Please tell me his message."

"That he'd like to come to Toronto if only you'll give him your royal permission to help."

"No!"

"I take it you don't want him to find out you really did it. What he calls 'the heinous deed Mara could not possibly have committed.'"

"It's not that at all. I simply do not want him to come here."

"I'll go help myself," I tell Mara, and go into the kitchen for that refill. What goes on between Mara and Albert has nothing to do with me. What, when you come right down to the last note, does any of this have to do with me? Piano keys have something to do with me, yes, and how soon I can connect up with some, never to leave them again. Yes! But can you play piano with limp noodles where your fingers are supposed to be?

I head back into the living room. Mara looks at my glass, which is brimming.

"You do drink rather regularly, then?"

"Just call me Ted the Barbarian."

"I beg your pardon," says Mara. "It's none of my business, of course."

A quick smile and then she tells me: "I went to your Maple Leaf Gardens."

"Really. What was going on? No hockey this time of year. A boxing match? What?"

"The Lions were gathered there to hear a speech by George Wallace, governor of Alabama."

"Wait a minute. You went to a Lions' convention at Maple Leaf Gardens and heard George Wallace speak?"

"Yes, it was most interesting. All around the outside, there were hundreds of people carrying signs with slogans: 'Wallace Racism Breeds Hate and Bombs Children,' and so on, but inside, people applauded what he said. More than once."

"What did he say?"

"Oh, I barely listened. George Wallace is a hate-promoting racist and therefore utterly predictable. But your Canadian Lions! They are fascinating. They have invented a civilian attire which stops just short of being a uniform. Inevitably, such conformity leads one to think 'herd,' but a 'herd of lions'?"

Definitely a twinkle in her eye.

"I know the get-up, Mara. You must have stuck out like a...a..."

"Oh, no. Not at all. I was invisible."

She throws me a quick look, checking my reaction. No idea what she got off my face, but she smiles.

"I'll be happy to show you one day. To become invisible for you. No, no, it's not a matter of magic or anything hocus-pocus. It's research-based, but really quite elementary. You'll see."

Then a sigh, a serious look.

"I must confess, however, I do find Canadians confusing."

"You find Canadians confusing! Holy shit, woman, why the hell would you want to go to a Lions convention? To hear George Wallace?"

"I was told that any jury of my peers might have Lions on it. I was doing research for my court case."

That nugget of reason and logic felt like a drop of balm, at the time, landing on nerve ends that felt raw. Chafed raw by all the confusion.

Meantime Mara is shifting in her chair, putting her hands in her lap, one holding the other. I remember that pose. She's looking down at her hands, then up at me and this time she's definitely heading for a hurdle.

"Ted, your landlord telephoned."

"What the hell for? And how did he get this number?"

"Your landlord said he was renting out your flat. It seems you forgot to pay rent for a while."

“That horse’s ass was just waiting for an excuse to get rid of me. If he’s shoved my piano into some hole in the wall, I’ll singe every dyed hair on his head with a blowtorch.”

“No, your piano and organ are both safe, Ted. I made sure of that.”

Before I can ask where exactly they are safe, before I can thank the woman, Mara shifts herself to look past my shoulder. Deflecting gratitude, I thought. Or maybe deflecting any talking she and I might do about our “instrument.” The whole subject of her music is under wraps, and that’s one of the mysteries I want cleared up. But first, a surprise skirmish!

“Mara, tell me what you said to Eva’s husband. The guy who informed on you to the SS but then only told them you might be a Communist.”

Mara laughs. Pleased with herself.

“I told him that if he informed the SS that I am Jewish, then I would reveal to the entire town what his wife went out to do every Thursday afternoon while he himself was out at the races.”

“Eva? But Helga said Eva was completely besotted with her husband.”

“And so she was. But he was a very stupid man, you see. He watched her curl her stringy hair and try to hide the wart on her cheek, and he didn’t know it was all for him. And he couldn’t bear to become known as a cuckold. For a small-town man there is no escape—he would consider himself a target for ridicule for the rest of his life. Well, he did not go to the races for several Thursdays, I heard. He stayed home and he beat Eva more often than before, but he didn’t dare ask anyone about her activities on Thursday afternoons. And so he never found out that on every Thursday, his wife was at the hospital, rolling bandages for the war effort.”

For a minute there, hearing about Eva getting beaten more often, I was going to climb up on my high horse, but I remembered just in time: Mara’s game there was life and death.

“And what, after all that, did you tell the SS to clear yourself?”

“Ah, Ted, that is a longer story. Perhaps another time...”

Mara looks toward the door and suddenly I get the feeling she’s going to dismiss me. Like the hired fucking Joe she thinks I am.

“No! Hold everything, Mara. Maybe that story can wait for another time, but here’s one I want to hear about right now: the one about you cutting off your own daughter’s earlobes!”

Mara is sitting very still, looking down at her hands. She starts shaking her head.

“No, Ted. I cannot possibly speak to you about that. But if you must hear about it, Lena will tell you.”

Mara gets up and goes into the kitchen. I can hear her opening the kitchen window, then talking to Lena.

"Lena, Ted would like to hear about Michelle, if you would. But nothing about the other matter, please. You understand!"

Mara comes back and says to go on up, Lena will speak to me in her apartment.

I made a detour to the Scotch and then climbed the stairs. Lena was already up there, squatting on a cushion. We both know this is going to be rough, so there's no point in long intros. I plunk myself down, facing her.

"Lena, why did Mara cut off Michelle's earlobes?"

Lena frowns.

"Listen, Ted," she says, speaking slowly like she's having to pull every sentence up from a well. "Michelle was my best friend. I still miss her every single day. Her voice, her way of listening to music, the way we could walk a mile without chitchat. Her earlobes? I can barely even remember what they looked like."

Lena is sad as hell. That makes it a lot harder to push on. On the other hand, if the earlobes are merely bits and pieces to her, why not tell me what she knows?

"When did you find out that Mara cut off the earlobes?"

"I knew right away because Mara started screaming. And calling me. She hadn't expected all that blood. She'd cut herself, too."

Pictures start pelting in—scissors, mothers, hair flying, bloody lobes. Quick: ask more questions. Get the facts.

"Lena, were you the one called the police?"

"No."

"Well, somebody did. Who?"

"Mara, I suppose. They came quite quickly. Oh, I remember. When they came in, Mara said: 'But I wanted an ambulance.' Maybe the ambulance people call the police?"

"Did an ambulance come?"

"Oh, yes. And Mara insisted they take her. But she didn't need stitches."

"Who, Lena. Who went in the ambulance but didn't need stitches?"

"They took both of them, of course. Mara didn't need stitches. It was just a small cut, on her left forefinger. Michelle—well, she was long gone. She'd stopped breathing at least two hours before the ambulance took her. I was up here, making some Valerian root tea for Mara, for her nerves. Then Mara started screaming..."

Lena's eyes are closed. She is rubbing her forehead like she's trying to rub away memories: a lot of blood and screaming.

I gulp the rest of the Scotch and it lands right on top of old screams of my own. Screams all over the house the night my six-year-old sister died. Everybody pulling me out of every hiding place—my father clutching me, "she was an angel and she left us"—and altogether too much careless splashing of drunken tears. And my own screaming—raging at that terrifying hole left by my little sister's forever absence. Until somebody grabbed me and held me so tight there was no breath left for screaming.

A few days later they told me: "Your mother went away for a while." I was so little and so stupid, I didn't even get suspicious. Maybe mothers were supposed to go away after their little girls died. Maybe all mothers do that. Mind you, "went away" is something they said about my little sister, too, and she was dead. I knew that. But when they said it about my mother, they leaned on that *for a little while*. So I waited for my mother to come back. Waited for two months for my mother to come back. Then waited another month to at least hear from her. Waited and waited and waited. And then she finally did come back. My brother and I were already in bed and there she was, standing in the doorway. Saying: "Shh, don't get up, boys. Go back to sleep. I'll see you in the morning."

But we didn't. We never saw her again. In the morning, I overheard my father on the phone and that's how I found out my mother was dead, too. Killed herself during the night. Left behind two kids, one eight years old and me six, and went and killed herself. End of waiting.

I heard a groan, like a fading echo, and I remember asking myself one more time: how in the blazes of hell did I land way back there again? How many times, sleeping or waking, do I have to claw my way out of that same cave? This time I know the groan is my own.

I open my eyes and I'm still sitting among the cushions and Lena the neighbour is looking down at her toes and she's hiding something. Believe me, I'm an expert in people hiding stuff and Lena was definitely doing that. All of a sudden it occurs to me I don't even know for sure why Michelle died. I'd assumed she OD'ed, but I really didn't know that for sure. So I had to ask.

Lena looks at the flute up on the wall.

"Michelle had a bad cold, then bronchitis and pneumonia. She was in the hospital, of course, but as soon as she started recovering, she insisted on coming home. Mara arrived the same day I brought Michelle home. For four days, whenever I heard Mara talking, she was trying to convince Michelle to go back to the hospital. Mara wanted me to talk to Michelle about it, too, but—I didn't. I really thought she was better off recuperating at home. I stayed with Michelle quite often. I was with her when she died. She just stopped breathing. Her heart gave out, the doctor said. Apparently—Michelle never told me—she'd had a bad heart all along."

Lena takes a long breath.

"I had to tell Mara that Michelle—that her daughter was dead. Mara wanted to be left alone with her for a while. I went up and started making the tea for Mara, and well, you know the rest..."

"What did Mara say when you told her daughter was dead?"

"Nothing. Not one word."

"Well, could you tell if she was deranged or not? Over the edge with grief?"

Lena is shaking her head. "I worry about Mara," she says. "Because she keeps herself so tightly under control."

"So you really have no idea why she cut off the earlobes? How she could even do such a thing?"

Lena is still shaking her head. I can't take it. I've jumped up and I'm on my way to the door.

"I am going to find out." I'm muttering, mostly to myself. "I'm going down there and I'm going to find out. Right now!"

Down the stairs, two at a time. Mara had better not even try telling me to wait to find out. I flew to Europe so I wouldn't have to just hang around and wait and I'm not about to do it now.

Mara is standing at the window, turning to face me.

"No waiting, Mara. And no lies. I want an answer right now: were you deranged by grief when you did it?"

"Deranged?" she says. Voice cold, eyes like a wall. "Certainly not!"

I turned and was out the door, getting away as fast as I could. Away from the woman who cut off her child's ears in cold blood. Not deranged by grief. Certainly not!

LENA

I could have screamed and screamed and screamed. Loud enough to drown out Mara playing the Rachmaninoff Prelude as if it's wedding music for demons. I wanted to scream at Mara for so coldly asking me—practically ordering me—to tell Ted about Michelle dying, and I wanted to scream at Ted because he was really interested only in hearing about Mara. I wanted twelve old women with me, beating our chests, moaning and ululating and screaming. In our culture, alas, the loss of a best friend warrants at the most a day off work—the day of the funeral—and perhaps holding the hand of a close family member and empathetically nodding. A bereft dog is admired for lying down and howling at death. I envied dogs.

And I wanted to rage at Mara. At her control. Why are you not howling, mother of Michelle? Why are you not crying out and sinking to your knees and stifling sobs in pillows?

Then I had a thought I'd been dodging for a while: What if it isn't control? What if the shunned and bitter truth is that Mara neither loved her daughter nor mourns her death?

A monstrous thought.

There are such mothers, of course, and in our world a mother without love has the lifelong burden of hiding that horrible secret. That deformity.

I remember thinking, going down the back stairs, going back to my tree, that I had a clear choice: Tell Mara, Ted, the world, to disappear from my life so I could live in solitude, so I could throw fits, kick and tear and scream till my voice gave out. How tempting that was: to live in solitude. The only other choice was to reinstate Lena the anthropologist, to observe, to forgive other people for being alive. Obviously, I chose the latter.

TED

The van's engine has been cold for a week so it takes some coaxing, but now it's rumbling and we're moving. Man, I don't know what I'll do when this old honker rattles off to junkyard heaven. She's not only the one that gets me to gigs and back; sometimes she's all I have for a roof. Never for long, mind you, because home is where my piano is and that old sweetheart won't fit in here.

At my own pad on Woodbine, I park the van in the driveway, which no tenant is allowed to do, and jump up the stairs three at a time. But, Jesus! My room key won't fit! I don't believe this. I really do not fucking believe the old bugger changed the lock just to keep me from getting to my piano.

"Come out, you asshole!"

I'm yelling down the stairs and at the same time I'm banging on the door and I keep right on yelling and kicking till I hear police sirens. Chickenshit has called the fucking cops on me. I jump down the stairs and into the van and hightail it out of there because I'm in no mood for jail. You go in on a Saturday, you don't get out till Monday.

Shit. Now I have to put in at least an hour farting around before I can go back and pull that chickenshit landlord out of bed and make him open the door to my piano.

Meantime, I need some sounds in a serious way. Archie Shepp, with all of New York's underbelly blasting and screaming through his horn. Ornette Coleman wailing on his electric violin. And I want booze. To dissolve all the fucking needles and knots. And I want grass. No, hash. Some of that black shit that was around a couple of months ago, mellowed out a whole room full of heavy smokers so they just lay there, grinning. But first of all I need some sounds and it's too goddamned fucking early for the clubs.

So now I'm driving around, just me and my van, free to go anywhere but nowhere to go. Can't go to Bear and Alicia's because I'm never going back there. I do not need friends who make conditions. Who tell me not to come around till I'm a good boy. I'm so fucking pissed off I can't think of one place I want to go. But then, hey, wait a minute—if it's Saturday (how did I know it was Saturday?) there just might be a jam going on at Henry's. It's possible. I yank the van around a corner and just about run the curb. I'm the one who used to tell Henry that Saturday is a lousy day for getting good people to come out and play, because everybody's out on a gig. Now I hope like hell he wasn't listening. He usually doesn't, which is why playing with him is such a drag. But he's got this basement...

It takes me about six minutes to get to Henry's place on Sherbourne and climb down into the basement. Just three of them down here: Henry, little Jay on the drums, and Rex on bass, looking half asleep like he always does, but swinging it. No fireworks, though. They close the tune and take a break.

Rex pulls out a joint, which he and I share. Little Jay's got a bottle beside him, in a brown paper bag so it won't get slippery with sweat when he puts out his hand and picks it up and sucks on it. Like he does after every tune. If you want Jay to be sober enough to still play after the first set, you'd better make sure you stretch out on every tune and don't give his hands a break. Henry, of course, is pure. No booze, no drugs, and by now everybody's given up trying to loosen his tightass.

"I hear Hamlyn wants you, you lucky sonofabitch. When are you heading out?"

"Jesus, Henry. I haven't even called Hamlyn back yet. Bear the one who told you?"

"No, man. Haven't you heard? Nobody's seen Bear for days. He didn't show for a gig, didn't send in a sub, didn't even call."

"Yeah, well, don't look at me. I've been away."

The grass tastes fine—Rex grows his own and it's light and tasty stuff, smooth and mellow, but today it's making me jumpy.

"Come on, Rex."

I like piano and bass together, and Rex and I are good, playing duos. We move together. Not the way Bear and I do, but then Bear and I have practically been living in each other's pocket, musically speaking. I sit down at the piano and before my ass is settled, I ram into the nastiest discords there are for Monk's "Crepuscule with Nellie." And Rex picks up his ax and we're off and riding wild howling winds, black clouds on every horizon, closing in fast, till suddenly there's no light anywhere and only the immensity of space can absorb the chaos and the final wail, slowly fading away.

Somehow, the piano survived. I take off my shirt and wipe the keys with it and the stains of sweat are a surprise. I expected blood. Judging by the way Rex and Henry look at me, I must have been playing some weird shit, but I can't remember one note of it.

I roll another joint, courtesy of Rex's generous pouch, and after a couple of tokes my scalp stops feeling like it's too small for my head.

"Okay, get your ass over here," I tell Henry. If you keep the host on ice too long, he might freeze you out altogether, next time around.

Henry picks up his tenor and says: "Dona Lee." He thinks it's one of his best tunes. He woodsheds on it regularly. "Measuring my growth with it," he told me one time, in confidence, like he was measuring his dick.

Rex starts out and he's playing Eddie Gomez style. That usually cracks me up. My fingers are stabbing chords into the tune. They're keeping to the right changes okay, but that's all. Not one note takes off, not even one phrase gets born.

Take it easy, I tell myself. Just coast on this one. Be cool!

We must have got through somehow because "Dona Lee" is over. And Henry's wife Sara is coming down the stairs. I like Sara. I used to think that Sara was the perfect jazz musician's wife. Then I watched her wearing herself out, supporting Henry's love of purity: he won't play anything but bebop and that does reduce a man's earning power, to practically nothing. Sara works a lot of overtime as a research assistant at U of T. By now she's looking years older than Henry, and Henry flashes his teeth at girls in clubs.

"Hey, guys," says Sara. "How about something mellow. I want to get some sleep tonight."

"How about a solo number," Sara says to me.

"Okay, lady. What do you want to hear?"

"A Monk tune. 'Misterioso.'"

"Done."

Sara pulls over an old chair and sits down beside me. I slide into an intro, very quiet, just a secret little silver moth, dancing, shimmering...but before I'm all the way in, there's a crash. Like the lid of the piano suddenly slammed shut. I've pulled my fingers out fast and I'm sitting there with all ten of them in my lap. Then I look and see the piano lid is still open! What the fuck is happening here?

I don't know. Don't ask me what happened. I still don't know. What I remember is saying out loud:

"Shit man! You've gone and cut off your nose to spite your face!"

I remember saying it but after that, everything's a blank. Till I woke up, lying on an old couch in Henry's basement, my head totally fogged, my tongue sucking on the roof of my mouth. I pulled myself up the stairs and into the kitchen. Nobody there. Henry and Sara were out, which was nice of them. I drank two glasses of water and ate two bananas. Then I saw the note stuck on the phone:

"Dear Ted, help yourself to breakfast. Back around 2. Your grandmother called. She has an urgent message for you. Sara."

My grandmother always has a list of telephone numbers for finding me, but this was the first time she called one. God, let her be all right! Just let her be okay and I'll even say yes to the damned family reunion she keeps wanting.

I dial her number and hold my breath.

"Hi, Grandma."

"Ted! Are you all right then?"

"I'm all right. Sure. How are you doing?"

"Fine, fine. I've been waiting for your call. There is an important message for you. From a woman called Lena. She said 'it is absolutely urgent that you come back right away.' Sounded to me like an emergency. What have you been up to, Ted?"

"Not guilty, grandma. When did she call?"

"Last night, quite late. You are all right, you are sure?"

"Yes, grandma, definitely. I'll talk to you later."

All the way back to Mara's house I keep shaking my head. Trying to get the crick out of my neck, the fog out of my brain.

I park the van right in front of the house. Lena is already opening the door.

"She's upstairs, in the bedroom."

I'm about to run up there but Lena holds me by the arm.

"Mara wants me to tell you about it," she says. "We had to go to the hospital, last night. Mara was hit by a rock thrown through the window. In the left shoulder. No dislocation, said the doctor, only bruises. But Mara insisted that I leave a message for you at your grandmother's."

Lena looks at me to see if that was all right. I nod. Lena says:

"Ted, there was a note wrapped around the rock they threw in and it's really frightening."

Flying up the stairs to Mara's bedroom, I'm Ted the Ferocious Avenger. Minutes later, I'm in a bathtub.

MARA

Dear Theodore,

Two days ago I emerged victorious as well as wiser from what is surely one of the antechambers of hell. Imagine this: Filth-encrusted cement floors and filth-coloured walls, crumpled paper and cigarette butts strewn everywhere. Big wastepaper baskets here and there, all filled to overflowing so that they sit in a ring of debris. The air is cold and stale. A cloud of smoke and sweat hangs under the ceiling like an emanation of the prevailing mood. An oppressive silence is regularly punctuated by moans and curses.

The people all have eyes like boiled onions. Clusters of them stood watching little screens fastened high up on the walls; others walked in, pushed money into small openings in cages, and walked out again. One man stood eating a hot dog, dribbling orange mustard and moss green relish. Two corpulent men in bright yellow vests were rolling fat cigars between their teeth.

The purpose for this afternoon's excursion was twofold: to go forth undisguised, to see whether the Canadian public recognizes me, and if yes, with what consequences, and also in order to observe Canadians who might be called upon to do jury duty. (Lena had assured me that nearly anyone there could appear on my jury.)

"There," as you cannot possibly have guessed from my description, is the Racecourse. Or, as they say here, the racetrack. I had imagined the milieu familiar to me from the times when you played the young rogue, skipped your classes at the university, and took me along to the Racecourse. So when I set out this afternoon, I anticipated a scene of fashionable people, both amused and amusing, delighting in an event of beauty and grace. You can imagine my shock!

I have not as yet had the leisure to think about possible reasons for this utterly dismal version of "going to the races." Only one surmise has risen: that religion took hold of the gambling aspect of it and, by way of guilt, turned the experience into something sinful, furtive and ugly.

Meantime, there I stood, wearing an elegant white linen suit with lime green piping, a lime green silk scarf at my neck, high-heeled white pumps, white gloves, and a somewhat large white braided straw bag. I had decided against wearing a hat, the better to expose my face for possible recognition.

As I entered the cement cavern, the clacking of my high heels caused all the men at the monitors to take their eyes off the screens and to look at me. With exactly the same vacant expression and for exactly the same length of time. Then their eyes glazed over again and returned to the screen. I decided that there was little point in studying these people since they could not possibly be fit to serve on a jury.

Signs indicated that there was an upper level, called the clubhouse, and a lower one called the track. I climbed the stairs to the clubhouse and there found a small table with a good view of the horses just as a race was about to begin.

After the race, after the groans and laughter had subsided, I noticed that my opera glasses were causing a stir. I immediately lowered them and then saw a very large man, a veritable giant, standing in the doorway of the clubhouse, looking at me. Recognizing me.

How long had he been standing there, formulating a plan to deal with me, the mother abhorrent to all nature? What conclusions had he drawn from observing my mien, my interest in the people around me?

The giant launched himself from the doorway. He had had enough beers to make him unsteady on his feet. He reached my table and stood, slightly swaying.

"Say, you're that Mara Deejohn, right?" Putting his giant hands flat on the table to steady himself while peering more closely into my face. "Yup. That's you all right," he said. And then, with a smirk: "Say, lady, come here to taste some horse's ears?"

I kept my gaze steady, looking into his face.

"Why?" I asked, in a completely calm and serious voice. "Are you volunteering?"

The man stared at me in astonishment for some seconds, and then he opened his mouth again and this time he laughed and guffawed loudly enough to draw attention from all eyes.

"That's me all right," he bellowed, "a horse's ass!"

Yelping and hooting, he headed back to the door where he stuck his head out to tell the joke to somebody just outside. That somebody pulled him right out the door, but not before I caught a glimpse of red hair belonging, no doubt about it, to Louise, the young woman who should by now have returned to her old home town. Obviously it was she who had instigated this little episode, which left me with the question: Would the giant have recognized me without the pointing finger? And with the certain knowledge that Louise might be more than a distraction and a nuisance and must be dealt with accordingly.

As soon as the two, Louise and her giant companion, were far enough away, I went into the lavatory (here called "Ladies"). I reversed my jacket from white to green, changed from my high-heeled pumps to open-toed sandals, removed the silk scarf and put on a dark blond wig. I returned home without further incident.

It has become clear and imperative that I hide my identity when going about in public. I also see that some excursions require that I have an escort at my side.

As always, your beloved sister,
Mara

P.S. Events march on. More soon. M.

TED

Up the stairs and into Mara's bedroom storms Ted the Avenger.

"Are you okay? Can I do something?"

I must have expected to see Mara propped by cushions, murmuring, and shaking. I mean, the woman was attacked and threatened and had to go to hospital, right? But here is Mara sitting up in bed, calm as can be. Tilting her head ever so slightly towards a chair, and my butt just moves itself right over there and sits down.

Now I'm close enough to see dark rings under her eyes. Her left arm is in a sling, the other arm cradling it. Hands under the covers.

"Mara, is your shoulder still hurting? Can I get you something?"

"No, no, I'm fine, Ted." Mara's tempo is her own and no fool rushing in is going to change it.

"Please, may I have some fresh water?"

Mara has slid that one in for Lena, standing in the doorway, who takes the glass decanter and departs.

"Now, Ted," says Mara, as in Let's Get To The Important Stuff. "Please read the note. It was thrown in through the window, wrapped around the rock."

The note has turned up in my hand. I look at it.

The paper is not crumpled, not dirty, but neatly folded in four—nothing to show it arrived by way of broken glass and bruises. I'm about to mention that when I see the printed letters. Big and ugly:

YOU ARE AN EVIL WOMAN. YOU BELONG TO THE DEVIL. WE WILL SEE TO IT THAT HE WILL NOT HAVE TO WAIT FOR YOU MUCH LONGER.

"Hard to believe, isn't it?" says Lena, coming back. "But I saw the broken window."

Mara moves her head to look straight at Lena.

"Are you suggesting that I might have produced the note myself?"

I'm watching Lena's face, trying to get a handle on her expression, when I hear a quick little moan. Mara is looking down at her arm in the sling, moving it slightly, very cautiously. Her hands are still under the covers.

"Are your hands hurt, too?"

"No."

"When we came back from the hospital, Mara stayed up to supervise the emergency repairmen working on the window," Lena's voice. "She should have gone to bed but she wouldn't let me take over."

"I was not supervising the men," says Mara. "I was observing. Doing research, actually."

"Mara, have you been harassed before?"

"Only once. In future, I intend to make sure that I am not recognized when I go out. I may even buy a few wigs." Twinkling, like she's enjoying herself.

Then Mara offers me a coffee, which somehow reminds me that I haven't had my clothes off since Vienna. I could feel the grit and dirt clogging my pores and every orifice.

"What I really need," I tell her, "is a bath."

"Of course," says Mara. "I do want to discuss something with you, but it can wait until afterwards. I shall take a rest myself. Lena, if you would, please...?"

Lena heads down the hall with me following, and I remember getting pissed off at the way Mara had both Lena and me jumping around to her tune. Lena hands me a towel and splits.

So there I sat, in Mara deJong's bathtub, trying to remember exactly how I got from rushing to be of help, into hot water. Seemed like every time I saw the woman, I started ricocheting around like a bat on speed. The bathtub was old-fashioned: comfortable, deep, but too short, so either your knees or your chest stuck out. As soon as they touched the hot water, my fingertips tingled. Playing does that. I sat and tingled and tried to make sense out of what happened the night before.

Neither Lena nor Mara mentioned calling the police. I sure am no believer in those who claim to serve and protect—cops or politicians—but rock throwers should definitely be rapped on the knuckles. And obviously, Mara needed protection. From rocks, and notes, and assorted cranks. I should move her, I thought. To a hotel. The Park Plaza, say, or the Windsor Arms...anything downtown so I could pop over and help out if she needed something.

And while I was doing those good little deeds, helping out, I'd also be watching the woman. Slinging questions into every chink. I wasn't soaking my brains, you know. After that basement horror show the night before, with all my fingers playing sorcerer's apprentice, it was damned clear to me that I could not split this Mara scene. Not until I knew: if not "deranged by grief," then what? And another thing: maybe Mara just didn't *know* she was deranged at the time?

Then Lena knocked on the door. She's on a mission: wants to know sizes—shirt, socks, and ahem, underwear.

"It's no trouble," she says. "Mara already gave me the money."

My gig bag is in the van out front, but nothing in it is clean. Still, I don't like Mara sending Lena to run around for me.

"It's just a few blocks," says Lena. "Don't get excited. I can use the walk."

So I tell her some sizes and off she goes. A woman of goodwill whose voice today is vibrant and lively. A few minutes later, I hear church bells—four of them and only one out of tune—telling me it's Sunday. All the stores are closed! What the hell did Mara have in mind, sending Lena off on a wild goose chase? Is this some kind of addiction she has, playing puppeteer, with everybody dancing at the end of her strings, fetching water and popping around the world?

I almost break my neck stepping out of the tub onto wet tiles. I grab the towel to wrap around my middle and go slurping down the hall. Mara's bedroom door is ajar; Mara is leaning back into pillows. Her eyes are closed. She looks calm. No way of telling if she's asleep but one thing is sure: the woman's a trouper.

("You're a good little soldier," my father said. Telling me I was doing it right: not crying any more, not screaming—bloody knee or dead little sister—no tears where they show. Even stupid praise hangs in there, I guess, and if you're not careful, it gets repeated. Mind you, for Mara it would have to be "You're a good little general.")

On the floor beside her bed is a black metal box with a gold rim and a small gold lock. Looks interesting. I didn't get as far as this room when I was snooping yesterday, or I'd have checked out this box for sure.

"I'll be taking it to the bank tomorrow," says Mara, eyes open. "To remove temptation."

So, I thought. She knew about me ferreting in her rolltop desk but she isn't going to mention it. Maybe she wanted those "Dear Theodore" letters found? I finally remember why I padded in here.

"Mara, why did you send Lena to the store? It's Sunday."

"Lena knows it's Sunday, Ted. I made preparations and arrangements. I have no doubt that we'll be successful in buying some attire for you." She throws me an amused look. "Much easier, I suspect, than procuring—what is it called in Canada?—an 'alcoholic beverage' on a Sunday. I understand it is possible only if you bring along a pickle wrapped in a permit."

No way am I getting goaded into defending Ontario's liquor laws. On the other hand, I'm not skipping this opportunity to ask some questions. I sit myself down right at the foot of her bed, towel in place but just barely, could slip any second and then wouldn't her scientific assessment of people be getting a little poke in the confidence. General Mara, meet Ted the Mule.

Mara is still talking. "And here is another interesting social phenomenon. Apparently there are public places where people go in the evening in order to imitate a girl in a cage. Fascinating. The girl is dancing, you see. The music is recorded, and..."

"Discotheques. Those places are called discotheques." I've got this horrible suspicion they're going to be big. Another kick in the ass for live music. And way off the track, here.

"Mara, have you thought of asking for police protection?"

"Of course. But it's out of the question. I need freedom of movement and anonymity."

The telephone rings. Before I've even located it, Mara pops out a hand and picks up the receiver.

"Yes," she says, and listens for a while. "I see. Please keep them with you. I'll be there in ten minutes."

Mara hangs up and is about to throw back the covers when she remembers the existence of Ted O'Sullivan, near-naked man sitting on her bed.

"Excuse me," she says. "I have to go out now." And waits for me to hop to it and disappear, pronto. Oh, yeah?

I stand up and turn towards the door, pulling the towel right off and slinging it over my shoulder. Walking out bare-assed. Don't ask me what reaction, if any. Sometimes it's the gesture that counts.

The bath water is cold. I soap myself and shower off, pick the nearest bottle of shampoo, wash my hair and shower again. Feels good. I'm towelling myself dry with a nice thick towel. I think about shaving. Then I do that, too, and find a dry towel in the hall cupboard to wrap around myself. Then I go into Mara's bedroom, to have a look around.

The room is crammed and crowded. A stand-up wardrobe, two chests of drawers, a full-length mirror in an ornate free-standing frame straddling one entire corner. There's a table, with a mirror on it, too, piled with little cases and boxes, all covered in the leather of reptiles—snake, alligator ("From Indonesia," Lena told me later). An antique lamp hangs from the ceiling above the dressing table. The bed's a single, with pale yellow sheets and comforter. I don't know where in all this there was room for Mara's presence.

Before I can start looking for the black metal box no longer beside the bed, Lena is back. At least I think it's Lena, standing in the doorway.

"What the hell did you do to yourself?"

By the sound of Lena's laughter, I must have looked like the village idiot.

"It's not my stuff; it's all Mara's. She really wanted me to put it on—the clothes, the shoes, the jewellery. Then listen to this: she told me exactly what to say to the store owner. So he'd open up on a Sunday and sell me your clothes. Mara said it was 'an Experiment in Persuasion'."

Lena is looking at me again, but this time my face is not making her laugh. I've just flashed on Helga talking about getting coached by Mara, getting prepared to give testimony about her to the SS.

"Anyway," Lena is saying, "Mara's experiment in persuasion was successful. Here you go."

Lena is handing me some boxes and turns around to leave the room so I can get dressed. The one definite around here is that I'm nobody's stud. Relaxing in its way, but these women are carrying it too damned far.

"Except," Lena is turning back, looking ready to laugh some more, "the store owner forgot to switch off the burglar alarm before he opened the door for me, so just when I was on the phone to Mara, telling her that the experiment was a complete success, there they were, two policemen at the door."

"And you told Mara about them? On the phone?"

"Yes, and she insisted we all wait for her and came right down in a cab. Then Mara and the policemen went off together to the Don Jail."

Mara in the Don Jail! Man, I can still get jumpy, remembering those words.

No time to ask questions—I just rip the boxes open and jump into the clothes. Halfway to the Don I'm still buttoning my shirt while trying not to picture Mara stuck in there: drunk tank, holding cells for streetwalkers, druggies berserk with the first stages of withdrawal, every sound an attack, every smell an assault.

I drive like a maniac and pull right up to the main door—let them tow the van away, it won't be the first time—but before my feet even hit the sidewalk, I see Mara walking out the prison door. The door held open by two cops. Who practically bow and actually salute.

Mara catches sight of me and walks around to the passenger seat. Like my being there was all arranged. But her face is definitely pale.

She climbs up and settles herself on the seat and says, "Thank you for coming, Ted. Didn't you like the tie?"

You see what I mean by "ricocheting like a bat on speed?" I'm pulling away from the curb, heading back along Gerrard Street. I don't even try to fathom a woman just out of jail, asking about ties.

"Why would the cops take you down here? Isn't it just a fine to the store owner, doing business on a Sunday?"

"Oh, yes," says Mara. "And I'll pay it for him, of course. But the police officers were kind enough to give me a little tour of the jail. I told them I am most interested...involved in research..."

"And they just up and gave you a tour of the prison? 'Sure, lady, certainly, what would you like to see first, the hole? The electric wire fence?' Can you get absolutely everybody to dance to your tune?"

Mara isn't listening to me blathering. She says, quietly, seriously, mostly to herself:

"Now I know with certainty that if I had to go to jail, I would very soon be dead."

And what was I going to say to that? All the time I was racing down to the jail, I'd been thinking the same bloody thing. But I try:

"Well, you know, Mara, the Don Jail isn't our regular kind of jail. It's sort of a temporary way-station. Nobody stays there for long."

Mara doesn't look like she's buying it. Then she sighs, looks at me, and frowns.

"It will look better with the tie," she says.

When it comes to clothes, I do not understand women. Even my grandmother, Queen of Sensible, has been known to say something like "that's the wrong shirt" about a perfectly clean shirt that fits and even has all its buttons.

Mara is looking out the window at a particularly unappetizing prostitute on the corner of Gerrard and Parliament.

"In Vienna," says Mara, "especially on the Kärntner Strasse, the prostitutes are extremely well dressed. Good fur coats, in winter. The finest footwear. At the moment the fashion among them is to walk two small poodles on a leash. Or any kind of expensive small dog. You see, the dogs permit a dignified approach. The man bends and pats and says, *sotto voce*, what fine little dogs, they look very valuable, he is sure. Then the prostitute can mention her price. But who do you suppose would approach that garish person we saw on the corner?"

"Johns who are broke. I assure you, we, too, have our high-class tarts. Just like any self-respecting country."

"I'm glad to hear it," murmurs Mara, looking out the window again. I can't believe I've just listened to Mara describing how to pick up a Viennese prostitute. Not that I don't appreciate the information. I'd actually thought those elegant women were just out walking their poodles before turning in for the night. Though come to think of it, four a.m. is on the late side.

Meantime, Mara is off on a new tack.

"This van," she says, "must be exceedingly useful."

"It carries all my needs except my piano. That won't fit in here."

"It could serve you well, should you ever desire to pass unrecognized. All you would need is the hat of a delivery man's uniform. Put it on and no one would look at your face."

"Oh, I don't know. This is Canada. In a first-class train compartment in Austria I'd be faceless with a hat like that, but in Canada, today's delivery man is tomorrow's owner of a fleet of vans, then trucks, then cargo planes. Didn't you know? Here people zoom up the ladder so fast, they get dizzy. It's all that gold pavement."

"You are mocking the dream of every immigrant, Ted."

"Sorry. I just get a bit peeved at the thought of me driving my van in a delivery man's uniform. Every jazz player's nightmare, I guess."

"You have made a point I've become aware of myself. Class distinctions are far more difficult to read at a glance, in Canada. I'll certainly need help in that area."

"Sounds like you're planning to stay in Canada."

"Oh, no. Although certainly for a while longer than anticipated."

I've made a right turn on University Avenue by now, heading north. Let her see at least one proper avenue on the way home, wide, with a flower-planted boulevard in the middle. Mara is looking at a clump of people in front of the Sick Kids' hospital.

"Please, Ted," she says. Could you stop for a moment?"

I pull across two lanes and into the driveway in front of the Hospital for Sick Children. Mara is still studying the people near the entrance. "Tell me about them," she says.

By a lucky guess Mara has hit on one of my many talents: "making up people stories," my grandmother used to call it. "Make up a people story about that one," she'd say, pointing her chin. "But a true story!" This bunch was easy. Parents, two sons in their twenties just heading up the sidewalk to have a cigarette, a daughter.

"See the guy with the hat? That's the father. The woman in black is his wife. They're from Italy—Southern Italy. First-generation immigrants, but been here a while, maybe 10 years. He's a construction worker: heavy machinery, I think. Mama stays home, runs the house and family, and by the look of her, the families on either side of their house, too. Hardly speaks English, but that's okay, she has all the friends she needs in little Italy.

"They used to think they'd move back home one day, but their kids wouldn't dream of leaving Canada, so now Ma and Pa don't know any more. They might bring the old ones over instead.

"Now see Blondie, over there? The teenager off to the side? She's the youngest daughter and she's giving them a lot of trouble. She's been here since she was a baby, see, and she'd just as soon you didn't know she has immigrant parents. Won't speak Italian. Understands every word but won't speak it. She sulks when she has to go to family celebrations or to church and she's really pissed that she can't go hang out the way her Canadian friends do. Not allowed. The parents are terrified she'll start dating non-Catholics. Another couple of years she'll either run off with a low-life Anglo-Canadian and get pregnant, or she'll get hurt, turn back and marry a nice Italian boy.

"The trouble is, this second generation sees itself as Canadian, only the rest of Canada isn't ready for them. Still lively, you see. Might actually raise a voice, tsk tsk."

I'm just getting good and rolling here, but Mara says:

"Now, I shall go and test your assessment."

"You what?"

Mara is buttoning her blouse to the very top. Then she loosens her belt.

"Do you have anything black, to use as an armband?"

She glances at my face and smiles. Then looks into the back of the van.

"There," she says. "That will do."

She reaches back and an old black guitar strap appears in her hand. Mara winds it around and around her upper arm. The one in a sling.

"If I appear to be in mourning," she says, "no one will refuse to answer simple questions, even if they seem a little odd, from a total stranger."

"Wait a minute, Mara. Those people are here because a kid in their family is sick in hospital. What are you doing?"

Mara is already climbing out. She waves—"I'll be right back"—and walks over there. I don't even recognize her from the back: loose-belted and limping, looking not one bit like the woman I saw walking down the aisle in the courtroom.

"An experiment in persuasion," Lena said about the get-up Mara had her in. Now Mara's out there, doing a "Test of Ted's Assessment." Mara deJong from Europe sure isn't going for your usual tourist entertainments.

Papa is beckoning his blondie daughter to come talk English to the nice lady. Blondie hates representing the family but she's curious about Mara. Who gently touches the black armband and has father and daughter both talking to her a mile a minute.

"Yes," says Mara minutes later, climbing back into the van. "They are from Calabria. The daughter refuses to answer to Anna Maria. She wants to be called Annie. I was right; you definitely have the eye."

Mara's tone has just conferred upon me a great honour of some kind, which, however, does not stop her from pissing me off exactly one second later.

"We must talk," she says. "Today."

Like she's scheduling a meeting with somebody who is not presently sitting beside her. Like we haven't been talking ever since she stepped out of the Don Jail. Neither of us says a word the rest of the way back to her house, though I doubt it was for the same reason.

As soon as we get to her place, Mara says: "Please come. There is something I must show you."

Her tone alone would have had me follow Mara up the stairs, holding my breath all the way. I'm sure Mara is about to unveil one of the mysteries of her life. I follow her down the second-floor hallway, to the back. Mara unlocks a door, pushes it open and steps aside. And there, big as life and gleaming, is my piano! My own piano! And the piano bench is there, too.

"It has been tuned," Mara is telling me. "You see, Ted..."

"Later," I tell her. "You'll tell me all about it later."

I touch the keys and listen. Every note tells me all over again why I've been hanging onto this heavy old piano. The tuner was a good one, did some work on the action, too, and replaced the broken ivory on the middle D. My fingers are lying on the keys, all ten in a row like kittens lined up at the mama cat's tits. I am going to sound a few chords, just for the lovely familiar sound of them, and then the chords will start moving, travelling, off and away, an adventure in every phrase, and then we'll have a dance, uptempo, for the sheer joy of reunion. Oh, man! Like I've been exiled from my own life and now I'll be allowed back in.

I'm still looking at my fingers lying on the keys. All of a sudden they jump away like the lid is crashing down again.

But it wasn't the piano lid at all, just somebody knocking on the door.

"Ted? May I come in?" Lena the neighbour opens the door.

"Lena. Did you know Mara moved my piano in here?"

Lena nods. "And everything else," she says.

I look around and sure enough, everything's there: the organ, the boxes with sheet music, tapes, books. My crates full of albums...

"Yes, I knew about it," says Lena. "Actually, I helped pack up everything for the movers. Mara wanted to make sure that nothing was lost or damaged. That landlord of yours was hovering over me the whole time. He was afraid you might get angry. Mara told him: 'Mr. O'Sullivan would be most upset if his instruments were to be left among strangers. I shall give them safe storage.' The landlord did rent out your flat, you know."

"Sounds good. Sounds good. Also sounds fishy as hell. Movers want a lot of cash, Lena. More than paying the landlord a month's rent, for that pad of mine. I don't know what's going on here, but..."

Before I get any further, I see Lena is lifting both her hands, holding a record and there's something horribly wrong with it. Deep shocking scratches going right across all the grooves, like a recording crossed out. Mara's recording!

Lena is looking at me. She pulls something out of her pocket and shows me a stone the size of a watch, but with a sharp point. I'm staring at the record and the stone and I can feel my heart beating harder.

"Holy shit! Does Mara know about this?"

Lena says nothing. She's looking very uncomfortable.

"What? You afraid to tell her? You want me to? No, wait. You know who did it!"

Lena says, "I think Mara did it."

I grab the mutilated record out of Lena's hands to get a closer look, but before I can wrap my mind around what Lena just said, we're both yanked around by a sound. By Mara's voice, suddenly wailing up from downstairs.

Lena and I jump down the stairs and into the living room. Mara is spinning around the room like a human top gone berserk. Around the table, to the desk, around the couch. All of a sudden she stops moving. She's keening under her breath, a kind of wordless lament, holding herself very still. Then a short scream and she rushes to the dining table again and flings herself across it. Yanks herself up again, turns and rushes across the room towards the window. She tears the curtains apart, then turns and holds her head in both hands. Her eyes are open too wide, her breath is coming in gasps. She hasn't seen us and she doesn't hear me calling her name.

I go over and touch her arm. She pulls away and starts spinning around the room again with those desperate sounds wailing out. She nearly pulls the rolltop off the desk, yanking it open, then slams it shut with a crunch.

"Oh, my God, oh, my God, what will I do..." finally some words. But she's still breathing in gasps, hysterical. Sore shoulder or not, I have to stop her. I catch her from the front and hold her tight, confining her, forcing her to stop flailing, to stay still, to struggle for breath. A few seconds of that, and then she finally goes limp. I lead her to the couch. Lena covers her with a blanket and gets some brandy and I hold Mara's head so she can sip it, hiccupping and shuddering, her breathing still shallow and too quick.

"What will you do without what, Mara? What did you lose? Whatever it is, we'll help you find it."

Mara's eyes are opening wider.

"My scarf," she says and starts to cry. "My new scarf is gone."

I'm stroking her back, which seems to calm her some, and then I remember Helga in Bergheim talking about a broken handbag and Mara getting hysterical. With only the little girl to take the brunt of the storm, and how much wilder a storm then, with Nazis at the door.

"We'll find the scarf," I tell her. "You can count on it."

"Delayed reaction," whispers Lena. I don't know whether she means the rock and the threatening note last night, or everything back to Michelle's death.

Lena goes off to make Mara some Valerian tea for her nerves. I sit down on the couch beside Mara, who is quietly crying like there's no hope left in the world but it's not surprising her any more, and then the brandy reaches her eyes and closes them and she's lying there, limp and silent, sliding into the fog of exhaustion.

Lena comes to the door with a steaming mug, but I wave her away. What Mara needs right now is sleep. Everything else can wait.

The next morning I wake up in Mara's bed. Alone, except for my dick, hard as an iron bar. One good night's sleep and there he is, butting against the metal gate. Or whatever it is zippers are made out of. I go piss and climb back on the bed.

I'm wearing all my clothes. My shoes are standing at the foot of the bed, side by side. I'm in Mara's bed, so no wonder pictures of her start parading through my head: Mara coming out of the Don Jail, pale and taut as a drum skin, Mara flinging open the door to my piano, Mara wielding a rock, destroying her own recording. No, wait, that's a picture Lena put into my head. Why would Mara hack a gash into her own recording? I don't get any time on that puzzle, because one more picture just came in: Mara last night, spinning all over and wailing like a violin at the gravesite, but it's not her dead child she's wailing about, it's her scarf. If that isn't berserk, what is? Anybody now trying to tell me that woman last night wasn't deranged can go blow it on the mountain. Which was damned reassuring, I'll tell you. A mother deranged by grief, not a monster who doesn't give a shit about her own kid.

And where exactly is Mara now? And *how* is she?

I jump out of bed, into my shoes, and down the stairs. The apartment is empty. I look out the kitchen window and there is Lena the neighbour, sitting under her big old Maple tree, wiggling naked toes in grass, listening to something. The most peaceful nutcase on earth.

"I didn't hear you," says Mara's voice behind me. A quiet voice. A polite voice. Nothing like the screaming and wailing I can still hear from last night. I turn around and here is Mara, dressed and accoutered all over, telling me she is fine, thank you. And, by the way, she found the scarf she was looking for yesterday evening. It was...

Mara waves a hand at somewhere upstairs and that's it. As of now, scarf, hysterics, the real reason she was wailing and crying have all been sent to join the other subjects closed to mere Ted. And before I get a word out, before I even get to ask her, for example, why she moved my piano all the way over here, Mara is asking me to please come into the living room. "I would like to discuss some arrangements with you."

What kind of shit is this? One day she falls asleep with me stroking her head—the back of her head, mind you; she had her face in the pillow and I was sitting on the edge of the couch, damned uncomfortable after the first couple of minutes but never mind, she isn't crying any more, she's breathing evenly, she is falling asleep. And the very next day I'm Ted the butler, instructed to come into the living room to discuss arrangements.

Ted the mule starts twitching his tail.

I follow Mara into the living room and look here, no signs of spinning anywhere. Mara sits herself down on the dirty gold chair like she's the busy executive, head buzzing with strategy and tactics for the big merger. Mara's beautiful legs are crossed. Her arm is no longer in a sling, her hands are not swollen, her voice is reasonable as a bank clerk explaining the benefits of a savings account.

"...and so you see, you could play your music any time at all when you are not with me. I have spoken to Lena and I have bought earplugs for her and for myself, in case you have nocturnal habits."

Wait a minute. Earplugs?

"Once more from the top. Please."

"As you know," says Mara, "I am preparing myself for the trial. I have a new lawyer and it's going to be a trial by jury. Before it all begins on September sixth, I have a great deal of research to do and I would like you to help me with it."

"Mara," I tell her, "you can't be serious. I've got no training in any kind of legal field. I wasn't even good at doing research for essays at school. Unless it was on the one subject in a hundred that really grabbed me."

"The research required," says Mara, "has nothing to do with books and documents. It is simply this: the jurors will all be Canadians. By the time we go to trial, I must be able to look at them and to read them at a glance."

She takes a look at my face and starts frowning.

"Ted. I have been in court before and I won. My preparations are thorough and effective."

"You were in court as a witness, Mara. Not as the accused."

"I was able to get a verdict of 'not guilty' for three men accused of murder."

Mara looks down at her hands and sighs. She looks at me and her eyes tell me I'd better listen hard.

"I will do something," says Mara, "which I have attempted only once before: an illustration of my preparations and research. First, I shall describe for you the situation.

"When Albert and I lived on Java, Albert managed a very large rubber plantation. All the workers lived in villages right on the plantation. The engineer was a young man from Sumatra, a man not previously known to the workers on the plantation, or to their families. He did speak their language, as well as speaking English, Dutch and German. He was a well-educated man, softspoken, with beautiful hands, and he dressed meticulously, in Western-style clothes.

"Ram and his wife lived in their own bungalow on the plantation. He was my husband's employee, of course, but he was also a good friend and often walked over to our house in the evenings, to see Albert or to keep me company when Albert was away.

"One morning, he was to accompany me on a trip to our city house in Bandung, a journey of five hours. Just before the time of our departure, Ram came to tell me that he would not be riding in the car with me. There were rumours in the village, he said, that he and I were having an affair. He was most distraught about the gossip.

"To our chauffeur, Ram said that he was not coming with us because as a Muslim, he refused to sit next to my dogs. I set out for Bandung in our car, with the usual and necessary armed escort behind and in front of us. Two hours later, Ram left for Bandung, driving the plantation jeep himself. His body was found on the road 30 kilometres from the village, shot four times in the chest. The jeep, overturned in the ditch, had been stripped of everything that could be removed.

"No guerrillas had been sighted on that day, nor for several days before the murder. A search was made of all the villages on the plantation and several parts of the jeep were found in the possession of three men. The men were promptly accused of murder.

"The judge was an elderly gentleman who lived on his own rubber plantation. He came and stayed in our guesthouse for several days and he questioned every member of our household and many villagers. When the judge left, he was convinced that the three villagers had killed Ram. The motive: protection of their beloved General Director Albert from Ram—who they thought was going to take over Albert's job and force him to leave. And, a secondary motive: revenge on Ram for the cuckolding of their beloved Albert.

"That was the situation.

"When I did my own research, however, it brought to light the following: Ram was indeed being groomed as my husband's successor, but Albert was scheduled to be retired within the year, no matter who took over. All the villagers knew that this was the case. I was able to prove just how they found out: through our chauffeur.

"The chauffeur was not one of Albert's people, you see. He had been hired and brought in by the British plantation owners as driver and courier, and he greatly suffered from isolation among the villagers. He tried to ingratiate himself by giving the villagers information pertaining to their lives: a new school to be built on the plantation, repairs to the bridge, and so on. The chauffeur had also told the villagers about my husband's retirement. Thus the major part of the motive for killing Ram was gone. As for the secondary motive, I was able to prove conclusively that Ram was a secret homosexual and that his interest in me was platonic.

"Finally, as the judge himself should have known, in our area articles such as the parts of the jeep were communal property. Passed around as needed. They were found in the houses of the accused because they happened to be needed there on the day of the search.

"I talked to the judge privately before the trial, and showed him my evidence and documented research, and he saw that he had been mistaken. My speech on the witness stand was—what do you call it—window dressing. Of course, neither my private talk with the judge nor my speech at court would have been effective in influencing the verdict if I had not on both occasions meticulously designed my own appearance to..."

"Hold it, Mara. No need for another word. I have dropped any notion that you might possibly be whistling in the dark. But we're not talking gossip and customs and secret habits here. We are talking every Canadian likely to show up on a jury! How in hell are you going to research that? It's impossible!"

"Ted, the fact that I am alive proves that nothing is impossible."

That one, let me tell you, really got to me. Think about it: Soviet authorities, Nazi SS men, peasants and judges in Indonesia…

Mara's been waiting for her claim to sink in and now she takes off again, not swerving off-course for a minute.

"I have been going out every day, to do my research," says Mara, "but I need you to accompany me. To go with me to various places, to give your opinions, your knowledge of background and context: I need your Canadian eye."

"How about Lena's eyes? Lena is Canadian."

"Lena's opinions are useless to me," says Mara. "Lena makes no judgments on anything except food preservatives. Besides, it has to be a man."

"A bodyguard?"

"You have read the note, Ted. The next time they might wait for me in the street or come through my door."

"Okay, okay, Mara, I'm not saying I won't help out. Look, here's what I'm going to do: I'll get right out there and find myself a new pad. Someplace not too far so I can help you out any time you need me. All you have to do is call. I'll give you numbers where you can leave messages, too."

Mara is looking down at her hands, folded in her lap.

"I can even call in a couple of times a day to make sure you're all right. And here's another idea: I can move you to a safe place, like a hotel. Believe me, I will help!"

I hold out my hand, ready to make it a promise. But Mara isn't taking it. Her face looks like instead of an offer of friendship, I've just thrown her a rotten fish. She shakes her head.

"I do not ask for favours, Ted. Also, I know from experience that it is impossible to be precise when depending on friends. Surely you can see that I must take no chances. If I were to go to jail I would not survive even for one week. All my skills would be useless there, all my knowledge futile. I would be defenseless and very soon dead."

"Well, what the hell more can I do, Mara? What arrangements were you talking about?"

"Live here in the house, Ted. And work for me. I really would require only four hours of your time. The rest of the day and night would be entirely yours. I thought a salary of $200 a week..."

I couldn't believe it: The woman was hiring again! A part time, live-in Joe. Job requirements: Canadian eyes, some muscle, and flexible morals about the boss' earlobe-cutting habits.

My tongue started blistering: "You expect me to play errand boy till the trial? That's weeks away from now! And you and I living in the same house all that time?"

"I don't see any insurmountable problem in that, Ted. We are both adults, in a business relationship, and..."

"No, Mara. I see a whole flock of problems. Here's just one even you will admit is relevant as hell: I, Mara, am not a robot you can set for a four-hour day and then turn off."

Mara looks puzzled, then:

"Oh, yes, of course," she says. "All this is rather sudden. Perhaps..."

"You're missing the point, Mara. I'm not asking to think about it. I'm saying *no* to your entire proposition. Is that getting through all right?"

I lean forward to take a good look at this woman. Who has decided to take over my life. Who actually moved my piano in here while I was away. Who thinks she can tell me where I am going to live and how I am going to live. I cannot fucking believe it!

Mara isn't looking at me, and a good thing, too, because if my eyes ever did look scary, that must have been the time. I mean, nobody has ever told me how to live and nobody ever will! I'm about to blast off at the woman, to let her know just how wrong she is in her scientific assessment of one Ted O'Sullivan. But before a single word makes it out of my mouth, I get ambushed by a truly horrifying thought.

If there is anything worse than getting your life taken over, it's this: getting your life taken over with collusion from your own dick! And don't give me any of this bull about a good night's sleep.

Get out, Tedboy! I'm yelling inside my head. Get out fast!

And just to make sure this time you're not going to come back, no matter what, call Bear! Call him and tell him you're out of it. Say you're coming over for a beer right now. Call him!

I look up and see that Mara has been watching me think.

"Excuse me," I say. "I have to make a phone call."

I dial Bear's number.

Now this next part is a whole long story all by itself, and maybe I'll tell that one too, someday. Right now it's more like a little detour—if you want to call Bear and me almost getting ourselves killed a little detour. I have to tell you some of it because by the time it was over, we were all of us singing a different tune.

Okay. I'm still back at Mara's place where she's got my hijacked piano, but I'm about to rear up and rescue my life. I dial Bear's number. Alicia answers the phone. And she's crying!

Now, if you'd ever met Alicia, then you'd know this: something that makes Alicia cry, believe me, that's no chipped-fingernail kind of trouble.

"I'm on my way," I tell Alicia and hang up. Then I tell Mara I have to go, and jump out the door. I make it over to their place faster than ever and have to stop and cool myself down a minute before going in. Whatever it is, better not be revving in high.

The door is open. Alicia is sitting on the couch with the phone still in her lap, still crying. Quietly, and rocking, like she's been doing it for a long time.

"Alicia, what is it? Are you sick?"

Something is sliding around on my vocal chords, so I sound like a crow.

Alicia shakes her head.

"Is it Bear?"

Alicia leans forward, cradling the phone and crying harder, scaring the shit out of me. I sit down beside her on the couch and turn her head to face me and hold her hands very tight.

"Talk, Alicia. Start at the beginning."

And out it pours: Alicia has just found out that she's pregnant. Bear doesn't know yet. Because four days ago, Bear took off for Mississippi and disappeared.

Holy fucking Jesus!

No mystery now about Alicia's crying. I'm ready to do some howling myself. In Toronto, Bear teaching racist cops a lesson can get him some mighty bad bruises. In Mississippi, U.S.A?... he'll get himself killed!

Alicia pulls one hand out of mine and reaches for a newspaper.

"It's in here," she says.

The front page has no headlines about Mississippi that day—no big civil rights leader down there trying to pour oil on that broken dam, no new busloads of whites from the North trying to help blacks register for votes so they can choose which Whitey to vote into office.

Alicia is turning the pages one by one and slowly, so I know she's making a point. Whatever news Bear read before he split should be on the front page. But it's not. It's buried. As far down as they'd bury those black people who would try registering for votes without the protection of Whitey's media from the North.

Alicia is pointing to a couple of paragraphs on a back page. Just a tiny little drop in the ocean of news. Two black teenagers got blown away in a little place called Fauna, near Jackson, Mississippi, and nobody at all's been caught and hauled in for it.

"In a place that size," Bear told Alicia, "plenty of people have to know exactly who did it. But if they're white, they won't tell because they're too busy clapping, and if they're black, they're too scared because if they tell, they'll be next." Then Bear said he couldn't take it any more, seeing how deep and far two murdered black kids got buried in the papers, and he took off. To find out who did those murders, and to let it be known.

Sometimes I wish I'd learned how to pray. Right now was one of those times.

"When, Alicia? When did Bear leave?"

"Four days ago. Took all the cash out of our joint account and left. While I was at work. By bus or hitchhiking, I don't know."

"Either way, he could be there by now."

"Oh, he's there. He called me at work, yesterday morning. Just when I had the class out on a field trip. All I got was a message: he's in Fauna, Mississippi, and he would get in touch. That's the last I heard."

"Yesterday, Alicia. That's just one day ago. We know he was okay yesterday."

I can tell by the sound of Alicia's breathing that she isn't feeling any better. Her eyes start filling up again and her head is drooping again in that horrible hopeless way.

"I'm going after him!"

Alicia, bless her, lifts her head and looks at me and her eyes stop looking like a trapped rabbit's. She leans into me and talks into my shoulder:

"I don't have any money left," she says. That little detail hadn't even popped into my mind yet. I was broke, too, but I did have Mara's travel money. Which was now going to be mine for a while.

"No problem, Alicia, I've got all the money we need."

Alicia sighs and relaxes another notch. She's still inside the nightmare, but at least she's starting to kick.

"How are you going to find Bear when you get to Fauna?"

"Never you worry about that," I told her. "You think it's going to be hard tracing one uppity Negro from the North? Besides, we know what took him there so we know where he's likely to show. You rest easy now because I am going to find that bugger and I'll bring him back if I have to knock him out to do it."

Alicia hiccups a little laugh at the notion of me knocking out Bear—not exactly flattering, but hell, I was happy to hear the sound, if you know what I mean.

"Now here's what you do," I told Alicia. "Next time Bear calls, tell him you're pregnant—yes, damn it, over the phone. And tell him I'm on my way. Ask where I can find him, exactly. I'll call you the minute I get to Fauna.

"Now go make like a Hausfrau and get me something to eat on the road."

Alicia tweaks my nose, and takes off for the kitchen. Glad to be in action. Meantime, I call Mara.

"I'll be away for a few days," I tell her. "Can my report about witnesses wait that long, or do you want it fast, right now?"

"It can wait," says Mara. And hangs up.

Alicia has hauled out an old map of North America, so I spread it out and mark myself a route. Whichever way I go, it'll be a thousand miles.

Alicia is back in the room so I ask her if she happens to have any diet pills.

Alicia smiles at me. I have no idea why, but bless her again. I really hate to see that woman cry.

"Well, Ted," says Alicia, "Bear always says: half the time he's the only one who can make sense out of you. Did you say *diet* pills?"

"Yes, dear daffodilly, diet pills. They have speed in them. Amphetamines. To keep me awake. I have a one-thousand-mile drive ahead and I don't want to fall asleep at the wheel."

"You better not." But she's got no diet pills.

Alicia makes sandwiches, a big Thermos full of black coffee for the road and gives me a hug good bye. In my hurry to get going, I don't even stop to notice if there's a little bump on her belly yet or not.

ALICIA

As soon as the door closed behind Ted, I wanted to call him back. To talk to. I just had to talk to somebody. I was sitting there with the phone in my lap again, trying to come up with somebody I could talk to, and I sure was surprised at the name that popped up out of the blue: Lena. I'd never even met the woman at that point. We spoke on the phone a couple of times, that's all. But she was the one I wanted to talk to, and believe me, I was not in the mood for social niceties. So I dialled her number.

"Hi, Alicia, did Ted call you?"

"Yes, he did. He just took off, once again riding to the rescue, but this time I'm all for it. He's a true friend, is Ted, loyal and laying himself on the line for us...Oh, God, I can't believe I've been so rough on him lately.

"Lena, tell me the truth: do you mind if I talk to you? Do you have time?"

Lena said yes and suggested we meet in a restaurant she knows on Bloor called "The Hungarian Pantry." I didn't even bother to do anything about my swollen eyes. I took a taxi and got there first, and sat down where I could watch the door. I was sure I'd recognize her coming in, don't ask me how, but now it occurred to me: did Lena even know I'm black? I don't *sound* black, being third-generation Canadian. Island talk is what my mother and my grandmother used when I wasn't supposed to understand. And being a teacher who loves to teach and wants to keep her job, I erased the last vestiges of Grandma's lilt a long time ago.

Well, I thought, we'll just have to wait and see how she goes.

Lena arrived, and before she was all the way through the door, we recognized each other. Lena looked sad, back then, but always easy in herself and dressed for comfort. I liked that, and the way she didn't bother with small talk. Minutes later, sure enough, I was pouring out all over her. Starting with the pregnancy Bear knew nothing about and how it wasn't altogether real to me until he and I could look at it together.

Right then my heart got a cramp, I swear. Like a wall of fear hitting me in the chest: Bear in Mississippi!

Thank God Lena already knew what was going on down there for black people—so she knew I was right to be scared as hell and she didn't try to talk me out of it. She just leaned forward and told me: "I don't know what to say," and held my hands.

Look, I don't want to leave you hanging: Bear and Ted did come back from down South. Worse for wear and definitely wiser, so not exactly the same Bear and Ted who left here—but they did come back. And do not tell me I'm letting dramatic tension out of the story. I know something about storytelling—my grandma's stories were strong as bones and old as spiders.

"And I think Lena and I getting to be good friends all in a swoop like that is as much part of the story as your first time meeting up with Ted," I told Bear on the phone later that week. Bear groaned. "Well, it's true," I yelled into the receiver and slammed it down on him. Bear says he groaned because he could tell there was a "women are equals" involved, now not only from me but probably from both of us, and how would he cope with two uppity women, etc., etc. I didn't catch on right then that Bear was teasing. Must have been my Hormone Monster in play again.

Okay, back to the Hungarian Pantry.

"Well," said Lena. "Now you know why you haven't been your usual self. That must be a relief, to know it's not incipient insanity, only hormones, and that it's temporary."

"Do you know that for sure? That it's temporary? Oh, God, with nine months of this, who knows what future havoc I might wreak? I tell you, there's a devil riding me, twisting my thoughts and keeping me on this emotional roller coaster: one minute I want to stand up and sing a hymn to the bravery and nobility of "my men" gone down South to see justice done, and the next minute I want to kick their asses, and then I fall into sheer terror…nine months of this? I'll never survive it with my sanity intact."

"It may only last two or three, Alicia. And this tea will help…"

Lena was scribbling something on a napkin.

"This is a herbal concoction. A friend gave it to me. She turned into an emotional mess in the first months of her pregnancy…"

"I should talk to her."

"She lives in Indonesia."

"Of course! Or Fiji, or the North Pole. Oh, hell!" I was waving my hands around like the demented woman I was, and then burst right out with it and told Lena about the horrible feeling I'd carried around ever since Bear left. "Maybe I was such a shrew that I *drove* Bear into heading down South?"

"Alicia," said Lena, eyes open wide, "that's trivializing his quest, wouldn't you say?"

This time it was me, leaning forward and reaching to hold her hands.

"Thank you," was all I could say. "Thank you, thank you, thank you."

"Lena, could I ask you something about Mara?"

"Go ahead."

"Do you think she's evil?"

Lena raised her eyebrows.

"Well," I told Lena, "I don't buy into psychobabble. We've all got traumas behind us and reasons to howl, but we don't all go around mutilating dead daughters and messing with people's lives."

"Oh, I think we *do* all mess with people's lives. I mean, look at you, messing with my life."

"Lena! What are you talking about?"

"Well, just for one, you're making me consider Mara in a different light."

"What was your light on her? That the woman has problems due to prior hardships and is therefore to be excused for anything, forever more? Not evil, just sick? What?"

"Maybe there's something missing."

I had to pause and think and ask myself, "since when did superstitions ride me?"

"Lena, do you believe in 'the evil eye'?"

"Well, when somebody's directing nasty thoughts at you, you can usually feel it, don't you think?"

"Well, of course I can. I'm black, remember? I never go outside without a shield ready to raise, to ward off nastiness coming at me. Bear's worse. His shield goes up and all around him just automatically every time he steps out the door. But the 'evil eye,' that's different. That's jealousy of the gods, envy of one's good fortune..."

Lena listened, nodding, then she said, "I think of the evil eye as just being hostility of any kind."

"Like mine towards Mara?"

"Yes," she said, and smiled. That's Lena for you right there: Lena the Truth-Sayer.

"So, Lena. How do you reconcile your role as Truth-Sayer with 'do no harm'?" (Lena must have told me by then about how she and Michelle tried to live by the dictum: "do no harm.")

"Oh," said Lena without hesitation, "It won't do you any harm to look at your hostility towards Mara."

At which point I started laughing, something I really didn't think I'd be doing before Bear and Ted were safely home. Bless the woman.

Towards the end of that first time talking, I said to Lena, "If Michelle hadn't died, you and I might never have met."

"Oh, I don't know," she said. "Maybe Michelle would have introduced us one day when we both went to hear her sing."

I guess it showed that I'd been wishing Michelle into Hades.

"You didn't know her," said Lena. "You would have liked each other. I told you, Michelle did not ever, as long as I knew her, even bat an eyelash at a married man. And she knew Bear was married; he told her himself. The very first time they ever sat and talked. So get off that ride, Alicia. You made it up. Well, I suppose the Hormone Monster did."

We both laughed. Back then neither of us was doing much laughing and it sure felt good, so we kept on getting together to talk, perchance to laugh.

TED

I managed to keep up a pretty good show of confidence in front of Alicia till I was out the door and into my van. I couldn't start shaking then either, because I had to concentrate on driving for a long long stretch. By the time I got to the sign "Mississippi, the Magnolia State," I didn't recognize the guy looking back at me in the men's room mirror. As soon as I passed the sign for Fauna, I stopped and phoned Alicia. No word from Bear. Alicia was trying hard to sound calm, and so was I.

"I'll call you every few hours," I told her. "At home or at work."

Fauna, Mississippi is my idea of hell. One minute the sunlight makes you want to stretch and purr and the scent of blossoms—could be magnolia—invites you to open all your pores to the sweet air, and the very next minute you see a drinking fountain marked "For Coloreds" and the rage boils up so fast you can taste it. I was still staring at my first sign ever saying "Whites Only" when some caricature of a human being wearing a straw hat started drawling all over me about those rabble-rousing Commies come crawling around and how he hoped I wasn't one of them, for the good of my skin and keeping it in one piece.

I took one look at his sweating ham of a face, and then I kept my eyes off it, but I stuck around long enough to ask about the nearest place where rabble-rousers might turn up.

"You in the wrong county, boy," says pig face. "Ain't no place in this county for white nigger lovers from the North to sit and tell our niggers they got complaints and rights and shit."

"What about a meeting place for Negroes? Is there one of those?"

"Not any more," says pig face. "Not since they church burned clear to the ground 'bout a month ago. 'Less you mean that shack they took for a school, which is looking mighty dry and kindling-like, too, if you ask me."

The place wasn't hard to find once I'd been told it came after the end of the paved road, just where the hot dust took over and there were more chickens crossing the dirt road than people. It was a one-room wooden shack that had never seen paint, with a roof made of sheets of tin, and even from the outside it looked under siege, with signs and scrawlings and crosses and curses all over the walls.

Inside, there was no welcome committee for Ted Whitey from the North. There were four guys and two women, all black, all doing office-type work, though it sure had a different look about it in this unpainted wooden shack, and not a tie or polished nail to be seen. One skinny guy with glasses was talking to a big woman sitting on a rickety chair, trying to convince her about something, reasoning in a quiet voice, on and on, but the woman keeps shaking her head.

"The strategy is right," she says, "but the tactics stink."

I decide to pick on her to ask my question.

"Excuse me..."

She doesn't feel like listening. They're all going to ignore me till I leave. I try again. Louder this time.

"Look, this is urgent, I'm looking..."

In about two seconds flat there are four bodies practically up against me and four faces ready to swallow me whole.

Who the fuck did I think I was, raising my voice at anybody in here? (That was the polite stuff.)

"Look," I tried again. "This guy's never been in the South, he's mad as hell, and he is going to get himself killed around here for kicking some redneck's teeth in. And his old lady back home is pregnant!"

"Noble," says the skinny guy with an Afro twice his size and steel-rimmed glasses. "This brother, you say, came to fight for the poor ignorant black folk in the South, only he needs his Mammy to come and look out for him. So then the two of you get a medal on television and go back home."

"Let us give him a medal right here," says the big guy in overalls. "Let me pin it on him."

"Stop bullshitting around, you assholes." By now I was yelling. "You're wasting time and there isn't any."

Big Mama waves a hand and everybody stops to listen.

"What you gonna do when you find him?" she wants to know.

I know this isn't going to sound one bit brotherly, but I'm too hot and bothered to make a lie sound right.

"I'm going to make him come home to Canada. Somehow. Because he ain't gonna do anybody any good as a corpse."

"That's real smart," says the woman. "Now let's just have a quick look and see who you are." Like underneath these raunchy jeans and stinking shirt I might be wearing a dark suit and FBI tie.

The skinny guy goes through my pockets. The cash is counted: $200 left.

"Look at that," says the big guy. "He came to make a donation."

Just then somebody walks in the door and it's Bear. He sees me up against the wall and starts growling. Big and Skinny step back—about half an inch. Bear takes hold of me by the shirt and we start a hollering match like two trumpets snarling up and down the scale and neither of us listening and it's only when I have to take a breath that anything gets through and it's Bear, yelling at me:

"You are going to get yourself killed, down here! You expectin' me to spend my time saving your ass? Go home, man!"

I start to laugh. I mean that's *my* line, right? And everybody else there knows it and so they start shaking their heads and grinning. Everybody except Bear.

"Ditto," I tell him. "So we're *both* going home."

Bear is still puffing mad and it takes another second or so but then he simmers down.

Now everybody settles back to watch us two some more, but we're not in the mood to do a performance. The skinny guy hands over the cash—all except a fifty, but who's counting—and Bear and I take off in the van.

I'm looking around for someplace to stop and go sit over a cold beer and talk, but there's no place we can both get into, black and white, so Bear shows me the way to where he stayed last night: another one-room shack, but this one with a porch. We sit down on the porch steps. We're, both of us, tired to the bone.

"First of all, I have to call Alicia," I tell him. "Where's the phone?"

"No phone. And Alicia is all right."

"Did you talk to her today?"

"No, Ted. Nobody has to babysit Alicia."

So I let him have it. The pregnancy first. Bear stares at me, stares at the ground, then he shakes his head, grins, shakes his head some more. Then he does some serious thinking. Not about the baby to come, fruit of his loins, as it turns out: he is thinking about Alicia.

"She'll be all right," he finally decides. "She's going to be pregnant for nine months, right? I haven't moved here, you know."

So I let him have the rest. Stupid risks that produce only dead bodies, and that damned temper of his, keeps shorting out his brain. I talk—fast so he won't interrupt—about doing what he can from back home and staying alive for the long haul and all that shit.

Bear keeps shaking his head.

"You think I can't figure out any game except contact sport? Man, I've been around for nearly 30 years in this black skin, and now you're gonna preach at me about how to save my neck from the noose?"

"There's the noose and there's the bullet in the back, and about a hundred other ways to die down here. You've never tried surviving in the Southern states, Bear."

"You think I know less about it than you do, white boy? Shit, man, in all the time I've been around here I didn't even get close to starting a fight."

"You've been here, what—four, five days? And there's plenty of others to be starting the fights around here. Look, Bear, you think about it. Right now I am going to find a telephone and tell Alicia that you're alive. So far."

I left him sitting there to simmer and got into the van. It took me 15 minutes to find a phone, attached to some official building, and then Alicia wasn't home. I tried her at work and got a polite voice asking if it was urgent because Alicia was supervising the schoolyard.

"Just tell her, 'He's fine and will call later today.' Make sure she gets the message."

Then I couldn't find my way back to the shack. Like it disappeared underground. Two little girls in pigtails and no shoes were sitting on a stoop sharing a can of pop. They didn't know anything they wanted to tell me. A big man with a gray fedora and holes in his pants scowled as if I was spitting drool on his shirt. No doubt about it, I was good and lost.

"Just fatigue," I told myself. "You haven't really died and gone to hell."

When I finally did find the place, the porch was empty. Inside, Bear was lying on a cot, snoring.

I went back out to the van, left the rear doors open to that sweet-smelling air and lay down and fell asleep in about 10 seconds.

MARA

Dear Theodore,

As I surmised, the young man, Ted O'Sullivan, is superbly fitted for the role of Guide and Protector. He has the clear discerning eye of a man standing apart and the heart of a warrior, shielding the weak or troubled.

I cannot, of course, feign weakness, but it will be easy to demonstrate that I am beset by threatening ogres and sneering gargoyles. In truth, even my rare moments of doubt and trembling, if he should happen to witness one, can be turned to my advantage.

Lena is pliant though I can see she is not without intelligence.

Tomorrow, I am interviewing yet another lawyer. I pose my questions in order to elicit whether, being male and accustomed to wielding unquestioned authority, he is yet capable of following my directions. If not, he is useless to me. Equally useless is the one who is all too willing to bend because in the grip of enchantment, for he will surely forget to apply the knowledge for which I hire him.

Still, I am confident that when the right one applies, I shall recognize him at once. Lawyers, I am pleased to say, are predictable.

And so the preparations proceed apace and I remain,

As always, your beloved sister

Mara

TED

I'm down South, sleeping in the van, back doors open. The next thing I know, my head is bumping something hard, which turns out to be the wheel well because I am being dragged out of the van, legs first. Then two guys are propping me hard against the side of the van and one guy is flicking a belt around my head. Just teenagers, all three of them, but big white nasty ones.

The metal buckle hits my cheekbone a couple of times, making a sound I don't ever want to hear again. Kicking is all I have and even that only for one good try, then I'm lying on the ground and one guy is sitting all over me, and the belt is still aiming for my head.

Nobody sees Bear coming.

Bear charges into the two guys standing and the surprise gives me the advantage over the guy sitting on me. I roll and get him under me, but just for a second. Then we're both rolling and everything is happening too fast to remember except as a kind of wildcat struggle for air. In the end, the three guys up and split, leaving both of us lying on the ground with blood coming out of Bear's forehead.

I don't know how long we just lay there, the both of us. When I got to my knees, my head exploded and I almost keeled over, but then somehow I managed to haul Bear into the back of the van. There was blood all over his face from a cut over his left eyebrow, but when I propped him up against the back of the driver's seat, the bleeding let up. Bear groaned and grabbed his left thigh and opened his eyes.

"Don't move," I say. "Just tell me how to get to a hospital."

Bear tries to turn his head and passes out again. I have to find that hospital fast.

I'm slowly driving down the road, looking for anything on two legs to ask for directions. The first guy I see, a tall skinny black man, watches the van coming, too slow and driven by a white guy, and he starts running. I catch up and yell out the window. Something about help and death. He stops and listens.

"You'll want St. Joseph's Hospital," he says. "Two blocks after the pavement starts, then turn left. You can't miss it." The guy's about to take off again but I'm a fast learner.

"Wait, damn it. Is that a hospital for whites you just sent me to? I need one for black folk and I need it fast!"

Now the guy steps up to the van, takes one look through the window at Bear and then runs around the front of the van and jumps in. Five minutes later we're at the hospital. The guy helps me get Bear out of the van and through the door into Emergency, and then he disappears.

There's a line-up in front of the reception desk. Bear is hanging on me like a ton of potatoes, groaning and mumbling and going to pass out again any minute.

I see a guy in a white coat walking down the hall and I grab him and shove Bear up against him so the guy has no choice but to hold onto Bear's body. Then, Bear being no sparrow, the guy in the white coat has to find some place to put him down. And because white coat has turned out to be a doctor, he causes Bear to be deposited in an examination room. All right.

They don't let me in with him and they're taking a while in there, so I have time to notice there's a flap hanging down from my sleeve and just under it there's a flap of my skin hanging too, exposing bloody flesh, and my cheekbone is a pneumatic drill, threatening to pop out my left eye. A crinkly-faced woman sits me down and dabs and stings and tapes me together. I've got my eyes shut tight, concentrating on Bear in the examination room getting a passing grade.

White coat comes out and says they should keep Bear for observation in case of concussion, but not to ask him where they were going to find room for him. There are already three people on rollaway beds parked in the hall, so I know he means it.

Bear's cut on his forehead, I'm told, is stitched up and going to heal fine if kept clean; the leg was dislocated at some joint but is okay or will be—it's just this blow on the head ...there could be a concussion.

"What," I ask the doctor, "do you do if it *is* a concussion?"

"Make sure he gets bed rest, lots of fluids, pain reliever if necessary. That swelling on his head is already the size of a goose egg; we'd be putting an ice pack on that."

"I can do that," I tell the doctor, who gives me a look I can't read at all.

"If symptoms persist," he says, "he'll have to go to a doctor for a follow-up appointment."

"What kind of symptoms?"

"Confusion, nausea, vomiting, blurred vision..."

"Right. Would he be okay for now lying in the back of a van? On foam rubber? Smooth driving all the way, no bumpy roads, best of attention all the way to Canada? Would he be safe?"

The doctor thinks it over and decides it's safe as long as I pay close attention to his breathing.

"Then get somebody to help me carry him out to the van. I want to get him way out of town before he gets too active. How about giving him something so he won't wake up till Cincinnati?"

"No, no. In fact, you'll have to wake him up every couple of hours."

"Oh, shit."

"He won't be in any shape to fight you for quite a while," says the doctor, who either understands more than is likely or doesn't care as long as I get Bear out of there and vacating some space. Doctor gets me an ice pack, a couple of rolls of bandages, adhesive tape, a small bottle with some clear liquid in it, and a note with scribbles. Then he gets a male nurse to wheel Bear out and deposit him in the back of the van. I get directions from the male nurse and half an hour later we're on the highway and I'm hanging onto that white line like it's a rope in a stormy sea.

Something happened back when we were fighting off the Jr. KKK, but I'm not going to tell you about it right now. Because for that whole trip back, I was doing my damnedest not to think about it. Pretend it never happened. And when Bear was finally sitting up beside me, he didn't mention it, let alone ask me questions.

The first time I thought it was safe to leave Bear sleeping and alone, I called Alicia and told her we were on our way. No point in telling her more, right then. But Alicia, well, she knows the two of us. (Too smart for her own good, says Bear.) Alicia wanted to know how come it was so easy to get Bear to agree to come home. I told her enough to make it believable without getting her all excited.

I tried to find us a spot where I could park the van. I could have used a break to lick my own wounds, or at least a couple of minutes with my eyes closed. But there was no safe place for us, not even in a police station parking lot. So I got going again and drove as far away as I could hang in there, heading North, and when I couldn't keep my foot on the gas pedal and my eyes open at the same time, I stopped by the side of the highway, locked all the doors of the van, and to make sure I woke up regularly to check on Bear, curled up with my head under the steering wheel. That way, every time I took a real deep breath, I hit my nose. It worked. About four hours and one sore nose later, we were off and on the road again.

The trip back to Toronto took a lot longer than going the other way. For one thing, I had to keep stopping to check on Bear, get fresh water, hot soup and all that. Then, once Bear was sitting up, I had to let myself get barked at for a few hours before Bear simmered down. Every time I wanted to holler something back, I told myself: shut up, Ted, you don't have to answer any of that right now. He's alive and he's going to stay that way. Plenty time for shouting contests later.

First couple of times Bear stopped yelling at me, he had to because he was dizzy. A few more hours after that, it sank all the way in that I was not going to turn the van around and there wasn't a damn thing he could do about it. So then he finally switched to a different key and started telling me what was going on back there, in the South.

"It's guerrilla warfare, man. No other words for it. I spent every night guarding that shack—you saw it, the local headquarters for the campaign—and do you know what the subversive activities were, going on in there? Do you know what those terrorists were planning? Nothing less than getting people out to vote. Yes, sir. America, 1964.

"What the use was guarding that shack I still don't know, because if a mob did decide one night to register burning objections, all we could have done was run like hell. And the only reason it didn't happen is that the KKK is busy just now, watching the feds on television trying to find those missing nigger lovers from up North—if you've read the papers at all, two whites and one black kid."

By this time, Bear is sitting up beside me and I wanted to tell him about the warfare going on in my own gut, but Bear's on a roll, and there never was anything you could do about that except listen. Especially when he starts talking kind of low and slow.

"Let me tell you about my grandmother," he says. "A religious woman, back in the South. She practiced what the preacher sang, worked like a donkey all her life, and died saying 'Hallelujah, here I come.'

"When I was ten years old, my mother told me to fetch grandma. She was needed for a childbirth. I ran all the way to where grandma worked, in the white part of town. She was the family cook.

"I'm crossing the lawn, heading for the kitchen door, and the family's 11-year-old kid starts following me. As soon as I gave grandma the message, the kid starts yelling. 'You're not going,' he yells at my grandma. 'You're not, you're not. You're baking berry pie for me today.' Jumping up and down.

"Grandma was taking off her apron and all of a sudden the kid rushes over and starts punching her in the stomach. And my grandma was just standing there. Didn't protect herself, didn't even say anything.

"So I beat the shit out of the kid. He was bigger than I was, but he was soft.

"When I got home, I got a beating from my grandpa. 'Knocking some sense into me,' he called it. And the next day I had to go back and apologize to the little bastard and to the whole fucking family, so grandma wouldn't lose her job. That little episode sucked religion right out of me for the rest of my life.

"And the next day after that, my parents sent me North, to live with my aunt and uncle in Buffalo. Whose oldest son was a musician." Bear started hanging out with that son and his friends, and pretty soon he was picking up a bit of cash fetching them home brew after hours. One night he got caught by two cops and they beat him and kicked him senseless: permanent kidney damage, at age 15—and they left him on a back road for dead. Which he was pretty close to being by the time somebody found him.

In the hospital, Bear started planning how he'd kill at least one of the three cops: the kicker. But then, when he was back at his uncle and aunt's place recuperating, he started fooling around with his cousin's bass. Pretty soon he was really getting into it, doing nothing else but, and then one day, when he was finally on his feet again, he split. Headed for Niagara Falls and crossed the border into Canada.

At the border Bear told them he was a music student going to Toronto to study. And that's what he did, for the next three years. Earned just enough by working the trains as night porter, woodshedding every minute he had to himself—first on the electric bass he got from a pawnshop, and then on the old upright double-bass he bought on time.

One night on his way home—by now he'd already quit the trains and was playing music full-time—two Toronto cops stopped him. "Shit man," Bear shook his head. "Those pigs had me pushed over a cement post, searching me, foul-mouthing me, till I lost it and ended up in hospital again, with a guard at the door."

And that's how Bear met Alicia. She was visiting a neighbour of hers in the next bed. Two weeks later they were married.

Bear took a pause and turned his head, slowly, till he was facing me, and said:

"Here it is, Ted old buddy. Just so you never make a mistake about this: there's nobody in my life more important than Alicia, and that includes my own self. You get that?"

"Then what the hell were you doing, trying to get yourself killed down South?"

"Look, man, if everybody keeps on bothering himself only about his own life and his family's life," says Bear, "there never will be any progress at all. A person has to stand up and give history a shove at least once in his lifetime."

"You think everything's gonna be so perfect in a few years you have to get your shove in now or never?"

"You're missing the point here, Ted. I was telling you about Alicia. She's the one turned a raging animal into something human. I still *see* the world is infested with racists, but I've stopped saving up cash for machine guns. And Alicia knows I don't ever aim to do without her. No, man. I'm with Alicia for life. She knows that. But for some damned reason, Michelle made her forget that. And me not bringing the two together, to meet each other, that was a big mistake I made. Because I don't want anything getting in between Alicia and me. Not Michelle, and not even you, Ted. So when you went spinning out on Michelle's mother the earlobe freak right on top of the Michelle ice wrap I was getting from Alicia..."

"Forget it," I told Bear. "I'm way past that. And I sure am glad this trip of yours into Mississippi was a shove on history and not a countermove on Alicia. She's long gone and melted that old ice wrap. You should have seen her crying, man, then you'd know that."

Bear gave out a sigh and I probably let out one of my own, too. Whatever shape our bodies were in, whatever-all was going on in the world outside the van, Bear and I were cool.

Then Bear started in on the earlobes. Throwing me looks, checking how I was taking it, this completely new attitude of his about those bits of missing flesh.

"I know I made a big deal out of it, Ted, back when I was telling you about Michelle being dead. I mean, her mother actually cutting into Michelle like that. But you know what? I'm seeing the whole thing in a different light now. I mean, I'm thinking about the Rev. Martin Luther King. Thinking about how far along the road that non-violence of his is likely to get black people, without some kicks along the way from SNCC and from Malcolm X and his Black Muslims. Not even all the way to the paved part of the road, I bet. And I'm thinking about Vietnam and who is getting killed over there: poor black people, that's who. Poor black men wanting three meals a day for a change, and maybe learn some readin' and writin'. So when you're thinking about all that, and about how much too slowly the times they are a-changing, then the next time those two earlobes pop into your mind, you get one big surprise: those same two earlobes that were the size of elephant ears are down to being just two little bits of dead meat. They just aren't a big deal any more."

Bear stopped talking and I could feel his eyes burning into me without even having to look.

"It's okay," I told him. "Relax, man. I don't actually give a fuck any more how big or how little those earlobes were. And I'll tell you why, too: because I saw Mara with my own eyes, going totally berserk. She was spinning and wailing away, on and on, and all of it supposed to be about what? About losing a scarf! Even Lena said 'delayed reaction.'"

"Oh, man," said Bear. "This is you and your 'deranged by grief' again. Get ready for a kick in the pants, my boy. This whole Mara deJong thing has got itself all mixed up with your mama and what happened with her. Am I right?"

I didn't answer right away. You get a kick in the gut like that, it takes a minute before you can answer. Sure, Bear was right; I knew that. But I hated to admit it right out loud. I mean, I'm a grown man, and all that shit happened way back when I was still a kid. Then I said to myself: okay, so what?

"Okay, so what?" I told Bear. "This was my first chance since my mother died to figure something out. Something I never told you about, but here it is, okay? My mother knew, just like the rest of us did, that my little sister never, ever wanted her hair cut. She used to scream blue murder if anybody even mentioned a haircut. But when my little sister was lying there dead, my mother went and picked up a pair of scissors and cut off all my little sister's hair. So you tell me—the minute my little sister was dead, her own mother doing something like that."

I threw Bear a sideways look and he shook his head.

"Ted," he said. "I wasn't talking about hair. And you know it."

"All right, fine. But you were talking about 'deranged'—was my mother deranged or not. Well, I sure want to *know* if she was or not. Because killing herself and leaving behind two little kids is a whole different story if she was deranged than if she just didn't give a shit about her own kids. Wouldn't you say?"

This time Bear took his time, answering. But he still didn't get off the track.

"All I'm saying is this, Ted: what Mara deJong did or why she did it has nothing to do with what your mother did or why. And how about this one, buddy—something it seems never even occurred to you: maybe Mara deJong made a big wailing deal out of losing a scarf because she's a twit? Shallow as a birdbath?"

"Shallow? Mara deJong shallow?" That made me laugh, that one.

"Listen to this," I told him, "and you'll deduce yourself that you are full of shit."

And then I told Bear everything I found out about Mara in Europe. From Mara's own notes, from Mrs. Whatsnikoff and from Helga and from Albert. I remembered every bit of it, believe you me, and Bear—you have to give the guy his due—he can listen with more than just his two ears. And this time he finally stepped all the way in.

"I'll grant you that doesn't sound twittish," he said, thinking out loud. "Her listening to Allied Radio, and telling the SS to clean their boots, and defending those guys in Indonesia. But then how about this other stuff, Ted—like wandering around in the dead of night meeting black marketeers, and all for a pair of blue shoes? What's that, if it isn't shallow?"

"Oh, I get it. When you challenge racist cops, it's the act of a hero. But when Mara goes out and defies the Nazis, she's shallow?"

"Hmmm," said Bear. Slowly.

"So now," I told him, "you are getting some notion what it's like trying to fit everything I found out about Mara into one single person. There's always *something* goes squishing out the sides. Think 'brave woman,' and in a minute she'll be moaning about a broken glass and blathering about seven years' bad luck. Think 'poor woman beset by enemies,' and you find out she snuggled up with at least one of them. Think 'deranged by grief,' and find out she abandoned her little girl twice during the war. And then, when you're all set to stay in there till you figure out what makes the woman tick, she goes and fucks it up altogether so you have to split. I mean, she went and tried to take over my life!"

So then I told Bear the rest of it: Mara moving my piano and my life right into her house and then me taking off.

"That's great!" says Bear. "Glad to hear you're finally out of it, man!" Sounding like he was ready to celebrate something, which I sure as hell was not. And I was about to tell him why, too.

I pulled the van over at a truck stop and fetched us another couple of cups of coffee and we sat there in the parking lot and I told Bear the worst of it.

"Here it is, man. Ever since this Mara thing started up, I've been so fucked up, I can't play. There's no music coming in, and my fingers won't move on the keys. That hasn't ever happened to me before. What if the music never comes back, Bear? What if I'm through?"

I turned on the engine and revved it, wanting to get going, back on the road. Just so I wouldn't sit there and start howling. Bear took hold of the steering wheel and wouldn't let me yank it away.

"Man," says Bear, "this is bad. Now I get it why you didn't sign up for the Hamlyn gig. Okay, okay. I know you, Ted O'Sullivan. I know you when you get obsessed. You're a fucking monomaniac!"

"Hey, hold it. My grandmother did not bring me up to be a monomaniac. As she keeps telling me."

"Right, said Bear. "Mara deJong certainly is not an obsession. Anybody would hop off to Europe, if she suggested it." He's letting go of the steering wheel but keeps his hands ready to grab it again. "It's clear and obvious to me now that this whole fucking mess won't let you be easy in your skin till you know what makes Mara tick. Therefore I will have to go check out the earlobe freak Mara deJong. You just tell me what exactly you want to know, make a list, and I'll go find out. And after that, your fingers will be tickling the ivories again every single night in the glorious company of my bass. How's that sound, old buddy?"

"Good, good. That sounds good. What about Alicia?"

"Alicia, well...she'll be so glad I came back alive, she won't say a word about it. We'll play it like you got South just in time to pull me out of there in one piece. After that she can't say no to me giving you a hand, right?"

"First, she'll see right through the bull but then, yeah, I think she'll go along with it." Bear grinned from ear to ear. "Mara deJong," he said, "is as good as mapped with all her parts fitting in, in living colour. Now grab hold of that steering wheel and move it!"

So we finally took off again, and pretty soon Bear fell asleep. I let him stay that way for the longest stretch yet. I was fighting to stay awake myself every inch of the way.

Next time Bear woke up, he wanted me to tell him more about Mara's playing on that recording of hers.

"It was a Rachmaninoff Prelude. The one in B Flat Major. You know the piece?"

Bear shakes his head. "I only know the one you hear all the time. In C-Sharp Minor. So how was she on it?"

"First rate. Chops I'd give my kneecaps for, and a whole lot of storm, too. Not just notes. She was *saying* stuff."

"So what was wrong with it? Come on, Ted. What was it?"

"I don't know, man. I don't know. I sure hope I get to hear it again."

"We'll find a copy of the recording. I want to hear it for myself. And hey! She's got your piano in her house! Don't move it out till after I get her to play on it, you hear? Man—we're on easy street!"

Ha! I thought, but didn't say. We still weren't mentioning the elephant in the room.

Anyway, there you are. That was the first result of the detour we took down to Mississippi, and it was the best news since the whole blasted thing started up: Bear was finally going to check Mara out. The bigger change that came out of the trip, the elephant, well, that kicked in later. After we got back to Toronto.

On the fourth day, around dawn, we pulled up in front of Bear and Alicia's place. I stayed there just long enough to watch the two of them collide in the doorway. Then I split. They didn't need another body around just then, not even one sure to be asleep for the next week or so.

ALICIA

"Lena," I said, during one of our herbal-tea drinking talk fests, "do you think Ted is getting to the nub of it? Or is he improvising all around the theme without actually playing it?"

"I think he's playing it just the way it comes to him," said Lena. "One note at a time."

"Well, in that case, isn't he leaving out a lot? Like the weather, peeing, getting gas—you know: the telling-details-and-pithy-descriptions sort of thing?"

“He’s a musician, Alicia,” said Lena. “I think he’s actually doing very well.”

“Oh, yes, of course. That old stereotype: the grunting musician. Ted had an Irish grandfather, you know.”

“Oh, yes, of course,” says Lena. “A much better stereotype.”

I can’t remember exactly when we had that conversation, but I know by that time our laughing together didn’t surprise us any more.

“Anyway,” said Lena and cocked one eyebrow at me. A very eloquent eyebrow, saying: “Well, Alicia, you goaded Ted into telling the story, now you have to let him do it his way.”

TED

Now what?

I pulled the van around the corner and stopped. Here I was, back in Toronto, Bear delivered into loving arms, and now I had to figure out where I could go stretch out my body. I couldn’t go to grandma’s and scare her to death, looking like the one who started the revolution. Having to explain anything to anybody was out. Too damned tired. I just wanted to go to my piano. My piano that—hey!—actually had a bed beside it. The thought that piano and bed were both in Mara’s house rattled me enough so I came awake for about a minute, but then I figured Mara had to be asleep at that hour. I could quietly climb up and into the bed, sleep till I’d had enough for the first round, and then I’d quietly hoof it out of there again before Mara even knew I’d been *in* the place.

Then I remembered that I had no key to this place. Even though my piano was in there. Shit. No way was I going to knock on the door and stand for a hail of questions. Gravity was sucking on my bones, but my legs made it to the back fence where I had to haul myself over the top like a sack of squashy pumpkins. I remember crawling up the back stairs to the second floor and into the bed next to my piano, where I must have let out one helluva long breath and maybe even a moan or two, and then I was gone. Gone way under, and I still don’t know how long I slept in that one go.

The first time I open my eyes, there's Mara. Sitting on my bed. A white towel in one hand, a brush in the other. A delicate fragrance wafting. Mara's face is solemn and beautiful. She's looking at my piano but she's far away. Before she's even noticed I was awake, my eyelids give up the struggle and close again.

The next time my eyes open up, there she is again. Head bent, holding my left hand in both of hers. I don't move a muscle, don't even blink, so I can keep watching her. Then I notice that she's looking at my hand like it's a dead mouse. And all of a sudden there are hot arrows shooting up my arm. Just because I wanted to move my fingers. Holy shit, that scared me! That scared me all the way to hell and back. I closed my eyes so I could concentrate on keeping my fingers still as rocks till those arrows stopped rooting around.

And that's when I finally had no choice but to look at it straight: my hand was fucked. Two fingers on my left hand, to be exact. All the way back from down South, I tried real hard not to think about those two fingers, which looked more and more swollen, blue and green, and felt more and more like hot wires were strung through the middle of them. Bear did his best, too, not looking at them and not asking about them.

But this was it: no more ostrich time left on those two digits.

I opened my eyes again, and this time Mara saw it. She moved my hand very slowly, very gently, and laid it on my chest. I put my right hand over it, to protect it. Mara dove right in.

"Ted, what happened to your fingers? Did you fight? With your hands?"

Mara's voice does not say I'm a hero for risking my hands on behalf of life and death. No, her voice says she cannot believe that any piano player would be so idiotic.

I turn my head and the sight of my piano shoots lightning bolts of fear right into my heart. My left hand weighs a ton, lying on my chest, and my right hand wants to cry all over it.

I hear Mara getting up and leaving the room and then I'm gone again. Mercifully, as they say.

The third time I wake up, I'm hearing Mara's voice. A voice with layers, harmonics, internal vibrations. Plenty of listening you can do with that voice before you even get to the words.

"Broth," is what Mara's voice was saying. "Chicken broth. And a visit from the doctor."

My eyes shot open.

"No doctor, Mara. I do not let doctors mess with any part of me."

I tried to sit up. I had to make sure Mara got it. I was cradling my left hand, scared to move it or look at it. But at least there weren't any shooting pains; more like hot embers. My feet were trapped by the flannel sheet, tucked in at the bottom, so I yanked and pulled the sheet free, and that's how I discovered that under the flannel sheet I was naked all over. And colourful. Two purple brown bruises on my right thigh the size of grapefruits, one long white piece of adhesive tape all down my left shin and covering my right knee.

Meantime Mara's sitting on my bed, blowing into a bowl of soup. She sees me looking at her and lifts the soup spoon, ready for fencing.

"The doctor is on his way, Ted. Your fingers have to be examined.

"And then," she says, "your brother wants to come over. He's been calling every few hours."

"What? How the fuck did my brother get into this?"

Mara doesn't know.

As far as I remember, only Bear and Alicia would know how to find me...then it dawns on me:

"Mara, did this brother mention his name?"

"Yes," says Mara. "Well, his nickname, I suppose. He said to me, 'Tell Ted that Bear called and that he wants to come over.' And the last time he called he said, 'Tell Ted to do nothing till he hears from me. His brother.'"

"Oh, ah," I said. "Yes, that's fine."

"I suggested that he come tomorrow."

"Thank you," I tell Mara and then start wondering what Bear meant by "do nothing till you hear from me." Do not engage in those great and ancient rites which he was no doubt enjoying ever since getting home, but Tedboy has to wait for his approval? Did he think I was in bed for fun? Anybody could see that Mara was sitting on my bed because she had no choice. There's no room for a chair between the piano and the bed.

Anyway here is nurse Mara, holding a spoon under my nose, and my stomach laps up the first sip of the broth and yells for more. Mara spreads a towel over my chest and I drip and swallow till the bowl is empty. A few more parts of me come back to life.

Mara is bending forward, putting the bowl down. Her head so close to my chest, she must have heard my heart beat.

"Tell me, nurse Mara, who cleaned me up all over?"

Mara straightens up and away like that's an answer. Frowns at me.

"Ted, do listen, please: your brother agrees with me. He says it would be wise to consult a doctor. Your fingers really must be examined."

"Well, I'm not moving any part of me out of bed, and around here doctors do not make house calls—wait a minute. Did you say a doctor was on his way?"

"Yes. I spoke to the same doctor who looked after my shoulder. He was quite willing to come after his shift at the hospital."

"How is your shoulder?"

"Completely recovered, thank you. The doctor saw to it."

"Any more rocks and messages?"

"No more rocks. But mail. From the same people, I think. I threw it away."

Mara's voice is not concerned with rocks and messages. Her finger is not wagging at me for failing to protect her. She's not even asking where I've been. She's nursing me and she's doing it without one sour look! Now she's getting up, heading for the door.

"Come back," I tell her. "Something I want to explain."

Mara sits down again. On the far edge of the foot of the bed, this time. That's okay. As long as I can look at her instead of my left hand, as long as I can talk instead of thinking. Mara was probably expecting to hear about my trip and the savagery of the American South, but what she got instead was my tirade against doctors. How they had my grandmother all depressed for weeks! "At your age," they kept telling her, till they'd actually convinced the old tiger she was on her way out. Practically gone. When all she had was a fracture!

"I spent two weeks watching my grandmother getting turned into a limp rag. Then I finally had an idea that worked. I snuck a bottle of champagne up into her room, and we damn well toasted her health till that bottle was empty. We had one great old time, that night. Grandma cheered right up and in a couple of days she was hobbling around the hallways! Getting ready to come home.

"You can see why I've been telling you about this, Mara: if you let them, doctors will kill you!"

Mara is shaking her head.

"When I check into a hospital," she says, all serious, "I know that I am in the hands of scientific specialists and of experts. I know that I can leave all decisions to them and that I can safely pass the reins into their hands and everything will be taken care of." Mara sounds like she's been holding the reins to the universe, and she's longing to lay them down for a break.

"I don't know what hospitals you've been to," I tell her, "but around here, hospitals are run by the One Great Book: The Laws of Efficiency. They don't even like admitting patients. Patients are messy; they get in the way. And let me tell you about the hospitals in the Southern United States. Ha! The ones for black people are so crowded, they look like there's an earthquake around there every single day. And in the hospitals for whites, well, they just might decide you're not quite white enough and have a little accident. With you ending up as organ donor."

"I realize you've just had a difficult time, Ted..."

"No, Mara. Listen, you of all people should know what it's like to be the wrong race in the hands of murderous bigots. And all those hospitals in the South are being run by your 'specialists and experts.' Doctors! Who have sworn..."

The front doorbell rings.

"The doctor," says Mara and goes off.

I'm trying to decide whether to fake a coma or throw a fit when I hear Mara on the stairs, saying "No. No." As if she's heard what I'm thinking. And now here's the doctor in the doorway. Young Ivy League. Slick skin, blond all over, just out of the shower. Has come all this way so Mara will give him a gold star. From where I am lying with my two sausages, that intention of his does not constitute talent or ability, and when my fingers are involved, I like to be sure of some of that stuff. Or else you'd damn well better leave me and my fingers alone!

"Thank you, no, doctor," Mara is saying. "My shoulder really is fine. This is Ted O'Sullivan, Doctor Fulton."

Doctor Fulton frowns at me like I'm a bug in his soup. He's forgotten that he's here to look at my fingers. He is picking up my hand, probing, moving fingers. He starts up those horrible shooting pains again and I can't do anything but lay there, crunching my teeth.

"I'll have to make splints for those two," he says. "Lucky for you, Mara had the foresight to suggest that possibility."

"Use the splints on your dick, Fulty. I'd rather chew those fingers right off than have you practice playing superhero on them."

"Be reasonable, Ted," says Mara and puts her hand on my arm, which prevents me knocking out the doctor's teeth, and the next thing I know he's got a needle stuck in my thigh. And I'm falling into a swamp. A man's voice says, "You can't love somebody you don't know." Right away, Mrs. Whatsnikoff starts shrieking with laughter and pelting dumplings, and there's red gravy splattering everywhere. Mara waves and says: "No, no. A blank invites the imagination to play." Still in the dream, I knew I'd heard that before, but what did it mean?

I rise out of the swamp, out of the dream, and I'm staring at my fingers, taped to a splint, when Mara walks in the door. She sits down on the bed. She wipes my forehead with a washcloth, and says, "That's better."

Mara pours from a pitcher, holds the glass for me while I drink. She picks up the washcloth and wipes my neck and ears. A warm lump comes moving up into my throat and weighs down my tongue so I can't even tell her thank you. For doing all this for me. And bless you for doing it all without one sour word or sharp note.

Mara is shaking her head.

"I do wish you hadn't kicked Doctor Fulton," she says. "He hit his head on the corner of the piano and was most embarrassed."

Now it comes back to me:

"That ghoul! He stuck a needle into me! Without so much as a 'may I'! Shit, man, I'm not a child!"

Mara looks at me like "you could have fooled me" but there's a smile in it so I take a breath and I drag up something like a smile myself and tell her: "Mara, I really do thank you for everything you've done for me."

So there you are. Now you know what I meant by "a whole new tune".

All the way back from down South I was navigating around those two mangled fingers because they were scaring the hell out of me. Navigating around the simmering rage over the destruction of Ted O'Sullivan as we knew him. I could smell the insanity just around the corner.

Then Mara deJong, practically a stranger, who has a whole heap of trouble of her own, turns into the Lady of Mercy and Compassion, doing her best to rescue my fingers from permanent retirement and my piano from the ax, and yes, doing her best to save me from being forever incarcerated in a stage of rage!

So Big Gratitude. A whole mountain of gratitude!

And then I thought, yes, Ted O'Sullivan, and here's how you can start whittling away on that mountain-size debt of gratitude: you can take on Mara's gig and you can protect her!

That was it. That was the new tune I was singing: I was going to stick around Mara and protect her every which way, till the whole damned trial was over.

When Bear came over to cast his discerning eye on Mara and to deliver judgment, he sure as hell surprised both of us.

I was still sleeping or dozing most of the time. Then I finally got pulled up to fully awake by the sound of Mingus' "Goodbye Pork Pie Hat," and there was Bear, grinning at me from the foot of the bed, holding a bunch of red carnations, for heaven's sake.

"From Alicia," says Bear. "Me, I wanted to bring a bottle, but the woman put her foot on my wallet and said no bottle. Flowers. Pregnant women are fierce, man. They eat for two and fight for two and you can hardly get a word in. 'Serves you right,' she keeps telling me. 'Don't let me hear you bellyache about that little bitty cut on your head. Be happy you're alive.'"

Bear's way of telling me that all was well between him and Alicia.

"I can see you've got it real nice here, my man. Just looking at your nurse should have you up and dancing in no time."

"So you saw Mara. Did you talk?"

"Well," said Bear. "Mara said 'How do you do,' and then she said, 'You'll be pleased to know that in time your brother's fingers should recuperate fully.' And then she said she had to go, and split. I'm here babysitting."

"If you want to practice fatherhood, get yourself a doll. *What do you think*?"

Bear knows I meant Mara, but he isn't about to jump out any opinions. Which is not one bit like him, so I'm getting jittery. I pull myself up higher on the pillow, trying for one hundred percent alert.

"She's supposed to be 52, you tell me."

"That's what the numbers say."

Bear nods and rethinks his notions about middle age—just like I did.

"Listen," I tell Bear, "I've decided to take Mara's gig. I may even have to stay here in the house."

"Well, good, good," says Bear. "No, I mean it, Ted. Especially if you still think there's a connection between your playing and this Mara thing. Stick around her till you find out about the woman. She can't take over your life with me and Alicia vigilant and rooting for you. Not with ten bulls, she can't. What exactly is the gig again?"

"Protect her. Oh, and help her research Canadians."

"Including some in-depth research of one Canadian, Ted O'Sullivan?"

Bear and my grandmother have this thing in common: they both think Tedboy is clover honey and every female who catches a whiff turns into a hummingbird. Although right now I think Bear's just flapping his lips. He's used to getting a clear picture when he takes a good look at somebody, and Mara has messed him up.

"Maybe what you really want," says Bear, frowning at me, "is to be told it's okay for a woman to cut off her daughter's earlobes. So then you can go ahead and try and find the sweet, sweet woman inside that organized powerhouse. Maybe that's what you want."

"You are way off-course, Bear. Way off. You just get busy preparing those searchlights of yours for when Mara gets back, okay? Because I still want a report from you. Now change the record. And get me a Scotch from the kitchen. There's Bourbon, too, first cupboard on the left. Then come back here and sit and shut up."

All of which Bear did, so now we're listening to Mingus' "Devil Woman" and waiting for Mara to show. Bear and I never do much talking about the music we listen to. A few grunts here and there, a shake of the head or a nod, both meaning the same thing: you said it, brother. And sometimes one of us reaches over and puts the needle back a few bars to hear some phrase over again.

Bear's fingers play, when he's listening. Out of tempo, you think, till you catch his counter-rhythm, travelling with the piece and adding to it. Bear is a musician with first-rate ears, great chops, and a lot of ideas coming in fast. When we're playing together, sometimes I lay down the ground and he takes off and sometimes it's the other way around and either way the ground is solid so the ideas can take their time growing and that's why we're good together. Listening to this Mingus Sextet with Bear for maybe the fiftieth time, I forget all about how I haven't been able to play shit ever since I went to that courthouse and followed Mara home.

"You and I are going to get our asses in gear," I tell Bear. "As soon as my fingers are ready, we are going to play for 10 hours straight."

Bear nods his head, then pulls closer. "Listen, old buddy. The baby is due end of January so you'd better get those fingers of yours working real soon—we're going to be playing a lot of gigs. I put it to Greenberg that we're looking to be a house band any reasonable place and to get us the booking."

We drink on it and Bear taps me on the head, which makes my cheekbone ring in every sharp and flat on the keyboard at the same time.

"Some babysitter," I tell him. "Better start going easy on the violent emoting here, or you'll kill your kid before he's two."

"*She*. I intend to have me a daughter."

I could see a babysitting in the crook of Bear's arm, sucking on his callused finger, and it's a nice picture. I look up and see an even better one in the doorway: Mara.

Mara knocks on the open door and Bear stands up—would you believe it?—and offers her his seat on my bed.

"Perhaps...if Ted is able to come downstairs into the living room...?" Mara is pointedly looking around the bedroom we're in. My piano and three makes the room very cozy. Mara doesn't want cozy.

"No problem," says Bear. "I'll get him down there."

The jerk. Down there, Mara won't be anything but hostess, from across the room.

"Wait, please," says Mara. She's pulling something out of a box and she is presenting it to me. A man's housecoat.

"I think this shade of blue is a fine colour for you," she says, looking at the housecoat and then looking at my eyes like she's comparing swatches of rug. And now she's looking at Bear and again back at me.

"Excuse this personal question," she says. "But which parent do you have in common?"

I realize she still thinks Bear and I are brothers as in *relatives*, so I explain how "brother" can mean something besides blood relation.

Mara nods. "Ah, yes, I see," she says, and right there she builds up a couple of points with Bear and me, because she so clearly is no racist. On the other hand, it's also clear Mara doesn't give a hoot whether Bear and I are Siamese twins or a tandem bicycle, and that pisses me off. But then I see the reason for it: Mara already knows that whatever the relationship is here, Bear's word is going to have a lot of weight in it.

"I'll see you downstairs, then," says Mara, and is gone.

Bear steps closer and practically yanks me out of bed.

"Come on. Get moving. I want a good long look at this woman. She's got me guessing here. Man, I can't even tell if she's sizzling hot under all that snow or if the snow is covering ice!"

"Hey, easy, easy! Let me get these sausages through the sleeve."

I'm on my feet but my legs are acting drunk. Which they never do when I really *am* drunk, and for sure never after one small Scotch. I make it down the stairs okay and into the living room, but then I have to stretch out on the couch and put my head on a pillow.

Now I have a view of Bear and Mara like they're onstage and I'm audience. Bear is sitting in the big armchair, Mara on the smaller chair. They are facing each other. Mara's holding still, giving Bear a chance to look her over. Chitchat definitely not relevant.

All of a sudden, Bear gets up and goes into the kitchen. Not taking my glass with him.

"Hey!"

I called because I want to see his face but Bear keeps going. Mara is looking at her hands. Maybe she already knows what Bear's verdict about her will be? Me, I know nothing.

Bear comes back. He sits down, puts one leg over the arm of his chair.

"So," he says, facing Mara. "You're a piano player."

Mara turns her head and throws me a look, accusing me. Like I've hung her biggest secret out on the line and lit it up with floodlights for all to see.

"What the hell is going on with you?" I struggle upright to face her. "You still want to tell me you being a pianist 'just didn't come up'? That look you just gave me could wilt a jack pine!"

Mara is raising one hand—slow, heavy, like she's stopping the world in its tracks.

"No, Ted, please. I made a mistake," she says. "I should have been more precise. If you'll excuse me..."

Mara gets up and heads out into the hall. Closing the door behind her.

There's a twanging in the room, like the snapped string of a bass guitar whizzing around, could even spring for your eyes, so watch out. I look at Bear and he has no idea either what just happened here. I know this much: whatever it was, it's bad. And I can't jump up off this couch to do anything about it. Bear, however, is not lying down and he doesn't duck for any loose string. Bear sticks his head out the door and hollers.

"Madame Mara," he hollers up the stairs. Mara's voice comes back.

"Please, help yourself." Nothing in her voice but strictly polite. Bear can't believe the voice.

"Is that the same woman who just shot out of here? Like we offered her a recorded duet for bat and bullfrog? Like we offered her a pet scorpion? Is that the same woman..." Bear stops himself riffing and hollers up the stairs again.

"How about a drink for you?"

"Thank you. I'll have some mineral water, please."

Bear disappears into the kitchen, muttering. I let my head sink back down to the couch. I feel like an old-time weatherman, reading the winds, taking clues from sounds and atmospheric conditions. Trouble is, doing it from anywhere around Mara, lightning can strike you out of the clearest sky. Anytime.

Mara comes down the stairs and into the room. No sign of storm in her face, not even a breeze ruffling any part of her. But she's carrying a handbag.

"What. Are you going out again?"

"Yes, Ted. Later," she says. "I have an appointment." The same polite voice. Did she or didn't she just about scald and maim me, a few minutes ago? Because...why? Because I told Bear she's a pianist?

Mara puts the bag down and accepts a glass of mineral water from Bear. She thanks him and sits down. Bear is standing in front of the fireplace and he is watching her like she's a newly hatched specimen, never before seen on our planet.

"Mara," I have to ask her straight out. "Was that supposed to be a secret, your being a pianist?"

First we get Mara's silence, at least eight beats long. Then:

"I would prefer...that all revelation...be left to me."

"What," says Bear, "have we here? You didn't make any revelation at all. Ted found out in Germany that you're a pianist. So okay, you don't want to be talking about that right now, but reveal unto us this much: do you *think* of yourself as a pianist? A musician?"

"I think of myself," says Mara, "as a scientist." A slow smile. Mysterious, but promising further revelations. The smile of a Nobel Laureate.

"Hm," says Bear.

"Tell me something, Mara," Bear says. "Did you destroy your own recording of the Rachmaninoff Prelude?"

Mara goes still inside, consulting herself. Decides to answer:

"It was not a performance by which I choose to be judged and remembered."

"Did you make other recordings?"

"Nothing which has been allowed to survive."

Allowed by whom? Mara's hand? Nazis? Before either of us can tackle Mara on that one we hear the front door opening and somebody coming into the house. Bear and Mara turn and look toward the hall. I'm surprised there's still a world out there to come in from.

"That must be Lena, finally," says Mara and opens the living room door. Lena is dragging a huge canvas bag along the hall. She stops at the doorway and looks surprised as hell by the assembly. And before anybody drops a word, Mara picks up her little bag and says she ought to go now, waves, and is gone. The house door closing behind her makes a sound like a plug being pulled out of a bathtub. What's draining out is every last drop of awake I have left in me. I crawl up the stairs, leaving Bear and Lena behind, and it takes me another 24 hours before I'm on my feet again. Meantime, the couple of times I do surface, there are sandwiches and pots of herbal tea beside my bed. But no Mara.

MARA

Dear Theodore,

Ted O'Sullivan has returned from a short trip to America with two fingers (the middle finger and the ring finger of his left hand) severely damaged. Impossible to tell as yet whether they will regain the strength and agility necessary for playing piano. I observe closely for signs of anguish and desperation. So far he is keeping both at bay.

Do you recall those nightmares I had as a child, in which the piano (always the gleaming old grand piano we had in our childhood home in Leningrad) was chasing after me, like a dragon, with enormous white teeth in its vast open maw, seeking to snap shut over my neck so that my head would roll among the strings, with a horribly dissonant screech? And each time, the day after one of my recounted nightmares, I would be allowed to play outside with my classmates for two hours after school?

The dragon piano: my foe and my protector.

You, dear brother, better than anyone, know our father's tales, told and re-told, assuring us that there was only one saviour who saw him through revolutions, imprisonment and exile and every other danger and hurdle on his path. That saviour was his own life's work. And he was favoured: despite the dire vicissitudes of his life, he was never deprived of his work for very long.

He taught us well, our father. I had no life other than the piano until I married (two weeks without practicing) and bore a child (five days of restless inactivity). Then back to the single-minded dedication, to the dragon, to his ever-present voice: your work comes first, remember that, waking and sleeping!

The first sight of Ted O'Sullivan's two swollen immobilized fingers catapulted me in an instant backwards into the cave of my despair, pierced by the howling of Furies. They hurled their curses and screamed with demented laughter. "Your childhood sacrificed, every hour of your life spent on preparing for the world stage, and now? Arthritis! Stiff swollen joints refusing to bend for Chopin, let alone Rachmaninoff or Liszt. What now? What now?" they screamed. Intent on driving me into madness.

While I was playing and practicing, all was right with the world, for I was doing what was long ordained. Even in the midst of war, in Germany, while everybody crouched in fear of bombs, of Nazis, of hunger, of informants, I was tranquil, immune, for my entire self was harnessed to my work. But then, "Arthritis!" the Furies screamed. "Now look around and see and fear as other mortals do, and every fearful thought, long banished and subdued, will now spring forth ferociously and cling to you and as you spin and gasp, will multiply."

There was, of course, a brief period dimly remembered—a week? a month? a day?—when I was lulled into a shimmering world of deception. When Liberty seemed to be my newfound friend and I was free to dispense hours at a time for simple pleasures never tasted. Going for a walk, attending a party, reading into the morning hours, all without once hearing that dragon's voice: "You should be practicing, your work comes first, remember that, waking and sleeping. You should be practicing!"

But all too soon I saw that liberty was as likely to drive me mad as were those Furies, mocking the failure of my life. I saw that with my Self no longer dedicated, my discipline dissolved, my daily victories over keys and fingers withdrawn, I was spinning in my life, without direction, without anchor, without sails.

And now the Furies' laughter was truly terrifying and I was fearful for my sanity. I cannot tell you, never could, how long I dwelled in that cave of no hope, where all my dreams, like mutilated snakes, writhed about my feet until they died. But one day…there came a Saviour.

There is no one else, not then, not now, to whom I can confide the identity of that Saviour. It was the SS. Yes. The very worst of the Nazi persecutors, perpetrators, devils, it was said, incarnate. Yes. They were my Saviours. Like this: Suddenly informed that I was to present myself for interrogation by the SS, I had to, life or death, harness my energies, recall discipline, dedicate myself to the cause of survival. And so I did. And the Furies retreated.

And furthermore, having first become the saviours of my sanity, the same SS was to serve me in the role of midwife! Assisting me at the birth of my new life's purpose! Not that either of the two SS officers in uniform who sat behind the massive desk intending to ask me dangerous questions were in actual fact anything but two men promoted beyond their skills and susceptible to manipulation.

For the first interrogation, my goal was simple: the appearance of total and complete confidence. A Woman of the World. The very antithesis of "victim." I achieved my goal perfectly though, at the time, I had to rely on instinct and intuition. By the second

interrogation, four months later, I had reached a degree of knowledge based on experiments, so that the victorious outcome was precisely attained. The suspended food-ration cards were restored to us and I was free to live on, free to undertake my true Life's Work. More on this anon.

And I must tell you of one very practical result of being afflicted by arthritis. Teaching, which was previously not permissible as it was a certain sign of failure for a concert pianist such as I, yes, teaching was now permitted. Not for money, of course. Money was worthless. But for food. So that when the SS cut off our food rations, the payment for piano lessons which I gave to a farmer's fat son—the jars of real butter, the Liverwurst, the bread and cabbages—kept starvation from our door.

And now I must return to my role as nurse and overseer, ensuring that Ted's fingers at the least show hopeful signs of recovering their former state. For if Ted should fall into the cave of despair, he would be of no help to me at all in my present endeavour.

As always, your beloved sister,
Mara

TED

There came a day when I was standing peacefully pissing, wide awake and going to stay that way. Maybe not all the snap and sizzle I was going to need for the gig, but it would have to do.

The gig was whittling. Chipping away at that mountain of gratitude owing to Mara, my Angel of Mercy and Many Kindnesses. So I'd better locate the woman and start.

First I had to pull on my jeans with one hand. And with a minimum of vocalizing, because I wanted to surprise Mara by appearing downstairs, ready to boogie. Downstairs: no sound or sight of Mara.

I start rooting around in the kitchen, looking for coffee. I feel a shift in the air and when I turn around, there she is in the doorway. Leaning against the door frame, looking at me like I'm a horse and she's checking me out so she can decide, race him or shoot him? I give her a nudge towards my own preference.

"Hello, Mara. I think I'm about to rejoin the human race."

"Yes, you almost look it," says Mara. "Perhaps we can begin working together tomorrow, if you are feeling well enough?"

"Why not today? Right after I've had a coffee." I've shoved my left thumb into my jeans to keep the sausage fingers from bumping into every thing within 10 feet, and I'm pouring myself a cup of something so black it looks like oil but turns out to be tea, and I'm just putting the teapot down when I have to yank up both my hands and clap them over my ears to shut out the screeching.

"Well, well, well, will you look at this! Isn't this cozy! Louise, she says to me. You'll be better off at home, she says to me. You'll be better off with your family and friends, Louise. Sure, I will. And you'll be better off without little old Louise bothering you in your cozy little nest!"

It's the Tic! Standing in the doorway of Mara's kitchen, spewing like a snake on uppers.

"What the fuck are you doing here?"

"Why don't I ask you the same question, Teddy darling?"

"Excuse me," says Mara like she's interrupting a duet, which is not the case and I want that clear.

"I'm telling you for the last time, Tic, get away from me and stay away!"

"Louise," says Mara. "I was under the impression that you were pleased to go home."

"You were under that impression, were you? Because you were so hot on having lover boy all to yourself. You think bus tickets can't be sold, if somebody decides they don't want to go back where they came from? Because it took them for bloody ever to get themselves out of there in the first place?"

"But you do have family there, Louise, and friends..."

The Tic was definitely on some kind of upper, speeding up what she calls her noggin.

"Oh, sure I do. My mom and pop, the both of them boozed up or out cold. My sister who's got a husband she hates and four kids she hates. And my big brother who thinks he's got to be my almighty father and give me a beating any Saturday night he can catch me out of the house. My bloody relatives. But yeah, I have a friend. A real good friend. A nurse. The only friend never charged little old Louise for all those red and green and orange and yellow pills. But don't you worry. I'm okay without her. I'm learning the ropes around here. You liked that little round friend I brought you, didn't you, Teddy darling? Didn't hurt a bit, taking little old Louise home that night, did it? Hey, let go!"

I've got the Tic by one elbow, turning her around. Mara puts a hand on my arm and says to wait.

"I want to assure Louise," she says, "that the association between us, I mean Ted and myself, is purely a business arrangement."

"That's got fuck-all to do with her!"

"Oh, sure." The Tic sneering is a sight to scare anybody but Mara. "Business arrangement. Oh, sure. Moving his piano in here, and all his stuff, so you can have business meetings any time day or night, right?"

Mara is sighing.

"Nobody here you need to explain anything to," I tell Mara. "She's gone, never to return."

This time Mara lets me walk Louise out into the hall, to the front door, the Tic spewing all the way.

"Don't be so sure! Don't be so sure I'm never coming back. Maybe I'll even bring along my brother sometime when he's in town. He's a little old truck driver, weighs 250 pounds, and he thinks all mothers are angels, that's right, and if he gets to hear what *this* little old mother..."

I've got her out the door and the door closed behind her. Mara is standing in the hall, and by the frown on her she has decided that Louise might just be a serious nuisance.

"Her home town evidently was not the right destination," says Mara. "I shall have to look for another solution. Now," Mara turns and enters the living room and I get a flash that the Tic is altogether gone out of Mara's mind. For the moment.

"Now, Ted," says Mara, facing me. "I urge you to go to your family doctor so that he can look at your fingers."

"Not a bad idea. I'll do that. I'll pop over there one day soon."

Officially, old doctor Toller has not seen patients for about six years, but you can call him any time and he'll say "Come on over." I'd planned to go see him as soon as I had the guts.

"You have an appointment with Dr. Toller today at two o'clock," says Mara. "I'll be busy myself this afternoon, so it's an opportune time for you to go."

Still caring for my fingers, the angel, and also still arranging my life and times. I tell you it's not easy being indebted to a woman who tries to run your life. (And she'd be good at it, too—except in my case, it doesn't work. I mean, if anybody's going to run my life, it's going to be me—as soon as I figure out how. But for sure ain't nobody else even a *candidate* for that gig. Something I intended to make clear to Mara right after I decided whether to thank the woman or to holler at her.) Finally, I do get something out:

"Wait a minute, Mara. How did you know who my doctor is? Where did you get his number?" I asked her, and then remembered: of course. The woman's got my little black book. Has had it ever since she moved all my stuff under her roof.

"What else did you arrange for me today, Mara? I mean, a doctor's visit isn't going to take up my whole afternoon."

Mara has no trouble catching sarcasm, but she's not throwing it back.

"You might like to visit your friends Bear and his wife," she says, perfectly serious. "Perhaps they can make helpful suggestions for our work together? And please take the Bourbon with you. Well, until tomorrow, then," says Mara, and splits.

I'm standing in the doorway, all my muscles revved up for action, watching Mara's taxi drive off, and decide to start doing good on Mara right then and there, without her. And first things first, high time I found out what exactly Mara was going to be dealing with in her trial.

The Law Library was walking distance. My legs wobbled and complained all the way, but they got me there all right and in through the door, and then the library attacked me with a whole series of sneezes till my head was snapping. But they don't let you take books out of the place, so I had no choice but to smuggle the one I needed out under my shirt.

I sat down on the steps outside, in warm sunlight, with that dark and musty-smelling volume on my knees, and tried to figure out how to look up what exactly the courts could do to Mara. Ten years' incarceration? A fine? $100 per earlobe? The only thing I came up with for the crime itself was "Mutilation," so I looked that up.

"Mutilation of art…paintings…architecture…monuments…tattoos… self-mutilation." No earlobes. Nothing under "defacement of," either. I guess corpses don't get defaced, but what do they call it? They sure as hell don't just say "the cutting off of earlobes"! That isn't law lingo at all. I'd have to get the information elsewhere.

I wobbled back to Mara's place.

It's not anywhere near two o'clock but I'm off to see my old doc. Now that I've stopped making like an ostrich about my fingers, I want a verdict immediately. I'm driving right-handed, which is all right if you keep your mind on it. But my mind starts rooting into all the places I kept out of till now. What if…? What if…?

Dr. Toller's house isn't far, just a bit north on Ossington. His office is the size of a toilet and it's wallpapered in photographs. I can never stop myself peeping at the one of me, little Ted O'Sullivan, seven years old. Sure enough, there I still am: skinny kid, looking like somebody left him at the zoo and forgot to pick him up. I hate that picture, but I can never tell old Doc to take it down. He'd start clucking in his throat about my mother dying so young, and I hate that clucking worse than I hate the picture.

Old Toller's got me perched on a stool I remember except it's not as high as it used to be, and he's already taken the splints off my fingers as if he can tell I'm gonna burst if we have to chitchat. To get a good look, he has to bend close enough to lick them, but it's mostly his own fingers doing the work here, probing and reading the joints like some bony Braille, and all the time humming. This time it's "She'll Be Coming 'Round The Mountain," with pauses where there aren't any, but never a note out of tune.

When he finally straightens up he says, "No more splints." Nodding and looking me in the eye to make sure I get what he's saying. "No splints. Start exercising those fingers every day. But gently!" And raps me in the head with his knuckles to make it sink in. "Your fingers," says old Toller, "will be just fine. As good as ever."

He almost hugs me then, the old doc. We nod and smile at each other all the way to the door.

I climb into the van and suddenly I'm hearing a jubilation choir in my head. Full choir and organ and me jubilating over the top of it all: Your fingers will be fi-fi-fine. Hallelujah. Your fingers will be good as ever. Hallelujah. I opened the windows and let our voices jubilate all over the city.

That Hallelujah chorus goes on for a while, then I have to make a right turn with my right hand and that starts me thinking again: I sure do owe Mara one great heap of gratitude. Who knows what the verdict would have been if she hadn't called that Doctor Fulty. So any hoop she wants to hold up, I'll jump through it. That's a promise.

Back at Mara's, first thing I want is go up to my piano and start in on those exercises, but gently. Only something pulls me up, all the way up to Lena's apartment. I knock on the door.

"Come in."

Lena is sitting at her kitchen table, doodling on a large sheet of paper. When she looks up, her clear brown eyes are sad. Michelle comes popping into my head and I push her out again, and then try to slow down to doodle tempo myself. I sit down across from Lena and take a peek.

Lena pushes over the paper and it isn't a doodle at all. It's a drawing. Of a calla lily: tall, cool and luminous, and just might be poisonous.

Lena puts the drawing aside like she doesn't want comments and asks about my fingers. I'm glad. I really wanted to tell somebody. We're both looking at my fingers, lying naked on the table.

"My doctor's verdict," I say: "'Your fingers will be just fine. Good as ever.'"

Lena grins from ear to ear and says: "Phew!" The way she smiles, I swear she knows that it was a life-or-death verdict. I want to pull her up and swing her around the room, yodelling and trumpeting, but simmer down, Ted. You'll scare the woman to death.

So I take a deep breath and stick my two fingers into the front of my shirt, and ask Lena about good places to take Mara for researching Canadians. I can see Lena already knows about this "researching Canadians" business, and she's not looking at me like I'm a demented prairie dog, so maybe the whole thing isn't that crazy?

"I thought watching television might be helpful," she says. "I mentioned it to Mara and she made some calls and had a television set rented and delivered, all within the hour. Two hours later she sent it back."

"Couldn't find any Canadians on TV?"

"That wasn't the problem, actually. I was supposed to give a kind of running commentary for whatever we were watching, to tell Mara what was reality and what was fantasy..." Lena looks at me round-eyed, makes a funny balloon face and slowly lets the air out of her cheeks again.

"I couldn't find anything real. Not even in the news programs or the documentaries." Shaking her head. "Have you ever watched any of those?"

I put on my best newsreader voice:

"The U.S. Defense Department today conceded that napalm bombs have indeed been supplied to South Vietnam and dropped from aircraft with U.S. instructors on board, but the instructors at all times urge their South Vietnamese student pilots to use extreme care when bombing villages."

Lena groans. "Exactly. Try to do commentary for that! Then I thought, well, Mara should at least know what it is Canadians *watch* on television. For hours and hours every week."

"Smart. Very smart!"

"Sure, but what? "The Price is Right?" The Beatles on Ed Sullivan? "I Love Lucy"? That's one of the most popular shows in this country, you know. Lucy hoodwinking and tricking her husband in every show and he treating his wife like a bimbo. We ended up watching one of those detective shows, and then a documentary about Primates and Aggression. Same theme, but in the detective show, the primates were human."

Lena is grinning at me again. When she does that, you can't help grinning back.

"So that was it. After two one-hour shows and a few minutes on three or four others, Mara sent the television set back. She told me:

"Anybody who qualifies as a juror would not choose to subject himself to such drivel as the screen spews out."

That scared me. I mean, Mara may be sophisticated all over three continents, but sometimes she sounds newly hatched. And that, for a woman in her position, is dangerous.

I hear Lena offering food and then I hear somebody moving around downstairs. Has to be Mara.

"Thanks, Lena. Catch you later."

Now picture this.

I bounced my gratitude all the way down the stairs and into the living room. There was a woman standing in the middle of the room who turned out to be Mara—looking like she dipped her head into frosty dew and her face got pinked over by a rising sun.

"Mara!" I said.

"It's a wig," said Mara.

But that wasn't it. That wasn't the reason it took me a second look to recognize her. I mean, how can a woman so unique turn herself into somebody else? And don't tell me it's not possible, because I saw it. I juggled the hair and the colours and clothes and everything I could think of, to get back the Mara sitting on my bed, feeding me chicken broth, but I could not get her back. The only thing unchanged was Mara's voice.

By now we're both sitting down, looking at each other.

"Absolutely nobody would recognize you," I have to tell Mara. "Your disguise is first-rate."

"Oh, it's more than mere disguise," says Mara. "I have an appointment, and I wish not to be misunderstood. Ted," she says. "I know you have already formed an image of me, but try to envision meeting me for the first time as I look now. What would be your impression? Please try to imagine."

I tried. And what I came up with was, "Beautiful, of course, very chic and *au courant*, but dignified, too, and...well, that doesn't sound so different from your usual look, but..."

"Yes? Go ahead."

"Well... hard to put a finger on it. There's a...softness? Like you're wafting veils..." Mara's beaming away, thrilled to bits. Not looking one bit worried. And that, let me tell you, that worries me. Maybe I should remind her that jurors are not going to let her draw veils over the blood.

"Listen, Mara," I tell her. "Here's what I am going to do. Whenever we're out, I'm going to point out to you who-all could be accepted as a juror. You, my dear Mara, are going to be mighty surprised."

"Tomorrow," says Mara. "Let's discuss it tomorrow, please. It's too late now; I have an appointment." I'm about to squawk real loud, but then I remember my useful idea for another do-thee-good.

"Okay, boss. Go ahead. But first just tell me your lawyer's name and number. I want to have a talk with him."

Mara stands up. Now she's looking at me like I'm still a horse and I've just opened my mouth to sing "La Traviata." Off-key.

"Please, Ted. That is not amusing. I have to ask you most seriously not to speak to my lawyer. Not at all."

Mara sits down again and for a minute I think she's actually going to open her mouth and tell me something. I pop myself on the couch across from her, all ears. Mara is thinking, looking at her folded hands, shaking her head.

"Once, and only once," says Mara, "I made the mistake of trying to explain myself prematurely. To Tanya Volnikoff, as it happens."

It takes me a minute, then I remember this is Mrs. Whatsnikoff she's talking about. The woman who wants to kill Mara.

Mara is shaking her head again.

"I made some wrong assumptions, you see. I must have been swayed by the desire to be understood. Perhaps even by a wish for validation. But it was a mistake. My work was incomplete and therefore any explanation was premature. There was no understanding."

Mara is still looking at her hands, folded in her lap—a pose I've seen often enough to draw for you, if I could draw. Then Mara looks up and now she's smiling.

"Please, Ted," she says. "It would be most helpful if you made a list of the places for us to visit in order to do our research. And do let Bear help you with it; perhaps even his wife. The more ideas the better our choices will be."

Mara was standing up again.

"Please give Bear greetings from me and don't forget to take the bottle of Bourbon."

Dismissed. Oh, lord of gratitude, did I really promise to jump through hoops without even a snarl? Lest I say something altogether nasty to my

Angel of Mercy, I grab the bottle of Bourbon out of the kitchen cupboard and split.

So now here we are, Alicia and Bear and me, sitting around the kitchen table like we used to, feeling good. Alicia's made a pot of hot spiced tea and poured me a cup, and I'm to drink up every drop of it. "For your fingers." Just looking at Bear and Alicia is good medicine. There's a shine in her eyes and a glow on her skin, and all the moves are smooth and all the sounds in the room are music. Bear and Alicia at home where they live, out of sight of anybody putting labels on them, is a sight to make you get easy way deep in your bones.

Bear and I have toasted my fingers more than once, feeling mellow, and I could have just sat there all night long, lapping up the feeling-good-together, but then Bear gets up and leaves the kitchen to put on another record, and I grab the chance to ask Alicia a question, and then everything goes off-key.

"What," I asked Alicia, "did Bear tell you about Mara?"

"Nothing," says Alicia, eyebrows moving down. "It's like this, Ted: you do whatever you have to do around this Mara woman. I can see it's important to you, you know? But don't, please do *not*, bring it into my home. Any of it."

Bear is back, giving me the sign: shut up about Mara.

"And," says Alicia, "I want you to keep that Tic away from here. You can't do anything for somebody like that. She's a burning house, that one. Even if you run in, what's there to be saved or salvaged?"

Alicia sounding so cold it could freeze your spine.

"She was here again yesterday," says Bear. "Looking for you. You've got to shake that bitch, man. She's trouble. For one thing, she's so hooked on being high, she'll be walking the streets soon, getting bread for the buzz. If she isn't out there already."

"Tell me something new, okay? How about you giving me an equally penetrating character analysis of Mara?"

"No," says Alicia. "I don't want to hear any talking about that one in my house. You think I want to have nightmares? You think I want acid attacking my baby? I don't even want any *thinking* about that one in this house."

Alicia puts both her hands on her belly, just as if she's got one, and leaves the kitchen.

"Oh Lordy," says Bear, in a way that lets me know I heard all that right.

"It comes and goes," says Bear. "Alicia says for her being pregnant is like being pre-period all the time. Seven more months, man! Lordy, Lordy."

Then the door bell rings. We hear Alicia go down the hall, open the door, voice all happy, inviting somebody to come in. Then a second woman's voice and it's Lena the neighbour.

"Hey, I didn't even know those two have met up."

"Oh, fuck, yes," says Bear. "Just you hope the two of them don't start laughing about you." Alicia and Lena come into the kitchen.

"So you two know each other?" I want to take this one from the top.

"We do," says Alicia. "Lena and I got together a couple of times when you guys were gone down South. I would have gone nuts without talking to her." Alicia reaches over and squeezes Lena's hand. "In fact, if not for Lena I would have torn Bear from limb to limb for putting me through that trip. But like she said: you guys are the ones messed up the world, so you're the ones who should at least try and clean it up, right?"

Lena and Alicia think this is hilarious. They're laughing so hard they have to bend over and every time they look at each other, they start up again. Bear is grumbling, which they also find funny as hell.

"Come on, Ted," says Alicia, finally calming down some. "Let's see you come up with a smile. I promised Lena that you're not hang dog/hound dog on the trail all the time."

Alicia doesn't look any different, but her teasing sure is growing thorns.

"Before I forget," she says to Bear, "I want to go with Lena next time she takes off for the country. To get farm fresh eggs and real maple syrup—some friends of hers have a farm. Maybe we can borrow the van, Ted?"

"No problem."

"Oh, and herbs! We'll get herbs, too. Lena knows about herbs!"

"Not spices, though."

Lena and Alicia are laughing again. How many inside jokes can they have collected up in just a couple of weeks?

"Lena's a health nut," says Bear.

Lena doesn't seem to mind being popped into that bag. In fact, she doesn't give a flying fig about fitting into any bag at all. I like that, and I like the way she laughs.

Alicia gets up. She wants to go to the store for sardines. No, she doesn't want Bear to go for her, because he never brings her back the right sardines.

"What's a wrong sardine?" says Bear.

"Oh, my Lord," huffs Alicia, like Bear's been failing to notice some sardines wear little tiny swastikas around their necks. Or maybe tiny sheets and hoods like the KKK.

Alicia and Lena split. Bear and I decide against discussing sardines. Bear rolls us one with his own homegrown—growing in a basement cupboard with its own light, which Bear keeps forgetting to turn on or off so the poor weed looks like a beanstalk with hiccups—and meantime he asks me when I'm starting in on the gig with Mara. Researching Canadians.

"We're starting right now, you and I. We're going to make a list of all the places I can take Mara for researching possible jurors."

Bear hands over the joint for me to light up and gets himself a pad and a pen.

"I'm already on the case," he says. Flourishing the pen while he thinks up a heading: "Ted and Mara hit the town." Sub-heading: "Research in Canadiana." A couple of minutes later, we're on a roll.

Clubs.

Restaurants.

A laundromat.

A gym.

The race track.

Music stores.

Then we talk a bit about the new electric keyboard from Japan Bear saw at Long and McQuade's, and then Lena and Alicia are back. Bear doesn't get the pad out of sight fast enough, so Alicia leans over Bear's shoulder to take a look. And starts laughing.

"Music stores!" she says. "Why not lingerie stores?"

"Okay," says Bear. "We do need some variety on this list."

"Not to mention in your lives," says Alicia and points us into the living room. Bear and I move ourselves in there and settle in our usual chairs by the record player.

"See how unpredictable?" says Bear. "And this is Alicia! Zinging on and off like a bass string on a ukulele. Hey, remember the time Hank forgot to cut off the loose end on his string and it kept whipping at that hairpiece of his till it finally hooked it off right in the middle of a solo and looked like a squirrel dancing on a hot plate, and then..."

"Whoa, Bear. You think I have time to listen to old stories we all heard about a hundred times? Next you'll be telling about the time Al pissed in Butterfinger's alto."

"Tenor. He pissed in his tenor sax. Just about filled it up, he kept boasting, remember? Till..."

"You know something? I'm not surprised Alicia goes zingy around you. I'm surprised she comes back, after a sardine trip. Me, I'd buy one goodly supply of the little suckers and head out, never to return to have to listen to old stories while I'm sitting here, dancing on a hot plate myself but just don't want to be so rude as to send up a smell of burning flesh and singeing tail."

"Did you say 'singeing tail'? Why aren't you keeping it between your legs, like I would, around anybody given to taking knives to human body parts?"

"Shit, this is worse than getting no help at all. That's it. I'm gone."

I'm up on my feet, ready to split, when Lena sticks her head in the door and says: "Ted, do you think it's okay to get back to the house this early?"

"What are you talking about? Get in here, woman. What are you saying?"

"Well, Mara obviously wanted the house to herself, sending us both away for the evening..."

I'm out the door and in my van so fast, nobody even got to glimpse my idiot face. Jesus, I hate feeling stupid! But here I was, strings pulling my legs, my arms, my head and various other parts, and I couldn't even tell you when they got attached. Shit, I hate it! I hate it worse than anything.

I sit in the van for at least five minutes, talking to myself. Reminding myself that I had debts to pay off. That I have a promise to keep. And that I have to get answers to some questions I've been chewing on. Therefore, I have to stay strung. Strung out, as they say. But not, I swear to myself, *every* part of me. There have to be some parts, godammit, that nobody can move except me.

I drive back to Mara's house and jump in the front door. Nobody in the living room. Mara's silvery wig sitting right in the middle of the dining room table. Nobody in the kitchen. I clump up the stairs to Mara's bedroom door. No sounds. The door is not locked. I open it just wide enough to see the bed. Mara is fast asleep. Alone.

Once again I had raced over here full speed and right into a wall. With graffiti on it: "You will never know!"

I shut Mara's door and head up to my piano in the back room. There has to be some parts I can move on my own, and my fingers better be some of those.

"Let's get started," I tell the sweet old thing. "We'll just be exercising the fingers."

LENA

I caught up with Ted just as he was getting into his van and tried one more time to stop him rushing back to Mara's, but Ted refused to believe that Mara actually arranged for both of us to be out of the house that evening. So I went back inside and told Alicia: "You know what? I don't think Ted *wants* to see Mara any too clearly." Alicia grumbled something, pointed me to the couch, and went into the kitchen.

I don't know whether Ted described Alicia and Bear's place at all. The rich colours: cornflower blue and poppy red under amber light, the way it satisfies the eye, and something deeper, too. Having seen the three of them here—Bear, Alicia and Ted—I understood why Alicia wanted Mara utterly banished from this home. I also knew that it wasn't possible.

Meanwhile, Bear was listening to music on earphones and Alicia was making more spiced tea with honey. I sat back and enjoyed the fragrance of tea and marijuana and thought how smart Bear was, to refuse outright any participation in our "telling of the tale." It was not his idea of fun, he said, yakking about every little thing touching on this Mara scene. Interesting: the rest of us seem to be bound by some unspoken code to be honest. To tell the truth. (Except Mara, of course. She's not telling us anything.)

Alicia brought in the teapot and poured and threw me a look I recognized.

"'Okay, talk,'" she said. "'And no bullshit.'" I even knew what she wanted me to talk about, all her vetoes notwithstanding.

"Well, all right, Alicia, truth to tell, I was bloody fascinated by Mara from the beginning. From the day we met, when I picked her up at the airport. A lot of other reactions, too, but definitely intrigued. (I love a mystery. It's where surprises come from.)

"And yes, Alicia, Ted was interesting, too. But pretty soon observing Mara and Ted both was more than I could handle. I got swamped. So I dumped Ted. Metaphorically speaking."

Alicia started laughing again. Maybe we had a contact high? I remember thinking: yes, laughter is balm for whatever ails you. Alicia loves to laugh. And when Ted and Bear were throwing each other startled looks and most women would have toned it down, Alicia kept right on hootin' and cacklin', as she calls it.

"Seriously," I said. "I think Ted's obsession is demonic. As in 'ridden by a demon.' And the demon riding him is not Mara, you know—it's obsession itself. Trust me, Alicia, I know that one well, that…that…"

"Go, Lena, go," yelled Alicia, and I said: "Yes, I know him well, that *fucker*." And Alicia whooped and grabbed my arms and danced me around the room.

"Oh, Wise One," says Alicia, still grinning. "Knowing that fucker well, you really must do your best to help Ted out of all demon clutches, if you can. I know I can't. Even Bear isn't getting anywhere so far."

"Yes," I said, "it's hard to watch Ted racing out of here, hound dog on the trail, bound to rant and rail, hound dog bound to fail. Oh, great," I said. "I'm starting to sound like Bear."

"And what's wrong with that?" says Bear, who we thought wasn't even listening to us, but he was just changing the record.

"Put your earphones back on," said Alicia to Bear. And to me: "Something's bothering you. What? That you're having fun again?"

"No, no, not that, Alicia. It's that I lied to you." I pulled Alicia into her kitchen and we sat down at the round table.

"I lied when I told you that Michelle's earlobes were small potatoes compared to the loss of my friend. The truth is that I was hiding from the memory of Michelle's head without earlobes. Blood, yes, and screaming, yes, but not that image. Jesus, I wish I could work. Really get into my work and dive into some new image of my own making. Maybe then I could obliterate it…but I took that oath, damn it.

"I remember the first time that image ambushed me and I thought I'd explode with rage and wanted to find those earlobes and stuff them down Mara's throat till she choked. Then, of course, I was disgusted with myself. And then I could hear Michelle scolding me: 'Guilt and regret,' Michelle used to say, 'are such a crock.' And then she'd hand me another one of the books she loved to quote. Lately it was the one by that New York woman,

Betty Friedan. Have you read it? *The Feminine Mystique.* I should really read the book myself, now that Michelle's quoting is over. I will, as soon as I stop hearing it all in Michelle's voice."

Alicia nodded slowly, handing me a box of cookies. We went back into the living room. Bear was still on earphones.

"So," said Alicia, "you'd like to be working?"

"Oh, hell, yes. Not working drops me into a land where I'm a stranger to myself."

"That different?"

"Oh, yes. When I'm working," I told Alicia, "I'm an eagle: sharp-eyed and alive! Now? Now I'm floundering. A flounder out of water. No, worse: a lemming. Drawn to those who are intense with focus: Mara, Ted...but I really have a horror of being a follower. I do not, for example, want to follow in the footsteps of male artists, climbing the Ivory Tower and to hell with a friend's tears, with the rest of the world. I took that oath not to work for 100 days so I *wouldn't* turn into one of those. And I hate to tell you this: the result is that I feel like a hollow reed. At the least huff and puff...

"I've done my own thinking for too many years now. I *hate* turning into a lemming."

I had no idea what image Alicia had in her head, but her laugh was so infectious, I was now gladly lemminging along.

"Okay," I said. "No lemming. But no eagle either, let me tell you. And much though I like the stance of the 'anthropologist in the field,' it's not possible with friends. Though with Mara, I'm trying really, really hard to keep cool eyes in my head."

"You're going to drive me crazy," said Alicia, "the way you mix and mis-match images and analogies.

"Or," I said, "you could think of it as 'Verbal Dali.'"

"Verbal Salvador Dali?" Alicia practically hooted, waving her hands to stop me saying anything else she'd find funny.

I managed to keep my mouth shut—actually I was a bit taken aback by what-all I'd blurted out. Then Alicia tried one last time to get me to "rescue Ted from Mara's clutches," but I wouldn't even if I could. After the way he frowned and snorted at me when I told him Mara didn't want us in the house, Ted O'Sullivan was on his own, trying to fill in his picture of Mara deJong.

TED

What with Bear playing every night and me busy being bodyguard and Canadian eye during the day, we hadn't been our usual Siamese twin act, so we sat down at Miguel's and I filled Bear in on the last three days.

Miguel's is the place we go when we want to talk without getting distracted by music. A bar, about five tables, a lot of linoleum and bunches of coconuts hanging here and there. Bear just finished telling me how he's putting the shove to history off to the side for now so he can put all his attention on supplying the nest. After the baby's born, Alicia's going to take a year off teaching, for mothering and writing. She doesn't want to talk about the writing yet, but Bear knows she already has six finished short stories. Meantime she's still throwing up now and then, and still turning nasty now and then—but not as often, thank the Lord above. No, wait, says Bear. It's "thank the Lady Above." Did you know there's a black Madonna somewhere in...

At that point I took over. Come to think of it, I must have been downright mellow to let Bear do all the talking for that long. I guess after old Doc Toller's promise that my fingers were going to be good as ever, and after I found out that playing was improving them day by day, I definitely relaxed a whole notch. And then, knowing that Bear was going to be listening to me with both ears so he could catch all the clues to what makes Mara tick, and being sure that Mara wasn't going to turf me out, which meant he and I could ferret around till I got all my own questions answered—yes, no doubt about it, I was feeling mellow. Could even see a funny side here and there. Right up to the time everything came crashing down on me like a barrel of beef.

It's Thursday evening, and I'm about to take Bear back to last Tuesday, around noon. His turn to be all ears.

I came bouncing down the stairs, holding that list of places he and I made: Mara's course in Canadiana. Not the least notion in my head about what-all is going to blow that list away.

I get as far as the living room doorway when I see Mara sitting at the rolltop desk, her back to me—and looky here, today she's a redhead! What my grandfather used to call Irish red, like a just-peeled chestnut red, and nothing carroty about it. And this glowing chestnut hair is waving and curling all over the back of Mara's head and down to her shoulders. Now she stands up and she's turning around and she has a wide black belt around her waist, making it tiny between the busty white top and the billowing skirt. An hourglass with a wig on top. And Mara's face looking out of those chestnut curls is smiling at me, and the smile is sparkling.

She says to me, "Do you think it will work?"

By the sound of her voice, Mara is absolutely sure of success.

"Will it work as what, Mara? That's not exactly a disguise, you know. More of a come-on, if you know what that means. One way or another," I tell Mara the busty redhead, "everybody moving on two legs is going to want to take a good look and check you out."

Mara is nodding and sparkling away like I've just awarded her a prize. I figured we had to be reading off two different charts here. Maybe she was playing charades? And maybe my first guess was supposed to be, say, "wife of a famous quarterback?" No, that couldn't be right. By the look on Mara's face, she'd already won the game. So what was going on?

"Surely you can see?" says Mara. "As I look now, no one will pay the least regard to my face. No one who sees me passing will think: 'Ah, the mother.'"

Bear and I look at each other: She was right. I mean, think about it: can you remember the face of a peacock? The bird can't fly, and it can't sing, but don't it catch your eye, looking so flashy. I personally prefer Mara's own hair and her Angel of Mercy get-up, whatever that was, but I have to give the woman her due.

"You are one swift lady, Mara, and no doubt about it."

Which is when Mara gets serious and tops herself.

"Today," she says, "I would like to go to court."

As in court of law, she meant. Because when you're researching potential Canadian jurors, you go study some in action, right?

"Should have been the first thing on our list," says Bear, shaking his head.

"I know man, I know."

I told Mara the redheaded bombshell: "You are one amazing lady. We'll do just that, we'll go to court. Right after a cup of coffee."

My mistake. Two mistakes, actually. First, Mara pours me a cup of already-made instant from a jug. Lukewarm and bitter. And while I'm sipping this nasty brew and Mara is locking up the rolltop desk (where did the new lock come from?) something is going on outside. I don't know that. I'm busy being Wily the fox, trying to talk chestnuts out of their shell.

"Mara, now that I'm working with you, you really should be letting me in on your strategy. I can be a lot more helpful if I know what defence you and your lawyer are planning!"

"I shall have to tell you that later," says Mara. "We should leave now."

So out we go, out the front door and down to the sidewalk into another hot sunny day. Halfway down the block, I see somebody break into a run and disappear around the corner. Somebody looking unpleasantly familiar. And lucky for her, gone just in time. That little turd went and smeared up my entire van. Three "motherfuckers" on one side of the van. Big ugly oily letters. On the other side, a whole collection, including "Syko" and "Monsterfucker." And a couple of stick drawings supposed to show some human parts in action. Mara is heading around to this side of the van, which is not a good idea at all, so I step around the front to head her off. She raises her eyebrows and says:

"We have to suppose that was Louise running away?"

"Yes, Mara, we have to. And we'll have to call a cab."

Mara nods and says, "I shall have to talk to Louise. Very soon."

Mara turns and goes back into the house. I try rubbing at the artwork but like I figured, it'll take Varsol to get it off. And it'll take hours. And then it'll leave patches all over, like the van has leprosy. Jesus, I hate the Tic being a woman. I'd like to bust loose at least a couple of teeth.

"What do you think Alicia would say," I ask Bear, "about busting a couple of teeth on a woman if that woman is the Tic?"

"Try thinking with your brains, Ted," says Bear in Alicia's voice. "Give your knuckles a break." He's so right on, we have to laugh.

Then I excuse myself and head for the john. I don't want to tell Bear what happened next, last Tuesday; that was between Alicia and myself. I had just remembered that Bear was going to use the van that night, to haul a new amp up to his gig, so I went back into the house to call and tell him "no van." Alicia answered the phone. She'd felt kind of dizzy and had to stay home from work that day. I gave her the no-van message for Bear, and Alicia wanted to know if the van was on the fritz. So I told her about the graffiti and she hit the ceiling.

"What's happening with you, Ted? That monster mother Mara deJong, this fucked-up Tic... Are you the guy I know?"

"You bet I am," I told her, pissed off. "I've been trying to shake that Tic ever since she tailed me into TO. I have not said one word to her but 'go!' So quit riding me, okay? And the thing with Mara is something else altogether. So let me make sure you're clear on this one: you're not the old Alicia I'm used to, either. The old Alicia would have believed me that this thing with Mara is something else altogether. That I tried passing on by and leaving that scene behind. But I can't do it. I cannot do it. Not till I find out what I have to know."

"What, Ted? What is it you have to know?"

"How a mother can do such a thing to her own child."

Long pause. Long enough for me to ask myself: hey, man. I thought you stopped chewing on that one. I thought you settled it once and for all with "deranged by grief."

Alicia's voice on the phone came in again, real quiet:

"See you later, Ted."

We hung up and I turned, and there was Mara, standing in the doorway. How much did she hear?

Mara was pointing to the front door. Did she want me to get the hell out of there? No. She was letting me know the taxi was out front. We climbed in, and this time we actually made it all the way to the Provincial Court of Ontario.

When I got back to our table at Miguel's, Bear was downright eager-beaver to hear more about Mara, which mellowed me right out again.

Everybody's been to court for one reason or another. Big stone building on the outside, big wooden rooms on the inside. Great echoes because the ceilings are high and the corridors are long and narrow. Footsteps coming and going in counter-rhythms. Voices like brushes on the snare drum. Everybody whispering in little clumps, every group huddled away from every other one. Once in a while, somebody lets out a shout and then there's a half-minute silence and then all the sounds and echoes start up again. The mood in the place, way down—down the river, they used to call it. And even the mood has an echo.

So now, walking into the wide open central hall with all its little clumps of whispering people, here comes Mara. Everybody turns to watch. Some guys stare at her like they're memorizing her for a pin-up in their future abodes. Or else, if they're on what's called the right side of the law, they start hoping she's looking for a lawyer but can't pay cash. All of a sudden I see every male in the place drop down to all fours and come running. Sniffing and salivating.

I know some dudes would start strutting, right then, eyes sliding sideways, making sure nobody misses what they've bagged. Not me. I tell you, I was fucking disgusted. Because I've been known to do it myself: wag my tail over the curves and the curls and never guess it might all be camouflage.

Mara and I turn a corner and there's a clump of three black robes and all three stop talking to swivel and sniff. So I drop one step back, behind Mara, then I bare my teeth and snarl and snap at them.

Bear is laughing.

"You should have seen those faces, man, glaring at me, raising up their snoots and swivelling back to business."

Meantime Mara is walking down the corridor, wrapped in her Mantle of Great Purpose, and really, how would anybody *know* that woman could outsmart every one of them? That she has a will as fierce and as aimed as an arrow? Not to speak of such minor accomplishments as playing classical piano concerts. There wasn't a single person in our great echoing halls of justice who could have guessed the real reason I was proud to walk beside that woman.

Bear shoots me a look but I keep going.

Okay. So Mara and I come off the elevator on the fourth floor, and she's heading straight down the hall for courtroom five, where a trial with jury is in progress—something she found out from the helpful old man downstairs (a grump-faced guard, to the rest of us).

Mara chooses a bench near the back and we sit. The courtroom is the usual high-ceilinged room, wood panelled, with polished wooden benches for the folks and a box for the accused in the middle facing the judge's throne, which is tucked under a shield, gold and white, the size of a billboard. The shield is held by a unicorn on one side and a lion on the other. And look here: in the bottom left quarter of the shield is the picture of a harp. Music in the Court of Law!

Bear nods me past that surprise. Mara wasn't interested in harps, either. Mara is studying the jurors, one at a time, like she'll have to draw them from memory with every detail in place. I'll take a good look myself in a minute, and I'll apply every bit of The Eye which Mara has deemed me to have. Right now, I see something moving under the lion and the harp.

Black robes. The judge. Already sitting behind his shiny wooden altar. The Church of Justice trying hard to make its rituals look ordained. Everybody keeps dipping little bows to the judge, and when the judge rises, so does everybody else, and the solemn blue jackets dotted here and there keep a cloud of reverence hovering just above our heads. Churchly ritual is a damned good cover when you know you're making a lot of mistakes. Sometimes on purpose, as in plea bargaining: we'll let the assault back out on the streets if he'll help catch somebody pinching profits off the big insurance company. The pound of flesh can be real cheap around here. I know—these robes have messed with several of my own pounds.

"All of mine," says Bear. "Stop blathering. What happened next?"

Well, Mara tugs at my sleeve and tells me she wants me to examine two of the jurors very carefully. The two at the right end of the first row.

"And then, Ted, please report to me about them: what sort of people you think they are. Take your time. I have made my assessment and when I return, we can compare our findings."

I want to know where she's off to.

"I'll be fine," says Mara. I figure she really doesn't need protection in a courthouse. The Tic is allergic to courts of law and anyway, nobody would recognize Mara as a redheaded bombshell.

I watch Mara leaving the courtroom. A blue coat is holding open the door and then he watches her walk off down the hall. He is obviously harrumphing at the presence of sex at court. At least he could still recognize it when he saw it.

"I guess when men stop salivating," says Bear, "they start harrumphing. What about those jurors?"

Right. Juror one, the closest to me. A burly Greek dude with mustache. Been in Canada a long time, since he was a teenager, I bet. Hardworking. In his uncle's restaurant, when he first came over, and it took 15 years before he had enough saved to buy his own restaurant, and now he owns it and he's pretty content. A whole family to shout at and show off for, only gets drunk once in a long while now because the wife nags about his health. Custom-made suit by a Greek tailor. Soon they'll be going home to Greece again, for a visit, and maybe they'll bring over a distant cousin who just might turn out to be good marriage material for the daughter before she gets in too deep with those Canadian school friends of hers who are all lazy and have no respect. Ask him about being a juror, about this trial of a punk accused of murder, he is willing to allow anybody a burst of temper or two, but letting it get out of control like the punk did is a danger to society. He'll bet the punk grew up in one of those Canadian families, with too much freedom for the kids because the parents are busy with careers and cocktail parties and they just don't care. No discipline. Not that he believes in beating his children, he's not a barbarian, but once in a while—well, spare the rod and spoil the child, isn't that how they say it in English? That punk up there should be put away and kept off the streets so that decent hardworking citizens don't have to go around worrying about their daughters. Not that any daughter of his would be as silly as that empty-headed girl, who is looking at the punk like he is a great hero and she is Melina Mercouri ready to believe in him for the rest of her lonesome but active life. No, that empty head hasn't even heard of Melina Mercouri, and if he did, he'd have no idea that there can be such courage, such dedication. I say: jail the punk and keep him off the streets.

I could hear him in the jury room. "Guilty!" pronounced in a voice equal to the booming task at hand.

Bear does a quick drum roll on the table. Everybody at Miguel's turns to look at us and smile, and Bear says: "He's on a roll! Okay, my man, juror number two."

Well, I say juror number two was just thrilled to be there, in the courtroom. And on an attempted murder trial, at that. She's got a new hairdo and freshly done nails and an outfit she went and bought especially for the occasion. She's disappointed in the lawyers, mind you, they're so old, and they're not looking to her, as they should, for sensitive insights into the human drama unfolding. But it's early yet, and if she doesn't freeze up in the juror deliberation room later on, she'll certainly have something to say that will turn the whole case in a new direction, as she'll tell everybody at work over lunch in the cafeteria as soon as she is allowed to talk about the case. Keeping her excitement to herself, of course, as well-mannered people do. As for the accused, she is going to make her decision after she hears the judge's summation to the jurors because he is experienced, after all, and a judge.

By this time, Mara is back, sitting down beside me on the bench.

"Well, Ted, what is your opinion of the two jurors?"

I give her a short but pithy version of my penetrating perceptions. Mara listens like she's memorizing every word. Then she looks at me like I'm an escaped chicken with the pox. She absolutely cannot believe what she just heard.

"Well, all right, Mara, you obviously have a different take on those two jurors. Let's hear it!"

Mara thinks that juror one is a retired military gentleman, well-off, and either a bachelor or a widower. He'd want to send the accused, guilty or not, to a military academy, to be taught discipline and respect for authority. As for juror two, Mara thinks her family is of the wealthy merchant class and she herself is a young lady who lives a life of active leisure, playing tennis, sailing...

"Sailing! Mara, she's from Cabbagetown, or the East End. She fought her way out, taking secretarial courses, reading magazines for tips on manners and how to dress so she'd never ever again be called 'white trash'..."

Mara is no longer listening. Mara has suddenly developed rigor mortis. Her body is sitting beside me, stiff as a board.

"Mara, are you all right?"

No sign she can hear me. No sign she's even breathing. But the bench under us is starting to vibrate.

"Listen," I tell her. "Maybe I'm the one who's all wrong about those jurors. It's been known to happen."

Mara starts shaking. Something's got hold of her from the inside and it's shaking her and she can't control it. Oh, Jesus, is she going to start spinning all over the courtroom and shrieking?

I put one arm on the back of the bench, ready to clamp down on her shoulder. I don't dare touch her, maybe set her off. I start up a kind of drone in my throat, trying to sound like the afterglow of a gong, and I tell her:

"Mara, listen. Here's a good idea. You listening? Maybe the judges are more your cup of tea? Maybe you'll find those guys easier to read. You don't have to have a trial by jury." That was the one useful thing I got out of that law book.

Mara doesn't even look up. She's staring down at her hands, holding each other in her lap. But, slowly slowly, the bench is settling down. Whatever it was made her shake like that, she's coming out of it. And then she says something, slowly, like she's thinking out loud.

"The trial was to be a Testing Ground," she says, "...proving my Theories...but if the Principles are not...Universal, then it will be necessary to add Regional, perhaps Cultural..." something like that.

Mara doesn't even know I'm listening. Not that listening means I'm understanding what she says. All I'm really taking in is that she's stopped shaking. Then she stands right up and tells me, "I would like to go home now," and heads straight out of the courtroom.

I'm one step behind her, watching her like a hawk, all the way out to the street and into another cab. Mara's sitting there thinking hard and she definitely wants no interruptions from me. Out of the cab, into the house, and Mara heads right over to her rolltop desk and starts making notes. Like I went "puff" and disappeared into thin air.

"Wait a minute! Just hold on there a minute, Mara. What the fuck is going on?"

Mara turns on the chair. Halfway.

"Do you think I didn't see you shaking in your boots? I want to know what's going on with you, damn it. And this is 'later,' lady. You were going to tell me your strategy for defence, remember?"

Mara is holding a pen in her hand. She still hasn't bothered turning all the way to face me.

"No, no, Ted. I didn't mean 'later today,'" she says. "I meant: 'at a later date.' At this time not even my lawyer knows more of my strategy than the immediately necessary tactic. In any case, today I saw that I may have to make a further and very drastic change in my strategy. I shall make that decision at the end of the week, and you shall certainly know of it then. You go ahead and exercise your fingers, Ted. I'll see you tomorrow. Around noon?"

Mara doesn't even wait to hear my answer. She is back making notes.

"Let me tell you this, Bear, and don't ever repeat it to anybody and that includes Alicia. I wanted to go over there and rattle the woman till all her strategies popped out. I couldn't fucking believe it! Half an hour earlier, I would have licked her all over like a mother cat if it would stop her shaking. Now I want to grab her real hard and rattle her. The same woman! I couldn't fucking believe it."

"Man oh man," says Bear, shaking his head.

Thursday night. Bear and I are still at Miguel's, still sitting at a table, and both of us are facing the door— something we never do, but we didn't want to miss Mara coming into the place. Earlier that day, Mara told me she might come and see where Bear and I go. Had to be to study potential jurors, I figured, but I didn't tell her what she was likely to meet at Miguel's.

I'd stopped talking for a minute because somebody came in through the door, but it wasn't Mara. Meantime Bear sticks in some of his own blues.

"Playing cocktail hour," he says, "is the worst. Nobody there listens anyway, those fucking hotels, but Happy Hour! I mean, I'm not asking for actual listening here. Just shut the fuck up so I can hear my own self! Last night..."

When he took on that gig, Bear nobly decided he would not complain about it to Alicia. So I'm it and double-it. Basically, the same old jazz musician's lament and curse: this music you're not listening to is not background music, you ignorant puffed-up morons. Only right now I personally do not want to do that chorus. I want to get on with my own blues, which in my opinion are a lot heavier on the side of gnashing teeth and growling in your sleep.

"You talking about listening?" I tell Bear. "Do some, okay? That night, after we got back from the courthouse, all the time I was scrubbing the Tic's shit off the van, I kept thinking about Mara sitting on that bench and shaking, and then, as soon as we got home, sitting her ass down at the desk, all cool and busy-busy, telling Joe-boy to piss off. Just like I never zipped off to Europe for her, and my piano isn't under her roof, and I'm just hanging around her for the bread.

"Listen to what Mara told me, Bear. 'My strategy,' she said, 'is not known even to my lawyer.' Like why would she tell me, Ted Joe-boy, more than the guy she's paying 10 times as much as she's paying me. Maybe 20 times as much."

"Two hundred bucks a week ain't hay," says Bear. "You tell me you start around noon and get most evenings free, make $200 a week in advance, for escorting and guarding the boss lady. I'd call that not bad at all."

The waitress comes by but Bear waves her away. Bear isn't drinking, even though I've got cash. I'm halfway through my third beer. I wave the waitress back over and order a Scotch.

"Anyway," says Bear, "you are playing the whole thing too damned mysterioso. Mara's calm, Mara's shaking in court—who wouldn't be shaking now and then, facing a trial in a foreign country where she can't even protect herself with her own hunches."

"Scientific assessments, you mean."

Bear is cupping his ear at me.

"Okay, give," he says. "Where did Lady Mara want to go yesterday?"

"McQueen's."

"McQueen's? You talking about McQueen's, the strip joint? Mara went to a strip joint?"

"It's not a strip joint any more. Where have you been, man?"

"McQueen's. Ceilings so low you have to practically crawl around the place, darker and smokier and noisier than any other club on the strip? The owner, Big Louis, five foot two, dressed in a tailored suit and a fancy French accent, when he doesn't misplace it somewhere?"

"Big Louis is legit now. He's put in some lamps and some ceiling fans, and he's now running an 'establishment.' Actually, most of the clientele is the same, I guess, except the strippers are gone and there's a 'live music' policy. Yesterday it was Third River."

Bear groans.

Third River plays avant garde/third stream—don't ask me who made up that handle—supposed to be a combination of classical and jazz. If you ask me, it's a cross. Bear and I have both heard the group. Three out of the five players are classically trained musicians with technique coming out of their pores, which should impress Mara. The other two are sometime jazz players I know. Not one of the five swings and their idea of "playing free" is to do anything you want over the top of a beat with some pretensions of jazz ancestry. (Face it, jazz and blues are the Adam and Eve of most of the sounds flying the air waves today. Flying or humping or squeaking their way through. So why not this, too?)

"Afterwards, I asked Mara how she picked Third River to go hear. She said, "'I thought the music might be a bridge.'"

"What, to jazz?"

I don't know what she meant. This was her first time ever in a "public club" in Canada, and she would be using her eyes more than her ears.

"No doubt about it," says Bear. "That woman is smart! There's your first report on Mara: she is damned smart! Hey, here's a notion: bring Mara up to the hotel lounge! Music: easy listening. People: lots of juror-type Canadians. And I'll have Alicia come up the same night—she's been wanting to come out one night and make requests for all her favourite tunes. Give us a break from playing 'Abilene' and 'Days of Wine and Roses.' She says she knows all the nice polite Canadians aren't going to complain about a black lady speaking up in a firm voice."

"Tell Alicia to wear a disguise so they won't know she's your own ever-lovin' or she'll get you fired. They'll have no trouble at all saying 'scram' to your black ass."

"Well, hurry up with those precious digits of yours," says Bear, like I wrecked them digging in my own nose. "We'll put out the word we're ready to be a house band somewhere. Anywhere's got to be better than this hotel full of fucking conventions. Every night at least three requests for 'Happy Birthday,' four for 'Misty,' and the manager comes out regular as a cuckoo. First set: don't play too loud, people are dining. Second set: break's over, get back on stage. Third set: don't forget to announce last call."

(I'm bothering to repeat all this because it was leading Bear, step by step, to his moment of sheer genius.)

Bear is finally coming in for a landing: "Aw, to hell with it," he says.

"Right," I tell Bear, "Yesterday. You want to hear about me following Mara to McQueen's, to hear Third River."

"Did I hear you right? You followed her? Hiding in doorways and shit? Ducking behind lamp posts?"

"Jesus, Bear. Keep your quacking to pianissimo, will you?"

"Okay, okay," says Bear. "But how come you followed her? How come you didn't just escort the lady?"

"Because the lady didn't tell me where she was going. The lady only said she wanted to test some hypothesis or other and for that she had to go alone. Once again I didn't rate an explanation. 'See you tomorrow, Ted.' So I waited till she got into her cab, and then I followed it. I was practically right behind Mara, going into McQueen's. I watched her crossing in front of the bar, getting lots of barstool swivelling, but nothing to worry about. The place was still buzzing in low gear. Some rickety old stuff sputtering out of that same old lousy sound system they always had. Mara picked a centre floor table and sat down. In no way acting the tourist from more civilized parts, or the gaga-eyed looking for lewd and horrible. She sat down, poker-faced, calmly observing, or maybe just making sure she hadn't been recognized. No wig, this time, just a small clingy hat, looking cool. She orders. I'm still checking out the place. Have to because any old drunk could recognize her and maybe decide to give Mara a talking-to about nasty habits. I sit down on a stool far enough around the bend of the bar so Mara can't see me.

"Now I spot Katie, just leaving the other end of the bar. You know Katie?"

"One green eye and one blue eye and a knife scar under her right ear, real close to the vein."

"That's Katie. She went and sat on the arm of a john's chair but a minute later I see her pimp wave her off there and take her outside through the back door. So I popped over to Mara and took hold of her arm and practically pulled her out of the club. By the time we get to the front door, cops are milling around, about to raid the joint. Mara wanted to know how come I knew there was going to be a raid. I told her I had a tip-off."

"Why not tell her the truth?" Bear wants to know. "Why not tell her 'experience'? Paying dues in all those dives for all those years." Then he stops himself. He can tell there's more to last night and he wants me to get to it. I know this part isn't going to trip off the tongue like a nice clean glissando, but it's time to get on with it.

"Okay, Mara and I are in the van. Mara says she'd like to do some walking on the way home. No problem. I drive us to Dupont and Madison in the Annex, park the van, and off we go, heading south on Madison Avenue on foot.

"Madison Avenue?" Bear lives on Dupont, which is nothing like Madison Avenue.

"All big old houses and big old trees—used to be high-tone family houses, at one time, but now most of them are divided up—apartments, flats, even rooms. Rented by university students, professors with young families, some artsy types. Anyway, it's around 11 or so. Mara and I are walking south on Madison, still about three blocks away from the bright lights on Bloor Street. All of a sudden, it starts raining.

"Not a downpour, but it's no drizzle either, and Mara definitely should have an umbrella or a raincoat. In fact, I'm surprised she doesn't whip out one of each, because Mara listens to weather forecasts and really pays attention, like she's a farmer deciding when to bring in the hay. But here we are, Mara and I, walking and the rain suddenly starting and both of us about to get wet all over.

"That's the way it is for mortals like you or me, Bear. Not for Mara.

"Mara stops walking and moves herself under a tree. The rain is getting heavier so it's even coming through the leaves like they're nothing but a sieve. Mara looks around for a minute, then she says 'Excuse me,' and steps off the sidewalk and up a driveway between two houses. A bit darker there, but enough light to see what Mara is doing. She is taking off her dress, is what she's doing! Pulling it over her head, folding it, and tucking it under her arm. And then she steps back out from between the houses and onto the sidewalk, in her slip."

Bear's mouth is opening but I'm not even pausing for breath.

"This slip she's wearing is shiny, some light colour, almost as long as a dress, but the whole bottom part is see-through lace. And it's very skimpy at the top: two thin straps and some lace. You can't mistake the thing for anything else: it's fancy underwear.

"And no, Bear my buddy, it was not for lusting after me that Mara took off her dress and walked around downtown Toronto in her slip. Here's what she told me. 'My dress is made of a certain fabric no longer available. When this fabric gets wet, the colours and patterns all run together and, in addition, the dress shrinks,' she said. Five sizes at least, by the tone of Mara's voice. I was trying to remember the dress, now wrapped out of sight—darkish green with a pattern of white rings.

"It is quite an old dress," Mara told me. "Absolutely perfect for certain occasions." And then she muttered something about "further testing."

"What kind of occasion, Ted? Going to McQueen's to hear Third River? Was she pulling your leg?"

"Don't ask me. It sure had nothing to do with me, this special occasion. I wasn't even supposed to be there, remember? All I know is this: I was fucking amazed! I mean, here she is: walking down the street in her slip, knowing people might see her—slip, shoes, and handbag, with a man beside her—and I can tell you for a fact, Mara did not give one fine fucking hoot! Not one fine fucking hoot! So now, you try telling me that Mara is just an average person who happens to be beautiful and that I'm just in heat. Just try it! No, man. That woman is something else. I may have to start wearing a hat so I can take it off to her!"

Bear's mouth was open again. I figured this time it was the equivalent of a raised hat. He was definitely waiting to hear the rest, so I told him.

"We crossed Bloor Street, Mara and I, nobody close enough to catch sight of the lady in her underwear, and we walked back to her place. By then we were dripping wet so I was about to suggest a towel rub and a cup of hot tea with something in it, but Mara got her word in first.

"'Goodnight,'" she said. "'I'll see you tomorrow at noon, Ted.'"

"Oh, man," says Bear. "Oh, man, oh, man."

"Keep your groaning pianissimo, Bear. Mara is likely to walk in the door here any minute."

ALICIA

I was luxuriating amidst cushions the size of a nine-month belly, covered in a beautiful fabric Lena called Indonesian batik—burnt orange and sunlit browns with brilliant splashes of red and blue.

"This," I told Lena, "is not the scene I imagined when you said 'Come for tea.' Where are the watercress sandwiches?"

Lena set a tray on a low table between us, slid herself down to sit and pulled the top off a tall glass jar full of muffins, home-baked by the smell of them.

"You know," I told her, "there's always a chance I'm carrying twins, so I'd better eat for three. What you say, girl?"

"There!" said Lena. "Just now I heard it again: that ever-so-slight island inflection."

"You heard 'island'? After my mother practically beat it out of me? She didn't want me to be handicapped, don't you know. My mother's word. Hm, here is something interesting: I just realized I never talked anything but my home English with you. Usually, I sound more formal, you know. More literate. Ever vigilant lest I contribute to the continued existence of a stereotype, if you see my meaning."

"Ah, yes, of course," said Lena nasally, her lips barely moving. "I do see. Quite. But I must declare, I rather like the singsong sound of the native Island tongue."

"Stop that! You're making me shudder. But I'll tell you, it's a real hardship for me, not being able to speak it. About a year ago I started writing down my grandmother's stories. Great stories, but I found out they really should be written in the language they were born to. I had to find a way of telling them in *my* English without losing their heart and soul. Slow going, I can tell you. And lately, nothing. Nothing burbling and brewing inside at all. I miss it. I miss having the stories brewing inside."

Lena was nodding. "Sometimes," she said, "life takes over. I haven't worked since Michelle got sick."

"And now you're helping Mara—about whom we shall neither speak nor think." I took a long breath and confessed: "When you invited me over for tea, my first thought was, 'yeegawd, go to Mara's house? What if this is a set-up, Lena staging a face-to-face with the one whose name I shall not speak?' I tell you, if you're black in this society, paranoia is never far away."

"Hey, you're the one who keeps bringing her up. Not that I think meeting her is a bad idea. At least you'd know she's no devil woman. And yes, right now I am helping her out instead of working. I don't ever want to start working every day, including Christmas, including all summer long, and to hell with everybody. That was my father's modus operandi. He wrote history books. When he found out he had only weeks to live, he spent every waking moment and drop of energy he had on finishing a book he was writing. That's how he spent the last days of his life! I never ever want to be like that."

"Then how do you answer this one, Lena: do you think it's possible to do first-rate creative work without being obsessed by it?"

"You bet it is. Look at all the artists who had day jobs or other obligations. It's probably harder, but it's definitely possible. I am not giving up living. Not for anything."

"Oh, that is reassuring, girl. I think I was beginning to listen to old wives' voices nattering about how you can't have it all. Okay then! Here I am, Alicia living 'pregnancy time.' Let the writing wait in the corner for now. Tell me this, Oh Wise One, do you think Bear and Ted are obsessed with their music?"

"No, I don't, actually. I don't think Bear would have headed south if he was. And Ted wouldn't have gone after him. By the way, I've heard Ted play. He's really good, isn't he?"

"Oh, he's more than good. What else about Ted?"

"Nothing else. Ted doesn't know I exist except as Mara's handmaiden."

"Not so. Not at all. Ted knows you have a sense of humour. He says you're a nut— which is a compliment, of course—and he knows that you are kind and generous."

"I sound like Auntie Mame."

"Wait. Not finished. He told me, with his own intermittent eloquence, 'She's the most peaceful human being I've ever met.'"

"I wonder what that means to a person who is trying to ride a hurricane?"

"Oh, I like that. Trying to ride a hurricane. Can I tell him that?"

"Hell, no. If he doesn't even know that much…"

"Oh, he knows. Trust me, he knows that much and he's not enjoying it."

"So it's not his habitual mode?"

"No, no—ride the wind, maybe. And I'm doing my best to pull him off this ride, believe me."

"Careful how you go about doing that, Alicia. Men are fragile."

"True, true. But now there's a real child on the way, these two have to get their ass in gear and grow all the way up. Bear is actually trying on the paterfamilias bit. Like: am I not being hasty, getting too close too fast with brand-new friend Lena here. Not that he doesn't like you."

"Oh, I know. He doesn't want you hurt, that's all."

"I know that. But I jumped on him anyway. 'Do you have any idea what shape I was in when you upped and disappeared on me?' I believe I credited you, dear Lena, with saving my eyesight, my sanity, and especially his hide."

Lena is shaking her head, laughing. "No wonder he wants to protect you."

"Yeah, well. To tell you the truth it even felt cozy for a bit, like great big wings covering you to keep you warm and safe. Then you notice that with those wings all over you, you don't get to see much. No horizon. Then you remember: hey, wait a minute. He used to trust me to know what I'm doing. Lawdawmighty, I wish my belly was sticking way out to there to keep reminding me: one day you'll be able to think straight again."

And that's where everything came to a sudden end: our tea and our chatting, and enjoying each other's company. There was a loud knocking on the door, startling the hell out of us, and then the voice: "Lena, this is Mara. You wanted to see me?"

Mara just outside the door!

I looked at Lena and she looked guilty as hell. It was a set-up.

By the time Lena reached the door to open it, I was out and gone.

TED

Bear and I are still at Miguel's and I'm still filling him in so we're both playing from the same score, but now Bear's gone tooting off on his own solo and I don't know when he'll be back and listening.

"Oh, yes," says Bear. "This is a whole lot worse than I thought. Here a woman walks half-naked around town to save some old dress from getting wet, and what do we hear from Ted? Ted is proud of her! This is serious, man. Listen up and pay attention! That's your cock sweet-talking you blind!" Bear taps his temple. "Why you don't recognize that voice by now, I do not know. It's not like you never heard it before. Mind you, this is a good one: she's walking around half-naked because she *what*? Needs the dress for special occasions? Almost as good as some of the stuff my own head came up with, trying to outsmart me on quitting tobacco. "Don't interrupt. That's a terrible habit you have. Just sit tight and listen, for once. I," says Bear, "am going to get you out of this! Yes, I am. You're the one got me out of that swamp called the South, and now I'm gonna get you out of the one called Mara deJong."

"Whoa. Hold it. You're forgetting something here, Bear, old buddy: I do not want out. Not right now. Something I have to do first, remember? I owe the woman. I owe her two fingers and a life."

"Hey, I wasn't exactly standing on the road with my thumb pointing to Canada when you moved right in and hauled me out of there. Yeah, yeah, I know. This is different. This thing with Mara, you get to pretend it isn't life or death. Even if what's surviving here is nobody even resembling my old buddy Ted."

"I bet you were a little fuckhead know-it-all even back in kindergarten."

Bear holds up one hand and lets out his favourite curse: "May beavers sharpen their teeth on your old piano and mistake the keys for a heavenly set of beaver dentures and may they yank them out and cart them off one by one to beaver grandma's hot dam."

He turns around and starts grinning at me.

"What we need," says Bear, " is fortification. We need fortification, and we need clarification, and we need elucidation. And then we need action."

Bear pulls out a joint—you can do that at Miguel's, as long as you know who's there and who isn't. Right then, the place was empty except for the one table at the back with regulars talking, laughing long loud thigh-slapping laughs, one guy flipping way up into a hooting falsetto, and a couple of chairs tipping back so far you'd be expecting disaster if you saw it for the first time. But these were regulars, like us, and they were passing around a joint three times the size of our puny little stick, a real island dooby, so nothing there to stop us lighting up.

Which Bear does. First sniffing all along the seam, then sticking the entire joint in his mouth for the moistening and sealing, and finally lighting that match. We toked a couple of times each and then Bear sucked on it for a bit, to catch up. All this time, I'd been imbibing the good stuff while he'd been filling up with water and juice. Or maybe Bear's hogging the joint because I'm the one who's supposed to be keeping it together here, in case we go wandering off-course. Fat chance, baby. There is no off-course. Even when I *want* to get back to the feel of my own life when it isn't spinning around somebody else.

We see the door open again and a woman comes in. She goes to the far end of the bar and sits down. Nobody we know.

"All right now," says Bear like he's presiding over the resumption of a meeting. "Are you telling me that bombshell on her elegant legs has never set your dick a-dancing? And are you also telling me a woman walked around in her slip beside Tantalizing Ted and she had nothing on her mind but keeping an old dress from getting wet?"

"Oh, yes, I'm telling you. And I'll tell you one more, too. That same woman saw me butt-naked and believe me, it didn't set anything on her a-dancing."

So then I told Bear about leaving Mara's room when she was in bed with her injured arm. Slinging the towel over my shoulder and exiting bare-assed.

"Well, says Bear. "I've seen your bare ass and it's just an ass. At least it's not wide as your shoulders or flat as a barn door. It's an okay ass for a white dude."

"How long you want to discuss my ass here? I'll refresh your memory in a minute."

Bear holds up a hand. "Let me do some thinking, okay? I've still got to get you out of this before you lose something you'd rather hang onto."

"Get me out of what, for Christ's sake? Bear! You still aren't listening to me! The woman does not let me get *in* anywheres! I cannot *get* to this woman, nohow. Is that enough clarification for you? Today was, what—one two three—the fourth day I spent with her, and what I got in all the four days was Mara the boss lady. A great boss, like you say, but I might just as well be a fucking monk in Tibet!

"No, wait." I'm not about to let Bear interrupt me now that he's introduced this prickly theme. "Let me tell you: Today I actually thought I was detecting a faint glimmer of curiosity. In Mara, about me. Around noon, the two of us are having a coffee at her dining table—I swear that coffee she's got doesn't even smell like coffee. Mara puts her cup on the table and she skims her eyes once over Ted lightly and she says:

'May I ask please, Ted. Are your interests engaged?'

"She wants to know if I have an old lady."

Bear holds up his hand and does Alicia's voice again.

"An 'old lady'? You mean a girlfriend, don't you? No, wait. A woman friend."

"Skip it. Just let me tell it to you, will you? Mara wants to know if my interests are engaged. So then my mouth takes off. 'Dear Mara,' I said. 'When would you suggest I might have been pursuing such an interest, in your opinion? While escorting Madame herself about town? While torturing my fingers at the piano, right here in your ears? Or perhaps secretly, at night, creaking down the stairs to the telephone and tiptoeing out of the house for a snuggle in the lane? My interests,' I told Mara, 'just in case this has escaped your notice, my interests have been real busy lately.'"

Bear nods: "That laid it out pretty clear, all right. Four to the bar, straight ahead. Okay, my man, what was Mara's line on that one?"

"Just as straight ahead. 'Well, Ted,' she says, 'You might be engaged in a relationship that is of great importance but that does not need daily reaffirmation.' And she sure has a point there, right? She's figured it out (like Dona never did, by the way).' Mara knows I'm not the kind of dude 'when I am not near the one I love, I love the one I'm near.' But how come she has failed to see all the 'personal interest' that's coming right at her?'"

Bear is definitely paying attention.

"So there I was, thinking 'finally! The woman is finally curious about me—Ted. Asking do I have a woman.' Then boss lady Mara says to me: 'I had to ask you this, Ted, because it is essential that I know whether you are likely to divulge anything which you and I might discuss. Anything pertaining either to the case, or to myself."

"Right," says Bear. "Did you blow?"

"No, man, I stayed cool. Where it showed, anyway. I told her, 'Yes, Mara, there is actually one person I talk to about most things. And I intend to keep right on doing it.' Mara just nods at me. Probably knew already I meant you. In fact, the way she's nodding, she's already made a decision about it."

Bear snorts. "Planning to have my tongue amputated, that's what. I mean, we do know that cutting off little parts here and there..."

"Stop fucking around, Bear. She was nodding because it's okay by her that you know what I know. Just a clause in our contract and she can live with it, that's all."

Bear groans and gets up.

"Oh, Lord above," he says. "Don't move. I can see this is real serious and that I absolutely have got to get you out of it," he says. "Right after I get back from the john."

Bear pops off like he's been waiting to go for a while. The guys at the back table are all in a clump, looking at a scrap of newspaper, shaking heads. The woman at the bar is sucking on a straw. The whole place starts feeling like it's underwater, a cave, and we're all trapped in here by the tides. Soon we'll be gnawing on the coconut shells.

Bear is coming back, sits down, and before he can start in on me again with his "I've got to get you out of this," I grab his ear and take off.

"Thursday, Bear. That's today. You listening? I'm coming down the stairs, and I stop in the living room doorway because I can hear Mara talking on the phone. Talking to her lawyer. And the way she's doing it, her voice, her concentration, reminds me that Mara really is kind of busy these days. Trying to save her neck from having to move to jail. See, Mara is convinced going to jail would kill her. What kind of jails does she think we have here in Canada?"

"Good question," says Bear. "Very good question when you come to think about how many people have accidents in our jails. Showing up in court with bruises because they've been falling down stairs and bumping into steel doors. And how about all these people with sudden urges to hang themselves? In other words, you're saying that Mara is fighting for her life and Tedboy here, the man she hired to help her, is being nothing but a bloody nuisance.

"Not too hard to handle, though, or she'd have fired you by now. Or maybe she's caught on that you're not in this for the bread?"

"I don't know, Bear. I can't get through to the woman. It's like I'm behind a steel door —no, not steel. She can hear me okay, but anything I say gets bent out of shape."

Bear is looking at me like I'm the one went off the rails.

"Try this one for why you can't get through to the woman," he says. "Letting people in on what she's up to is not a habit she would have developed, is it? Not as a young girl in the Soviet Union. Not as a young woman in Nazi Germany. With a German husband and neighbours who might turn her in for two eggs and a bag of coal.

"And that reminds me," says Bear. "Do you know what Alicia came out with this morning? Listen to this: 'There are evil forces in the world,' she said, 'and don't you think you can be safe, if they're out to get you.' Does that sound like something that might come out of Alicia's mouth? Today she's in a blue funk, close to tears all the time, muttering about trusting nobody. I'm getting worried, man. It's like she turns into somebody else. And she talks a lot more than she used to, did I mention that?"

"Is that why I'm getting all this dropped on my head right now? Because at home you don't get a word in edgewise?"

"What am I supposed to do, till you people get yourselves back to so-called normal, if ever? Turn myself into a tape recorder permanently set on 'record'?"

So I let Bear carry on for a bit—only fair, sometimes grass takes me all over the dictionary, too, and meantime I'm trying to catch why those "evil forces" of Alicia's gave me a jolt between the ears. What comes up is Mara, lamenting broken glass for fear of a whole year's bad luck. Evil forces with a calendar. Call it superstition or well-oiled intuition—you show me a human being and I'll find you the don't-walk-under-the-ladder, don't-open-an-umbrella-in-the-house, don't-make-faces-because-the-clock-will-strike-and-you'll-stay-that-way, don't-step-over-a-child's-body-or-it-won't-grow, and all the other vampire scars. Dona used to keep a bedside lamp on at night and I never once told her she was getting a bit old for the bogeyman.

Besides, that little white lamp of hers sometimes brought on my mother's voice, sweet and soft: "Turn off the light, Teddybear, I'm right here in the next room." I like that memory. One of the few. Most of the time it was: "Ted, please! You are making my nerves scream!" It took me six months living at my grandmother's before I came down off my tippitoes and used my whole foot, walking indoors.

Now my ears get yanked back to our table at Miguel's by my own voice: "Hey!"

Bear's stepped on my foot so hard, I yelled out. I check out what his chin is pointing at: the woman at the bar. Looking at us. And all of a sudden, something about her is familiar.

Now she gets up off the stool, waves, and heads for the door. Waves again. Goes out.

"Holy Shit! That was Mara!"

By the time the both of us make it to the door and jostle and push outside, Mara is in a cab and the cab is pulling away.

"I don't believe it," says Bear. "It's like she was invisible, sitting at the bar right there, and then, all of a sudden, she wasn't."

"Shit, man, I should have known she'd pull something. That must have been the experiment she planned for tonight. She even told me she was going to show me one day how she makes herself invisible. What was she wearing?"

"Who can remember? Something brown. Or grey. Everything the same colour."

"A hat? No, no hat. Hair colour? Okay, okay, let's remember her coming in. We saw her come in, for Christ's sake. A woman, not young, not real old, no colour, no kind of *feel* to her."

"Makes you wonder how many invisibles there are all over the place, don't it? Let's go out on the street! Let's go and check out the Invisible Ones!"

"Wait, man. Listen up. Don't you want to hear about Mara and her music?"

Bear heads us back to our table, orders a Scotch after all, and cups his ear.

"Mara," I told him," never touches the piano. I invited her to play my piano anytime I'm not actually doing it myself but she has never touched it."

"Never?" says Bear. "Not once? What does she listen to?"

"No listening. And no talking about her music. Not even 'I'm acquainted with the feel of keys under my fingers.'"

"Yes," says Bear. "Right there 'mysterioso' does fit."

"And how about this one, Bear: Mara told Michelle, 'Don't become a musician.'" Lena says that's what Mara told her own daughter. 'You practice all your life and then the world puts a cork in it and it all turns to vinegar.'"

"That's it, man! I've got it!" Bear is somebody who does not lose his cool and yell out loud. Except sometimes around cops. But he sure is sitting on the edge of his seat here. "I've got the cork, man! Mara's not playing or talking music because it got corked. By World War II, in Germany. She had to hide out, right? Couldn't give concerts and draw attention to herself, right? She must have gone gaga around the bend way back then! Think about it, Ted. Risking her life in the middle of the night for what? A pair of red shoes!"

"Blue. Blue shoes."

"And losing it over a broken handbag—that's nuts, too. And disappearing on her kid, not even telling people where she went and when she'd be back. Think about it, Ted! The woman went hoot-owl nuts and bonkers during the war!"

Luckily, even Bear has to stop and take a breath sometimes.

"So nuts, she outsmarted the Nazis? Knowing what to say and what to do, even training others how to testify? So nuts she could listen to Allied Radio and not get caught? So nuts she was the one who called a doctor and saved my two fingers and my life?"

Bear is deflating like a tire with a slow leak.

"Anyway," I add a little kick. "She couldn't give concerts, maybe, but she could still play. She had a piano. She even had a piano in Indonesia."

We stop talking to think about that. I toke well and deep and hold up the second joint, already down to a meagre roach. Bear takes it and pops it into his mouth.

"But listen," he says, thinking out loud, "maybe classical concert pianists don't ever just play? Maybe, by the time they're ready to do concerts, they've got to do just that or else they're like racehorses, trained and trained and led to the gate, but never allowed to race. Except, how about recording? Oh, shit, Ted! The recording. I forgot to tell you something Lena said about Mara's recording. The Rachmaninoff Prelude."

"What about it?"

"Mara recorded it when she was twelve years old."

"Don't fuck with my head, Bear."

"Twelve. There was a date printed on the record."

"Twelve? Twelve years old? Man, that's something! Mara was a Wunderkind!"

"You've got it! That's it! She was one of those freaks."

"What the hell does that mean?"

"Hey, take it easy, Ted. I mean I saw one of those Wunderkids up close, once. A little boy playing a little violin. Ordering his parents around like they were his slaves. And the parents so scared he'll refuse to practice or refuse to eat or refuse to stay a Wunderkind, they did everything he wanted, pronto. A ten-year-old jerk of a kid running the show. And he sure did enjoy pulling everybody's strings, the little power freak. Who are you frowning at?"

"I think I just got it, Bear. What was missing in Mara's playing. Years! That's what was missing. At least ten years. Of living!"

Bear is watching me, expecting me to go on, but something's gone and sloshed all over my brain. All the hanging coconuts are sprouting evil masks under their hair and they're muttering at me: *you will never know.*

Bear throws me a look I know and don't like and tells me to go throw some water on my face. As soon as I'm back, coconuts all innocent decorations again, Bear gives me a different look altogether. Crafty? Triumphant?

"Okay," says Bear. "Recap. We have here the mystery of Mara's missing music, and we have the two of us high, and in your case, drunk as a skunk. And we both want to entice the Lady Mara into revealing her true nature. Therefore," says Bear, doing his preacher-uncle-at-the-pulpit "we will march forth and slay the dragon of ignorance, yes, we will. We will gather up our forces and gird our loins, yes, we will. And the air shall be filled with the beating of mighty wings, and then we will behold the message, clear as lightning from the skies, and we shall be enlightened! And we shall be released!

"In other words," says Bear, "On Saturday I'll get a sub to take over for me at the gig, and I'll get Alicia to come down with me to the Empire Club, where you shall be seated with the Lady Mara, awaiting us and the meeting of the Two Mighty Women. And then we shall all listen, are you ready? To the great Dizzy Gillespie and his band! And together we will behold the Message of Truth about Mara! Yes. And one way or another, all ye who art enslaved shall fucking well be released!"

Remember what I told you? Genius!

ALICIA

I had jumped to the conclusion that Lena plotted my meeting with Mara, rushed out of her place, and landed myself in a tub of misery. But Bear and Ted were both so sure Lena would never set me up. When I phoned her, Lena sounded sad and I nearly burst into tears.

"Oh, Lena, I am so so sorry. It's just—you looked so *guilty* when Mara..."

"Alicia, I didn't feel guilty. I was upset. And confused. I didn't leave any message for Mara."

"Oh, hell, Lena, I am so sorry."

"I guess we're still getting to know each other."

"Bless you, girl, for saying that. But you're disappointed. I can hear it."

"Disappointed with myself, Alicia. I broke my oath..."

"Your oath of 'no working'? What happened?"

"Well, I kept losing confidence, till I was doubting that I have any talent whatsoever. So I brought a couple of pieces home from the studio. Just to look at now and then, just to reassure myself. But then I started feeling that brewing inside, you know. That bubble of excitement you get with new ideas. So I've already broken my oath, you see."

"I do. I do. And I'm coming over right now, to give you a spanking. Bad bad girl!"

We laughed, both of us relieved that our friendship was alive.

TED

The next morning nobody woke me up, so I got to surface slowly for a change, and floated for a minute or two. Then I remembered the secret and subversive plan Bear and I had hatched for when Dizzy came to town and decided I'd better have a coffee and think about it stone-cold sober. When I hit the kitchen, the stove clock read one, and I'd once again forgotten to buy some decent coffee. At which point I heard a yoo-hoo, and it was Lena leaning in the doorway. Her hair loose, something colourful on her body, sandals on bare feet.

"So we'll see you later," she says.

"Sure, Lena. Later," I say. Then I realize she's not just saying so long.

"See you when, Lena? And where?"

"This afternoon, at Varsity Stadium. Louis Armstrong. The blood donors."

Lena sees I have no idea what she's talking about.

"The Red Cross organized it. A whole lot of people giving blood, a whole lot of entertainment for the donors, to pull them in. Judy Garland's daughter, Liza Minelli. And Louis Armstrong. Alicia and I are going because Alicia wants to see Louis Armstrong up close. Bear won't go."

Bear's take on Satchmo was well known to me. We argued about it often enough.

"And what makes you think I'll be there?"

"Mara told me. You know she's going to be a blood donor, right?"

"Oh, God have mercy on my head."

"Yeah, I think I better," says Lena and disappears. I make my cup of instant and take it over to the phone and wake up Bear. I don't want him to start another bout with me about Louis Armstrong, so I jump at him fast.

"Bear! Pretend Satchmo doesn't mug, and he doesn't entertain when he plays and then tell me that he isn't a great musician who gave the history of jazz an important chapter."

"Then," says Bear, "we would at least have something to talk about. And I am not discussing Satchmo for the second time today. Alicia woke me up at ten o'clock this morning; she wants to go line up. Line up! To get to see the dude. She loves him. She's going to hide her future belly and she's going to fake being a blood donor, to get in there. Oh, shit, now I'm awake. What do you want, anyway?"

"Mara is going to be a blood donor. You believe that? She's going right into the middle of that circus at Varsity Stadium. What the hell kind of tactic is that?"

"Jesus, Ted. You have to wake me up to ask that? It's bloody obvious: she's going to get her photo taken as a good Samaritan, donating her own blood. No, wait, you're right. That's too obvious. Nobody would buy it. Okay, you've got me," says Bear, catching up with my own wide-awake state.

"Unless she's going do more 'research.' You know: potential jurors."

Took me a while to notice that neither one of us assumed she was doing it out of the goodness of her heart. I tell Bear I want to go down there and check it out for myself.

"And, hey, maybe I can get Mara and Alicia to meet up. 'Accidentally.' You coming?"

"Give me time for a shower. But do *not* expect me to pick up Satchmo's hanky for him if he happens to drop it."

Fifteen minutes later Bear jumps into the van and we head for Varsity Stadium. There's a long line of donors outside, waiting to get in. Bear and I head for the corner of Bloor and Bedford and hang around there till we see a couple of musicians coming along. One of the guys looks familiar to me, but it's the other one who recognizes us. He lends me a flute case to carry past the guard at the entertainer's entrance. Bear being black, he's just assumed to be one of the musicians.

We make it into the stadium, Satchmo nowhere in sight. We start looking around for the women.

About twenty or so cots for blood donors are set up in rows in the far area of the arena. People lying on them, nurses attending, a registration table on the right... Bear and I don't want to get grabbed and laid low, so we hold our arms like they'd already milked our blood, and we reconnoiter, looking for the women.

We see Mara first. Just arriving at a cot in the back, sitting down on it. She's looking mostly like herself, though she's wearing a big straw hat that hides half of her face. Bear and I stay where we are and watch.

Mara gives a little wave to a guy standing nearby with cameras. He comes closer and starts taking her photo. Mara is not posing, but not turning away either. The photographer looks familiar to me. Then I remember: he was the guy in front of the courthouse the day I met Mara.

She nods the guy back to the side and talks to a nurse, explaining something to her, then takes a mask out of her handbag, covers her eyes, lies down on the cot, and the nurse starts the blood donation process on her.

"She can't stand the sight of blood," Bear is explaining the mask. "Well, the sight of her own blood, anyway. Look, this bloodletting is going to take some time. How about some juice?"

We turn towards the juice table and see the man himself, Louis Armstrong, come walking into the arena. One look at him, the beaming teeth and beaming heart of the guy, and even Bear had to see the man is no Uncle Tom. I add a little dig: "As if Alicia would come out to see *your* version of Louis Armstrong."

"All right, Ted. Okay. He's the saint came marching in. That does *not* make Miles Davis the devil."

I can only shake my head over that one. I mean, hell no! The cool dudes like Miles, not smiling from ear to ear, not tolerating chitchat over the music, wearing their sober suits— those dudes are demanding the respect they deserve. But just because Louis, and even Dizzy, let it *show* they're having a good time up there entertaining folks, that doesn't mean they don't deserve respect.

Bear pokes me in the ribs. Louis Armstrong is handing a bouquet of flowers to a nurse. Bestowing them. Cameras flashing, including the *Toronto Star*, but not Mara's guy. That dude is watching Mara, who is just getting up off the cot and wobbling a bit. Her face is definitely pale—not something you can fake. Bear and I are on either side of her in a flash, ready to hold her elbows.

Mara smiles like she expected us.

"A little dizzy," she says, and sits back down on the cot.

We hunker down to avoid being conspicuous.

"Are you here to acquire a goody-goody image?" Bear does not tiptoe around the bush. "Because if you are, Mara, the jurors are going to know that's what you're up to."

After which Mara—must be her weakened state—actually spills something.

"Oh, no," she says. "Not if they think I tried my best to remain incognito. There will be no public photographs of me. Only private ones that we can produce at court, if need arises. They will show me with my face half hidden by my hat—my effort to be anonymous while giving the gift of life—but I will be recognizable, of course, on closer scrutiny."

"You sure are a piece of work!" says Bear. "Are you aware," she says, "that your wife is just now gaining entry into the stadium?"

Sure enough, Alicia and Lena are coming into the arena. Both of them laughing, as usual. They haven't seen us yet and they stop and case the joint. It takes them less than a minute to figure out the same ploy we used: Alicia starts holding her arm like she's already done the good deed.

Then I see that Louis Armstrong, in among the cots, has spotted Alicia—a beautiful young black woman in a sea of pale faces, and he's heading straight for her. Lena spots him coming and whispers to Alicia. Next I see Mara raising a hand at her photographer and pointing him towards Alicia. By the time Louis is there, shaking Alicia's hand for a good long minute or two, the photographer is over there too, taking pictures.

Meantime, Mara is up on her feet again, and we're holding her elbows just in case, and we're heading over there, just getting close enough for Lena to notice us coming, and for Louis Armstrong to catch sight of Mara and to demonstrate he's a lively old fart, and then the whole scene revs up and changes tempo.

I see a different photographer, "press" all over him, start snapping all of us together, including Mara, who is not even wearing her hat. Mara turns her back to the photographer and says to me, quiet but fierce:

"Please be sure to acquire that film before it can be developed."

I look at Bear: "did you catch that?" He has. And what's more, he's getting off on the notion. Which suits me, because nobody is better at pulling off shit like that than Bear. Only did it have to be right then and there? We haven't even had a close look at Louis Armstrong, let alone shaken his hand, when the press guy takes off and we have to leave this whole scene and follow.

"Be well, be happy," says Bear to Alicia. "Take Mara home," says I to Lena, and we're off. Chasing after the photographer, who's heading out of the stadium and east on Bloor, walking. Based on the look of his nose, I'm willing to bet he's headed for a drink, and sure enough, the dude turns left and steps into the Pilot Tavern. Must be this photographer has ambitions to be an artist; the Pilot is where painters hang out. Or maybe it's just where he gets to run a tab. Which he certainly proceeds to do.

He sits down at the bar and so do we, right beside him, and now we figure it's just a question of waiting for him to leave the camera behind when he goes to the john. But he doesn't. Oh, he goes to the john. More than once. But he never leaves his camera behind. Meantime, we sit and talk to him. About this and that, looking for an angle. And we find out that he has no idea he's got a shot of Mara deJong in his camera. Which means he has no idea what Mara looks like. I check him out on it, just to make sure.

"Say, did you ever take photos of that woman in the papers a while ago, the one who cut off her daughter's earlobes? Mara deJong?" He shakes his head.

"Nobody's got pictures of her. She's impossible to find."

"What are you talking about?" says Bear. "We just saw her, less than an hour ago. Sitting outside at the Penny Farthing Café. Come on, if she's still there, I'll point her out to you."

Five minutes later, the three of us are approaching the outdoor café on Yorkville, packed to overflowing, it being about 80 degrees out. We stand at the corner, looking over the clientele on the Terrace, and then Bear points.

"There. That's her, see? The woman with the hat."

The woman doesn't look the slightest bit like Mara, but press dude doesn't know that. He starts shooting, first with a wide lens, then close-up. The woman catches on and starts preening and press keeps shooting until he runs out of film and has to reload. And before he's slipped the film into his pocket I've grabbed that arm, and Bear, all excited, is pointing him off in another direction and meantime I poke a finger and push the film right out of the dude's hand and take off. Bear follows fast. We're moving at a clip the press dude can't equal, hampered by bouncing cameras. We streak around the corner of Bellair, head across Bloor, down St. Thomas, and in a loop back to the van parked near Varsity Stadium.

We sit there in the van, catching our breath, laughing like two apple-stealing kids.Eventually, I drive us back to Mara's place and Bear hands her the film. Mara says "thank you" politely, as if we've just bought it for her at the corner store, then goes and locks the film into the rolltop desk. Then she asks us to please sit down. She's still looking pale, fragile, but not wobbling. She sits down and says to Bear:

"The photograph for your beautiful wife will be ready in a few days."

"Thank you. Alicia's going to love having a picture of herself with Louis Armstrong."

"Perhaps then she will see me with more friendly eyes?"

"Let's hope so," says Bear, grinning at Mara.

Mara sighs. "Women so rarely do."

("That," Alicia told us later, "is because she can't pull male hormones over our eyes." Bear groaned: "Oh, no, not more hormone talk.")

Something has just occurred to Mara, and she goes back to the desk. She pulls a folded sheet of paper out from under a pad and hands it to me.

"This letter is from Tanya Volnikoff," Mara says. Meaning Mrs. Whatsnikoff.

The letter has only one sentence. "I hope you go to jail because I know it will be the death of you."

Written in English. I hand it to Bear and ask Mara if she has the envelope. I want to see the Paris postmark with my own eyes.

"Oh, I threw it out," Mara says. "And now I would like to rest. Could one of you please pull the Band-aid off my arm?"

Mara sticks out her arm and turns her head to look the other way. Bear steps up and yanks off the Band-aid. Mara does not look at it, or at her arm.

"Thank you," she says. "Thank you both for everything." And heads towards the stairs.

Bear and I watch her go, and the way her body is moving makes us both think "delicate" and "fragile." Bear and I look at each other and we don't even have to say it out loud. We both believe that the note is right: jail would be the death of her.

That same day around midnight, I was playing my old beauty, when somebody starts knocking, then pounding, at the front door. I figure Mara must be asleep with her earplugs in, so I hop down the stairs and open the front door, and the Tic practically falls into the hall. I grab her just in time and deposit her on the hall chair, and Jesus, she's all bruises and scrapes.

"Who the hell beat you up like this?"

The Tic is high, pupils huge and vibrating; who knows what she sees standing in front of her.

"Answer me, who did this to you?"

The Tic smiles and it's a horrible sight.

"I came to say goodbye," she says, and then she starts crying like we're Siamese twins about to get ripped apart.

"Come on, Tic. Tell me who's been beating you!"

She stops crying and hisses at me:

"Louise. My name is Louise."

She's high all right, but not on speed.

"Okay, Louise. I want an answer, Louise. Who has been beating you?"

"My brother, who else?"

"The truck driver?"

"Who else? But now I'm going someplace he can't catch me at ever again."

"And where's that?"

"Saudi Arabia."

"Saudi Arabia! How the hell would you get to Saudi Arabia?"

The Tic pulls something out of the pocket of her jacket—a very clean and very new-looking white jacket—and waves it around: an airline folder. It slips through her fingers and lands on my shoe. I pick it up, look inside, and see an airline ticket to Riyadh, Saudi Arabia. I put it on the hall table beside her.

"Where did you get this?"

The Tic pats her red mane down with both hands. Her fingernails are filthy, as usual. She's wearing the longest skirt I've ever seen on her. Beside her on the floor is a new-looking white leather bag.

"Come on, Louise, talk to me."

"Do you want to snort? I have some right here."

She's about to reach for the bag but then she forgets.

"I'm getting married," she says. "As soon as I get to Saudi Arabia."

"Congratulations. Who's the guy?"

"I've only met him," she says, nodding sideways at the plane ticket like it's got a gender. "His cousin."

"Listen, Louise, what do you know about those guys?"

I can't believe I hear myself saying something that might stop the Tic from taking off for faraway lands.

"Why not snoop around a bit about this guy and his cousin? Check them out."

"You don't want me to go," she says. "You want me to stay? With you?"

"No. Listen to me. That is definitely not what I mean. You listening to me?"

She grabs the ticket, grabs her bag, gets to her feet and walks out the door. A little stagger here and there but not hitting the doorpost.

I let her go. And then feel shitty about it.

I was back upstairs sitting at my piano when something came sliding into my head: the day Mara went off to meet somebody, all sparkly and wafting veils. Meeting with the owner of the television rental place. Who was from Saudi Arabia!

I don't remember when Mara told me that, but just in case there was a connection, I intended to hear all about the meeting with that guy, right now.

Mara is fast asleep, lying on her side with one arm above the cover. As soon as I touch her, she wakes up into full alert and pulls out the earplugs, looking at me. (How does she do that: asleep one second, completely awake the next?)

"The Tic was here just now," I tell her. "Louise. Waving a ticket to Saudi Arabia. What do you know about that?"

"Ah, success," says Mara. She sits up in bed, pulling the covers up with her, and looks pleased. More than that: she looks triumphant!

"If you recall, Ted, Louise has on several occasions been an unpredictable element, disturbing our plans. Lest she continue to interfere with them in future, I took steps to send her far afield. Even if she were to find a way to return to Canada, the trial should certainly be behind me by that time."

Mara reaches over and pulls a flimsy something around her shoulders. She's not looking at me, and let me tell you, right then that was a damn good thing.

"If you recall, Ted, I had a meeting with a Saudi gentleman. He mentioned that his cousin was looking for a wife. I arranged an interview for

Louise as potential bride. Then I spent three mornings preparing her—appropriate clothing, coaching her in the manners that would be expected, in what to say, and so on. It was difficult and arduous work and I did actually have some doubts about the outcome of this particular undertaking, but it has brought the desired results, yes? The gentleman must have assumed Louise is the kind of young woman he is looking for: attractive, respectable though impoverished, and willing to move far from home. The fact that he bought her an airplane ticket proves that the experiment was a complete success."

I have been watching Mara like a hawk and I know that not even one doubt has crossed her mind. Not one. She is convinced that she's been successful with a social experiment, and that's all she can see. I am holding on real tight, trying to keep my voice under control.

"Mara, *what about Louise?*"

"But, Ted," she says. "I thought you didn't care for Louise." Puzzled but reasonable, looking at me.

Well, that blows me sky-high.

"Mara! She's a human being, for Christ's sake. A living breathing person! You do not send somebody from North Bay, somebody who's addicted to all kinds of shit, off to a country like Saudi Arabia! To marry a complete stranger. And probably a Muslim. You just do not treat a human being like she's a pawn in a game or a guinea pig in an experiment! Who in the name of Lucifer do you think you are?"

I can't stand to look at the woman for another second, so I slam out into the hallway and lean against the wall, trying to breathe without shaking the house down. Finally, I get the breathing to stay in my chest and the roaring in my ears down to forte, and I get myself down the stairs, out to the street and into my van. Next thing I knew, I was climbing a bar stool, ordering a double and pouring it in.

I was sitting on that bar stool, staring at my hand curled around a glass. It was a sight that was getting to be too damned familiar. What happened to the dude who never drank three days in a row? Obviously a question I was going to have to look at one day real soon. But one addiction at a time, Ted O'Sullivan, and right then it was the Mara jones.

Oh, yes. I was sitting there, glass in hand, finally forced to admit: I was addicted. To a woman who didn't even know I'm an air-breathing mammal with pretensions of being human and persistent symptoms of being male. I'd been deafened by all those loud roaring questions in my head, and blinded by my sweet-talkin' cock, but now I finally knew: I had something gnawing at my gut and I couldn't get rid of it, and that is an addiction. And whether your jones is booze or drugs or Mara deJong, if you don't kick it out, your jones will kill you. Just like it killed Fats Navarro, and Bird, and Billie Holiday.

It won't kill you right away, mind you. First it fucks you around so you're strung out and sick, like they say Bill Evans is, and it makes you play shit, like Bud Powell did the last time I heard him and he used to be one of the best bebop players you could get to hear, and it will make you rip off your best friends and jerk them around, like Bird did with everybody he knew, even borrowing somebody's sax to play on a gig and then instead of giving it back, hawking it to cop some cash for running down more drugs.

Well. There was only one medicine I ever heard of that works for getting rid of an addiction: cold turkey.

I'm sitting there with my ass on a bar stool on Yonge Street and my empty whiskey glass slips and slides out of my hand and into my lap. That's how much my hands were sweating. Because I know about cold turkey. I took somebody through it, once. It was so bad, I didn't know if either one of us would come through it in one piece. A three-day inferno of vomiting and shaking and screaming down the house, and none of it easier because he knew he was the one who put himself into that hell. We never talk about those three days. It's something even Alicia didn't know about back then.

I put the glass on the bar, wiped my hands on my jeans and started rehearsing what I was going to say, cold-turkey-talking to Mara on the telephone. Every time I got to the part where I say "goodbye, Mara" and hang up, I had shivers and sweat crawling up the back of my neck and rats gnawing a hole in my belly. Say, Mara, know any wise old Russian ways to help cut me loose? Then my two fingers twitched. Reminding me: hey, fuckhead! You are forgetting something here. You *owe* the woman! You don't have that option, just cutting out!

So then I started rehearsing a different intro. "Mara, I am going to do my job, just like I promised and like I owe you. I'm going to help all I can, but from now on it's going to be nothing but a gig. And to make that absolutely clear, to both of us, I'm going to move myself out of your house."

That actually sounded like I could make it happen. I pried myself off the bar stool and by the time I stopped in front of Mara's house, I had it mapped: I'd leave the piano and the B52 till I had a place of my own, but everything else, my boxes and crates, I'd get out of the house and into the van. Then I'd go crash at Bear's place for the night, and look for a pad first thing tomorrow. Considering the shape I was in, I was damned proud to have a clear plan of action like that. Maybe cold turkey' was going to be easier than I thought.

By the time I was carrying the second crate down the stairs and into the van, I had to sit down a minute; my stomach was burning me like a leaking battery. When was the last time I gave it some solid food to work on?

I was heading around to the front of the van, planning to go get something to eat, and saw Lena coming up the street.

"Hey, Lena. How about grabbing a bite to eat?"

Lena says she has something to do right now, but to come on up to her place if I want, and forage. She walks ahead up the stairs and into her apartment, points me in the direction of the kitchen and goes off into the living room. I find juice and a big piece of cheese and eat it right there in the kitchen, chewing and swallowing and chasing the cheese with more orange juice, and it occurs to me that it's been a long time since I tasted anything at all. Tasting is good, I tell myself. Tasting again so soon is very good.

I step into the living room and see Lena standing in front of a big easel, looking at a drawing. Watching it like the lines on it are the tracks of an invisible creature, moving and leaving a trail. Then Lena lifts her arm and draws one curving line. Slowly and smoothly, one long curving line on the right side of the drawing. Then she stands back and watches again. I look at the drawing too, and I swear, I hear it make a sound. The sound a great old tree would make, from deep in its roots. Suddenly I remember Lena sitting under the big Maple in the backyard, listening. Remember thinking she had a crack somewhere, but who doesn't? One thing I knew for sure about that drawing: it made you feel strong as a tree.

Lena still hasn't heard me, so I start backing away, quiet as I can, and my damned feet get caught on something, and I stumble backwards. Lena turns around.

"Shhh," says I. "Never mind. Just go back into it. I'm not here." Idiotic stuff like that.

"It's okay," says Lena. "I'm done. Actually, I thought it was finished this morning, but something brought me back to it. Anyway, it's done. How about some..."

Lena hesitates to offer it but henceforth I'll accept herbal shit from her, any time.

I follow her into the kitchen and watch her move around in there like she's slowly dancing, humming under her breath, sticking a piece of crust in her mouth while buttering some grainy-looking dark bread. Thick slice, thick crust. And Lena is once more the picture of the most peaceful nutcase on earth. Except now I know she's no nutcase at all.

"Does that drawing have a name?"

"I don't really do drawings. They're only preparations for my batik paintings. That one," she points her chin towards the easel, "will be called 'Roots of Sound.'"

Three beats, then Lena starts laughing out loud. At me. At my face, which has just found out by way of Lena's title that Tedboy is not a total art-ignoramus after all. So now we both have a laugh. And every time we look at each other, we start laughing all over again.

All of a sudden, there's a knock at the door. Loud and urgent. Lena calls out: "It's open," and goes to the door, and there's Mara in the doorway. Looking pale. Throwing me a heavy look. Then she turns to Lena and asks to borrow large scissors. Large and sharp.

Lena says she doesn't have any. She doesn't ask why Mara would want scissors in the middle of the night and Mara doesn't explain. Me, I've just had a flash of the Tic, bruised and scraped all over, and I bark: "What are you planning to cut off this time?"

Mara turns and is gone.

Lena can't believe what she just heard coming out of my mouth and she's ready to go after Mara but I stop her. It really has to be me.

"Don't worry," I tell Lena. "I promise I'll apologize for that nasty cutting question. But then I'll be talking some serious turkey."

Downstairs, Mara is sitting at the round table in her dining room. She has both her hands on the table, palms down, fingers spread, and she is staring at them with total concentration. I don't think Mara has heard me come in, so I stand there, watching her. She doesn't move, doesn't even look like she's breathing. She and her hands have turned into a statue.

And then I see that four of her fingers have thick and swollen knuckles. Arthritis!

Seeing Mara's fingers swollen with arthritis hit me so hard, I froze. I remember thinking: "She wants to cut them off. She wanted to borrow scissors so she can cut off those knuckles!" That's how crazy it made me to see Mara sitting there, staring at arthritis.

And then came: what to do, what to do? Suck on her fingers till the knobs came out? Ax a piano? Howl? What if it gets me, too?

I want to go closer and put my hands over hers but my hands won't move. I know arthritis isn't catching, but my hands just want to creep out of there and get away.

Mara and her gloves. Mara and her not practicing piano. Mara answering Bear's question about being a pianist with "not at this time" and then escaping up the stairs...Maybe it was WWII put a cork on her concerts, but the playing, that was killed by arthritis. Oh man!

You hear about athletes struck down in their prime and forever out of the game, and you hear about dancers breaking ankles and musicians getting wasted, but Mara's swollen knuckles—that was the closest I ever came to believing in the devil.

Mara is sitting still as a rock. My two fingers are twitching. Reminding me that all digits are frail, but reminding me about something else, too. Something I discovered when I started exercising them on the piano keys: the music isn't in your fingers. Even if all ten fingers are lying dead on the keys, the music will bloody well find a way out. Would blast itself out, if it had to.

But wait a minute, that doesn't hold for classical pianists. In Mara's music, there are those who write it and those who perform it. And Mara is a performer.

Then what about at least *listening* to music? No. If I could never play again, listening would be like sticking red-hot pokers in my ears.

Mara is still staring at her hands and doesn't even know I'm standing here. What is she thinking?

"Don't jump, Mara. It's me, Ted."

She doesn't move. Not even the slightest change in her breathing. Did she know all along I was standing in the room? Was she *showing* me her knuckles?

Now she's pulling her hands off the table. Slowly, like they're empty gloves. Puts them in her lap, holding each other. The swollen joints are completely hidden.

"The bloodletting didn't help at all," she says. "Nothing helps."

Then both of us are silent, because what can you say?

A few beats later, there's a change in the silence. Mara gets up, goes to her favourite chair in the living room and sits down. And waits for me to come sit down, too. I do, and lean forward to look right into her eyes.

"Mara, please. What are you doing about your hands? What do the doctors say? How often does it flare up? For how long?"

"It varies," says Mara.

I am ready to lay down my head and howl. Mara sits there, calm and cool.

"All my life," she says, "since I was three years old, I practiced piano every day. Several hours, every day. All my life was spent in preparing for a performance. Even after all concerts stopped, during the war in Germany, and when I was in Indonesia, I still practiced. Because if I didn't, I heard those voices, berating me: 'you should not be walking your dogs on the beach, you should not be reading, or socializing, or shopping. You should be at the piano, practicing.' And even—" Mara's eyes are finally meeting mine—"even after I began my Work, I still heard those voices. But since the arthritis began, I am finally free. Free to do my more important Life's Work!'"

Mara sits back and waits for me to say something. I'm trying so hard to catch her perspective, my head is spinning. First, she was chained to the piano, condemned to a life sentence of playing. Then she gets rescued by arthritis. And now she has something else. Something more important... Try wrapping your head around that!

"Mara, tell me about this more important work of yours—are you *writing* music? Composing?"

"No. My Work has nothing whatever to do with music."

"Does it have to do with the trial?"

"Not originally. The trial was an interruption. But I decided to turn it into a valuable testing ground for my Work. I really cannot tell you more than that, Ted."

Mara gets up and walks towards the kitchen.

"I am going to have a drink," she calls back. "A Scotch for you?"

I'm still tapping around in the dark, trying to guess what work can be More Important than her music, when Mara gets back and there is a glass in her hand, and in it, Vodka. She hands me a Scotch, a triple at least, lifts her own glass and speaks into it:

"Lena says alcohol is bad for arthritis."

She raises her glass higher and says: "A toast. Yes, I would like to make a toast. To the man who will be the very first to hear about my Work!"

Mara is looking at me. Ted the hired man instantly promoted to best friend and confidante.

"When, Mara? When am I going to hear about your real work?"

"After the trial, Ted."

We're standing, facing each other. I feel like I've been handed a dissonant chord that I have got to resolve.

Mara is heading to the kitchen for a refill, which means she toasted me well. I go sit down. Mara's second glass has Vodka in it, too. Neat. But she's not sipping on it, enjoying the taste. She's gulping, intending to get drunk.

"How often do you drink Vodka, Mara?"

Mara flashes me a wide-eyed look.

"Not as often as you drink water," she says. Then she raises her glass again, ready with her next toast.

"To arthritis!"

"No!"

I'm up on my feet, pulling down her arm. Some Vodka splashes out. The streaks of Vodka on her dress look like tears, running down. Mara drops her arm, drops the glass, and slumps down to the couch. Her body looks like she's been deboned, and on Mara, that scares me shitless. She starts hiccupping and yawning, hiccupping and yawning. Can't even talk.

"Come on," I tell her, pulling her up on her feet. "You're going to bed."

She heads for the stairs, ignoring my arm, and starts climbing. I walk up behind her, just in case, but her legs seem steady enough. She goes into her bedroom and closes the door.

I didn't set eyes on her again till two days later. Nothing but short notes left on the kitchen table. Including one that said Louise was not, after all, going to Saudi Arabia. Nothing about her hands, nothing about how I was supposed to keep myself busy without touching the piano, which I couldn't do, in Mara's house, now that I knew why she never played it.

The next day, I drove Bear to his gig, and on the way I told him about Mara's arthritis and everything she told me about it. Bear slumped down in his seat, and I knew all his insides were twanging. Arthritis of the hands will do that to a musician. Even somebody else's arthritis. I remembered one more thing Mara said.

"She told me, 'The bloodletting didn't help at all.' She must have meant giving blood at Varsity Stadium, right?"

"Must have," Bear says. "Man oh man, how many birds does that make for one stone?"

"But you know what is really bloody unbelievable, Bear? Mara isn't doing the least bit of whining about getting fucked by fate. She didn't even sound pissed off. Like I told you, she claims the arthritis gave her freedom from slavery. Freedom to do her More Important Work."

"What? What *is* this 'More Important Work'?"

"No idea. Not a clue. Except it's not composing; she made that clear. She says she's going to tell me what it is, but after the trial."

Bear is slowly shaking his head. "The woman is planning to run for president of the world. Has to at least be something like that. Hey, wait a minute!"

Bear sits up straight.

"Liszt," he says. "A dude who played piano like a mother, and he composed, too!"

"Liszt is no news to Mara, man. If he didn't pop her cork so far…no, wait. You've got something here! Only what's needed here isn't Liszt. It's *something completely new*. Something she's never heard before. Something so new and exciting, it will set her own music bubbling and rising up till it has nowhere to go but burst out!"

Bear and I look at each other, grinning, remembering Bear's brainstorm.

"Dizzy Gillespie!"

I want to pull over so we can get out and jump around for sheer relief, but Bear can't afford to be late for this gig, so I keep going.

"Oh, man," says Bear, "Mara has no idea how lucky she is. Dizzy with his own band coming to the Empire Club this week. What if it was Archie Shepp, or Ornette Coleman? You don't tell somebody 'Learn to swim' and then push them into a tidal wave. Never mind. It's Dizzy we're going to hear and that's damned near perfect."

I had to agree with him. Real perfect for Mara would have been Bill Evans with his beefy hands and the touch of perfect pearls, or that master Oscar Peterson...well, you can't always get what you want, my grandma says, but if you try, sometimes, you get what you need.

For the rest of that ride, Bear and I laid our plans, and I'll just move right on to how it all went down that Saturday night: smooth and easy to start, till all hell broke loose.

MARA

Dear Theodore,

I recently arranged an opportunity to speak with a Canadian woman of education. (The "old money" kind I have described to you.) At first she was reticent, because I do still have an accent in English, though faint now, I am told. Then she recognized that I am nevertheless a person of stature and so we sat on a park bench while she held on to the baby carriage of her sleeping infant and we talked.

In the course of our conversation she revealed to me that most Europeans who come to Canada are perceived as poor and uneducated immigrants. A very few—orchestra conductors, for example—are highly respected because they clearly hail from the Greater Civilization. The Arts and Letters of Europe are still revered here above all others, although I understand that some support for a fledgling Canadian culture is beginning to emerge. One wonders: why now, in 1964, rather than at any earlier time?

I happen to know, by way of Albert's interests, that the truly indigenous Canadian cultures are ignored. How Albert used to fume and pontificate on the subject of colonial arrogance and how it reduces indigenous cultures to their artifacts.

The educated Canadian woman said she had to let her children's nanny go because she never knew how to speak to the woman, who had a thick accent but who was once a pediatrician in her own country. "So unsettling," said the Canadian.

I can't help wondering how my court case will be affected by such unease in the face of complexity.

As always, your beloved sister
Mara

TED

So now it's Saturday, around eight. Mara's been upstairs getting ready for too damned long, but I refuse to let the waiting blow our brilliant plan. When I told her, "Tonight I'm going to take you to a jazz club," I had a whole recitative ready in case she balked: all the people you can find in a jazz club who just might show up on a jury.

Mara said: "I am most interested in coming to a jazz club tonight." Then she went upstairs to get ready.

The van is parked out front where I can keep an eye on it through the living room window. All my toes are crossed against the sounds of interference—phone, doorbell, rock through window, the Tic, or flying saucers. I am sitting and sipping, waiting to take Mara to hear her first real jazz! Trying not to let the waiting get to me.

Mara upstairs has no idea that she is getting ready for a whole new look at life! Oh yes, she is going to be meeting up with sounds so new that all her blinders are going to fall off, and the saddle of her long past will loosen, and the short reins of classical European music will drop, and she'll raise her head and toss her mane and take off for the hills. With Tedboy right there beside her, of course, galloping and grinning. Oh, yes, it's going to be one fine evening at the club, listening to jazz alongside Mara's virgin ears.

Now mind you, losing any kind of virginity can be a pain so I don't usually rush right over and volunteer, not even for virginity of the ear, but then, Mara is a different case in every way.

I'm just pouring another Scotch in the kitchen when the phone starts ringing. I grab it before Mara can get sidetracked off the brilliant plan.

"It's me," says Bear. "Bad news. Rick called and he's sick. And every other bass player in town's got something on, or else they're not broke enough to stoop. I can't find a fucking sub to take my place tonight!"

"What about Alicia? Is she still coming down?"

"Ted, my buddy. Crying bitter tears for his good friend Bear not getting to hear Dizzy. I'll tell you straight: Alicia comes if I get a sub. So get out your fucking union book and thumb up to bass players, and call everybody who is likely to be sober enough to hold onto an upright bass tonight—which you, by the sound of you, are not."

Bear hangs up. Pissed off. I would be, too, if I had to play "Misty" instead of going down to listen to Dizzy. I'm standing there, trying to think up bass players to call, and does it have to be on acoustic or would electric be all right, and then I remember my union book's lost again. This time somewhere between my old pad and Europe and Mara's place. And I can't call the union office to get numbers because it's closed by now—wouldn't you think a musician's union would have different office hours than the government?

In the middle of all that I hear footsteps. Hallelujah, Mara is coming down the stairs. She comes as far as the living room doorway and stops cold.

"It's difficult," she says. "I have only generalities to lean on for my decisions."

Decisions, she'll have me believe, about what to wear.

"What you have on is fine, Mara. Practically anything's fine. It's not a fashion show, for Christ's sake. More like a muskrat ramble."

Mara frowns.

"All right, Mara. Some women do come out to strut their finest. But some wear jeans. It just doesn't really matter a whole lot."

"It always matters, Ted. Appearance always matters. Although not always at the obvious level of perception." That's when I finally get it and just about laugh out loud. Sheer glee at having made sense of something: Mara doesn't want to be recognized!

"Listen, it'll be pretty dark at the club," I tell her.

Mara, still standing in the doorway, says, "It's wrong. It's all wrong." Talking to herself. "I have to make a change." She turns around and goes back up the stairs. Back straight, head high, like she's going to start a major change in the universe.

I figure she must have had an omen. Some old Russian superstition. And decided that whatever Mara was wearing the next time she came down those stairs, I'd tell her it was perfect. That she'd hit it exactly right so that nobody would recognize her. And off we'll go.

As for that sub for Bear, he has his own union book, let him make the fucking calls. And Alicia was not about to miss Dizzy for no good reason. But what if Alicia took one look at Mara and screamed, "It's the devil!"?

Jesus, this waiting sure has got me by the neck.

I finish the Scotch, which is definitely going to be my last, and start some up-tempo pacing. And pretty soon, I start feeling better. Maybe, I think, the music Mara's about to hear for the first time is not only going to blow the cork right out and set Mara's bottled-up love of music flowing again. Maybe the music will blow off a whole layer of straight and narrow, so I could actually have that laser-sharp look into the woman? I mean, almost anything I know that's worth knowing I've learned by way of jazz and I'm not the dumbest kid on the block, so after tonight, with Mara listening to jazz right alongside of me, I'll be able to see through her like through a glass-bottomed boat.

At that point, completely out of the blue (or maybe out of the Scotch), I get attacked by a horrible thought: What if Mara hates the music?!

No! Impossible. Absolutely impossible.

The attack lasts just long enough to get me another Scotch, and then the phone rings and it's Bear again. He's got a sub. A new guy in town Henry knew about.

"Get down to the club soon," says Bear. "Get a good table. Alicia's not back yet, but if she doesn't make it home in ten I'll just leave her a note. And you had better get Mara prepared so she doesn't expect the Viennese Court Kapellen orchestra. I'm not coming down there to sit at your table and listen to her talk about cacophony and the aesthetics of the avant-garde. These ain't no clever little bleached-out fugues she's gonna catch tonight. She ever even heard a 12-bar blues with New York sirens at the head? Well, see you at the club, if you make it there."

I hang up and go into the kitchen, to the cabinet where Mara keeps the liquor. It has a key in the lock. I lock the cabinet and go to the window and throw the little key way out into the backyard. Someday, we can have a treasure hunt out there: find the key in the grass. Right now, waiting is over!

I walk out into the hall and holler up the stairs, and this is what I get back from Mara:

"I think you'll be pleased when you see it, Ted."

"It" being what? The ancient heirloom opera glasses sitting on her desk? Maybe an ivory hair clasp with inlaid rubies? Why not a tiara?

Temperr temperr, says my grandma, nattering in my ear again. Only my grandma doesn't natter—she sort of shoots a chuckle. I still haven't told her about this gig and how come Mara prefers a hired hand to a friend. I mean, my grandma has a childhood friend she last saw about 45 years ago, and she still writes her a letter every week.

Well, yes, grandma, but this is Mara's life, remember? Nobody survived where she came from by being friendly, trusting people.

And what grandma would say to that is, all you are telling me is that

Mara has had many opportunities to learn how to tell the fox from the chicken.

Obviously, my grandmother has never met Mrs. Whatsnikoff, or she wouldn't be saying things like that. Mrs. Whatsnikoff may look like a demented chicken but she's fierce and she's smart. And I'll bet all my Monk albums that as a friend, Mrs. Whatsnikoff with her hot little eyes is as loyal as a burr. And I bet something else: Mrs. Whatsnikoff would like Thelonius Monk! Or does she listen only to dead Russians?

"Mara! Get your ass down here, damn it, or I'll go up to the piano and I'll murder a Beethoven Sonata!"

I could, too. Murder it, I mean. When it comes to *really* playing, it's jazz and that's all I can do and all I want to do.

What gets to me is the way it all disappears. No wonder so many jazz musicians fall into booze or harder stuff. Some do it early, trying to follow giants' steps. Like: if I get stoned enough, I'll fly like the Bird—Charlie Parker, dead at, what, 36? With the body of a 65-year-old, sayeth the doctor, popping a pill to steady his pronouncement.

Some players make it through for years, and then one day they hear themselves repeating a phrase they once discovered all new and shiny, find themselves walking in their own footsteps around and around the same licks, clubs, streets, trying to play a keyboard missing three keys, looking at another generation of foot-tappers and faces waiting to be turned on, oh yeah, and that player thinks: what kind of life is this, when you're losing your teeth and hair and the music keeps disappearing into the air?

Recording! That's the answer, of course. What would we do without albums of Tatum? Yes, catch it on tape, make it permanent, sell it, and sit back collecting percentages. Ha! I've played on one album, so far. Bought me the B52 organ and a trip to Germany for grandma. Grandma came home sorry she went. My name is on the back of the album cover, collecting dust.

I hear some sounds and right now they're just the music I want to hear: Mara coming down the stairs! I see her in the doorway, and the sight of her doesn't exactly make me feel sober. There's a kind of shimmer coming off the woman. It makes you forget you've just spent half your life waiting and it makes you get up and follow her and stand there watching her climb up into the van's passenger seat like it's one of those thrones carried on poles through teeming streets to the sounds of chimes and bells.

I jump into the van and off we go.

"Sometimes the best-laid plans are as mouse turds in a hurricane." (To quote Alicia.) On the way to the club there was not one road sign reminding me of that fact. True, I was being cautious as hell. I even parked the van, not in an executive spot one knows about and borrows now and then, no, I drove right into a parking lot and paid with paper money! What will I do next, buy a powder blue suit?

Okay, I'm walking from the parking-lot booth back to the van. Mara is standing there, waiting for me. And all of a sudden the Scotch in my blood starts racing. Mara is wearing no kind of disguise at all. Her own hair, her own face, and that mystifying brain-addling cool and classic beauty which is unmistakably Mara's. Especially here, on hot and crowded downtown Yonge Street. And it's my own Scotched brain I have to blame! I could have told Mara anything: to a jazz club you wear a surgical mask. A sandwich board. Anything. Now it's too late. No way we can go back for her to change because we'd miss the opening set.

Three blocks to the club. Summertime Yonge Street is the usual freak show on parade. I start steering Mara through it. Lucky for us, out here nobody lets on they're watching anybody. Too cool. Except the kids who come in from the suburbs. Man, those tiddlywinkers will step on your toes, so busy checking out the boys with Beatles hair. Every now and then I want to grab one of those teenage boys and ask: does this long hair mean something, or are you just another kind of sheep?

So far, Mara and I are manoeuvring nicely. The road is full of crawling cars, stinking up the air so everybody walking gets drenched in fumes and loses brain cells with every step. What if the fumes give Mara a headache? Shit! I should have left the van at home, called a cab and had it drop us at the door to the club.

Mara says, "I see that most of the drivers are young males, with short hair, looking at the young males on the sidewalk who have long hair."

"Long hair is like antlers on the head," I tell her. "They're trying to get to be adult males but there's no territory for them except a car or their hair. To tell you the truth," I confess to Mara my less-than-perfect understanding of Yonge Street '64. "I don't know whether these youngsters are actually rebelling or whether they're just genuflecting to the god of a different fashion."

Mara nods. Now she's looking at a woman lumbering along just ahead of us, in pants tighter than skin. "What do you think she had in mind?"

Mara wants to know. "I mean, how does she picture herself?"

The woman weighs about 300 pounds and she's balancing every ounce of them on stiletto heels, and points so long she must have sharpened her toes to get them in there. And right there I stop believing in the theory of evolution. It makes no sense. Not when you're watching yet another human being determined to self-destruct. Or maybe those pointed shoes and stiletto heels are a secret weapon, slowly disabling the feet of women, destroying their minds by torture... Has to be a secret weapon from China, now that Russia is supposed to be so peacefully co-existing with America.

"Perhaps she models herself on a movie star," says Mara. "Many women here do seem to follow fashion whether it suits their bodies or not."

"You mean we in Canada have more sheep than Europe does?"

"Only the women," says Mara. "Men conform everywhere. Though here they are more naive."

"We're all just overgrown babies, I guess. Must be boring for you."

I sure am sprouting some surprising quirks here: paying for parking and now, making like a Pekingese lapdog with its nose out of joint. Mara moves on down the street, stops to look at the window of a new record store. Lately, new record stores are popping up like gophers all over this strip. High school girls milling around in front of them, big Beatle posters in every window.

"Tell me, Ted, do adults listen to this music?"

"If you mean the Beatles, yes. They're not bad, for pop music. Some nice tunes. And they're not playing three chords over and over and then add a fourth one and call it a bridge."

Mara looks at me like this is all foreign gibberish. Music is supposed to be the universal language, but that obviously doesn't hold for talking about it.

"The lyrics," I tell Mara, "are a nice change from June-Moon-Cottage for Two."

Actually Beatlemania drives me crazy so I'm not exactly in the mood to wave Beatle flags. I change the subject. To a European pop star.

"Did you know that Marlene Dietrich is visiting Russia?"

"I hope they keep her," says Mara. "She has become a fool."

"All in the interest of international peace and co-existence, Mara."

"Ah, yes. Politics," says Mara. "Soon now Canada will have its very own flag and its own national anthem."

I take her elbow and steer her down the block all the way to the Empire Club and through the door. Then past the barflies and it's like I'm leading one of those silky Persian longhair cats past a dog pound full of mongrels.

I spot the only good table left. It's a bit close to the drums and it only has two chairs, but we'll find more for Bear and Alicia when they get here. We sit down. There's a group of five students at the table in front of us, half-conked and not looking like they're here for the music. They may have to be re-arranged. Meantime, Mara is looking around the club.

Around twelve years ago, the owner of the Empire Club came across the word "décor," so he hung bunches of coloured balls from the ceiling, like obscene grapes, and put framed photos of jazz musicians all over the walls. The rest is still comfortable chairs, heavy round tables, and cheap glass ashtrays. You know the kind of place. If you've never seen it with the lights up, you don't know the colour of the walls is a disgusting dirty green and you don't know that the big yellow stain near the kitchen door is chicken broth. Sprayed there late one night by a trombone player who was expecting a glass of after-hours Scotch but somebody'd decided warm chicken broth in his glass would be funnier. The curses that trombone player let fly are still making the rounds.

"It's dark in here," says Mara. "And noisy."

Not noisy for a club, I didn't tell her. And not dark enough for me and you.

For people-watching—and juror study, I tell myself—the place is a beauty. A smorgasbord. At the front tables you get the suburban couples in foursomes, suits and hairdos. Then you get dating students in pairs: he hoping he looks cool and that he'll have enough money, and she hoping he looks cool and has enough money. And you get the steady customers, unsteady since 6 p.m., mostly businessmen and at least half of them legit. And then of course you get a few working girls strutting their colours. And right in the middle and everywhere, the jazz freaks, who come in all shapes and sizes. And, as far as I can tell, nobody anywhere showing signs of recognizing Mara deJong. Once the music starts, we'll be okay. Most people's eyes will head for the stage. Even those that don't listen but just nod their heads to the beat and watch the players' fingers, or expressions, or crotch.

Jim the waiter brings me the usual. He's about to plunk it down on the table when he sees Mara. And puts my glass back on his tray.

"What can I get for you?" he says to Mara, which from Jim is like bowing and scraping. Jim usually just barely slows down, passing your table, and you'd better be quick about grabbing a beer off his tray or he's gone. Mara asks for a Brandy Alexander and I reach up and take my Ex back off Jim's tray. Mara is looking around.

"How will the musicians be able to concentrate under these circumstances—the clatter, the smoke..."

I shouldn't be surprised by the question. I mean, we've all been to classical concerts: if you have to cough during the music, at least three people blast you with nasty looks, and if the music moves you and you dip a shoulder or tap a toe, three rows of people jump on your head.

Mara receives her Brandy Alexander and sips and wants to know when the music will be starting. It's around nine and the musicians probably won't be out much before ten, if then.

"They're preparing," I tell Mara, and I don't go into details of what that might mean. No point in getting her prejudiced against the music before it starts. Besides, Dizzy is clean.

"Any other questions, Mara? Better now or else afterwards. I don't talk through the music."

Mara looks at me like I suggested she trims her toenails in church.

"Okay, let me tell you about Dizzy. Dizzy Gillespie is an innovator. And a genius."

"I would have thought," says Mara, "that you would be passionate about great pianists." As I told Bear later, there wasn't anything in Mara's voice to remind you what was under those little white gloves she was wearing. I skimmed over piano-playing.

"Well, Mara, I'll talk about them, too, till your ears beg for mercy, but right this minute you and I are about to hear Dizzy Gillespie. And this dude is one of the originals...never mind all that. Listen. Tonight, just keep reminding yourself of one thing: they're improvising up there. Improvisation based on harmonic progressions, and some of them damned tough and tricky ones, too..." Oh, sweet Jesus, have you ever tried to describe be-bop to a classical Mara? Better switch over to Dizzy the person who, thanks to the Great Bandleader Up Above, is not into needles, and with that goatee of his and maybe wearing his beret...

Mara's been listening like she'll have to pass an exam on every word. I still don't think she was just trying to forget about her knuckles.

"Never mind," I tell her. "Forget everything I said. Just keep your ears open."

Three of the five students in front of us are quiet and drinking fast, because every time they raise their glass it gets them a look at Mara. I can't tell if it's plain horniness or if they keep checking: can that really be the Mother Who...? They're all engineering students, by their jackets and beefy thighs. Not enough facial hair to make a decent beard between them, but they've got daddy's car outside and no exams in the summer, so yahoo. There's five of them, so I'm glad to see Bear coming along the bar towards our table. Tall and fit and walking through the club like he walks everywhere: "This is my turf and if that bothers you, tough shit!" Bear never has to look down to see where his feet are going—just like he never looks at his hands, playing. He's got the coordination of a cat and he holds his head like an elk, high and alert. But why the hell is he alone?

Bear hoists over a chair and I point him to the other side of Mara. Sitting there, his Afro's going to shield her from about one-third of the club.

"She's coming," he says to me. "She's coming, okay?"

Mara's head swivels—to me, then back to Bear who is winking at me.

Then he gets halfway off his chair again to shake Mara's hand.

"It's my wife who's coming," he says to Mara. "Alicia. Who, by the way, already has herself up on the wall with Louis Armstrong at her side."

Bear has had a taste of the weed and he's in the mood to talk. Which suits me, because I'm still trying to catch the exact drift of those students and their bleary eyes.

"How's the research going?" Bear starts in on Mara. "Find out yet what Canadians are all about? Do you realize every second conversation in this country is about 'what is Canadian'?"

Then Bear takes off on CanLit people, sitting so high in their towers, dreaming about prairie childhoods, and the few who look down at the teeming multicultural life below, getting dizzy... "Alicia says things are changing, though. Definitely, she says. She's going to give it two more years, then she'll start sending out her stories to Lit Mags."

Mara is listening to all this like she has to pass an exam on Bear's riffs. Then she asks:

"How many American Negroes are in Canada, would you say? Among Canadian citizens, that is?"

Bear looks like all his strings just went way out of tune. I jump in and explain what's on Mara's mind.

"She wants to know how many Negroes are likely to show up on the jury. I.e., does she have to sit down and study you, or can she skip it?"

Bear chuckles. Then he says:

"There'd be a lot more of us American Negroes here in Canada, if the rest had any sense. But you know what they say about us black folk—happy-go-lucky wherever we are as long as we got our music and enough dope and a little old shack roof over our heads."

Mara doesn't have a clue what he is talking about and Bear can see that.

"Well," he says, "It's not the Garden of Eden, here in Canada, but I'll tell you this: before I left home I took a real hard look around the globe. Europe was out because everybody there hates everybody else. So Canada was it. The best I could come up with."

Mara nods. Don't ask me what she has fished up out of all that. Bear isn't done talking.

"Now you," he says to Mara, "you are tying up a lot of my brother's time here. I hope you're showing your appreciation the way he likes it?"

Mara looks at me.

"Mara is paying me a generous salary, Bear." I shoot him a look, trying to paralyze his tongue. Bear ducks.

"You should know," he says to Mara, "I had to get my old lady pregnant to keep her safe from this Don Juan of the Digits."

Mara looks confused, and who wouldn't be, in her place? I mean around Mara I hadn't even been my own self, let alone Bear's operatic wolf.

Mara's confusion, it turns out, has nothing to do with me at all. Mara is struggling with language.

"Your old lady?" says Mara. "Pregnant?"

"My wife Alicia, to you," says Bear. "And don't either of you let on I called her 'my old lady.' Yes, Alicia's going to be here any minute, little belly and all. Not that you can see it with her clothes on. Hey, guess what we're going to name the baby if it's a boy. Go ahead, guess. It's going to be Ted!"

How about that! Bear and Alicia naming their baby after me, that blew me away.

Bear is grinning at me. "I actually had my heart set on Junior. Start a Bear dynasty. But Alicia wants to make Ted here into a godfather."

Bear bellows at the thought and I have to smile some myself. Mara is nodding her head again.

"Names can be very important," she says. "I have changed my own three times."

"Why?" Bear and I are ready to settle back and listen to a good story or two, but Mara is doing shorthand.

"Once for professional reasons, once to take on the identity on my false papers during World War II in Germany, and then once more when I tried to find a way to escape from Germany."

"Was that in 1940 and '41? When you left your little girl behind in Bergheim?"

"Ted," says Mara, "Why don't you ask the waiter to find another chair, for Bear's wife? I have to excuse myself for a moment." And off she goes.

The students are watching her go but they're too drunk by now to cause anything except their own departure. Assisted by Jim the waiter. Jim enjoys deftly dislodging drunks like they're just one more bunch of obscene grapes.

Bear is rumbling into my ear. "Did you see her reaction when I said *'she's coming'?* The woman is definitely checking out your nooks and crannies, man."

"She's checking out if I'm going to be distracted, is all. Don't you figure I can tell when a woman's got her eye on my crannies?"

Something catches my own eye—Alicia, coming through the crowd. And right behind her I see Lena the neighbour. Alicia's had her hair cut short and it fits her fine head like a sparkly black cap, and around her high neck she's got a band of something red and she sure is not looking like any morning sickness. And neighbour Lena has a blue bandanna tied around her hair, and she looks like she's already having a good time.

Bear takes off to find more chairs. Alicia sits down and leans into my face.

"You make sure," she says, "that Mara and I are not sitting next to each other. No touching."

"Jesus, Alicia. What is this? The woman is not a leper. Or a witch."

"How do you know? I'm taking no chances on anything with this baby inside me."

"Then maybe you should do Lena's gig, for the next nine months. Sit under a tree and make like a female Buddha."

"You flatter me," says Lena, laughing.

Mara and Bear get back to the table at the same time. Mara does not offer Alicia her hand to shake, which is unusual for Mara, and also smart. Alicia has gone very still.

I put Mara across from Alicia and Bear so they can keep their eyes on Mara and watch her reaction to the music. I'm beside Mara. Who is looking at Lena, on her other side. Lena is taking the bandanna off her head and shaking out her hair, a whole shiny mane of it. Mara leans and whispers a question into Lena's ear. Neighbour Lena looks at Mara like she's just turned into an acrobatic lizard. Then Lena catches my eye and blushes. And then she laughs and I'm willing to bet my Evans albums that Mara just asked Lena about some graffiti she saw on the toilet door. Mara waves away the graffiti and moves to another question.

"Were you able to arrange that meeting for me, Lena?"

"Not yet."

"It is an urgent matter. Could you perhaps try again tonight?"

"No, Mara. I'm staying here to hear the music, tonight. I'll try again tomorrow."

Mara wants to insist but thinks better of it and looks away. The nerve of the woman, trying to send Lena off on an errand when Dizzy is about to play. Alicia was whispering to Bear. Bear puts his hand over Alicia's. Mara turns to smile at the two of them.

"Your child," she says, "will be exceedingly beautiful. No matter how they are combined, your features will create beauty."

Now wouldn't you think that would have caused Alicia to lay down her sword and shield? Not a bit.

"Don't talk about my baby," says Alicia. "It's bad luck. Don't even think about it."

Mara nods. "In Russia," she tells us, "it is bad luck to buy baby clothes before the birth or even to make preparations in the house. Constant complaining about the baby also helps to avert the jealousy of the gods."

Does Mara believe those old wives' tales? Nobody knows. Least of all me, having heard Mara talk about scientific assessments and then lament a broken glass for seven years' bad luck. Mara is talking about beauty again.

"In human life," she says, "to be beautiful is to be privileged. Unfortunately, many of those who become aware of their own beauty while young, fail to develop any capacities other than gliding through life by means of their beauty. You and I," says Mara to Alicia, "have escaped that fate."

Alicia is struck dumb. Bear starts laughing. "What are the rest of us? Beautiful but never-grew-up babies? Or just dogs?"

Now everybody is laughing, even Alicia. Mara is smiling. Sitting tall and calm. It's a round table, but she's definitely at the head of it. At least until the music starts up. Then it's every pair of ears on their own.

Lena is sitting back into her chair like she's getting ready for milk and honey to come lapping over her. I flash on her drawing, the Roots of Sound. Suddenly I feel Mara beside me getting tense.

I shoot a quick look at Bear and he's grinning. "I told you so," he says. "Nooks and crannies." So now I'm confused as hell. I mean, if I can't even depend on knowing that much—whether a woman is checking me out—then, Jesus, I'm really and royally fucked! And if I've been reading Mara wrong and she is interested, then I'd better let her know that I like it, pronto! Or is she playing some kind of game here?

Jim the waiter comes over and I pass. Lena and Alicia both ask Jim for soda water. Jim is too distracted to snort his disgust at such an order. Distracted by Mara pulling something out of her bag. A magician producing a silver light, shimmering and enhancing the beauty of all you see. Well, of Mara anyway. It's that silk kerchief she's pulled out, the one that was a "perfect find." The one that set her wailing and spinning when it went missing. Mara wafts it out of her bag and around her neck. And looks at me. Checking for my reaction.

So I let her see it, of course, full force. Yes, I like it that you're interested, Mara. Me, too. Let's be interested in each other together!

And Mara smiles! A smile I have never seen before: full attention, with a sizzle, and definitely personal.

Nobody can convince me that was just a satisfied boss lady smiling. No way! I'm high and I'm happy, and to top it all up, I'm about to hear great music.

Now there's movement on the stage and the musicians are drifting on, one at a time.

Everybody at the table is getting quiet. Alicia and Bear are holding hands, something you don't see them do much in public. Mara is shimmering. Just possibly leaning a bit my way.

I hear a sound from the stage and it's Becky Thompson, already up there, tapping his snare and settling in behind the drums.

Bear says: "Will you look at how high that guy's got his cymbals, man! What's he trying to do, hide?"

Only we both know Becky does not have to hide from anybody because he already thinks he's invisible. Right now he's sounding out the skins and moving something a millimetre this way and tightening something there and he already doesn't see any audience, so how could any audience see him?

I'm glad Mara isn't asking questions right now—like how come these guys sauntering onto the stage look nothing like the Vienna Choir Boys. Becky's clean these days, mind you, but he'll never lose that junkie look, like he's a ghost on loan from a forced labour camp. Of course the minute he starts playing, you don't see it any more.

The piano player is somebody I've never laid eyes on before. Bear hasn't either. Probably one of the altogether too many hot young players from New York, who'll stay with Dizzy for a while, if he can cut it. The guy looks young, bright-eyed and in great physical condition. He's not going to die like Charlie Parker, not him. He's with Dizzy, who exercises and drinks carrot juice and tries not to inhale his own cigar smoke more than once.

Dizzy walks out on the stage—applause, applause, and—oh shit, he's got a cold! He's sniffing and snuffling and his eyes are watering and he checks his pockets for Kleenex and walks right off again to get more. I'm pissed off as hell that Mara has to hear her first jazz from Dizzy-with-a-cold, but what can you do? Well, in Dizzy's case a lot, actually, because the man's been around a long, long time and no cold in the head is going to wreck his show or his blow.

Lena and Alicia are quietly talking. Bear and I are glued to the stage. And Mara still has no idea what she's in for. That's okay. I'm revved enough for both of us.

Dizzy's back and he's not waiting for the band to open the set without him. He's right up there, swinging his ax, looking out at the crowd he probably can't see except as dark blobs, all waiting. The piano player is dangling his arms, and either the stool is low or his arms are extra long, his fingertips are practically touching the floor. Becky is tapping the high-hat pedal so lightly there's no sound at all. They're all waiting for the bass player, who's got one ear snuffling at the G string, tuning it.

Then Dizzy counts them in and I can't believe it! It's "A Night in Tunisia"! The Gillespie tune I first heard over ten years ago, way back in '53 in Massey Hall when 5 Giants of Jazz played and turned on one Ted O'Sullivan so he can't ever be happy doing anything else but play jazz.

I look over at Bear, who knows I'm thinking "Massey Hall," and we grin and turn back to the stage. Where it's only the first tune in the first set and they're already starting to cook! I glance at Mara and she is listening, eyes wide open but glazed so the ears don't get distracted. Listening like a musician.

"Remember all this," I tell myself, and then I finally give my ears to the music one hundred percent.

And then, not more than three minutes into the tune, the piano player just getting into his solo, something yanks me right out of the music. A guy is standing in front of our table. Real close. A big mean-faced dude, looking like his mouth is going to bust wide open and spew poison.

I'm up on my feet.

The guy puckers up, and spits Mara in the face.

Don't ask me if it hit her or missed. All I saw was red.

And the next thing I saw was hospital white.

ALICIA

A couple of days after Ted landed himself in hospital, Lena and I were in my kitchen finishing the post-mortem on our visit to the Empire Club. I wanted to know what Lena thought when Ted up and rammed into that huge man-mountain who spit at Mara.

"Out with it, woman!"

"Okay, okay. My first reaction was, 'Good for you, Ted.'"

"So spoke Lena, 'the most peaceful nutcase on earth,' according to Ted."

We both laughed till we remembered Ted, lying in hospital.

I got up and started making Ted the first soup of many. Lena moved to where she could stand and watch me. And tried to sneak in a Mara question.

"What do you think Mara made of Ted's Great Defender act?"

"Well, you know, I wasn't looking at *her* when Ted and Bear were both likely to jump up and get us all landed in jail. Though I have to tell you, Bear has been mighty calm ever since he got news of his woman being 'with child.' Is that part of the deal? Woman gets pregnant, loving husband turns into over-protective caveman? And here's another question: do I or do I not like it?"

Lena wants to know if my father was over-protective when I was a child.

"All I know about my father is that he died when I was a baby and my mother refuses to talk about him. I've given up trying to get behind that mystery. Well, given up for now. What about your father?"

"My father?" Lena says. "My father only remembered that he had progeny when said progeny, being me, got under his skin. Like an irritating recurrent itch. My father's method of seeking relief was to buy me heaps of presents. Apparently, I used to destroy them on sight when I was a toddler. Not willing to be bought off. God, kids are so bullshit-free before they get indoctrinated. If I ever go out there and march holding up a sign, it won't say anything about the war in Vietnam. It'll say: 'Freedom from Indoctrination'!"

"Not as catchy as 'Hey! hey! hey! How many kids did you kill today.'"

I was stirring spices into the soup and I don't know if it was the smell of those old-home spices, or what, but I let out a big sigh and a gnarly old question: "Do you think my mother will ever stop thinking that I shouldn't have married Bear because 'his skin is too dark'? No, never mind. I know you can't answer that."

"Well…the times they are a-changing…Hey! Maybe she'll change once her grandchild is born."

"Not if the grandchild comes out dark-skinned. Aw, shit—I don't even *want* her to come around because of a grandchild. I can't be family with my mother thinking like she does."

"Do you realize," Lena says, "that every one of us lives apart from family? Sorry, Alicia. My anthropologist mind. Always rears its head when 'family' comes up. Thank god." Lena looks at me and she's grinning again.

"Right," I told Lena. "Start writing down ingredients. You may have to make a pot of soup too, now and then. It's what we do in *this* family." I meant the four of us, and Lena knew it.

It was a fish soup, by the way, with herbs and spices.

TED

There are some big gaps in the first couple of weeks after I landed in hospital. What I do remember, I'll tell you. But first, the last few minutes in the Empire Club.

I'm sitting in the Empire Club beside Mara-with-smile, sparkling and yes, very personal, and we're listening to Dizzy Gillespie's piano player nattering on the ivories, and I'm feeling great. Really great. All of a sudden, a big barrel of a guy is standing in front of us. He puckers up his ugly mug and spits at Mara. I've jumped up and I punch the guy. My fingers start screaming to cut that out, so I switch to kicking his legs out from under him. Kicking so hard that I lose my balance and fall over backwards. Meantime my kick makes the guy go down forwards. He grabs the table—and that's a heavy table we're talking about, with a serious edge. The table cracks right across my legs, breaking them in a couple of places each. The guy's full weight, a barrel of pork and beans, lands on top of me, and bounces my head on the floor, which fractures my skull. Slightly, they tell me. A slight fracture of the skull. Like being a little bit pregnant.

It's true though, my brain didn't actually come off its hinges and go squishing out any gap. It just went on a little vacation. In other words, all the time they're shovelling pieces of me into an ambulance, I'm not even there to supervise! And while I'm out and gone, they X-ray me into radiation shock, fill me with dope, do some cutting and sawing and sew me up again, and then they dip both my legs in plaster and string them up over the bed.

When I finally come back, I'm on Demerol. Strung up by the legs so I can't move, and now the walls start shifting and the ceiling is sprouting hideous faces and all of them have fangs that grow way down all the way to my screaming bones. Man, it's hard to believe some people go to that Demerol shit for a high.

After three days of that I quit Demerol and the hallucinations stopped. But then something worse started up, which is that recurring dream I used to have. About my little sister wanting to fly and jumping off the cliff and me not able to run fast enough to catch her. Two nights of that and I suddenly saw the scientific brilliance in a little blue pill they offered me every evening. I swallowed it and put myself out for the night and dozed a lot the rest of the time, too.

Thinking back on that time now, I am bloody amazed at myself for not flipping right out and landing in the booby-hatch. Because what went on in that hospital—the one long nightmare thing that went on—was waiting, waiting, waiting. And as if that weren't enough, I was feeling like shit about leaving Mara on her own, with rocks through the window, and arthritis in her hands, and the court case coming closer every day.

They told me that Mara sent a message every day, wishing me well. Then, one day, they plugged a phone in beside my bed and Mara came on.

"Hello, Ted," said Mara. "Tell me, please: do you trust your doctor?"

"It would help a lot," I told her, "if I could get one clear word out of my surgeon, the star. Why do you think they call operating rooms 'the theatre'? Ever since he finished rummaging around my insides, the closest he'll come is the foot of my bed, and as soon as he sees a question trying to get popped, he's gone. Try to catch me next round."

I would have kicked that surgeon's ass to Orangeville except he was also the dude who pulled together all the pieces and made my legs come out, they tell me, looking pretty much the way they used to, and would soon be functioning that way, too. In other words, in addition to wanting to kick his ass, I also wanted to kiss his hands because without him I might never have made it into the upright position again.

Mara sighed into the phone. "Hospitals," she said, "are such a temptation."

And then she told me how she'd been in hospital three times in her life: the first time for a small orthopedic operation (I would have guessed bunions, except it's impossible to imagine bunions on Mara). The second time was for typhoid, when she was in Indonesia, and the third time it was ten days in a Viennese hospital to clear up an infection.

"Each time it was the same," said Mara. "Experts and specialists in charge. Nothing to worry over, nothing to decide..." Mara's voice sounded like she was talking about a haven, an oasis, a temple. "Yes," she says. "Hospitals are a great temptation."

That's what I think I heard. You can't be one-hundred-percent sure of anything when you're coasting on painkillers. Maybe Mara was actually making some kind of sense? Or maybe she was trying to cheer me up? I didn't know and I didn't ask. No point in passing out invitations to observe my mental state while I was trapped in here. It might just have led to shock treatment. There are a number of white coats, and even a few pastel ones, in that hospital who'd be happy to see me fry.

Anyway, after that first talk, Mara phoned me every day, and she wasn't just being polite. She was asking real questions, and listening to what I came up with in the way of answer.

I didn't ask her anything about herself. All the questions I used to have for her were hovering off in the distance, in a holding pattern.

Here's something I remember clearly and always will: Lena sitting beside my hospital bed, telling me the Spitter—that barrel full of phlegm—was the Tic's brother. Which meant that whole disaster was my own fucking fault. If I'd taken care of business with the Tic right off the bat instead of letting it hang, waiting for the wind to blow her my way again before I cut her out of our lives, this whole mess wouldn't have come down on my ass.

Man, that was it, I promised myself. No more letting things slide! Like the time I got called to do a tour with D.T. Lobby, and when I called back he wasn't home, and instead of keeping on the case, I figured: "If he really wants me, he'll call back," and then I find out because he didn't hear from me he hired somebody else, so I lost out on getting to play in Paris and New York and maybe even on his next album. I tell you, that is never going to happen to me again. These two broken legs are forever gonna remind me: Tedboy, stop making like an amoeba hoping to end up in warm water, and fucking well *take care of business!*

Lena wasn't through with the saga of Mara and the Spitter. "The Spitter was all set to sue you for assault," she said, "but Mara went to talk to him in his hospital room and after that he changed his mind and dropped all charges."

"The woman is amazing!" I said, for maybe the hundredth time. "Mara takes care of business like nobody I ever met."

Lena was looking down at her own toes so I couldn't tell whether she was done with revelations.

"By the way, what did I do to the Spitter to put him in hospital?"

"He cracked his jaw falling forward on the table," Lena said. "It's been wired up ever since, but he'll be talking again before too long. Mara wants to use him as a witness at her trial."

"The Spitter as a witness?!"

"A character witness," Lena said. "I don't know. I suppose the Spitter could testify about how reasonable a person Mara is in the face of crisis."

"Why? What was Mara doing when all that went down, the spitting and hitting and punching and crunching?"

"I have no idea," says Lena. "There was so much screaming and yelling and jumping…who knows? Maybe Mara wants the Spitter to testify to the 'quality of her character'? How good a friend she must be to you, talking the Spitter out of suing you, and if a good friend, then surely a good mother? I don't know, Ted… Anyway, Mara's lawyer refuses to have the Spitter as a witness and now Mara is thinking of firing her lawyer."

Was Mara rescuing me from a lawsuit just because it would be good for her court case? But Lena left before I could ask anything more and the next time she came to visit me, everything changed. Not only for my time in the hospital but for the rest of my life.

LENA

Bear told me he didn't want Alicia going to the hospital to visit Ted, lest she catch something there. I suspected that Alicia wasn't going for her own reason: she didn't want to run into Mara. So I gave her Ted reports.

"He's still doped up a lot and the rest of the time he's earning himself a reputation as Tantrum Ted."

Alicia laughs. "How about Tirade Ted? How about Tempest in the Pee Pot?"

"All of the above. What does Bear think? He visits Ted every day. With a thermos full of one of your delicious-smelling soups, I happen to know."

"Oh, Bear. He still feels bad that he wasn't fast enough to get to the Spitter before Ted went down. Let me tell you, I'm sorry Ted's in hospital with broken legs and all, but if it was Bear, he'd be in *jail* and who knows for how long. I do not intend to have a child whose father is in jail."

"Alicia, I never even thought of that!"

"Wasn't much time to think. But now I wonder if Ted jumped so fast to keep Bear from doing it. Well, most likely it was Ted rushing to Mara's rescue."

"There you go again: Ted, the knight on the white horse. But he may be changing: Ted has not asked any questions about Mara, for ages."

"Now that *is* good news. Did Mara give him the boot now that he can't be useful to her any more?"

"Oh, no. She calls him every day."

"Oh, hell. Honestly, Lena, I wish you'd known our Ted before Mara..."

"I do get a glimpse now and then."

"And...?"

"And what? Alicia, are you matchmaking?"

"Perish the thought."

"Yes. Let it die for lack of oxygen. Because there never will be a pre-Mara Ted again."

"True. Post-Mara, then. Oh, Lena, I can't wait for a post-Mara world.

When none of you is doing Mara's Danse Macabre. And we can all be totally pre-baby."

Alicia takes a deep breath and changes the subject.

"Lena, are you going back to work in your studio, after the trial?"

"Yes, I expect to. Not much urge right now."

"What about…being afraid? I'm afraid that by the time I can get back to the stories they won't be there. Or they won't be alive any more. Know what I mean?"

"Sure I do. Sometimes that does happen—an idea loses its sparkle. But then there's always something else, some other idea that comes up glowing, or hits you over the head."

Alicia isn't even chuckling. Really worried.

"Listen, Alicia: that's one I trust by now and you'll find it's true. There's always something going to tug at you to get back to work. You'll see."

Alicia sighs: "Poor Ted," she says. "All this time stuck in hospital waiting and not even getting to play his piano... Does he at least get to *listen* to music he likes?"

"I don't know, but you, Alicia, have just given me an idea. Tell you later."

TED

Okay. I was still in hospital and by this time I was getting damned close to the loony bin. Think "upside-down turtle." Think ants crawling around under the plaster casts. Life was one long wait and I couldn't even holler any more because the guy next door was real sick, and I couldn't kick anything because I couldn't kick, and I was about to commit mayhem and inflict gross indecencies on the next sticky voice to touch me, and then, on my fifteenth day in hell, everything changed and my life started up again.

That day, there's a dull thump on my door and Lena walks in, carrying something big and flat, saying: "Pull out your table, Ted."

I swing the tray table over me and Lena lays the big flat thing on top of it. It's wrapped in an old blanket and I think maybe I know what it is but I don't dare believe it.

Lena kneels on the bed and unwraps the thing and it's a small electric piano plus headphones! And what with the table and piano between us I can't even hug the woman, so I grab her hand and kiss it. Inside that hand it's warm and cozy, and the wrist is strong, and so are the fingers pinching my cheek. We're both laughing like a couple of kids who just did a magic trick and conjured up a treasure chest. And then Lena jumps off the bed and plugs the cord into the back of the keyboard like she knows what's she's doing, and she does, she does, the guy at the store where she rented the keyboard told her exactly what and how, and Lena plugs in the earphones and pops them over my ears and steps away from the bed and throws open her arms and goes: Ta-da!

I can't stop shaking my head.

And then Lena says goodbye. No, she absolutely has to run off.

She knows I can't wait to play.

And she was right. I played and played and played, all that day and into the night. Earphones on, no sounds escaping, throwing looks like spikes to keep everybody far away. I played and played like any minute now somebody might grab the keyboard away again. My two fingers hurt some but nothing I couldn't handle, and every time they touched a key, they got a jolt of joy.

8:30 p.m., drug-pusher nurse comes by, wagon loaded up with little paper cups piled with pills all the colours of the neon rainbow. Some patients live on those pills. Some survive.

"I am not taking one more pill," I tell the drug-nurse. "Not till I know exactly what's in it."

She bumps a chair closer to my bed, talks in a nighttime voice, and tells me everything I want to know. So now I can prescribe for myself, and I do.

Nurse leaves, satisfied I've taken my pills. I spit them out, stash some, and swallow three. One of theirs to help me stay awake so I can play at night when there aren't so many interruptions, and two of the ones Lena brought me—vitamin pills. I'm starting on those because I don't want Lena to be all alone, out there in health-nut park. In a hospital, let's face it, people don't even *talk* about health. The best they can do is "going home soon."

Never mind. I don't have to sing the old hospital blues any more. I'm playing on the keyboard, till pretty soon I'm not a live bomb anymore, trying to keep from detonating. I'm "Ted, the guy who used to be a real pain but now he's got this piano to play with, he's a regular charmer."

And next thing I know, I'm hearing some weird new shit coming out of that keyboard. Shit I've never heard before, and it's leading me, taking me out. Like looking down an alleyway and seeing out into wide open spaces beyond, where the only rule is to fly by the seat of your pants and so you do it. You fly!

I phone Bear to bring me some music paper and he goes one better and brings me something brand new called a tape recorder that plugs into the keyboard. So I play some of the new shit onto the tape and Bear takes it home and listens to it and comes rushing back in, way after visiting hours, and grabs my face and kisses my nose so hard my eyes start watering. Then he's out in the hall, trying to find the head nurse. He wants to bring his bass up to my room here, to play with me. Head nurse says: "under no condition." I can hear her voice through the door and the tone of it says: "One more word out of this guy and I push the button for orderlies." Hospitals don't believe music and healing have anything to do with each other. Isn't that sick? I mean when and where else in the whole history of the world can you think of that music and healing didn't come together?

On the other hand, when you hear their idea of "music to help you relax"—the stuff you hear at the dentist's, and in the elevator, or cafeteria—you get downright scared to think what they'd pick as "music for healing."

Never mind all that. Bear and I are going to play plenty, very soon! Because the next step is to get myself out of this hospital.

I'm eating Alicia's soup by the gallon, and I manage to corner my doctor and tell him I want early release with parole. The doctor looks at the latest X-rays and charts and says yes, I am doing very well. All surprised.

"You'll be able to leave sooner than expected. Perhaps next month."

"I give it ten days," I tell the dude. "But we'll discuss it."

Doctor smiles like I'm joking and zips off.

"We'll be playing together in two weeks," I promise Bear the next time he shows up.

"Meantime," says Bear, "fill these up," and starts pulling empty tapes out of his jacket pockets!

"Hey, man, you spent a lot of diaper money there."

Bear says no. He got them through a connection for a buck each.

"Just you make sure," says Bear, "that these tapes stay as hot as they are."

So now I'm the busiest patient in the hospital and Bear keeps saying: "I don't know what shit they've got you on in this hospital, but I want some of it. Could it be Lena's vitamins?" And then he pops a couple of them and grins a lot.

I tell him to get his own. And that it was Mara—the same Mara on whose behalf I punched my way into this place—who always says "nothing is impossible."

Bear says, "You would have punched anybody spitting at anything female." Bear still thinks of me as some fool Galahad. I tell him, I would punch anybody who spat on Bear, too, so what did that make Bear?

Bear wraps a towel around his middle for a skirt and does a fast shimmy. Just then, Snaptidy-nurse comes into the room. Bear points his shimmy-ass right at her, causing Snaptidy to gasp. Because the towel he is using as a skirt is a hospital towel.

So I'm the star pupil in the physio room, developing strength and dexterity in every part that moves, and I'm playing and filling up the tapes, and discussing the future with Bear, making lots of plans for when I'm out of here. And then, one day, I get two new visitors one after the other and life takes off in yet another direction.

ALICIA

I phoned Lena to give her a message from Bear: "He says you are a 'real Susan.'"

Lena guesses being "a real Susan" is a good thing.

"The best. Bringing Ted that keyboard was not only the act of a kind and thoughtful friend, Lena my dear, but according to Bear it was also the single most important thing to have happened in Ted's adult life. Oh, yes. Ted is writing music again, composing directly to tape, and Bear says it's great stuff. And since Bear is sure that music is the healing force of the universe, you are Muse and Good Witch of the North and "a real Susan," above which there is no greater praise.

Lena says: "But, Alicia, you're the one who gave me the idea to get Ted a keyboard."

"Not me. I thought "poor Ted, not playing" and I would have said it more than once, very sincerely, but that's all. You are the one who went and did it and, believe me, Bear is your friend for life! Are you purring?"

Lena says: "I am, I am," and I can hear she's got tears rising up.

"Happy tears?"

"Happy," says Lena. "Yes."

TED

I am playing "Roseland Shuffle" for some tiger lilies dancing on my windowsill. Then Lena comes in, bringing me a pot full of boiled gravel she calls seven-grain cereal. Hello, hello and then a question: Would it be all right if Albert came up to visit me? Yes, she is talking about Mara's husband number two from Vienna. He's in Toronto, staying at the Park Plaza Hotel, and he is wishing to come and see me.

"Of course," says I, "I like the dude. Tell him any time."

"He's downstairs now," says Lena. "I'll go get him."

While I'm pushing the keyboard to the side waiting for Albert, Helga comes sliding into my mind. Helga in Bergheim. I'd like to see her again, too. How about Helga and my grandma meeting up, and the two of them doing a *Kaffeeklatsch mit Bienenstich*? Stories about canaries and mules. And even Mrs. Whatsnikoff. I wouldn't mind exchanging a few more cackles with that one, just to keep me from ever riffing pablum. Mind you, not likely Mrs. Whatsnikoff would show up in Toronto, unless the prosecution brought her over here, but I sure intend to ask Albert if Helga is coming. A question I completely forget the minute I see him standing in the doorway.

It's not the same Albert. He looks older and slower-moving, and there's something gnawing on the man. Something besides being in a strange place he can hardly see.

Lena kind of eases Albert along to the chair beside my bed, says she'll be back, and splits. Albert and I shake hands and he says:

"I am sorry about your accident."

What accident? Who is telling the man bullshit stories? Albert is glad I'll soon be well again. Then he takes a short pause and a long breath and asks:

"Has Mara come to pay you a visit?"

"No," I tell him. "I haven't actually been in a receiving mood."

"Mara," says Albert, "is not nervous of contracting a disease, you understand. Nor is she afraid of the ill, as some people are. But for Mara, hospitals are..." Albert is fishing around for words.

"...hospitals are what, Albert? Spit it out. Dangerous drug depots and just stepping near the place gets you hitched up to cloud nine? Was Mara ever...?"

Albert shakes his head. Not like I'm way off-base, wondering about Mara and drug addiction. More like it's one of the guesses he's already checked out and eliminated.

"I don't know how to explain it," he says. "I have seen Mara walk several blocks out of her way to avoid the sight of a hospital. She invariably turns her head away when passing one by car. And yet..."

"Yes, Albert? And yet...?"

"Well, when she herself was in hospital, in Indonesia and later in Vienna, too, I visited her every day, of course, and I can only say that she seemed...as much as I have ever seen her, before or since... I would say Mara was lighthearted. I would even say 'happy.'"

Albert's eyes can't send much to help you out, but his tone of voice is saying: "I'm totally puzzled by this one, myself. Puzzled and bewildered."

Albert, I remind myself, is the guy who has Mara's piano in his apartment. And keeps it locked. Still, he knows more about her than anybody else around and *he* is puzzled and bewildered!

"Ted," he says and lets out a deep sigh, " I guess you know by now..."

Albert has found out that Mara did it. That she committed the Heinous Deed.

"Hold on, man. Mara didn't actually *hurt* anybody..."

Albert is not listening. Off somewhere among his illusions, trying to save them from this new shrill light. Later, Albert. Right now, he has to answer a question for me.

"Albert. *Why* did Mara do it?"

He shakes his head. Hell and damnation, Mara hasn't told him, either.

"What about her defense? What's she going to plead? Have you talked to her lawyer?"

Albert brings his very serious face closer and says: "Ted, it is of great importance that Mara's lawyer not try to push her into an insanity plea. Not even temporary insanity. I have met with him and I have tried to convince him that the results of such a plea would be disastrous. I am not certain that he took my point. He did say it would be a last resort, but I want it entirely eliminated from the list of possibilities. He and I will be meeting again."

Albert stops. It's not fun to see this fine old dude all agitated and stirred up so I try to reassure him.

"I can tell you one thing: Mara has that lawyer of hers well trained and under control. He won't do anything she doesn't want him to do."

"Mara would certainly never agree to a plea of insanity. Never."

Personally, I don't see the fuss—if it keeps you out of jail and leaves you clear of a criminal record, hell, a speck of insanity on your reputation is no worse than a case of acne. Albert and Mara obviously don't see it like that, so I let it rest, because following my first couple of questions, a whole tangle more of them landed on me. Except right then Lena comes into the room, saying she and Albert should be on their way if they're going to be on time for their dinner reservations.

Albert wants to freshen up. He gets himself out the door and Lena stands in the doorway and watches him walk down the hall to find the men's room by himself.

"He hates to be babied," she says.

"Come back in here. Does Mara know you are dating her husband?"

Lena looks at me like I've just sprouted six warts on my nose.

"Mara's husband?" she says." Mara is refusing to see Albert. Won't agree to meet him at all. I am having dinner with the man. What is eating you?"

"Nothing. Forget it. Just wishing I could come along, I guess."

Lena smiles like I'm ten years old and shouldn't be asking for lollipops at my age. Then she looks down the hall again.

"I worry about Albert. His eyes are not going to get better, and Mara... You see," says Lena, "Albert will always do the Honourable Thing."

"Is that right?" says I. "Did you know that he is the one who left Mara? I don't find that so very Honourable."

"You mean," says Lena, "that Mara and Albert no longer live under the same roof."

Albert came back and then they were both gone. I really wanted to think about Lena's comments. Albert...the Honourable Thing...not living under the same roof, and about Mara and hospitals. But I'd spent all night playing, like I do these nights, so I'd barely started in on the thinking when I fell asleep. And while I was asleep, Mara came out of the nook she'd been occupying when everything was on hold and she spread herself all over every inch of my mind. No room at all for my keyboard, which stayed closed and I didn't even hear it knocking. And so when Bear came by the next day to pick up a tape full of new music and found out I hadn't been playing, he was pissed off.

"'Mara on my Mind' is not exactly an original any more," he says. "What will make you get back to playing? A few more broken bones?"

"Some answers," I tell him. "For example: exactly how long ago did I tell Mara not to come visit me just yet?"

"Hey, Ted," says Bear. "You're not what I would call fond of hospitals yourself."

Bear should know. The first day we met, I ended up handcuffed, arriving at a hospital at four in the morning, and the next day Bear had to come and spring me out of there.

Bear jabs at me. "I suppose you're back to hassling everybody in sight for doing the job they were trained to do? I suppose you're back to that old chorus: 'What would make a mother do such a thing'?"

He takes a look at my face and raises both hands.

"Okay, okay, don't start growling. Here's what we'll do: you make a list of your questions about Mara and hand it over to me. I'll go heat up fingernail irons, or maybe earlobe clippers, and then I'll go to Mara's with that list of your questions to get you the answers. And I'm doing all that because another dry spell from you right in the middle of this fertile season is not going to be tolerated."

"Unfortunately," I have to tell Bear, "neither of us gets to make the weather on this one." Bear talks about fertile seasons because he has them. Fallow ones, when he does nothing but play the best jazz bass around, and fertile ones when he holes up and pours out music, from his head directly onto music sheets.

"But," I tell Bear, "that list of questions actually is a good idea. Why don't you be the one starting it off with some of the questions about Mara you've got to be carrying around in your own head by now. Just you make sure you start out with a 'why.'"

Bear takes off like a giant cat on the hunt, muttering under his breath. I decide to by-pass the waiting until he gets back and swallow three downers to knock me out, but this time they're not working for me. I finally give up and open my eyes, and I get a big surprise: Mara. Standing at the foot of my bed, watching me.

"I am glad to see you are doing well," says Mara. Then, like she's come to give me a report: "The preparations for the court case are going well, also. I am confident that everything will work perfectly."

I don't want to shake her off her confidence, so I can't ask where she's getting it.

Now Mara takes a step backwards and stands there, completely still.

"What do you think?" she says. She turns around, slowly, and then stands still again.

"Mara, let me see if I've got this right. I haven't laid eyes on you since we were at the Empire, listening to Dizzy together, both of us more or less in one piece. Now, here you are visiting me for the first time and you want me to comment about *what you are wearing*?"

"Yes, yes," says Mara. "Is it perfect?"

I knew by then she wasn't just fishing for compliments. "Perfect for what, Mara?"

"Oh, I'm so sorry, Ted," says Mara. "Of course I should have told you that. It's for my first day in court. Tomorrow."

"*Tomorrow?* Your first day in court is tomorrow?"

I can't fucking believe this! Not one of my so-called friends has told me. They must have actually conspired to keep this from me! Even Lena hasn't told me tomorrow is Mara's first day in court!

Mara is giving up on me, turning away.

"Wait, Mara," I tell her. "You are amazing. What are you doing here, visiting me the day before your trial starts? I'm all right. Go home and rest, or wash your hair, or go out to a movie or something. Whatever you have to do to be cool tomorrow."

Mara gives me a little smile, waves a graceful hand.

"Oh, I am entirely prepared, Ted. There is nothing left to decide or to do. Everything is arranged perfectly. The trial will not be a long one, I think. A few days, perhaps. And then I shall be acquitted."

This time I can't let it pass.

"Tell me about those preparations of yours and what makes you so confident you'll be acquitted."

"Oh, I can't possibly go into it all now."

I suspect more conspiracy. "Did somebody tell you not to tire me or some shit like that?"

"No, Ted. Nobody told me anything. They could not even tell me when you'll be well enough to leave here."

She can't mean well enough to be of use to her, because my job is supposed to be over once the trial starts. In fact, it would have been over today.

"Mara, I'm really sorry I couldn't stick around to do my job..."

Mara nods. And says: "I did have to alter my strategy again. It will not be a trial by jury." She gives me a little smile. "Perhaps," she says, "this necessary change will be for the best."

"Well," says I, "I am certainly glad to hear that some good has come out of me getting myself broken in pieces and stuck in here."

As soon as I hear myself say "in pieces" I feel useless. No help to anybody, and not even looking good. Every time the mirror catches me, I have to ask myself: how long till my face stops making like the bare ass of a monkey?

Meantime, Mara has come close enough to shake my hand and wish me *Gute Besserung*. She says it means "good recovery" but in English it sounds awkward.

"So, if you are interested in the proceedings, I'll let you know how the case is developing."

"Interested in the proceedings? What kind of bullshit is this? You really think my interest was tied to your chequebook?"

Mara smiles one of those "how charming of you" smiles at me and starts heading for the door. Which makes me realize in double time that I'm not ready to have her disappear on me again, so I say the first thing that comes to mind:

"Wait. May I give you a ride home?"

"Yes, thank you," says Mara. She is actually twinkling, remembering our first meeting. Then she shakes her head. "Unfortunately, your doctor said 'no.' I asked him myself but he said 'on no condition.' Not even with a hired nurse by your side at all times."

I am speechless. I want to hear Mara say it again: that she tried to spring me out of hospital, and I want to thank her for it. But before I can do that, Mara goes and spoils it all.

"Well," she says, "You are probably enjoying your stay here..."

She does not seem to be joking.

"What in bloody hell can you possibly mean by 'enjoying my stay'?"

And Mara tells me for the second time how she has always enjoyed her sojourns in hospitals. And how, watching me sleep today, she was reminded of being in hospital with typhoid fever when she was twelve, her hair falling out, an endearing lace bonnet to cover her head, and how, ever after, she felt hospitals were havens. The only place where nothing was expected of her. No practicing, no decisions of any kind. Where even later, as an adult, nothing at all was left up to her to decide, to arrange, to bring about...

I wasn't really listening any more by then and when Mara started to leave, I didn't call her back. I had some very urgent business to take care of. Preparations to make. Because the next day, one way or another, I was going to move all of my pieces out of the hospital, and over to the courthouse for the opening day of Mara's trial.

MARA

Dear Theodore,

Whenever a quavering note arises in my confidence during these days of preparations for my trial, I remind myself how my powers of precise observation and decisive action have been honed since the long-ago time of my second interrogation by the SS. The proof that I was successful in orchestrating the proceedings is in my sitting here, alive, free and able to write to you.

Two men, that second time, and strangers both. Tall, eminently Aryan, astounded from the first sight of me: sailing in wearing my high-brimmed hat and looking around the office for a suitable chair. I wore my blue silk blouse and pearls, the suit I have described to you with the tailored slim skirt and feminine curve to the jacket, which is long and bell-shaped. Gloves, handbag and shoes in a rare and subtle blue-green to complete the picture of accustomed elegance. No excess of any kind, lest they think: Aha! A foreign strain. Not even a daring contrast, not even a touch of the playful. And not a word more than necessary.

My papers examined again, my origins gone over again, my reason for coming to Bergheim...obviously not a likely place for such as I unless I had come to ski, which they certainly knew I had not. Everyone here knows I have never skied.

I repeated the old tale of concert tour and rheumatic trouble and the baths at the spa. Then: the beauty of the area, the climate, the health of my child, the friends I made. I mentioned Herr Hauser's name whenever possible. Though I don't know what exactly his position is, I know by his very appearance that it is pro-Nazi and high.

They did nearly startle me off-course once, with a sudden question about Eva. Do you remember her? Father's legal secretary in 1930. A young Russian-German woman of great energy who used occasionally to come for Sunday dinner. You'll remember her by the big wart under her left eye.

I never paid her attention, she was so utterly dowdy and provincial, but now, it seems, she lives in Bergheim and has recognized me. She wanted her husband, who is a Nazi, to report me. When he refused, she herself went to the SS to claim that I am Jewish. Imagine!

The only incident I can recall which might have sparked that atrocious act took place one Sunday, when she and I were left alone for a short time and she tried to tell me that my hairdo was severe. (You remember the fashion: short, straight and smooth as glass. Very chic.) I threw her an eloquent look, taking in her entire unspeakably boring appearance, and opened a magazine.

In the interrogation office, with a picture of Hitler framed by two Swastika flags, the men watched me closely. I smiled.

"Yes," I said. "Of course. Eva. I remember her well and I liked her immensely. My father had to let her go, unfortunately..."

I sighed, implying that polite silence about Eva and her untrustworthiness was my lofty intention.

It was a gamble and I won. The men exchanged looks and told me to return the next day.

You see, dear brother, how the study of appearance has stood me in good stead. Eva, if you recall, has one eye which wanders when she is agitated (a physical trait often mistaken for a trait of character) and which thus gives the no doubt perfectly honest woman a shifty look.

When I recall that victory, I am again tranquil and am even anticipating the trial with some excitement.

As always, your beloved sister,
Mara

TED

I would just as soon skip what Alicia calls "Ted's latest escapade," but she wouldn't let me. For one thing, she was the only one who wasn't there and she wants to hear all about it with every detail in place, if you please, and for another, how else would I explain the decision I made that day? According to Alicia, the most important decision of my life.

Well, okay. First of all, I had to find out what my so-called friends were keeping frm me so I sent Bitsy to get me newspapers. Bitsy is my only ally inside the hospital: a shy little mouse named Bettina, so scared she might drop a dustcloth or sweep away somebody's penny that she creeps around and sidles her eyes, and from the first time I saw her, I wanted to make her stand tall and listen up while I recited a list of all the rights she has just for being a two-legged animal on this planet.

Bitsy came back with an armful of newspapers and I scanned through them, reading headlines and the captions under photos.

OPINION POLLS SHOW 85% OF AMERICANS SUPPORT PRESIDENT JOHNSON'S DECISION TO BOMB VIETNAM

THE BEATLES ON ED SULLIVAN

(Not in the Entertainment section of the paper, mind you, but on the front page. And not a word about the music. No, it's the hair and all the screaming girls, and those four fabled youngsters from Liverpool...oh, get on with it, Ted.)

BLACK MUSLIUMS: "F-INTEGRATION, WE WANT HUMAN RIGHTS"

CHINA REJECTS RUSSIA'S "PEACEFUL CO-EXISTENCE" AND GOES IT ALONE

Ringo, when asked "are you a Mod or Rocker?" said "I'm a Mocker."

U.S. AIR RAIDS DESTROY HALF THE NORTH VIETNAMESE NAVY

STREETCAR SEVERS TOES OF 4-YEAR OLD BOY

CHINA WOOS AFRICA AND ASIA

(I thought China was going it alone?)

MOST POPULAR T.V. SHOW: THE FLINTSTONES

Malcolm X is the second most popular speaker at colleges and campuses, after senator Barry Goldwater.

Holy Belinda! That doctor could be right: maybe I wasn't ready to leave the hospital. Because I sure as hell was not ready for the world out there. Malcolm X and Senator Goldwater? Mind you, now that I remembered it, Barry Goldwater did say, "Extremism in the defense of liberty is no vice." Pretty soon Goldwater and Malcolm X are gonna be a double bill and everybody will pronounce that a sign of progress. Debate your views. The more talking, the less jumping around. No rocking, no rocks.

LONG HOT SUMMER; 276 ARRESTED IN HARLEM RIOT

PRESIDENT JOHNSON IS PLAYING POLITICS WITH POVERTY, SAYS SEN. GOLDWATER

(I hate having to agree with that fucker Goldwater.)

TORONTO MAPLE LEAFS, WITH THREE CONSECUTIVE STANLEY CUPS...

Testing the Civil Rights Act of 1964: three judges order a restaurant in Atlanta, Georgia to admit negroes within 20 days.

TIED FOR MOST POPLUAR: THE PRICE IS RIGHT, I LOVE LUCY

LENNY BRUCE ARRESTED ON OBSCENITY CHARGES

(I couldn't tell whether the world picked that month to go berserk or whether it was the world as usual. I'd never been stationary long enough to get bombarded by all the bad news in the world at once. And some of it damned confusing, like this one:)

Prime Minister Lester B. Pearson on Aug. 6th, in a statement to the Canadian House of Commons: his government urged Washington to stay clear of any action in Vietnam that could lead to war.

In the same paper they gave the body count of Vietnamese dead, which sure sounded like war to me. Something to ask Bear about. Which I do when he arrives, as usual with one of Alicia's soups, and while I'm spooning up tongue soup Bear explains to me why the killing in Vietnam is not a war.

"It's a 'Police Action,' you ignorant blob. And a Police Action is entirely different than a War, see? The corpses are just as dead but that's only because they don't know any better."

Bear is doing his "White House Public Relations man" and I am just glad to hear it isn't myself gone nuts. That it's still the Out There that's really way out there.

"And what we have going on in the States," says Bear, "is not a revolution, you understand. It's some 'Racial Unrest.'"

Bear is off and running and there is no way I can introduce my personal unrest and my plans to overthrow hospital law and order the very next day until Bear comes to a stop on his own.

"Listen to this," says Bear, grabbing a paper: "Rochester, New York. Population 320,000, 40,000 of them black. New York National Guard units and State Police called out. Ten hours of fighting. Tear gas grenades thrown by the cops were picked up by youth and thrown back. Three hundred and fifty injured, one white man killed, 400 blacks arrested. Eight p.m. curfew imposed and ignored by hundreds. Rockefeller called it all 'clear evidence of extremism' and sent in one thousand, you hear that? One thousand more National Guardsmen, steel helmets, bayoneted rifles and all.

"However," says Bear, "lucky for us, President Johnson and Senator Goldwater have met and they have reached an agreement: That 'racial tension should be avoided!'"

Now that I've started looking past my own bed rails again, I have to admit that none of this is totally new.

Then Bear starts talking about opening a civil rights chapter right here in Toronto and how he's having a hard time choosing an organization. CORE? ACT? NAACP? SNNC? Not the Black Muslims, because Alicia would kick him off the planet before she put up with long sleeves in the summertime. But there is this new one Bear is looking into: the Mississippi Freedom Democratic Party. They have a black panther for their emblem, so the press started calling this group the Black Panther Party. Bear is checking it out to see what they're fighting against and what they're fighting for.

What I really want to say to Bear is this: Forget it. Tear yourself right off that manure pile called U.S. of A. and settle into the compost heap called Canada. But the U.S. of A. is and always will be the home of Bear's gut. So I just tell him I'm into playing music and raising bread for any bunch of letters he decides to pick, as long as it's going to be fighting racism right here in Toronto the Good. By now a big bowl full of that hot spicy tongue soup is inside of me and is causing my eyes to close, so if Bear could just stick around for about ten minutes because I have something else to tell him, something very very important...

When I wake up, Bear is gone. While I'm dialling his number, I see my flowers, dancing their colours all over the windowsill. It suddenly hits me that I haven't once asked where all the flowers came from. Who is bringing them? I yell for Bitsy and she's in here like a flash—sometimes I think she lives just outside my door—and I ask her about the flowers.

Some are from "her," says Bitsy. The "her" dripping with significance.

I ask Bitsy to describe this "her." I can hardly wait to hear Bitsy describing Mara, but it turns out to be Lena, the lady who also brings vitamin pills and herbal teas.

"Some of the other flowers," says Bitsy, "they're just sent through a flower shop. They always have a card with good wishes from M."

Bitsy's voice has dismissed those other flowers and has also made it clear that Bitsy does not think "M" stands for mother. The flowers are from Lena and from Mara, and I have never told either of them how much time I spend with my eyes hanging on those blossoms. Even when I'm playing music, on the keyboard or in my head, my eyes are on the flowers.

"And the rest of them," says Bitsy, "are stolen."

"How do you know they're stolen?"

"Well, where would you buy bunches of garden flowers in this city? The stems all different lengths, too."

"You could grow them? In your garden?"

Bitsy titters. "Using her fingernails for a hoe?"

"Okay, Bitsy. Out with it. Who is bringing me garden flowers?"

"Garden flowers, park flowers, even dandelions. Your friend with the dyed red hair and the white lipstick and..."

"The Tic! Still at it. Holy shit, that woman never stops asking for trouble!"

"Actually," Bitsy sighs because she doesn't know any way around honesty. "She isn't trying to make trouble. She's trying to make up for something. She told one of the volunteers that she's the one landed you in here."

"Well, the Lord above save me from the penitent. Look, Bitsy. If you ever see this redhead, tell her to just get out of my life and stay out of my life, and all will be forgotten. Okay? Tell her that."

Bitsy wanted to sit down and hear all about it, but this wasn't the time.

I felt like different pieces of my life had been off on different journeys, and now they were all floating back in and I had to catch them so I could put them together again. But right then, all I could really get a hold of was this: I had to be there for Mara's first day in court. Somehow I had to get myself out of the hospital and over to that courtroom and be there.

I phone Bear and he's home by now. And pretty soon he says okay, he's into it. He'll get me out for tomorrow, as long as I promise to get back to the keyboard the day after. Promise on my grandmother's head. Swear on my own ten fingers. I call Lena and she doesn't exactly hug the idea to her bosom, but eventually she promises to come and help get me out.

"Because healing," says Lena, "is not promoted by the state of mind of an addled goat."

I've told them both I'll call back just as soon as all my plans are made. Strategy, tactics, and time of action. Probably around 7:45 a.m., I figure, when the nurses change shifts.

And then the Great Trickster Up Above saw fit to warn me off the whole thing: don't do it! don't be an idiot! stay put!, but I wasn't paying attention. I was sitting up in my bed and I was the general about to come up with his brilliant campaign. No notion at all that this was going to turn into a caper. Of the sort I would just as soon not hang out on the line. Except maybe for my grandma, for laughs, just as soon as I get brave enough to tell her I'm in hospital and haven't even let her know.

Here is how it went:

It's evening and the night nurse comes in. The skinny one, with a little round belly and green-blond hair. She hands me my sleeping pill and I make like I'm swallowing it but I palm it instead. I've been doing that a while now because I need my nights for playing. I'm just slipping this one in with the others I stashed in a former vitamin bottle, when I see the nurse is still standing in the doorway watching me. Now Miss Little-Belly comes back in and points to the pills:

"You want to trade some of those?"

"What have you got?"

"You name it," she says. And frowns like she disapproves of a hospital where this sort of thing goes on.

"How about some speed?"

Speed has its uses. For instance: when you've been playing a gig and then have to pack up the instruments in the middle of the night and drive somewhere else, sleep two hours or none, do a sound check and start playing all over again.

Miss Little-Belly hands me four big white capsules. Speed by a fancy medical name. I give her something, too. Not the sleeping pills she expects, but some of Lena's vitamins, which, I tell the nurse, are a new street drug. She's about to study these long speckled pills but there's somebody out in the hall, coming closer, so she pockets them and off she goes.

To stash the speed, I empty the last few pills out of one of Lena's little bottles, figure I might as well swallow them, and did. And that was it. The very next thing I know, Bear is shaking me. Refusing to let up. Saying things like: "Come on, man, wake up! It's 7:30 in the morning and I fucking well didn't get my ass out of bed in the middle of the night so I could come over here and watch you sleep. So get up!"

Bear has to keep on shaking me because every time he stops, my eyelids fall down again. Because the pills I thought were vitamins were actually some of my stashed sleeping pills. And these sleeping pills were four and they were strong, and I was one and very weak, and so to stop Bear shaking my teeth out of my head, I open the other little vitamin bottle and make damned sure it's the right one this time, and take the speed by a fancy name. To wake me up. And the speed is very strong and I am very weak, and on top of all that other shit I'd been taking lately, and all that lying around on my ass with even the weight of the casts suspended in a sling, well, let me tell you, I can hardly sit up, let alone march at the head of the parade.

It's nearly eight o'clock by now and Bear is rarin' to go. It turns out that Bear and Lena have gone ahead and made plans all on their own for getting me out of hospital, and Tedboy is just the goods to be transported. What the hell!

Except that things don't exactly go according to their plan, either. Because the goods they are transporting have turned into one revved-up mess, wracked by bouts of inconvenient laughter. Tedboy on a chemical roller coaster.

Anyway, here we are at 8:00 a.m. Lena is waiting outside with the van. Bear has pushed a wheelchair into the room and he's brought my own clothes. What he didn't bring is scissors for cutting open my pant legs—there's no other way you can get into jeans when your legs are two fat plaster mummies. We can't very well call a nurse, so Bear takes the tiny penknife off his key ring and starts slitting the legs of my jeans. He hacks away, one side and another, till they're ragged flaps and so now my crotch starts playing peek-a-boo. I'm all for trying again with Bear's jeans, but Bear says: "You'll never be able to get that white ass of yours into my jeans." This from the guy who's been sharing a pair of tux pants with me for at least a year, fitting both of us just fine.

"Man, you sure do love that ass of yours."

"Better than being one," says Bear. And right about then the amphetamines hit and reveal to me that our usual ribbing each other is the hippest repartee on the Avenue. I hoot and snort and holler out loud and Bear has to rush out into the hall and make sure that all the nurses are still at the nurse's station.

Bear tells me to pipe down and that I'll be sitting anyway, so he'll cover me with a blanket.

But the blanket makes me itch, especially under the casts. Bear tries a pillowcase pinned around my lower middle, and that looks exactly like a diaper and sets me to hooting and hollering again and now Bear is getting pissed off.

"Okay, okay, the blanket."

So now he's got me in the wheelchair and decently covered up but the damned casts on my legs won't bend. They stick out higher than the footrest of the wheelchair and it hurts like hell, all that weight pulling on my hip joints. So Bear comes up with another one. He unscrews the lid of the keyboard and rigs it up like a platform extending out from the seat of the wheelchair so my legs can rest on it, sticking out ahead. Then he yanks the cord out of the curtain they pull around the hospital bed, and he ties the piano lid to the wheelchair and my casts to the lid. Bear covers it all up with the blanket, and now we really are ready to roll.

Then Lena comes in and wants to know what the hell is keeping us. Bear tells her I'm ripped on something.

"You can't be serious," says Lena.

"That's right, I can't be serious," says I and start hooting all over again. Long and loud.

So now Lena gets to work on me and she forces me to eat soup. The last of Alicia's tongue soup, but cold, which isn't fair. Then they make me drink a lot of water. All that fluid makes me heavy enough to sit still and bloat for a while, and Bear promises me a joint to slow my head down. He says he's stashed one in the van. All we have to do now is get out there.

"Okay," he says. "Hold on tight."

Down the hall, no problem. Waiting for the elevator, no problem. Going down, we're alone in the elevator and Bear reminds me: Lena's piled that bag and a couple of my flowerpots on my lap so we can pretend this patient is moving out. Nobody at the reception desk raises an eye from their papers so out we go, around to the side, where the van is waiting with the back doors open and with the organ dolly making like a ramp. No snags. They roll me into the back of the van, with me pretending to be my own organ and squawking some enthusiastic scales and arpeggios, and here we are.

"Man, if it's this easy, we could have got me out of that hospital to play a jam session, or just to go for a ride!"

"No, thanks," says Bear.

All of a sudden the outside world is all around me, zipping in every direction. Bear is in the back with me, lighting a joint. I take two good long tokes and start slowing down a bit. And next thing I know we're in the courthouse parking lot and bells are gonging somewhere and my wheelchair is moving through some big doors into a lofty hall with lots of echoes and one skinny escalator going up. There's a black crow crossing in front of me. He sees another black crow going up on the escalator and calls up: "Harold!"

Harold looks down like he's perched on a branch and croaks: "I got your message."

The crow beside me caws back up: "Can we get the deferment?"

And Harold croaks: "Yes, I'll arrange it."

I don't understand a word of it, but I get the feeling somebody's fate has just been decided in thirty-seconds, between escalator crow and chum.

Right then I get an attack of crow phobia because they're everywhere, popping up from behind groups of people and walking briskly along, black wings flapping...

My mind is jumping around like a demented frog. And then it lands smack on a what-if: What if something goes wrong and Mara is convicted?

Bear's voice says: "Close your mouth, Ted. And sit up. We're out in public now!"

I'm tied to the wheelchair, getting rolled through open double doors and right into some experimental music. A rhythmic squeal cutting into a sustained baritone drone. The squeal turns out to be my wheelchair and when I locate the baritone, it's a male voice, droning out a stream of words. We're in the courtroom, and the fuckers have obviously gone ahead and started the trial without me. Now I actually catch some words:

"Please, your Honour, could counsel speak more slowly."

Said by a woman with a face so dead white, I expect her to start jumping for butterflies, like that French mime with a flower standing on his head.

"Yes, Whiteface," I tell her. "I, too, wish counsel to speak more slowly."

"Shh," say Lena and Bear, one in each ear.

"I would submit, your Honour," says the drone, and "with the greatest respect, your Honour, as I indicated to the court..." and more stuff like that. Then a phrase jumps out at me: "prior undertaking."

What is that? Getting buried before you're dead? Or some kind of bargaining? Like: we've agreed to plead guilty to one earlobe, if you let us off the other?

I want to ask Bear what's going on here—it sounds bad. So I turn my head, and that's when I see Mara. Sitting right there in the front.

I keep looking at her: is that really Mara's back? Or is that maybe some kind of replica they've put there, to represent the real Mara? Do they do that?

I want corroboration. Maybe those tokes of weed on top of all the chemicals have taken me so far out, I am now hallucinating Mara's shape.

"Look down there," I hiss around my shoulder at Bear. "What do you see?"

"No doubt about it," says Bear. "It's Mara."

"I've got to get a look at her from the front," I tell Bear.

He starts pushing me down the aisle—wheelchair squealing—then all the way across the front to the other side, passing right in front of Mara.

It's her.

But she's not there.

She is sitting, facing front, eyes looking down at her hands. Her body is present but the rest of her has gone somewhere deep down inside. She hasn't even seen us going by.

Bear parks me beside the fourth row, and sits down on the bench.

"Man, that's a new one on me," whispers Bear. "I've seen people in church go into a trance, but this isn't anything like that. Maybe she's *on* something?" Bear's head keeps shaking.

Me, the second I look at Mara from the front, I can see the Magic Mantle all around her, and Mara, deep inside, spinning it. It's a big relief.

I look up at the altar and there's the judge, preaching. "If the Crown has any knowledge or evidence which will expedite the trial of this case then we would all be obliged if we could hear it and hear all of it, now. We are not in a television courtroom drama that is best served by intermittent surprises. We are here in a court of law."

Bear bends over again and translates:

"The prosecutor wanted to keep a witness for later but the judge says now. Must be dynamite."

The witness is moving into place on the right, just lower than the judge.

"Holy fuck!" says Bear. "Look who's up there as a witness for the prosecution.

The witness is Lena!

"...the material facts involved in this case are not in dispute...blah blah blah...I have brought this witness in for the purposes of determining the nature of the relationship between the mother Mara deJong and the daughter, Michelle." The talker swivels towards Lena. "Your friend," he says to her.

Mara's lawyer objects. Blah blah blah, Lena's testimony would be hearsay.

So far I've been staring at Lena. Now my eyes are caught by Mara's lawyer, turning to look at Mara. So I look at Mara, too, and I see her left hand lightly tapping the arm of her chair. Two times. Very precise little taps. And her lawyer stops his objecting right then and there. He drops his head. He mumbles something like "Sorry for the interruption, your Honour," and he sits down.

"Did you see that?" says Bear. "I hope you saw that. Just in case you've got a single doubt about Mara ruling the world. Tap, tap, lawyer changes course..."

"Shut up, Bear. I want to hear the judge."

The judge says to answer the question. What question? Concentrate!

Lena says, "I actually know very little about the relationship between Mara deJong and her daughter Michelle."

"That's very hard to believe," says Crown. "After all, you and Michelle were close friends, were you not? You lived in the same house for four years, did you not? You took a vacation together two years ago, did you not? You sometimes had dinner together at the Blue Cellar Room, did you not?"

"Yes," says Lena. "Yes, we did. But Michelle didn't often talk about her mother."

"Didn't you find that curious? Why would a good friend never mention her mother?"

"Michelle did mention her, when she'd receive a letter, for instance. Sometimes she quoted her mother on some subject. But neither of us are—were—given to talking much about our childhoods."

"Because your childhoods were so unhappy?"

The Crown Crow is practically hopping. Lena says: "No, that is not correct. My own childhood was not without joy. I don't know about Michelle; we never really talked about it."

"Well, what *did* you talk about?" Crown Crow is starting to flap. The judge has something to say, but first he wants to hear what Lena and Michelle talked about.

"Our work," says Lena. "Our life. Men."

There's a pause, like a smile all around the court. The judge waves the Crown Crow and Mara's lawyer up to the altar. They talk to each other so quietly I'm not catching any of it. And all of a sudden, my ears start buzzing. A loud, hard buzzing that completely drowns out everything else. And right after that one voice starts up, from inside my own head.

"Ted O'Sullivan," the voice is yelling at me. "This is the absolutely last fucking time you are going to be high and buzzed and floating around right when you need both of your feet on the ground. Don't you ever even go *near* any chemical fucking launching pad again! Shit, man, you are sitting here with about ten percent of you present and accounted for. And the rest buzzing so loud, you can't even *hear* what's going on, let alone figure out what's happening. And you did that to yourself! What the hell gave you the notion that you, Ted O'Sullivan, can just keep on popping a pill here, toking up there, and hoisting a few any old time—how long can that go down without it fucking you up for the rest of your life?"

I didn't have an answer for that voice. All I could do was sit there and promise yes, yes, yes, absolutely for sure, that was the last time. I made that promise over and over till the voice finally stopped attacking me, and then I finally hear something coming in from the outside again. It's Bear, saying:

"Ted, are you paying attention here? That prosecutor didn't get a thing out of Lena. Not one bloody thing. Question is, why would he even call Lena as a witness? Maybe he just figured she was Michelle's friend so she'd be bound to want to do some cutting on Mara? Anyway, Lena did good. Now everybody's thinking, 'If there'd been bad stuff to tell, then Michelle would have told Lena and if Michelle didn't tell her, then there was probably nothing much to tell.' Very together, our Lena. And a real Susan."

I can't even see Lena any more and anyway, I'm still pissed off at myself. What if I miss the explanation about why Mara did the heinous deed? I knew they weren't going to give the true reason in court, but hell, I was even curious about what Mara and her lawyer would come up with for a defence. Mara is sitting upright and very still. She's not wearing gloves; I checked her hands as I was going by. I take some deep breaths and concentrate my available ten percent hard as I can and I guess the high must be levelling out because it's starting to get easier.

Somebody new is in the witness box, swearing to tell the truth. Tall and scrawny, yellow fangs, wispy hair over mottled skull. A Mrs. Heinrich Müller . Resident of Hamilton, Ontario. Originally hailing from Bergheim, Germany. One of those wire coathangers with clothes dangling from it. Small squinty eyes. She's saying something but her voice is so weak she'll likely drop dead before the next sentence. Wait—I think she just got an injection of venom to start the pump going. Her voice is picking up and a steady stream starts pouring out of the puckered hole in her face. A stream with a German accent.

The first words I catch are "we all." Said a few times over. Maybe the woman's a delegate from all the Bergheim housewives and bandage rollers who knew Mara deJong during the war. Not Helga. She's not representing Helga or others like her, but "we all" is at least a platoon.

"We all thought Mara deJong, as she calls herself these days—we all thought she would come to this, one day. High class, she thought herself, but she was a hussy. It's not like she didn't know he was a married man. We all knew, although he never went home on leave. And him with two children! He was supposed to be recuperating from something, even though he was a doctor himself. Had a duelling scar on his left cheek, right here..."

Mrs. Müller pulls a finger across a cheek and throws a look in Mara's general direction. The look says, loud and clear, "I may be old but my memory is clear, and it will bury you."

"And she certainly knew that he was a high-ranking SS officer. He was never out of uniform. In public, that is. The two of them used to go for long walks in the forest, both of them looking like they were parading along on some Berliner promenade. Of course, she always was dressed to the teeth—we all thought the whole black market for clothes must have ended up in her cupboard."

The judge says something I don't catch. Unfortunately it doesn't seem to be an order to hang Mrs. Heinrich Müller .

"Anyway," says scrawny yellow rat-snake, "this one day, the two of them had just left and the child had an accident."

A man's voice barks an interruption and she snarks right back.

"Yes, who else could I mean by the child except Mara's daughter? She lost control on her roller skates and she skated right into Herr Herrendorf's bicycle. They both fell over, Herr Herrendorf on top of the child, so only the child was hurt. Bleeding knees and nose. I thought there might even be concussion. So I sent my youngest to run and fetch them back, Mara and her officer at the Cafe Waldblick, and none of us could believe the message she sent back: 'Take her to the clinic.'

"The child's own mother! And he a doctor!

"In the morning, there was Mara, bringing a stuffed toy dog for the child, playing mother. Never an explanation about where she'd been all night. We all knew she was a hussy, of course, but after that we just shook our heads."

She's still shaking it, on and on, and then she straightens up and holds her head still to listen and takes a breath to answer the next question.

"No, we did not speak to her about it. We all had to live together, live and let live. Of course, we did not invite her to roll bandages with us. She was too good for that, anyway. Played piano for the wounded, she did, up in the mountain hospitals. Wearing evening gowns and high-heeled leather shoes and silk stockings, and God knows how she got those.

"No, we were always polite, as Christians should be, but we all had our private opinion, of course, and we were all agreed on that. And we all knew it would come to this, one day."

The hole has snapped shut but it's clear that if Mrs. Müller weren't such a polite Christian, she'd be cackling with glee.

I look at the judge. What's he making of mother Mara and her abandoned, hurt little girl? He's Jewish so he sure as hell isn't going to like the picture of elegant Mara and Nazi boyfriend.

The judge turns to the Crown dude and asks him something about relevance.

And out comes the Crown with something like this: "Mrs. Müller 's testimony proves that the relationship of Mara deJong to her own child, the victim, blah blah blah..." and then:

"...Mrs. Müller 's evidence proves that Mara's heart, in committing the crime, was not innocent."

Did I hear that right? Is this a courtroom where hearts are on trial? Where they look at the most relevant question of them all: whether Mara's heart is innocent?

Down front, an old man on crutches is manoeuvring himself into the witness box. Agile old bugger. Does he know the answer? The old man's voice is loud and the German accent is very faint. He is Heinrich Müller , Mrs. Müller 's estranged husband. He starts out like he's in the middle of an argument.

"Why would Mara come barrelling back for a scraped knee? She knew Helga was right there on the spot. Helga would be the one looking after the child anyway. Everybody knew that Mara couldn't stand the sight of blood. As for leaving the child alone, the whole house was full of women, for heaven's sake. Which is probably what drove Mara out of there in the first place. But women like my ex-wife," he says, "wouldn't understand that because they don't appreciate a man. They'd just as soon sit around and cackle about other women, especially if the other woman knew how to appreciate a man..." And more stuff like that.

Obviously, the old geezer has come down here to contradict his ex-wife. Mara is just a way for the two of them to do each other more dirt. The judge saw it. He's telling the old man to go ahead and crutch off. He wants Counsellor and Crown at the altar.

"Don't waste my time," he tells them, loudly enough for everybody to hear. Does he think Mara's case is worth only so much time and they were running out of it? Or maybe it's just that he has an ex-wife himself and that Müller duo made his teeth twinge.

"What do you think, Bear?"

"I think those two poisonous buzzards have everybody convinced Mara is a beautiful woman who prefers the company of men to that of women and children."

All of a sudden Lena's voice pipes up from the other side of me. When did she even get here?

"The impression on women," says Lena, "would be very different. Most women will think Mara was neglectful of her child and, well, pleasure-seeking and selfish."

I'm glad there's no jury and that the judge is a man.

Mara's lawyer is getting louder, nattering at the judge: "Would a woman who endangered her own life by listening to Allied Radio deep in Nazi Germany have a Nazi boyfriend? Only if he could provide protection for herself and the child."

The Crown: "Nevertheless, Nazis were the enemy. Of Mara deJong's own people and country."

The judge tells them both to stop. "We are getting altogether too far afield here. We are merely trying to establish the measure of criminal intent in cutting off her dead daughter's earlobes."

I'm starting to feel sick to my stomach.

"There's a set-up here somewhere," says Bear into my ear. "I can smell it."

Then Lena's talking: "I'll have to testify again later in the trial."

"You did fine this time," says Bear.

"Mara was sure I would," says Lena. "She coached me, you know. But I was worried."

Bear is looking around me at Lena and says:

"Are you impersonating a professor? No, wait. I know. A psychologist. A child psychologist!"

"Mara's outfit," says Lena.

Now I hear a voice cutting in from the front: "exhibit number one, your Honour, one pair of gold earrings."

Gasps all around the courtroom.

The judge takes the earrings, looks at them for a long moment, and then hands them over to Whiteface.

Meantime, the crown is telling the judge that Mara cut off her daughter's earlobes so she could get at those gold earrings! Jesus Murphy!

This was the first I'd even *heard* about those earrings, and I sure as hell was in no shape for a shock like that. Next thing I knew, I lost all connection with what was going on in the courtroom because I was so busy trying not to throw up. I wanted Bear to get me out of the courtroom before I puked, but I couldn't move or talk or it would have come spewing out all over. So I just sat there, still as a wall and just as deaf to what was going on. But my eyes were open and they fell on Mara and they see *earrings*. On Mara's ears. A pair of gold earrings.

And next thing I knew, I was horizontal, tipped way back, wheelchair and all, and whizzing along so fast my hair was blowing in the wind. Nobody got in the way of Bear racing a wheelchair up the courtroom aisle, with a wild-haired passenger hanging on, but just. In about a minute we were out on the sidewalk, both of us breathing hard. Slowly my head starts getting clear but I'm still horizontal.

"Hey, Bear. Put me back up!"

Bear tells me he's just trying to get some blood flowing back into my brain. "Lena," he says, "is getting the van. I'm taking you back to the hospital."

Now Lena stops the van a couple of inches from my toes and hops out.

I yell some more about going back into the courtroom and then I must have passed out. When I opened my eyes, I was back in the hospital bed, in the dark, trying to shake a dream out of my head. A dream about a pair of earrings.

And next time I woke up, it was daytime. And the earrings were not a dream.

MARA

Dear Theodore,

The first day is behind me. Since you already know my intentions for the trial, I can simply report that it passed precisely as designed.

The Toronto newspaper which will most assuredly try my case in public is often called "The Rag." This is a pejorative term. (It is always difficult to understand slang in a different language.)

Here is the headline from today's "Rag":

MOTHER MUTILATES DAUGHTER'S CORPSE FOR PAIR OF GOLD EARRINGS

And some quotes: "In the trial of Mara deJong, the Crown today shocked the court by producing a pair of gold earrings. The accused is alleged to have cut the earlobes off her daughter's corpse in order to obtain these earrings. Both the defence attorney and the accused herself sat calmly throughout the allegation."

"The Rag," conscientious to a fault, then described the earrings and even added a drawing of the fastener and safety clasp. Wrong side up. "The earrings are finely worked and of a delicate beauty, nearly one inch in length. Each earring is composed of a pearl, nestling between two half-shells of gold. The hook which goes through the earlobe is caught by a hoop from below and secured with a tiny safety clasp. This type of fastener is not unique to these earrings except for its unusually small size."

The judge, at this point, motioned my lawyer and the Crown attorney to come closer and asked, I'm sure, why, if it had been a matter of acquiring the earrings, didn't I simply *take* them off? Why cut off the earlobes? I am again quoting "the Rag." "The accused has arthritis in her fingers which sometimes causes them to become stiff and swollen and renders them incapable of handling anything so delicate and intricate as the opening of the earrings. And so, determined to have the gold earrings, the accused cut them off, earlobes and all."

Now, at my signal, my lawyer positioned himself halfway between the judge and myself, pointed, and said: "As you can see yourself, your Honour, Mara deJong has no need for her daughter's earrings because she owns an identical pair of earrings and is, in fact, wearing the identical pair at this very moment, proving that the earrings did not constitute a motive."

Excited whispering in the courtroom. The judge asked to look at the earrings again (while everyone else no doubt stared at the earrings on my ears). My composure was perfect. Then the judge abruptly adjourned court for the day.

Nothing more of interest has been printed as yet and I believe it best to refrain from reading newspapers in future. Since they know nothing of me or my purpose, they will inevitably be trapped in the darkness of ignorance.

As always, your beloved sister,

Mara

TED

The morning after I was abducted from the courtroom and dumped back into my hospital bed, I found out that they turned the hospital into a prison, just for me. I couldn't even burp without somebody sticking a head through the door, checking on Ted the Terrible. They ordered another whole series of X-rays (tried to get away? Fry the fucker!) and all the time I was being wheeled around, those earrings followed, crawling with questions. Could they have had something hidden inside them? Microfilm? Mara as Mata Hari? Bullshit! Nobody runs Mara but Mara.

Then Bitsy brought me the Rag and I read the story about the first day of the trial and then scrunched it into a ball and hurled it against the wall.

I refused to believe that Mara would cut off her daughter's earlobes for a pair of earrings. I mean, that's crazy. And Mara is not, definitely not, nuts. She was running her lawyer, she was running me when I still had legs that could run, she was running Lena, and God knows who else in Toronto, not to mention a judge in Indonesia and the SS in World War II. Does that sound like a woman who's nuts? Of course not. Which means that Mara knew full well, as they say, that earlobe removal is not okay. Piercing earlobes is okay. Chopping off bits of nose or tucking half your face behind your ears is okay. Walking around on secret weapons like stiletto heels, that's okay. Burning your hair into an electric frizz is fine, and painting your face is fine. But earlobe off-cutting is not fine. Not in this tribe.

I pull the phone over and dial Mara's number. I let it ring three times and then I hang up. Who am I to interrogate the woman? I'm the one who managed to be in court with her for less than a couple of hours and all the time higher than old cheese.

On the other hand I can't hang around here waiting for the next day's newspaper to find out more. I phone Lena.

"Did you know there were earrings on those earlobes?"

"Yes."

"Why the hell didn't you tell me about them?"

Silence. Lena thought the earrings were bad news about Mara, and Lena does not speak ill of people. The woman is a freak.

"Lena," I try, "it would really help my condition a lot if you could tell me whether she cut off the earlobes to get those earrings."

"I don't know that, Ted."

"Shit."

Lena wants to know if I'm going to be doing any playing today.

"You think my music is some kind of fucking therapy? Some kind of keep-Ted-calm self-therapy?"

Lena says, "So long, Ted," and hangs up. I dial her number again but she's not picking up the phone. Not then and not for the next dozen tries, made in between naps, every one of them a bumpy ride, shaking the drugs out of my system a bump at a time. Finally I wake up, feeling thirsty as the desert but fairly clear in the head, and there, waiting on a chair beside my bed, sits Mara.

"Hello, Ted," says Mara. "How are you?"

"Tell me, please," says Mara, "what did you think of my tactics, yesterday?"

Mara's face comes closer.

"Are you all right, Ted? Can you hear me?"

I manage something like a nod.

"Good," says Mara. "Tell me whether you think it worked. I believe that wearing the earrings to court showed everyone that they could be duplicated—that I didn't commit a crime in order to enrich myself or in order to be the owner of a unique piece of jewellery. Do you agree?"

I nodded again.

"At the same time," says Mara, "the earrings had the precise effect on people which they are intended to have. I suspect now that they failed their previous test because not all aspects of the situation were known to me. This time, they have certainly proved themselves to be most effective."

Dramatic pause, then she bends closer and says:

"They predispose people to be helpful. To go beyond their usual degree of willingness to help."

"Mara, let me get this straight: you are talking about a pair of earrings?"

"Yes, yes, Ted. That particular pair of earrings."

Mara looks perfectly serious, is expecting an answer. She is not wearing earrings now.

"Mara, I'll tell you what I think about the helpfulness of earrings if you tell me one thing: Why *did* you cut off your daughter's earlobes?"

Mara is looking down at her hands, which are wearing gloves, and it's clear she won't be answering my question.

"Not yet," says Mara. "But soon I'll be able to tell you. Very soon, I hope. Please be patient, Ted."

Now right there, when I'm told I have to wait, I usually get pissed off and do something stupid. But this time it all went a different route. I jumped straight over getting riled and when I landed, I was standing in Mara's moccasins. And I could see that what the woman needed right then was a friendly hand she could get hold of.

So I told her: "All right, Mara, some day soon you'll tell me. Meantime, yes, you wearing the duplicate earrings sure would have convinced *me* that you're not selfish or ruthless. But then, I never thought you were. After all, you're the one who grieved for weeks over a dog. You're the one who helped Mrs. Whatsnikoff get out of the Soviet Union. The one who went to bat for the three Indonesian peasants accused of murder. That does not sound selfish or ruthless to me."

Mara has been listening like I've been playing the greatest solo she's ever heard. Now she jumps up and says she has to go.

"Thank you, Ted. Thank you very much. I'll be back to morrow."

My tongue is still in gear, but she's gone.

Lena wasn't answering her phone. (Turned out later that she wasn't answering the phone because she was not allowed to talk about the trial, since she was supposed to appear at it one more time.) Bear called and said he couldn't come by because he had an early sound check. It's taking hours, he said on the phone, bored and bugged because the so-called fucking vocalist on the gig forgot to tell the so-called fucking leader that he was bringing two back-up singers along, a couple of hang-around chicks he'd promised a break, so setting up the mics... I think I fell asleep with the receiver still ragging at my ear.

And woke up the next morning with Bitsy rustling the early edition of the Rag. The front page had a huge black headline:

MARA DEJONG CONFESSES: SHE BEAT HER CHILD SENSELESS

Under the headline is a photo of Mara, but it's so smudged and blurred even I hardly recognize her. Then the Rag's version of the second day of the trial.

The Crown asked to submit excerpts of a letter but Mara's lawyer said no. No excerpts, the entire letter or nothing. So the Crown read out the whole letter, apparently with dramatic pauses and vocal italics here and there, and Mara and her lawyer sat through it like they were listening to a recital of the Toronto telephone book. The Rag printed the entire text of the letter, as read:

Dear Theodore,

Walking home after the second SS "interview," I planned the long night's work in preparation for the next day's interrogation. The number of details which had to be designed and orchestrated were myriad. But when I arrived at home, there was the child, hysterically sobbing. She had had a fight, I was told, with the neighbour's daughter Ruth. Ruth, in the heat of quarrelling, had screamed, "Anyway, you have a Jewish nose," and my daughter had responded to this by hitting and bloodying Ruth's tiny snout. And then the two of them had pulled hair until Ruth's mother separated them. Dealing with the still hysterical child must have set me off, because I proceeded to beat her nearly senseless. It was *one of only two times* that I have resorted to hitting the child. In these subdivided apartments little escapes people's notice, certainly not screeching and the sound of blows, and so I expect that some will think me cruel. But let any of them stand in my shoes for a day like today and see how they would act.

That night, I burned all the family photographs, even yours, dear Theo. The child loved to spread them out on the floor, to point to each face of a relative she has never met, and to recite the name and the person's relationship to us. In the morning, hours before the fight, our neighbour's daughter Ruth had come in during one of the child's recitals, and Ruth said: "Your Aunt Tanya looks Jewish." I sent both the girls out to play and when I looked at the photographs with Nazi eyes, I saw that in our family, everybody is either very blond and blue-eyed, or else black-haired and dark-eyed. Our father and several others on his side of the family have rather long noses, which, thank goodness, neither you nor I have inherited.

In any case, there are already enough suspicious circumstances surrounding me. I burned the photos and told the child that I accidentally threw them into the coal stove. She cried and cried but never doubted my word. I don't dare to tell her the truth.

The big modern textile store I wrote to you about is in new hands. The Sachs family who owns the store disappeared overnight. The new people who are there behave as though they are now the proprietors.

I must go and bury this letter to you with the rest, before the house wakes up.

As always, the sister who misses your Love,
Loyalty and Understanding, your beloved Mara.

"How did the Crown get hold of that letter of yours?" I asked Mara when she came by after court, but she just shook her head. Sitting on the chair beside my bed, Mara—the same Mara who went out in the dark of night to bury letters to her brother—shook her head and said, "That is not important right now," and started right in complaining about how very difficult it is, here in Canada, to research people like the judge. Because there are so few house servants.

"In Indonesia," she says, "it would be easy to discover a judge's predilection in women. I could send my cook's boy, for example, to find out what the judge's laundress knows—about that or anything else. Ah, well...

"I do know," says Mara, "that the judge's parents came to Canada from Germany. From Hannover. I often took the train to Hannover because it was the nearest city with fashionable stores. Before they were destroyed in the bombing raids."

Mara is not reminiscing; she is thinking out loud. About how to use the judge's background in her favour.

"Perhaps," says Mara, "I should fly Helga to Toronto, after all...?"

"And what, Mara? Have her bake some *Bienenstich* for the judge?"

"Or perhaps," says Mara, "there are some customs of the area...I know of one myself: the burning of a witch. An effigy, of course. She wears the local traditional skirt, very full with a small apron over it, and a red kerchief on her head. She is attached to the ski-lift wires and rides on a broom all the way up to the top of the Burg mountain. It looks quite as though she is flying up there. And when she arrives at the top, she is thrown onto a large bonfire and burned to cinders, broom and all.

"Well," says Mara, "that particular ritual isn't perhaps relevant, but..."

But now, Mara gets an idea she obviously thinks will work. She's up on her feet and halfway to the door by the time she tells me she must leave immediately, and off she goes.

MARA

Dear Theodore,

All those who were in court today and hungry for drama surely began to enjoy themselves from the moment the Crown Attorney turned mauve. (On human skin it is a most unattractive shade.)

It seems the Crown Attorney had just then found out that a second "Dear Theodore" letter he intended to read was written later than the official time of your death.

Immediately everyone in the courtroom drew the conclusion that the letters are faked. Confusion and whispering. The judge retains some of his wits and asks to be told when the accused found out that her brother was killed.

"Soon after the war," the Crown Attorney told him. The judge looked at me, utterly at sea, and then I stood up and said, "Of course, I have never believed that my brother is dead and that is why I still write to him almost every day."

In the stunned silence, questions collide. Is she intending an insanity plea? Does she have reason to believe her brother is alive? Has there been communication? Is he in some prison camp, in Siberia? On the other hand, if he is dead and she knows it, have all the letters been fraudulently written for this trial? But if that is the case, why include incriminating material?

Again and again all eyes turn towards me, the accused, fly to the judge, to find reassurance. In vain. That somnambulant toad had awakened, but too fast. The best he could do was to croak "consultation" and disappear. The Crown Attorney and my poor lawyer followed him at a trot. I opened the book I take to court with me every day, a leather cover hiding author and title, and pretended to read.

My lawyer was the first to return. Why, he wanted to know in that whisper that threatens spittle, why had I not told him the truth about those letters and their dates. Why was I jeopardizing everything for these moments of temporary and childish triumph?

"But what does it matter," I asked my lawyer, "whether my letters to Theodore were written before or after my brother's alleged death? I never mailed a single one of them. Therefore their weight as evidence, such as it is, surely remains equal? Think of them as a diary, a dialogue with myself, or, if you like, think of them as fiction."

I had spoken loudly enough so that many ears in the courtroom were equally informed and after a moment I added, in a thoughtful tone: "I may in fact publish these letters. I have been approached about them and by a most reputable publishing firm. I am told these pages have historical value." Thus I reinforced the notion that all the letters might just possibly be fiction and upset everyone all over again.

The night grows short. Tomorrow, I must don an ensemble which neither you nor I could have imagined (nor would we have wanted to) when we used to sit up late into the night, designing gowns for my future concerts.

As always, your beloved sister,
Mara

TED

I'm back to waiting: for Bear's daily report on the trial, for Mara's visits, and then a whole day goes by without a word from Bear. When he finally shows up, I'm not in a mellow mood.

"Where the fuck have you been? Aren't you supposed to be my ears and eyes at the trial?"

Bear just bounces it back at me:

"Yes, I missed one whole fucking morning of the trial of Mara deJong. Not only that, I left town! Just hoofed it over to Niagara Falls, and cavorted about like nothing earth-shaking was happening here in TO and all over Ted O'Sullivan."

Boiled down, Bear had had to go to the Canada-U.S. border, to the celebrated Peace Bridge, to make sure a brother didn't end up in a U.S. deserter's jail, which, we've all heard, is no picnic.

Alicia and Bear are on a list of people willing to help Americans who don't want to go kill people in distant places to teach them democracy. Bear got called out to do something for this 21-year-old deserter. "The kid," Bear tells me, "was in an army camp near Chicago and was about to get shipped off to Vietnam when he ran across an old newspaper with a report of those little girls blown up in an Alabama church by a racist bomb. Alabama was the soldier boy's own home state in the US of A, and he started asking himself questions. Like, who was he going off to war for, to kill or be killed? He couldn't come up with an answer that made sense, so he walked out. Out of the army camp, out of the state, hitching rides. And ended up riding on a chicken truck to the Canadian border. The guards asked for papers and were getting ready to push him back out to the American side, so somebody called Bear, who hauled his ass down there in triple time and now Bear is a sponsor and responsible for the kid for a good long time. The kid's parents told Bear on the phone that they no longer have a son. Bear says the kid's still in shock and sleeping round the clock, or maybe just lying there in bed, waiting for his hair to grow in.

"Let's hope he doesn't turn out to be an asshole," says Bear. "So now go ahead and hassle me some more about that pair of earlobes."

Then Bear finally gets to his report on the trial. "Something's going on there, man. I can smell it. I'm willing to bet my upright bass on it, and you know I'm not a gambling man. I have never seen a trial like this one and I have sat through many a trial. Like the one when Alicia was accused of shoplifting. Did I tell you about that one?"

About a dozen times. Alicia getting pulled into the police station because a saleslady described the thief of a bracelet as "a black woman." Oh, Canada!

"And what about the time I got hauled in for harassing that white girl on the bus?"

That was a few years back, when Bear had a shitass job in a plant on top of late nights playing. So he never had enough sleep. So he'd climb on the 5:00 a.m. bus, head for the bench at the very back, and sleep for the 35-minute trip till he had to change to a second bus. It turned out there was a young white woman who also sat on the back bench of the early bus, and one day she claimed to the police that Bear always sat beside her and often touched her here and there. Where? The shoulder. Sometimes he put his head on her shoulder. And sometimes he touched her thigh. No, not with his hands, with his own thigh.

Bear couldn't even remember this person he was supposed to have been touching. He just always headed for the rear, sat down and fell asleep. And he went to court, on Alicia's account and on his own, because nobody was going to get away with shit like that.

Like I said, Bear has had lots of court experience, and when he says something is going on, then something is *definitely* going on.

"I keep seeing strings," says Bear. "A whole lot of strings, and all of them leading to Mara. Like she's a spider in the middle of a web and she wiggles this thread or tightens that one and directs the whole drama in that courtroom from where she's sitting. Looking calm and like she's doing nothing at all except following the proceedings.

"There's a lot of stuff going down," says Bear. "For one thing, that judge is awfully willing to listen. Like no judge I ever saw. He sounds like a bored father presiding over the Sunday roast, but underneath, that judge is personally curious! Damned curious."

"Well, hell, I should think he would be, sitting across from Mara all day long."

"Another thing," says Bear. "Did you notice how fast Mara's trial date came up? A poor maid accused of pocketing change in the couch would have had to wait a year and a half to get a chance to clear her name."

Although Bear is willing to concede that maybe Mara being a non-resident has something to do with the early trial date.

"At one point the prosecutor..."

"Crown Attorney, Bear."

"Yes, he claims he has evidence of a reputation for violence. Mara hitting the kid and threatening to leave her, and screaming at her—stuff like that…

"Now Mara's lawyer starts jumping up and down, objecting. And he starts reciting a list, too. Mara deJong, says her lawyer, is a warm-hearted woman. Why even the death of one of her dogs had her grieving for weeks. And Mara deJong is a generous and kind woman, who brought a colleague of hers out of the Soviet Union and into the West—a Mrs. Vovlikoff or something like that, living in Paris to this day. And Mara deJong is a woman of principle and courage, as she proved in Indonesia where she fought for justice on behalf of three poor villagers wrongly accused of murder. I. e., the lawyer starts the usual claim that his client is an angel."

"Whoa," says I. "Hold on there. This tune sounds mighty familiar!"

I think about it for a minute and sure enough, all three parts of that lawyer's claim were in that riff I played for Mara the day before.

I tell Bear, "Grieving for the dog, bringing Mrs.Whatsnikoff out to the West, and helping to clear the three peasants in Indonesia, they all came out of *my* mouth yesterday when I was trying to show Mara she was no cold bitch in *my* eyes."

Bear stares at me like my eyebrows are on fire.

"So she *is* pulling all the strings," says Bear.

"Maybe not every single one of them," says I.

Bear isn't listening. "Yes," he says. "Mara is directing this entire show. And you, Teddyboy, are part of it. Any idea yet what role she's got you playing?"

Not something I intended to think about right then. After Bear left,

I was actually kind of relieved. I could tell his own curiosity had finally dropped him into the drink—hook, line and sinker.

Day five of the trial, 5 o'clock. Mara steps into my room looking like she's auditioning for an operetta.

"A *Trachtenkleid*," she tells me. "A copy of the traditional dresses worn in Hannover. Hometown of the judge's parents." A triumphant twirl of the full skirt, flip of a little apron. Then Mara tells me: "There must certainly have been old family photographs in the judge's childhood home with just such dresses in them. They haven't changed for generations."

"Jesus, woman! Why not just sing the judge a medley of German nostalgia. And where the hell did you come up with one of these dresses?"

"I found exactly the right materials for it yesterday just before the stores closed. The seamstress worked all night. I drew the patterns for her, of course. The neckline is a little too high but otherwise it is quite perfect."

"A seamstress? How did you find one of those?"

"Oh, I engaged her weeks ago, to stand by in case of necessity. Last night was the first time she earned her fee. She did very well, I think."

Mara turns around again, twirling her skirt, giving me a Cheshire cat smile.

"You are enjoying yourself!" There I was, stuck, lying around on hot nails, and the Countess Mara looked ready to dance at the ball.

"Be serious, Ted," says Mara. Countess and Cheshire cat both gone. This is the General, sitting down on the chair beside my bed. Talking strategy and tactics.

"I requested a postponement," says Mara, "Because I wish to hire a new lawyer. But their decision went against me."

"Why?"

"Because I am, as they put it, 'on my third lawyer now.' I find it odd that even in a courtroom people do not refrain from colloquialisms and imprecision."

"What they meant is that firing three lawyers is not a good thing. Especially for the lawyers."

"Well, you saw the first one yourself, Ted. He had no understanding at all of a very important aspect of his profession."

"Ah, yes. The jacket sticking out over his ass. And the second lawyer?"

"Oh, he was very dedicated and certainly tried very hard to make the right impression. Unfortunately he was not directing his efforts towards the judge."

In other words, the second lawyer couldn't concentrate on the court case because he was smitten with a severe case of Mara-itis.

"And what's wrong with the lawyer you have now?"

"He is refusing to put me on the witness stand!" A frown to scare the feathers off a duck, a short pause, then all of a sudden she starts in on a completely new tune. No wonder my brain has ricochet-fatigue every time she leaves here.

"Tell me, Ted. Which would most Canadians value more highly, a woman who is a good homemaker and mother, or a woman who makes a major contribution to the world of science?"

"The scientist will get the prizes," I tell her. "The homemaker will get more valentines. Which do you want to go for?"

"Oh," says Mara, "My own path has been clear to me for a very long time. At the moment I am trying to assess the relative weight of earlobes."

Mara is looking down at her folded hands, thinking hard, her face wearing none of its usual confidence.

"Listen," I told Mara. "The weight of earlobes is relative to what goes onto the other end of the scale. Is it a dozen eggs somebody broke on the way home from shopping? Or is it a hole burned into the piano? Or are we talking about piling up bombs and warheads?

"I've been reading the papers," I told her. "In Vietnam, U.S. navy planes bombed 100 miles of coastline for five hours, destroying half the North Vietnamese navy. No mention of how many people were killed. In Mississippi, the bodies of three missing civil rights workers were found by FBI agents. Three kids, two white, one black, trying to help black folks get registered to vote. They'd been shot and dragged into a swamp. And in Rhodesia, listen to this, a Lumpa student was slapped for truancy. Alice Lenshina, founder and leader of the Lumpa cult, proclaimed a holy war and the Lumpas went on a murder rampage. Five hundred villagers were slain.

"So you see, Mara," says I, "if they put that kind of thing on one side of the scale and a pair of already dead earlobes on the other..."

Mara is pulling on a pair of little white gloves.

"Thank you, Ted," she says. "Thank you again. I'll be back tomorrow."

Off she goes.

The next day, Bear comes in and repeats that whole list of insanities as having come out of Mara's lawyer's mouth. Who then asked the judge to weigh any of those atrocities against the deed of removing one pair of earlobes, already dead. The judge apparently shook his head and said to put it on hold for the summation.

Bear looks at my face, raises his eyebrows, and says: "Give." So I tell him how I made that very same argument to Mara the day before, with the very same list of stuff I'd pulled out of the papers.

"There you are!" says Bear, with awe in his voice. "No doubt about it: that woman is a major fucking powerhouse!" Then he leans over the foot of my bed:

"And you know what else, Ted, ole buddy? Mara is up to something new. I can feel it."

ALICIA

Lena and I were at her place, sitting among the bulbous cushions, and Lena wanted to know what made me change my mind and go to Mara's trial and then to the hospital to visit Ted.

"Well, Bear had to go off into the bureaucratic maze for our deserter boy and somebody, it seems, absolutely *has* to be in court so Ted can get his daily report. What are you grinning at?"

"You completely forgot to mention 'curiosity,'" Lena says.

"Sure. But with Ted and Bear going on and on about Mara as puppet-master of the entire trial, *somebody* had to go take an objective look. Don't laugh, Lena. Somebody who is not trying to see Mara in a rosy light just because she's beautiful."

"Come on, Alicia. You know there's a lot more to her than that. There's her music, for one. The mystery of a good musician, possibly a great one, who does not make music or listen to music. Doesn't even want to!"

"Ah, yes. Mara Mysterioso. That's another one I'm sick of and wanted to see through."

"So did you?"

"Did I? Hm… I'll concede this much: the woman is remarkable. Whether evil or not is yet to be determined. You know what Ted says: 'The deciding factor is whether the heart is innocent.' I may have to agree with that, in the end."

Then I gave Lena pretty well the same report on the trial that I gave Ted. Starting with the first drama of the day: the judge asking Mara's lawyer, "Does the accused wish to take the stand?" The lawyer shakes his head, emphatically, but the voice we all hear is not his voice. It's Mara's, saying: "Yes, your Honour, I do wish to speak on my own behalf."

Mara is on her feet, walking straight over to the Bible, swears, etc., etc., but I'm still watching the lawyer. Because, Lena, that poor man couldn't even sit down, he was so totally surprised.

Meanwhile, Mara has arranged herself on the seat up there and she's making a little speech. "…it is also true," says Mara deJong, totally calm and reasonable, like she's been on trial every day of her life, "…it is also true that I could not remove the earrings because my fingers were swollen. I must confess, however, that I did not expect blood. Certainly not so much of it. If I had known in advance of the blood, I might have hesitated, but in the end…Well, I would have had to find a way of retrieving those earrings, or of having a jeweller come to make sketches and to take imprints so that he would be able to make *exact duplicates*. Because, you see, your Honour, the earrings are absolutely essential to my Work. Absolutely essential to it."

At that point, I see something out of the corner of my eye so I turn and catch it just in time: a man sitting in the second row has raised his hand in front of his chest, clearly giving a signal meaning "Stop!" Mara's lawyer sees the signal, and a second later he's swivelling towards the judge, interrupting Mara in mid-sentence. The lawyer insists that he must come forward and speak to the judge. The judge says okay. The lawyer and the Crown step up to the altar and the three of them rumble away up there. I look at Mara, still on the stand, and she doesn't look like she's even trying to listen in. I sure as hell had *my* ears trying hard, but I could only catch a word here and there. Finally, the judge stands up, he thanks Mara, practically bowing to her, and tells her she may go. The court is adjourned for lunch.

And right after lunch, half an hour of legal blah-blah, and that was it. The whole trial finished except for the sentencing. In one week.

I went straight over to the hospital to tell Ted.

TED

"One week. Nothing to do but wait for it."

That's what Alicia left behind when she split. And that "nothing to do but wait" jumped right into a tape-loop in my head and it kept playing under all the questions kicking me back and forth. Like, are you sure Mara really ever smiled like you think she did, that night in the club? Maybe it was just a waiting-to-hear-Dizzy-Gillespie kind of sparkle? And, was Mara really deranged by grief like you keep telling yourself? What if she wasn't? Then maybe a short break with: remember how Mara looked after your fingers? And she respects you, think about that; she had her lawyer quote you in court! But then, why hasn't she told you the reason she cut off her daughter's earlobes?

I could have popped a few downers from the hospital drug cart, just to take the edge off, but I swore that day in court that I was never again going aboard any kind of chemical roller coaster, and I meant it.

Somehow I made it through the rest of the day after Alicia left. The next morning, the phone rings and it's Mara. "I will be unable to visit you for a while," she says. "There are matters which need my attention. However, I shall have excellent news when we meet again. I wish you '*gute Besserung*.'"

And she hangs up on me. I couldn't believe it.

Then the door opens and Lena walks in. Now that the trial is over, she tells me, she can come and talk about it.

"I thought you might have some questions," she says.

Do I!

"Lena, you told me you don't *know* why Mara cut off the earrings. But why do you *think* she did it?"

Lena does not pretend she hasn't thought about those earrings.

"All I can tell you," she says, "is what I *used* to think. And you'd better be patient because I have to go round-about, by way of our neighbour, Mr. Hathaway."

"The Mr. Hathaway Alicia told me about? Wants to cut down a living tree so he can have a tidy lawn?"

"That's the one," says Lena. "One day Mara told me, 'Mr. Hathaway is going to be upset tomorrow morning. The cleaner didn't deliver his brown suit, and he always wears his brown suit on Thursdays and Mondays.' And would you believe it, the next morning, Mr. Hathaway slammed his house door so hard, even our place was rattling.

"I started watching Mr. Hathaway from my kitchen window in the mornings and here is what I spied: Mr. Hathaway, every single morning, steps out the front door at 8:30 sharp, briefcase in his right hand. He closes the house door, switches the briefcase to his left hand. With the right he taps his breast pocket, two times. Then he walks to the garage door, pushes the button, and while he's waiting for the garage door to creak all the way up, his right hand taps his hip pocket. Three times. He mutters something, too; I can't hear it but it's the same thing every time. Then he steps into the garage. On the count of 35 he is backing the car out of it.

"And that is what Mr. Hathaway does every single work day of the week!"

"Wonderful," says I. "How exciting."

To Lena, sarcasm is a housefly passing through.

"You and I," says Lena, "have no such routines to give us the illusion of safety and continuity.

"You and I," she says, "do, however, have our own magic activities. Sometimes called passions. Your music, my batik-paintings—our work. Then there are some people who have magic objects. You know, rabbit's feet, medals of saints... So that is what I used to think about those earrings. That Mara has magic objects, and that the earrings were among her magic objects."

"Wow, lady! You're fishing in deep water here!"

But Lena has more to tell, and the rest is harder.

"Here's why I thought those earrings were magic objects. The day before Michelle died, I'd been with her all night, so in the morning when Mara took over, I went up to my place and took a nap. I was just getting up again, around noon, when Mara came up the stairs. Would I please put some earrings on Michelle? I told her I didn't think Michelle would want to be bothered with earrings. But Mara was...well, you saw her that night when she couldn't find her new scarf? Almost like that. Frantic. Insisting over and over that I put the earrings on Michelle. So I did it.

"Mara watched me do it—Michelle was barely conscious—and Mara even checked the safety catch to see that I'd done it right. She couldn't have put the earrings on Michelle herself because her fingers were swollen that day and she couldn't manage the tiny clasp."

"Wait, Lena. Slow down a bit. Say you're right and Mara thought the earrings had magic powers. But the magic didn't work, did it? The earrings didn't save Michelle's life. So why cut them off?"

"I don't know," says Lena and sighs.

"At the beginning," says Lena, "I thought maybe Mara got mad at the earrings for not doing their magic for her. That she had a fit. She couldn't take them off and stomp on them, so she cut them off in a fit of rage. Because they didn't save her daughter's life.

"Then I thought: maybe Mara wants the earrings because she thinks that, even if they did nothing for Michelle, they will work for her...?

"But now that doesn't make sense, either. Because Mara makes no distinction whatsoever between the *original* pair of earrings she had me put on Michelle and the duplicates Mara had made. The day she wore the earrings to court, she told me herself that she wasn't sure any more which earrings were the originals because they were so wonderfully and exactly duplicated. But you see, Ted, for my theory about 'magic objects' to make sense, the earrings can't be duplicates; they have to be the original magical pair. And Mara would have kept track of the magic pair! So there it is, Ted. The earrings are still a complete puzzle."

Both of us nodded, completely stumped.

Lena was the first one out of the funk. Wants to know how I am doing, "otherwise."

"Oh, great," I told her. "Except for being a magnet for questions pinching my nerve ends, and Bear expecting me to produce tapes full of original music, and now, on top of everything else, my grandma is squatting in my head."

Lena wants to hear about the grandma part so I spill that whole bag: I call my grandma at least every Sunday, even when I'm on the road. And here it's been, how long? and me in hospital all this time. How do I even tell her?

"You haven't missed that many Sundays," says Lena. "Why don't you call her today and tell her you're touring and you'll call again when you get back home?" It's a shock, Lena of all people advocating lies to my grandmother. I've never yet told my grandma an out-and-out lie, but now I'm willing to give it a try. I dial her number.

"Hi, grandma, how's it going?"

"Is that you, Ted?"

On the other end of the line I hear a sea lion, blowing through a bullhorn stuffed with cotton wool.

"Just a cold," says the sea lion, "but it's been keeping me inside for a week now."

Yes, she's seen the doctor—a bad sign in my grandmother, she has to get dragged to the doctor—and this one, young enough to be her grandson, gave her cold a fancy name and told her to take aspirin and rest. No, she doesn't need a thing. And I'm to make sure that this tour I'm on doesn't include too many sleepless nights and chili con carne (which once gave me a bellyache and has ever since been on my grandmother's list of poisons) and this call wasn't getting any cheaper, so...

So here we are; grandma is one sick sea lion pretending all she has is a cold, and I'm stuck in hospital and can't even go see what's what. Lena has caught the drift and offers to go to my grandma's house. She'd be an emissary from Touring Ted, bringing flowers, and she'd check the old lady out for me.

"What do you think? Will your grandmother go for it?"

"You know what? I think she would. Last time she was sick, I brought her champagne. Right into the hospital."

Lena laughs and takes off. I spend the next couple of hours wearing out my dialling finger, but Mara is not answering the phone. When Lena calls me, she's back at her own place and grandma, it turns out, really did have just a bad cold.

"And a severe case of impatience," says Lena. "She hates to stay home, stuck in front of that darned humidifier spitting steam at her."

Lena sounds like she already knows my grandma.

"She was full of questions," says Lena.

"Like what?"

"She wants to know why you haven't found the right woman so far. Are you just too picky?"

"And what did you tell her?"

Lena claims she said to grandma: "Ted is travelling in strange lands right now, and there's no way of predicting what he'll be like, when he comes back."

"Well, let me know," grandma told Lena. "And remind him for me to choose his manias with care."

"What does your grandmother mean by that?" Lena sounds intrigued, so I tell her about my grandmother's attempts to swat me away from monomania.

"'Don't be like the man who was so obsessed with his work, he forgot to eat,' grandma told me.

"'What kind of work?' I asked her. Grandma got mad. 'You're supposed to ask, What happened to the man?'"

"Okay, grandma, what happened to him after he forgot to eat?"

"'He died,' she said, like it's a victory." I asked Lena if she ever read the book about the little boy Struwelpeter who got himself dead because he wouldn't let them cut his fingernails. Accidentally dead, of course. Lena hadn't.

"Never mind. What I told my grandma was to spare me her German cautionaries. I like Irish goblins a lot better. Grandma told me she likes them better, too, but sometimes she still gets trapped in the Black Forest. 'Black Forest ham ain't bad,' I told her. 'And the cake is damned fine!' And then Grandma and I both remembered how Grandpa used to call her 'my Black Forest Beauty.'

"Anyway, for years, grandma tried to keep me from turning into what she calls a monomaniac. Then she gave up and started telling me: 'If you can't help being one, then at least choose your mania with care.'"

"Ah," says Lena. "Now it makes sense."

While we were still talking I'd reached over and pulled the keyboard around to the front and after we hung up I started right in doodling on the keys, and when the memory of Mara's smile came in, all personal and sparkling, I took that smile all over the keyboard and played with it till I found the melody that caught the feel of it so I could get it back any time I wanted to. A ballad, it turned out to be.

When I played the tune for Bear, he said, "Hey, man, that's beautiful! First time I've known you to write something like that."

"What do you think? Too romantic?"

"No, man," says Bear. "I like it and you know me, I hate sentimental shit. No, man, this is one fine ballad."

By the time that tune was pretty well together, I started taking all my old questions to the keyboard and I was still reeling in a piece I call "Danse Diablo," when the shit hit the fan again.

Visiting hours were just about over for the day when the head nurse came in and said she was willing to give permission to one visitor if I wanted him. "A distinguished-looking gent..."

I pushed the keyboard to the side and there was Albert, coming in the door, shaking my hand, telling me:

"We have the sentence."

"Well," I tell Albert. "You'd better sit down and let me have it pretty quick."

Albert sits down. I pull myself up higher so I can hear him over the racket my heart's making in my chest. Albert says:

"Temporary insanity plea accepted. Four months under psychiatric observation, and a report to the judge."

"Whoa, Albert. That's too fast for me. Have to back way up on that and start over again. First of all, what is this temporary insanity shit? Aren't you the dude who said no plea of insanity for Mara? *Ever?*"

"Yes," says Albert. "But Mara left us no choice. Let me explain.

"We had an agreement," says Albert. "Mara complied only after much persuasion, but she did agree. If Mara mentioned her work, that was to be the signal that the lawyer should enter a plea of temporary insanity. Well," says Albert. "Maybe it's for the best."

And pauses like that's a statement of great significance.

"As for the sentence," says Albert, "Mara will be spending four months in a private clinic founded by a Dr. Hunter, who is to be Mara's observing psychiatrist. In four months, he will report to the judge. I am entirely confident that Mara will then be cleared and everything will be over.

"And the clinic," he says, " is 'The Greening.' A former estate, now a flourishing private clinic. Just outside Toronto."

I've heard of it. The inmates are called "clients" and they're mostly rich, depressed women recovering from breakdowns due to weight gain or divorce. Along with a few people with embarrassing problems like kleptomania and a few other quaint little manias and phobias.

Mara was not exactly going to the Don Jail.

"I believe it is generally referred to as 'the Retreat,'" says Albert. "Mara herself has visited the establishment and has had an interview with Dr. Hunter. She is quite satisfied. And she is pleased that the retreat is located in the country because she intends to concentrate on her work."

"Is that the work Mara says is more important than music? The work used as the signal for switching the defence and copping an insanity plea?"

"Yes, Ted. But Mara herself will have to tell you about the *nature* of her work."

Mara did say that I was going to be the first one she'd show it to. Maybe she actually meant it?

"And you're sure she's getting out in four months?"

"Yes, Ted. So you see, it's all for the best."

"I still don't get it, Albert. Last I heard, temporary insanity was the Evil that Ate the World, and now it's been pleaded and you're not even looking riled."

"I am relieved, actually. I was afraid that even a mere mention of temporary insanity might send Mara over the edge."

"What edge? Are you saying Mara is close to teetering off her rocker?"

"That," says Albert, slowly, "would not be an accurate description. No."

"Well, how would you describe it? Accurately?"

"Mara's perception of human society is, er, unique. It is unlike anyone else's."

"That is what 'unique' means, I do believe. So you're saying that Mara marches to a different drummer. Is she claiming the world is out of step with her?"

"Oh, not at all. Mara is even, at times, frighteningly accurate in her perceptions. But...well...she is somewhat extreme in the application of her theories. Even her research and her experiments sometimes ride a very fine line..." Albert is sighing and he doesn't even know about Mara's little experiment with the Tic, trying to turn that drug-addled redneck into a prospective bride on her way to Saudi Arabia.

Albert perks up. "All in all," he says, "I am very pleased with the outcome of the trial. And Mara is in good spirits, Ted."

"Not freaked out by being labelled a freak-out."

"Quite," says Albert. "And she asked me to give you a message: when you leave the hospital, please go to her apartment and take care of it until she returns. She would be most grateful."

Then Albert has to be off and away, back to Europe, going to do a one-semester teaching stint at a university in Belgium. He would keep in touch.

Albert waved from the doorway and I started dialling Mara's telephone number. And did it again and again until a cabby the size of a mountain walked into my room and handed me a note:

Dear Ted,

I am going to work very hard for the next four months so I will not be receiving visitors or even phone calls. I shall be pleased to think of you in the apartment and shall see you there in four months.

Yours, Mara

Here's something everybody knows: four months can go by dragging their ass over every ever-lasting minute, or they can zigzag by you like a rabbit. What I'm just finding out is that sometimes they do both at the same time.

After I read Mara's note, I started planning to storm "The Retreat." That place where they were supposed to be testing Mara's wits—and would find themselves, I was damned sure, outwitted.

I had Bitsy bring me a road map and I found it: Greening Hill. Not that far from Toronto. I was pretty sure I could convince either Bear or Lena to drive me up there. Meantime, Bitsy, at the other end of the map, pipes up:

"The Retreat must be good for her nerves," she said.

"You mean the trial was that hard on Mara?"

"I'm sure the trial didn't help," said Bitsy. "But we think her nerves must have been close to snapping for years."

And on what did Bitsy base this astonishing diagnosis? She got all miffed about my tone of voice and wouldn't say another thing. Except then she did:

"Everybody in the hospital thinks that wasn't the first time Mara's nerves snapped, when her daughter died and she cut off her earlobes. Everybody in the hospital thinks Mara's probably been snapping for years and years. It's just that maybe this was the first time she did something really weird like that and so now she finally got the attention she was really asking for all the time."

My toes were curling so hard they made my hips hurt, but I just couldn't yell or shout at Bitsy. She scares too easy. But what a bunch of fucking Donas on staff here, chain-smoking themselves yellow on their break, yakking about Mara's bid for attention. If anybody gets plenty of attention, from men and from women, too, then it's Mara. And none of it has to do with knives and earlobes.

It wasn't a knife, anyway. Or scissors. Mara went into the kitchen, the Rag said, and she picked up those bone clipper things, those shears for dismembering chickens, fowl scissors—you know what I mean. The Rag had a photo of one, with a few dark drops on it—we were supposed to think it was the same one Mara used, still dripping blood. Sometimes that Rag is enough to convert you to censorship.

Anyway, Bitsy didn't think I should try to visit Mara at the Greening, and let's face it, she was right. Mara did not need a report to the judge that included a man on crutches climbing in through her window. I told Bitsy to take away the road map and to tell the psycho-diagnosticians at the nurse's station not to retard my recovery with the sound of their voices.

You know what the old Ted would have been up to right after hearing Albert deliver the verdict, "four months," and then getting Mara's note: no contact for all that time. The old Ted would have blown like a typhoon! Driven everybody nuts who slipped as much as a toe in the door. But not the new Ted. The new Ted concentrated every waking minute on getting out of hospital soon, and in good shape. I practiced the crutch walk, swung on the bars like a ding-dong bell, worked out till my upper body started looking like somebody else's. And just to make sure all those muscles weren't going to impede the nimbleness of my fingers, I played the keyboard the rest of the time.

And then, one day, I finally got out of there. Released into the custody of my crutches. Bear picked me up with the van around noon, dumped me and my stuff in the hallway at Mara's place and said he'd be back. And there I was, sitting on the couch in the living room, smelling not-hospital smells and hearing not-hospital sounds, and seeing not-hospital sights. Hallelujah!

I was looking around the place and I still didn't see anything you could point to and say, that has got to be Mara's, but somehow every bit of the room was filled with Mara anyway. No. Not with Mara. With the *absence* of Mara. And with waiting! But hey! This was no endless waiting; it was going to be over in four months and that was that.

I settled back down on the couch, and something on the right caught my eye. A screen. All three panels are covered with batik in bright swirling colours—definitely Lena's handiwork. And about as different as you can get from anything you see in a hospital. Except those flowers of mine on the windowsill.

Then Bear was back, with a 12-pack of brew, and crowding in right behind him, Alicia and Lena. Alicia was wearing a short tent in bright colours, and she and Lena were carrying so much stuff, I couldn't even get close enough for a decent hug. Man, it was great seeing everybody together, sitting around a table covered with food and flowers. And my friends all busy organizing the life of Ted the Invalid O'Sullivan. I ignored everything they said and just listened to the sound of their voices, the tones saying: we're thinking about you, Ted. We want to help. And Alicia gave me a second big hug to tell me how glad she was to see me out of that place.

"Listen, Ted," she said. "You'll have to sleep on the pullout couch down here. Unless you want a bed brought down?"

"The couch is fine, Alicia. But I can get up and down stairs okay, you know. You just put both the crutches in one hand, see, and with the other one you're holding the banister..."

"Not in the middle of the night you don't, when you're half asleep and heading off to pee," said Alicia. Bear was grinning. "Alicia," he said. "You're forgetting there's nobody sitting on Ted's bladder. He doesn't have to go piss every half-hour."

Alicia did her most wicked smile and said: "He will when he starts eating all the soups I'm going to teach him how to cook."

"Hey, Alicia, what if it's a girl? What are you going to call a girl baby?"

Bear and Alicia looked at each other, both of them laughing.

"It's a raging battle," said Lena, finally getting into the fray. "The last defeat was Bear's so she will not be called 'Marylou.'"

"A great pianist," I reminded her, "and a pretty name, too, in my opinion."

"Moving on," said Bear, "I want to see what you two women were cooking up here last weekend, and I don't mean the soup."

Lena picked up my crutches and carried them out into the kitchen. In two minutes she was back, hanging on my crutches, with a contraption dangling from her neck. A small basket, it turned out, dangling from a guitar strap at chest level.

"We designed it," said Alicia. "So you can crutch around the kitchen, putting stuff into the basket for making soup, and everything. And see the hook on the side of the basket? You can hook your tape recorder on that and play your tapes while you're cooking."

"Sheer genius," I told them. "You two are something else. Hand it over!"

To demonstrate the contraption and how much I appreciated it, I started clearing the table into the basket on my chest. The second trip out to the kitchen, the basket was still working great, but the apple cider in my legs was pushing me right over to the couch.

"You sit right there and don't move," said Bear. "Time for the unveiling."

Now Lena and Alicia went and stood at either side of the colour-popping screen. Bear did a drum roll on the table. Alicia and Lena pulled the screen to the left and there it was! My own piano! Sitting right down here in the living room where I could play my old beauty any old time I felt like it! Including, that very minute! So I sat down to it.

By the next morning, the day after I came out of hospital, I woke up and I didn't exactly hear "Freedom Jazz Dance" in my head. The only tune playing in there was a new one on me, called coming up with Big Bucks for the rent.

Mara actually left an envelope on the desk with my name on it and the rent cheques for four months inside, but those are staying right where I put them, inside the rolltop desk. Bear said he has some gigs lined up for us, but later. I needed that first month's rent now.

Then, while I was still sitting at the kitchen table over my first cup of coffee, real coffee, the phone rang and Alicia said:

"Let's have a rent party!"

ALICIA

I'm the one who is telling you about the rent party because, as I said to the guys: "This party is not about who played on which tune and whose solos were 'way out there.' This party is about two things: about paying the October rent, and about having Fun!" Anyway, it was my idea. And it turned out great. I don't believe in modesty as a great virtue, do you?

Mind you, it took a bit of persuasion.

"A rent party?" said Bear, like he couldn't believe his ears.

Ted said: "This isn't Chicago's South Side, Alicia. A rent party in Toronto? That would be like Mardi Gras in Sudbury."

Lena said, "I think it would be great to have some celebrating going on in the house. Some live music in Michelle's place."

What can I tell you? It was a great party! Mostly other musicians, so it turned into a jam, of course, and that's all a party really needs. The other ingredients were the table piled with food, and bottles in the kitchen. Honestly, I had more fun that night than in months. And ditto for Bear, so we did a lot of flirting with each other and a lot of grinning. ("Okay, okay," says Bear. "No need to get into every detail, you know." But I'm really only giving you the highlights.)

Early on, Lena drove Ted's van over to pick up his grandma and bring her to the party. Grandma handed me a huge apple cake and then she shook hands with everybody in the room like the regal old lady she is. Then she sat down on the couch and patted the cushion beside her for Bear to join her. Those two have the same funny bone. Bear started right in on the tale of "getting Ted out of the hospital for a day." With himself as hero, of course. So Ted had his go: "Grandma, remember who is telling you all this: Bear, the friend who tilts a helpless man and wheels him into the van like a slab of beef. I'll give you the real version another time." Seeing Bear and Ted jivin' like that, it was good old times.

A bit later, I saw Ted whisper something in grandma's ear. She started smiling and kept on smiling all through Ted and Bear doing a slow-swinging "Satin Doll." Afterwards she winked at me: "'Satin Doll' is the first jazz composition Ted ever played for me." A brisk nod, trying not to get sentimental, but still smiling.

"Is that what Ted was whispering about?"

"No," says grandma. "He was telling me: 'I'll come to your damned family reunion and I'll be as good as I *can* be.'"

"Well, he can't promise better than that, grandma." I said, and now we're both nodding and smiling.

The music never stopped—people came and stayed, or went, but there was always somebody playing. And Ted was so greedy to be doing it with other people again, he hardly got up off the piano bench.

Around ten, Lena took grandma home. I was in the hall when Lena got back and I was about to tell her what a fine person she was, but then this same fine person tells me she invited the neighbours.

"Why in the blazes of Hades would you invite those Nutters from Squaresville?"

"Because," says Lena, the imp: "I happen to know Mr. Hathaway is in insurance so I thought, why don't we get some? Insurance, I mean. We don't want them to call the cops and shut the party down at 11:01, do we? And here they come," says Lena and opens the door to Mr. and Mrs. Hathaway.

She bearing a casserole dish with bits of something beige floating in whitish stuff, and he sticking out a bottle of French white wine like it's a stop sign. Lena introduces them around and then I lost track of them for a bit. The next time I see Mr. Hathaway, he's sitting in the kitchen, eating goat curry and drinking rum. Meanwhile Mrs. Hathaway is in the living room, giggling and dodging some guy nobody knew who'd blown in early and was still around the next day, sleeping behind the couch. We never did find out who he was because around noon when we started the clean-up, he woke up and walked straight out of the house.

At some point, I climbed the stairs to go to the bathroom and there, in the upstairs hall, is Mr. Hathaway, listening to Bear telling stories. Just then, Hathaway starts laughing so hard he keeps bending forward and straightening up again, tears and snot flying all around, mostly landing on his tie. Now, I'll grant you that Bear can tell a good story, when in the mood, but the way Mr. Hathaway was laughing, I would have bet anything, the guy was high. Not a booze high, either.

I signal to Bear behind Mr. Hathaway's back: "Did he smoke the herb?" Bear signals back: "He doesn't smell like it." Then, Bear told me later, he got curious himself about all the laughing because the story he was telling wasn't even a funny one. Bear and I sniffed around a bit, ran into Lori just sitting down on the top stair, looking glum, and pretty soon the mystery of Mr. Hathaway's jolly mood was all cleared up.

Lori is a drummer who doesn't smoke the weed or hit up but, Bear told me, he does carry a vial of crumbs wherever he goes. Crumbs of hash brownies with the emphasis on hash.

"Hey, Lori," says Bear. "Got any crumbs on you?"

"Not any more," says Lori. Seems he had his vial with him all right, but he accidentally left it behind in the washroom and when he got back to it, it was empty.

We told Lori what happened to his crumbs, but Lori didn't think it was funny.Around two o'clock I passed the hat around, and in ten minutes Ted's October rent was covered. A great party all around.

After that I must have dozed off a bit on the couch, but Bear filled me in on the rest of the party. He says they played their best set that night around three. "After Henry quit trying to ride the Bird's tail and Sammy came in on soprano sax." It's not Bear's favourite saxophone, but that night Sammy made like the angel Gabriel and woke up every sleepwalker on this planet. "Move over, Ornette Coleman, or stick to the electric violin, there's a Sammy on the way."

When I woke up around five o'clock in the morning, the last musicians were just packing it in. There were two guys sleeping on some blankets on the floor, Sara and Henry were crashing in Ted's bed upstairs, and Ted had apparently crawled up to Lena's living room at some point and fallen asleep among the cushions. Bear raised his eyebrows when he was telling me that but I I had not raised one matchmaking finger all night.

Bear and I headed home in a cab, both feeling fine.

TED

Alicia told my grandmother: "Ted is euphoric." Just a fancy way of saying "high" and sure, I was high. High on being out of hospital, high on playing whenever I felt like it, for hours and hours—solo or with the cats Bear and I called out—high just on being able to get up from the piano and walk around the apartment without stubbing one toe on the fridge and the other on the bedpost. And I was swinging from my crutches, cooking Alicia's soups with those great soup smells, and going walking and talking with Lena. Sometimes I even forgot about that low drone going on under everything else, coming from that one part of me sitting there on the couch, waiting for Mara to come back. Because I really had to see the woman face to face so I could figure out what is going on between us.

In the meantime, I knew two things for sure and both of them new in the life of Ted O'Sullivan: one, I'd be playing jazz for the rest of my life and, the second thing, I wasn't ever going to go down the chemical drain. So with a clear-eyed look at all that, I figured I was all set to be a candidate for survival, and for writing some serious shit while also taking care of business, instead of floating like a leaf on the river. (You know, sometimes the Great Roulette Spinner Up Above has a way of letting you win a while, till you get to feeling lucky. Sometimes he lets it go on for months before he gives the wheel a mighty turn and spins you right off.)

One evening, Bear and I went to Miguel's and we sat and talked all through the night. About music, what else? Yes, we made a lot of plans that night, and they were not dreams that come out of pipes or bottles or anything but our unadulterated, rarin'-to-go selves. Well, we did have a toke or two, though my sweet herbal friend is practically invisible around these parts. Seems like the days for growing your own are gone and the hip thing to do is to spend cash for imports supposed to be Colombian and could just as easily be London, Ontario. I guess I'm just belly-aching because I actually had to lay out ten bucks cash to buy an ounce and then it didn't smell right.

We've been rehearsing and jamming around three times a week and sometimes at the weirdest hours, like 10 a.m. *You* try getting four guys together when one of them has a part-time straight gig on shift work and another plays a dance gig on weekends, etc. etc. But it won't be long. Soon we'll be going full-time, playing nothing but music we want to play. What the hell else am I in this for? An early pension? Fainting teenagers? No, man, I'm in it to play jazz. And if I have to play some pablum to pay the rent now and then, or because Bear's baby needs braces on his teeth, hey! My own music is not going to disappear. Not in my lifetime.

After a few weeks I switched from crutches to canes and Lena and I went walking all the way around King's Circle and back. One day we sat down on the grassy hill beside Philosopher's Walk to enjoy the last bit of warm sunshine and I pulled out grandma's letter. I'd found it when I was doing the pre-laundry pocket-check grandma drilled into me and I'd read it at least ten times by then. This time, I read it out loud, to Lena.

"My dear boy! I hear this Mara deJong woman has you stuck in that old nightmare: 'how can a mother do such a thing.' But your mother and this Mara deJong have less in common than a rabbit and a Tasmanian devil.

"Your mother was a very pretty, very young girl who had never yet had any serious trouble in her life, and who hadn't even had a chance to grow up yet. The death of her little daughter sent her into the darkest depression, and she couldn't see how she would ever climb out of there again. She had to go into the hospital for three months. When she came back, she was supposed to stay on her medication but she didn't, and so she went right down into that depression again and that's when she gave up and took her own life.

"Now you know why I always say 'never give up.'"

Signed with grandma's squiggle, which I'd recognize anywhere.

I folded the letter back into my pocket and told Lena I thought grandma was right. That I'd even half-known it wasn't my fault I couldn't save my mother.

Lena was looking at me, brown eyes wide open.

"And you didn't know any of this as a child?"

I shook my head. "My father told Grandma never to mention my mother. He said it would upset me." Lena was still looking at me, so I told her the rest.

"After I read her letter, I went over to grandma's and we talked and I asked her: why did my mother cut off my little sister's hair right after she died? Grandma told me "Ah, Teddy, people do many strange things after a loved one dies."

Lena nodded. I could swear she knew how grandma's letter made me feel. So on the way home, I even talked to Lena about waiting.

"Life is damned good," I told her, "except for that one part of me, still sitting on the couch, waiting for Mara. But I mean, look at me. I'm playing music, enjoying life… The old Ted, if any part of him was waiting, he'd be wreaking havoc, getting drunk, getting into fights, getting fucked up one way or another, and by the time Mara stood in that doorway, I'd be too strung out to know what really was happening with Mara and me."

And then, the very next morning after that, there came a knock on the door and Lena stuck her head in and said:

"Well, I'm off."

She couldn't tell me when she'd be back because she was going off to her studio to work. She had a deadline—an exhibition of her work coming up—so she was going to be sleeping in her studio. Right up to then, on our walks and while we were cooking and eating together, Lena had definitely done her own share of talking, so how come this is all news to me?

"Oh," she says. "It's a new development," and hands me the key to her apartment, a note with instructions about watering her plants, gives me a quick peck on the cheek, and then she's gone. No phone number, no address. Every time I think about her going off like that, I start getting pissed off, so I go up to her apartment to take another look at her batik, "The Roots of Sound," leaning against the bedroom wall. To remind myself: Lena has other things to do in her life besides walking and talking with Ted Terrific.

But she sure picked a rotten time to go into heat for her work. Not that it hasn't happened to me. A couple of years ago I was in that state and in the middle of it I tried to take Dona's kind of holiday. We almost split up the third day in. Here's Dona, saving our money and planning everything and really looking forward to it all, and then, when we get there— some tourist beach in Mexico—Ted the mule gets turned on by some local musicians with lousy technique but great feel, and hangs around the dark hotel dining room all day, playing that wreck of a piano, trying out new ideas. Dona's plans included walking hand-in-hand, lying on the beach and baking ourselves to a crisp, and exploring the quaint little town full of bargains. All I wanted to do was play. The third day we had a row, with banging doors and shouting, and then we worked out a compromise. I got to play two hours in the morning and two hours in the late afternoon. The rest of the time was hers. A couple of days like that and the music dried up, so after that we spent all the time walking around, hand in hand.

Anyway, here's the point: if Lena doesn't want to be interrupted then I sure as hell am not going to bother her. I know one thing about the woman: if she says she's working, that's what she is doing. Lena would starve before she'd lie.

Only what about when she's done working for the day? Or the week? What is she doing then? With me, as soon as a great jam or gig is over, I'm horny as hell. I used to have a helluva time with it, too, because if I had a steady woman around, I'd come home and find her mad. I'd have been gone for too many hours or days and I'm not to mistake her for an old sofa, the way I walk in the door and want to climb all over her. Mostly, there's been no woman at home when I was done playing, and the ones I knew would likely be fast asleep or otherwise engaged. So mostly, I just walked it off.

ALICIA

I was just back from work when Lena phoned.

"Hi, Alicia. I wanted to let you know that I'll be staying at my studio for a while, so..."

"Staying there? You mean, sleeping there?"

"Yes, for a while. I've started working towards a show. With a deadline."

"When did all this happen? And why aren't you more excited about it?"

"Well, I actually have a standing agreement with a gallery: when I feel ready, they give me a show. It's a sweet deal but now that I've told them 'Okay,' I'll have to work pretty hard."

"And you decided that right now was a good time to be working very hard? Suddenly? A yen, an urge, an avalanche of ideas, what?"

"My hundred days of no work are up, you know.

"You're bullshitting. Something's happened. Out with it, Lena!"

"You're a hard hard woman, Alicia. Okay. Yesterday, Ted told me: that a part of him is sitting on the couch, waiting for Mara."

"Shit shit shit! I knew it had to be something to do with that woman. So now you are clearing out to show Ted how much he'll miss you? Which he will do, of course."

"No, Alicia. I'm just not willing to be in any kind of relationship with obsession. Not even when it's somebody else flailing around in that swamp. Anyway, I wanted to let you know that I have no phone in the studio but you can leave a message for me any time with the corner grocer right next door. I'll call you with the number, okay?"

"Okay," I said and listened to Lena hanging up. What else could I say?

TED

Lena disappearing all of a sudden like that surprised the hell out of me, so I phoned and asked Alicia if she knew anything about it. Alicia says:

"You'll find out for yourself, if you *get off the couch*."

Which told me those two definitely talk about me, Lena and Alicia. I like it that they do, but do they have to talk about *everything?*

"So which one of you told my grandmother about Mara, you or Lena?"

"That one'll be easy to figure out, too, when you get off the couch."

"What kind of chorus goes with that, Alicia? 'I'm pregnant, so I can be bitchy'? Lena doesn't have any weird shit about Mara, you know. Lena doesn't think Mara's a devil out to get your baby."

"No, that's true. Nobody's perfect."

That was the end of that call and it didn't help me out one bit.

MARA

Dear Theodore,

I rarely speak to anyone these days (except you, of course), being so pressed for time as I near the inevitable moment when I must leave this haven. I have been able to pursue my Work almost without interruption and so I am very close to completion of the first and seminal part. Exhilaration grows.

What was once only a surmise, has grown into conviction: that there must be a Great Purpose and a Comprehensive Mind at work in directing my life. Every experience since earliest childhood seems, in retrospect, to have served in preparing me, in providing me with the indispensable abilities necessary for the Work.

Now that the revelation of the First Part is at hand, I must be prepared, also, for the adulation which will inevitably follow.

As always, your beloved sister,

Mara

TED

It's five-thirty.

I tried calling Mara earlier today. I wanted to drive out and pick her up at the Funny Farm. Mara didn't even come to the phone. Somebody with too much honey in her voice told me: "She'll be taking a taxi at three in the afternoon."

That means Mara should have been here an hour and a half ago. And I can't even play the piano till she gets here because when Mara comes walking in through that door, I want to be standing right here, one hundred percent, looking at her.

But I sure as hell am not used to this shit any more. I'm supposed to be all done with feeling like an ostrich on hot coals and can't get off till somebody else says the magic word.

Right after my coffee I moved all the furniture back where it used to be. Except my piano. No point in moving it back upstairs, because I do know one thing for sure about what's coming: I am not going to live in a room in Mara's apartment. In fact, I've already got my eye on a pad. And now her trial is over, no more Joe-boy, the hired hand. High time to get that straightened out between us. Whatever this between-us turns out to be.

I sit down on the piano bench, my back to the keyboard, waiting to see Mara step into the room.

Bear and I stopped talking about Mara a while back, and Lena hasn't been around to talk about anything at all. She must be into her work up to her eyeballs; she hasn't even phoned the last four days. Her last call, I asked her if she was going to be around when Mara gets back.

"No," she said. "I won't be there. Mara isn't going to miss me." Which was probably true. So it's just me, sitting here, waiting for Mara.

I start pacing. Wearing a fucking groove into the living room rug. Maybe I should transfer my pacing to the outside. Cool off the brain cells. I've already got one arm in my jacket when I hear the taxi drive up in front of the house. I pull my arm out again and sit back down.

I hear the front door open. Mara is stepping into the hall. I see the taxi driver bringing in two huge suitcases and a fat briefcase. Mara steps into the doorway and sees me sitting here, watching her.

Mara's eyes are shining, looking at me, not jumping away. Mara is glowing.

"Ted!"

We must have taken some steps. I take her hands and look at them. They look fine. She gives me three pecks on the cheeks, left, right, left, and then we stand there like we've just met and don't know what to say to each other. For about three seconds.

"Mara," I say. "How's it going?" Or something like that. "You look good! Why..."

Mara holds up her hand. She's right—plenty of time for questions later.

"Do you remember my promise?" she says. "My vow that you will be the first to hear about my Work? Well, Ted, now you will!"

Mara turns back towards the hall. I walk past her and pick up one of the suitcases.

"Upstairs?"

"No, thank you, Ted. The briefcase, please. If you would bring it into the living room."

I pick up the briefcase and bring it in. Mara wants it on the couch. She sits down beside it and opens it. Inside I see a photo album and under that, a typed manuscript. Both fat.

"How about a cup of tea, Mara? A drink of mineral water? Not to mention Vodka. Or maybe a chat?"

Mara looks confused. She is offering the universe and I'm asking for a box of popcorn.

"Okay, Mara," I tell her. "Let me get myself a Scotch and then I'll be back to hear about your work."

In the kitchen I pour myself a Scotch and stand there for a minute. Then I pour the Scotch down the sink and all of a sudden, I'm pissed off! Which is not exactly a new one on me, with Mara. I leave the bottle of Scotch standing and go back into the living room. Mara doesn't notice I've come back without a drink.

We sit down across from each other, me on the couch and Mara on her chair, and Mara is looking straight at me. Excited. And finally about to spill something.

"Ted," she says. "Today is a very important day. Some fundamental changes in society are about to begin. The full reverberations won't be felt all at once, but today we drop a stone'—a gemstone—into the water, and the circles will begin to rise and to spread."

"Better give me a description of this gemstone we're dropping today. Or give it a name."

Now Mara is gleaming and sparking.

"My Work, Ted! Today I fulfill my promise to you. I shall unveil my Work and you will be the first to have seen and heard. And so your name, too, will be remembered."

Getting my name remembered is actually something I'm aiming to do for myself. With my music. Climbing to where the music is growing, and adding a leaf or a bud of my own. But I'm not going to get sidetracked here. I'm too damned curious about Mara's Work.

"Okay," I tell Mara. "Drop it in."

And she did that. Smoothly. Sliding it. A few ripples to start with, but then—just like she said—a whole world of changes.

"Please, Ted, first look at the album."

Mara lifts the album and presents it to me. I take it from her, thick and heavy, hold it on my lap, and quickly flip through a few pages. Right away one thing jumps out at me:

"Every one of these photos is a picture of you."

"Yes, yes," says Mara. "But of course I am incidental in all of them."

Mara leans forward and opens the first page of the album. A picture I already know. Mara, age three, in the red-and-white embroidered dress, standing on a chair. Princess as round-cheeked little girl.

"And how exactly are you incidental in this one?"

"No, no, Ted," says Mara. "Don't ask questions yet. Look at a few more."

So I do.

Second photo, Mara as a young woman. Big eyes, straight bangs, short smooth black hair. A shawl over her shoulders and across her breasts. Left hand playing with the fringes.

"Mara, is this the shawl Mrs. Whatsnikoff burnt a hole into?"

"It is, Ted!" says Mara. "Yes, yes, you are beginning to understand."

She's wrong. Mrs. Whatsnikoff's curse is still working: I understand nothing. I turn a few more pages of the album to a snapshot of Mara leaning against a rod iron garden gate. Cool, elegant, self-conscious pose. I've seen this one before, too. In Helga's album. But Helga's photo showed somebody beside Mara: the Nazi boyfriend. This picture has undergone a complete amputation of the boyfriend. Interesting but right now, I want to find out how exactly Mara is incidental in all these pictures of herself.

Next page, Mara is in a red-and-white flowered skirt and white blouse, one hand on a weathered old fence, the other holding a wicker shopping basket. Like she's got a part in a musical—pardon me, an operetta. Simple Maiden, played by Prima Donna. Mara would be elegant bare naked in a grubby old sleeping bag. Bare naked is one thing she isn't in any of the photos.

This next photo looks definitely familiar. A photo I've seen before? No, an *outfit* I've seen before. On Lena. That time she went to buy clothes for me on a Sunday. The "Experiment in Persuasion." I'm about to open my mouth, but Mara turns the page and here is another familiar outfit of Lena's. The one she wore to court as Mara's witness. Worn here by Mara, of course.

Mara doesn't give me time to settle on that one, either. She flips a few pages and stops at a picture of herself on the first day in court. Silver scarf and all. Still no solution to the puzzle, but now I notice there's a series of numbers under each photograph.

"Yes," says Mara, finally answering a question. "They are reference numbers to indicate the appropriate pages in the manuscript. Let's look up one of them. Which reference do you wish to see?"

The one that goes with the photo of the missing boyfriend. I check back and tell her the serial number and Mara opens the thick manuscript and finds the right page.

"One of my early successes," she says. "Go ahead, read it."

So I do.

Impression:

Cool elegance, but of the fragile kind, inviting protection from harsh realities. A hothouse flower, denoting exotic riches and also the need for careful protective tending.

The suit: well-tailored long jacket with waist, slightly flared from the hips. Medium tight skirt without slits. Background white, with delicately coloured stripes so thin that they give the impression only the greatest of care will keep them from chaotic webbing.

Silk stockings: of flesh tones, with a very fine seam. The fit is very important so that the seam on the back stays precisely in line, slimming and elongating the leg but above all, reinforcing fragility.

Hat: wide brimmed, white—delicately hovering like the wings of a butterfly, shading the eyes which thus take on a darker hue and glow.

Neckline: Collar of blouse and jacket both form a V, the neck exposed, the décolleté hinting but never revealing.

Gloves: white, of course.

Shoes: high heeled, as for most occasions. In any light colour which is already present in either the blouse, handbag, or stripes of the suit.

Handbag: no heavy-looking metal clasp or handles, nor anything glistening.

Handkerchief: peach-coloured, silk, with narrow white lace edge.

Jewellery: Earrings: small pearls nestled in gold, of delicate design.

Hair: no tight curls nor severe straight lines. Best: large upswept waves. If pins or comb are used, they must be the colour of the hair, thus making them invisible.

Lingerie: white or peach silk. If not obtainable, fine white cotton with thin lace edging. Do not neglect this aspect merely because it cannot be seen. The effect of, for example, black silk lingerie is subtle but strong, even if not visible.

Optional additions: a delicate wristwatch with very difficult clasp, making assistance desirable, or an ancient Persian coin, pierced, of dull gleam, which can be carried pinned to the lining of the handbag.

Occasions: of dire and secret necessity.

In order to establish indirect control not otherwise obtainable, strong invisible reins permitting optimum manipulation and maneuvering, without detectable signs at any point.

End of page.

I look up and Mara is walking around. Waiting for me to finish reading. Nothing more than a glimmer has got through at this point, but I don't like the feel.

Mara says: "Go ahead. Look up another one."

I can't. My eyes won't focus.

"Mara, "I say. "The jewellery for this outfit. It sounds like the same pair of earrings..."

"Yes, yes, Ted. The very same ones and they are available for study!" Mara comes close enough to put her finger on the album page. "This second set of numbers under each photograph, you see? It always refers to specific items and artifacts which are available for study. At first hand!"

"That means the same pair of earrings you cut off..."

"The originals," Mara nods. Smiling.

"Yes," she says. "I knew all along that you would be the one to understand. When I saw that the earrings had failed in the effect they should have had on Michelle's doctor, it was as though a pillar threatened to collapse and to bring down the entire edifice of my Work. Everything was shaken to its foundation. All the work futile, all the years wasted, the horror of that...I must have started to scream...

"You see, I had no duplicates. And I had to subject those earrings to further tests immediately. Immediately. I had to find out why they didn't work. Now, of course, I have duplicates of the earrings, in fact of each one of the major items and artifacts. All precisely labelled, as you will see. All stored in a safe place."

Mara goes to the briefcase, zips open a side pocket and takes something out. A small case, like a jewellery box. She's opening it and I almost jump in with: "No, no, no. I don't want to see the earrings." But thank God I first looked at what Mara was holding out in her hand: three little keys.

"I want to be quite certain," she says, "that the entire set is available to future generations. They will surely be eager to see the originals of those artifacts on which the first Manual is based. At the moment they are all in three trunks, in safe storage."

One little key is now in the palm of my own hand. It weighs practically nothing.

"Oh, Ted!" says Mara. "You haven't seen the title of the Work. Look. I would like to hear what you think."

On the manuscript cover, thick black letters read:

Manual for Survival

"I had to choose from among many possible titles," Mara tells me, thank God not waiting to hear what I think. There is no thinking going on.

"'Manifesto,'" she says, "has the wrong associations; 'Treatise' sounds far too theoretical; 'Rules for Survival in the Western World' was too long. So is 'A Comprehensive Plan for Survival and the Improvement of Life.' My working title was 'The Secret Codes of Mara deJong.' I still think of it like that, but it might give the wrong impression. It makes the work sound too fragmented, you see? It is not, after all, merely a set of codes. It is, as well as being entirely original, a very Comprehensive Work. The beginnings of an entirely new body of knowledge."

"You mean it's not an autobiography? With pictures?"

"No, no, Ted. Of course not." She sounds like I'm miles from solid ground, but in her present state of elation chooses to think it amusing. She indulges me:

"It is true that personal experience forms the basis for it but I have spent years in objective research. I have formulated theories and hypotheses and tested them. Of course, bits and pieces have been previously known and even applied, but there has never been a comprehensive system, and certainly no Manual. Just look at the chapter headings on page two."

Before I've got page two open, Mara is reciting them off by heart:

Chapter One: The Whole versus the Sum of its Parts.

Chapter Two: The Import of First Impact.

Chapter Three: Persuasion in Bureaucratic Settings.

Chapter Four: Invisibility when Crossing Borders.

Chapter Five: Designing for the Specific.

Chapter Six: Adjustment for Era, Size, Age, Colouring.

"And so on.

"You can see now: this Manifesto will hail the beginning of a new era! Further in-depth studies have to be made, of course. I foresee that before long, new departments will have to be set up at universities. Courses such as 'The Manual for Survival applied to History.' 'The Manual for Survival and International Relations,' and so on. In the end, I assure you, all the world leaders will concur that I have provided an alternative to war and revolution!"

At that point, I must have croaked something, or maybe I just held up my hands again. I had to stop the avalanche coming at me.

"Yes, of course," says Mara. "I understand. I am sorry to have overwhelmed you. I'll go upstairs now to give you time to absorb the magnitude of the Work. When I come down, we'll discuss arrangements."

I don't know how long ago Mara went upstairs. I don't know when I turned around on the bench to face the piano keys. I've been staring at them: they look orderly, familiar, solid. Every key one note, and I know every single one of them better than I know anybody else. We sing together. We tell stories with our guts. Right now, if I put my hands on the keys, all I'd get is noise. I want to find something I can pull out of the noise, some little part I can take a look at, to help me figure out what just happened here.

Out of the corner of my eye I see the photo album sitting on top of the manuscript. And on top of that, a pair of blue shoes…

Then my brain finally starts kicking into action, enough so I know the blue shoes are important. A reminder of Mara's courage, going out in the dark of night, blackout dark, during wartime Germany. And now there's something more. "Appearance," says Mara's voice in my head. "Never underestimate appearance." Those blue shoes came from way back, when Mara was just starting on her "more-important-than-music" Work.

And now I understood something about Mara more clearly than ever before: the sheer vast power of the woman!

Mara, in the middle of the war, living where anybody could denounce her and condemn her to death…responsible for a young child, too, like it or not, and the one thing that might save her from buckling under all that: playing the piano, that one thing she couldn't do any more. But Mara didn't buckle. Didn't go limp, didn't go under. Mara found some Very Important Work and dove into it. With passion and dedication. Then, at some point, it must have all tipped into obsession. (Don't ask me where that point is. Could be I'm right on the edge myself, and I don't exactly have wars and Nazis knocking down my door.) So Mara dedicated all that power—Jesus Murphy, what-all that woman could have done! But she had no choices. Only one thing at hand and Mara made of it a "Manual for Survival"! To benefit not just one human being, or just one country, no. To benefit all of humanity. A Manual for Survival. Although further study will be necessary.

And don't anybody tell me I'm admiring a woman who cut off her daughter's earlobes so she could save the world with a "Manual on Appearance"! I don't give a shit that I'm admiring a woman who is deranged. Who is definitely around the bend and off the rails.

My head seems to be working again but my guts are tied into some very complicated knots.

Mrs. Whatsnikoff jumps into my head again. Mrs. Whatsnikoff, who thinks Mara is evil, but Mrs. Whatsnikoff is wrong. Mara must have been deranged by grief! Starting way back when she lost her whole family in the war, including "dear Theodore." And there was the grief over the death of her music. Her chosen life. And there was the constant *threat* of death, hers and the child's, all through the war. And then, on top of all that, Michelle dies on her. Her only daughter. Her only child!

I put my arms down on the keys and put my head on top of them, but my eyes won't close. Then I remember Mara could come down those stairs any second. I swivel to face the doorway and wonder what I am going to see when Mara steps into it. Now that I know.

Before I can even imagine the answer to that one, another question pops in: what-all *didn't* I see? There must have been some signs! I mean, I lived here in the same house with the woman, and I was watching her all the time we were together, how come, in all that time, I never saw a sign?

Mara kept saying: "Never underestimate appearance," but hell, you can hear about how important appearance is all over the place: ads on TV, smiling at you with blinding teeth, every ad supposed to be the surefire road to success in business, in love, and in getting everything you want out of life, right? They have whole magazines about Appearance and how important it is, especially for finding your man. So how in hell was I supposed to know that Mara saying the same thing was different? That with Mara it's a decree! A Universal Law. So firing the lawyer because his jacket stuck out over his ass, that's not even bizarre. I bet even the lawyer's wife told him, "You're getting too pudgy for that jacket, dear. Never underestimate appearances." No, man. No way I could have seen *that* as a sign.

Okay, Ted. What about her getting the screaming heebie-jeebies because she lost a silk kerchief. That's getting pretty far out there. But I remember thinking that was just pre-trial jitters. And Lena saying "delayed reaction," meaning after the daughter's death.

I heard something upstairs a second ago, but now it's quiet again. I'm relieved it's not Mara coming back down. I'm not ready. There's still something hiding on me. Something important. Something I've missed.

All the knots in my gut are tightening up some more. Oh, hell! Here it comes: *Mara has to be watched over!*

A loud groan comes flying out of me. Yes. Even the judge knew it and sent her to the Funny Farm. For observation. To find out how far she'd been off the rails, cutting earlobes off her daughter's corpse. And, oh, sweet Jesus, I remember that her Work is not finished! More social experiments may be necessary. Like what? Cutting off a nose for her scientific research? Maybe deciding she needs a living nose?

Mara has to be watched over! She has to be watched over *all the time*. And that somebody watching over Mara will have to be *me*. Michelle is dead. Her other relatives are dead. Oh, shit, I wish I knew how to pray. Do I really have to make a choice? Choose to give up my life to watch over Mara, or choose to abandon Mara…and then what? Live half a life. Because sure as hell, if I abandon the woman, I'll have to veer around the memory of Mara every time I play, avoiding all the chords and notes and tunes that might remind me of Mara, and pretty soon I'd be playing pablum. Never going wherever the music takes you, free and travelling on paths unknown, oh, no! That way you might stumble onto the memory, screaming at you: you abandoned a woman in need and don't you ever forget it!

But if I choose to give up my own life to watch over Mara, how long before I go off the rails myself?

I've jumped up on my feet, then realize I heard the house door opening. Next thing I know, I'm shaking hands with Albert.

The surprise has snapped me right out of the state I was in. I'm leading Albert towards the couch, glad he can't see me too clearly. Albert points a finger at the ceiling, as in "Is she up there?" and I say, "yes." We sit down, me on the chair. Albert nods and says: "I see that you now understand, Ted."

"Oh, you do, do you?"

Albert hears that I'm pissed off, but he gets the reason wrong: he thinks I'm blaming him for something.

"Believe me, Ted," says Albert, "I have urged Mara many times to visit specialists…"

"You mean shrinks? Psychiatrists?"

"Yes, Ted. But Mara absolutely refused. She always said: 'There is simply no point in talking to anyone as long as I cannot yet talk about my Work. And the Work is not ready.' Perhaps now…?"

I hate to squash that faint hope.

"No, Albert. What's finished is only part one. How much exactly do you know about Mara's work?"

"I know its essence, Ted. Its hypothesis. I even know about many of the experiments. I…I'm afraid I snooped. There were so many signs, you see…"

"Signs? You saw signs? Why didn't *I* see any signs?"

"You would have very soon," says Albert. Kind old Albert.

But if nearly-blind Albert saw the signs, saw Mara, snipping shears and all...

"Tell me about the signs." I'm trying hard to sound calm. "What should I have seen?"

"Oh, it's not easy, in our Western culture," says Albert. "Mara's particular, er, orientation does not stand out in any stark manner, you see. Most of the time it fits into the prevailing attitudes and is barely noted. As long as the actual 'Manual for Survival' was not revealed."

Now Albert actually smiles and says: "Ted! You surely would not expect Mara to write a book on 'Dressing for Success,' would you? Or on 'Make-up for the Modern Woman?' Of course not. Mara would achieve nothing less than a *MANUAL FOR SURVIVAL.*"

Albert sounds proud of her. Makes me want to scream, knowing I sounded that same note not very long ago.

"Albert. Mara survived the Soviets, survived the Nazis while living right in the middle of wartime Nazi Germany, and this is what she dedicates her life to? Clothes?"

"A Manual for *Survival*, Ted. Who more in need of one?"

"Isn't that when people are supposed to turn to God?"

"A God who permitted WWII and the killing of Mara's entire family? In any case, Mara grew up in post-revolutionary Russia, remember? There was no religion."

"Okay, okay, not God. But this?"

"Ted, consider the situation Mara was in. What were the choices available to her?"

I groan and hold my head.

Albert says: "...Yes, yes, you see? You do understand that. Now consider the other part: how deranged the *world* was, all around Mara. In comparison to that world, gone entirely insane, her own, er, preoccupation was child's play. Later, of course..."

Albert pauses, remembering something. One of Mara's experiments? A scientific assessment? I'm glad for the pause because it's all coming at me too fast.

"Albert, knowing all that, why didn't you keep Mara safely on the plantation in Indonesia?"

"Oh, no, Ted. I encouraged Mara to return to Europe. Given her field of endeavour, she would quickly draw attention in most societies. Her best hope of escaping notice lay in our Western culture. That is precisely why we had to go back to Europe. When I let her come here to Canada by herself, I assumed that she would find more or less the same attitudes and priorities as those prevailing in Central Europe, and I still believe that to be so to a large extent, except to be truthful, I doubt that Mara would have been brought to a court of justice in Europe. Well, spilled milk and all that. But I shall certainly prevent Mara travelling anywhere alone in future."

Wait a minute. I thought it was Albert who was the tail, wagged by Mara's whim. Now what the hell is this? Somebody give me a Manual on these two. Please.

"Tell me something, Albert. Why do you keep Mara's piano locked?"

Albert shakes his head but he's smiling.

"There are some things you can't explain to the blind," he says. "So leave us our fantasies."

The fantasy of the beautiful Mara deJong, sitting at the piano, playing for him?

"Was she good, Albert? Was she...is she a good musician?"

Albert claims he isn't qualified to be a critic but that in his opinion, "Oh, she was a superb pianist," and then shakes his head. "Of course, she has not been practicing since arthritis crept into her fingers."

A superb pianist…not being able to play. That still feels like a mountain falling on my head. What a bloody amazing woman, making it out from under that. Albert is watching me, the kindly old dude. Expecting the next question.

"Which is why she started on her Work, right? When she couldn't play any more?"

"Oh, no," says Albert. "Mara was making notes for her manuscript years before the first signs of her condition appeared."

Years ago, when her handbag broke in wartime Germany and Mara threw a fit and even Helga knew there was more to it than a ruined purse? And was Mara conducting an experiment at that wedding, testing the effect of her new gown on six SS men come to arrest themselves some Catholics?

"Albert! Why the hell didn't you *tell* me?!" It bursts out of me and we both know I'm not talking about Mara's arthritis.

"Oh, no," says Albert. "I tell no one. On the contrary, I do everything I can to prevent anyone finding out. And, I must say, I was entirely successful in that until Mara rushed off to Canada without me. I fully expected, of course, that she would be protected, here as in Europe, by her best camouflage: her great beauty..."

"Are you saying I got blinded and bamboozled by Mara's beauty and that's why I didn't see that she's living in kookoo land!?"

Albert winces and sighs and is surprised that I'm pissed off again.

"Ted, imagine for a moment a woman in Mara's place who is...shall we say, bow-legged, barrel-shaped, squinty-eyed...see her before you and then hear Mara's words coming from that woman's mouth, and now tell me: can you not see the great difference?"

Albert stops and waits for an answer, but there isn't going to be one because I'm spinning.

Albert sighs and says: "Ted, in your case..." and I blow up again.

"In my *case*, Albert? What case? What kind of shit is that? I'm a case and you're her keeper?"

Albert sighs again and waits. Head down, now, looking at his shoes. He waits until I finally see it: I've gone and hit the nail on the head. Yes. Albert *is* Mara's keeper. Has been for a long time. And I am the case of the blundering fool.

Albert leans forward and puts one hand on my arm. "Ted," he says. "I am sorry. I had to leave you in the dark until the trial was over. It was essential that her universe remain intact until the report to the judge was behind us. Now that I am taking her home..."

"Taking Mara home? Wait a minute. Whose home?"

"To her apartment in Vienna, Ted. Where she lives. To her own home."

Albert looks puzzled. I must look like I've lost all connection with what's going on, because I have. Too fast. It's all coming at me too fast and furious. Albert is taking Mara back to Vienna...where she has been living in her own apartment...by herself...

"Albert. Haven't there been any...problems?"

"Nothing serious," says Albert. "Nothing that couldn't somehow be bridged, or explained."

By Albert, the ever-faithful.

"Mara," says Albert, "was and is the only woman in my life. I shall always..."

Albert stops. We have just heard Mara coming down the stairs.

Albert and I both turn in our seats so we're facing the doorway. Mara steps into it. She looks at Albert, getting to his feet, waves him down again and says:

"Hello, Albert." Pleasantly. Calmly.

She walks over to the little table with the manuscript and photo album on it. Every bit of my attention is on Mara, but I don't see anything different. She's still the same beautiful woman with a hum in her veins and the walk promising Drama Larger than Life.

Then I notice that there's been a slight shift in how I'm sitting, how I'm watching. Like I've just been turned into a spectator. Watching not only Mara, but all of it: Mara, Albert, the little table with the Work bomb on it, radiating…

Mara is opening the briefcase. She puts her manuscript inside, then the photo album. Locking the briefcase. Placing it on the table.

Mara turns to me and says: "I am sorry, Ted. There is no time now to discuss arrangements, after all. We shall have to make them by mail and by telephone."

Then Mara turns to Albert and says: "Our airport limousine should be waiting outside."

Albert and I get up. Mara goes into the hall, brings in her coat, gives to me. I hold it open for her. Albert is buttoning his overcoat.

"Is that a little tight?" Mara says to Albert, looking at his middle. Albert tucks his gut under his chest. He turns to me, smiling: "I wanted to tell you: Mara has finally agreed to choose a new dog."

"As long as he doesn't bark while I'm concentrating on my work," says Mara, to me.

"Work on Volume Two, Mara?"

"Oh, no, not yet," says Mara. "Amplifications for volume one. It's an ever-expanding field of knowledge, you see. Details proliferate. And the research is ongoing, of course, and sometimes it leads one to new conclusions."

Mara sighs, then looks at me and smiles. A beautiful, happy smile.

"You will be the recipient of the first copy of the printed work," she says. "Just as soon as it is published."

I thank her very much.

And then we're all standing in the hall, shaking hands.

Albert says he'll keep in touch, if I would like.

I stand in the doorway and watch Albert open the limo door for Mara. As she gets into the back, he holds her elbow. Tenderly.

Albert climbs in after her. The limo pulls away from the curb. Albert turns his head and waves to me. Mara sits facing front. From now on, if Mara thinks about me at all, it'll be as the Keeper of the Key, the one who will receive the first published copy, part of her important Work.

I waved until the limo turned the corner, and then I closed the house door and went and sat at the piano and stared at the keys. Finally I moved my ass out of the house and into the van and drove over to Bear and Alicia's place.

They're both home, sitting in the kitchen, and so is Lena. All of them at the table, eating something that smells familiar. Sitting there, eating, and smiling and living. Waving me to the table like I'm going to do the same.

Alicia goes and gets another plate. Lena and Bear are looking at me.

"She's gone. Back to Vienna. And that's all I can tell you right now."

Bear and Lena are still looking at me. Like they're checking to see if I've survived.

Then Bear says: "This is like old times," hoping for it. I'm willing to help out.

"Only better," I say. "There's more of us."

Alicia pats her belly and winks. "You mean the baby? Or Lena?"

Now all three of them are looking at me. I don't let them see I nearly forgot about the baby just then.

"Both," I tell them. "I meant both of them."

Alicia laughs and pulls me up, hands me the plate. I go to the stove and fill up the plate and sit down with it. But I can't eat.

Bear says: "You want to go play?"

"Hey, man," I tell him. "Don't be such a bloody monomaniac."

All three of them start laughing.

What a sound! What a great sound!

THE END

Acknowledgements:

My thanks to editors Joy Gugeler and Sandra Huh.
Gratitude also to Wayson Choy for his early encouragement.

And to the Helene Wurlitzer Foundation for the Arts,
New Mexico, for an Arts Grant.

Author bio

Lilly Barnes was born in Russia and had lived in three countries by the time she arrived in Canada as a teenager. She was educated at the University of Toronto and the University of Vienna. She was married to the late Canadian composer Milton Barnes and has two sons, Micah and Daniel.

Her poetry has been published in 7 editions of *Variety Crossing Anthology* and in *Chokecherries (*New Mexico). She is the recipient of the 2007 *Gemini Special Award*: the Margaret Collier Award for writing, for outstanding body of work.

She lives in downtown Toronto, in an old house full of music and stories.

Other titles by Lilly Barnes:
A Hero Travels Light
5 books for children, including 'Toe Tapper'

VARIETY CROSSING PRESS
PO Box 45035
5854 Yonge St.
Willowdale, on, m2 m 4 k3 , Canada
Phone and Fax: 416-222-7935
E-mail: dt_huh@yahoo.ca and
varietycrossing@gmail.com
Web site: www.varietycrossing.org

Recycled
Supporting responsible use
of forest resources
FSC
www.fsc.org Cert no. SGS-COC-003153
© 1996 Forest Stewardship Council

100%

MARQUIS
Marquis Book Printing Inc.

Québec, Canada
2009

100%
BIO GAS ENERGY

This book has been printed on 100% post consumer
waste paper, certified Eco-logo and processed chlorine free.